Former journalist S.D. Robertson quit his role as a local newspaper editor to pursue a lifelong ambition of becoming a novelist. His debut novel, *Time to Say Goodbye*, was published to rave reviews in 2016.

An English graduate from the University of Manchester, he's also worked as a holiday rep, door-to-door salesman, train cleaner, kitchen porter and mobile phone network engineer.

Over the years Stuart has spent time in France, Holland and Australia, but home these days is back in the UK. He lives in a village near Manchester with his wife and daughter. There's also his cat, Bernard, who likes to distract him from writing – usually by breaking things. *If Ever I Fall* is his second novel.

S.D. ROBERTSON

IF EVER I FALL

HarperCollins
PUBLISHERS
—— Since 1817 ——

This novel is entirely a work of fiction.
The names, characters and incidents portrayed in it are
the work of the author's imagination. Any resemblance to
actual persons, living or dead, events or localities is
entirely coincidental.

AVON

A division of HarperCollins*Publishers*
The News Building
1 London Bridge Street
London SE1 9GF

www.harpercollins.co.uk

A Paperback Original 2017

1

Copyright © S. D. Robertson 2017

S. D. Robertson asserts the moral right to
be identified as the author of this work

A catalogue record for this book is available from the British Library

ISBN-13: 978-0-00-810069-8

Typeset in Sabon by Palimpsest Book Production Ltd, Falkirk, Stirlingshire

Printed and bound in Great Britain by Clays Ltd, St Ives plc

MIX
Paper from
responsible sources
FSC
www.fsc.org   **FSC** C007454

FSC™ is a non-profit international organisation established to promote
the responsible management of the world's forests. Products carrying the
FSC label are independently certified to assure consumers that they come
from forests that are managed to meet the social, economic and ecological
needs of present and future generations, and other controlled sources.

Find out more about HarperCollins and the environment at
www.harpercollins.co.uk/green

For Mum and Dad

Also by S.D. Robertson

Time To Say Goodbye

PROLOGUE

I come round in stages, struggling to shed the cocoon of my dreams. They seem so real, so urgent, until the tug of daylight on my eyelids takes charge and one world blends into another. As my knuckles rub this place into focus, the harsh reality of a moment ago fades, filed away into a dark drawer.

'You're awake.'

The man's voice startles me. I move to sit up, only for a sharp pain to explode in my head, forcing me back down.

'Easy now. You need to take things slowly, lad. Doctor's orders.'

'What happened?' I whisper, wary not to bait the throbbing.

'You've suffered a head trauma. I don't know exactly how you did it. I wasn't there, but it looks like you fell off a ladder. I found you unconscious in a pile of soil. That cushioned your fall, but your head wasn't as lucky as the rest of your body . . .'

The voice continues, but I've stopped listening. My mind is on something more important. Something I've just realised. Something that makes my blood run cold.

I've no idea where I am.

The part of the room I can see from my horizontal position on the single bed is unfamiliar: mint green paint; a pine wardrobe and a matching bookcase busy with spine-creased paperbacks; varnished floorboards and a cream rug.

But that's not what's really worrying me. Neither is the fact I don't recognise the voice muttering away in the background. It's far worse than that.

'I don't know who I am,' I say. My voice echoes in the room.

Then there is silence.

on in my life, I suppose, and my reaction to it. Let's be clear: for this to work, I'm going to have to think of you differently. I need to be able to confide in you, to tell you anything and everything, and that won't be the case as things stand. So, to make that easier, I'm imagining writing to a future version of you, as if nothing bad ever happened. I know it's a bit weird, but I've given it a lot of thought and it's the best I can come up with. On the plus side, I think it will also make it easier to steer clear of the sadness: the black hole that threatens to swallow me if I think about it too much.

I want to tell you about what happened in the schoolyard today. I was standing apart from the other mums, as usual. I'll never be part of their little club and I've no desire to be. I'm pretty sure they all either despise me or pity me and, to be honest, I feel pretty much the same about them. The ringleaders – the overdressed, overconfident Queen Bitches, as I call them – make me want to scream. They're so damn snooty. And I feel sorry for the more timid, frumpy underlings for being at the Queen Bs' beck and call.

I missed my chance to join 'the gang' when Ruby started in reception and I was too busy working to do the school run. That already marked me out as a bad mum in their eyes. They'll always think so now, even though the new me is in the playground five days a week. It'll never make a difference. I'll forever be an outsider: someone talked about in hushed voices behind her back. That's small town life for you, I

4

suppose. We made the decision to buy this house – in a semirural spot within commuting distance of the city – and with that comes a specific type of people, people who have, shall we say, certain attitudes. I imagine it would be much the same anywhere in the country as it is here in the north of England. City folk are less judgmental in my experience, or at least better at minding their own business.

In the early days I made the mistake of trying to talk to a couple of them: a pair I later christened Horsey and WAG, not knowing their real names. I walked up to them and said something innocuous. 'Lovely weather today,' I think it was. Their response was simply to look down their noses at me for a horrified moment and then to continue chatting with each other as if I didn't exist. I shuffled away, turned back to watch them giggle. I couldn't believe it. I felt like I was back at school myself, but at least I knew to steer clear of them in future.

Not everyone is that way. There are people I could speak to if I so desired. I could always make small talk with the other outsiders: the grandmas and grandpas; the working parents on a rare day off; even the girls in the hi-vis vests from the nearby after-school club. I do occasionally, if I'm feeling chatty, but mostly I keep myself to myself. It's easier that way.

So there I was, standing alone in my usual spot near the dustbin, avoiding eye contact with everyone around me, and willing Ruby to be the first out. Then someone spoke to me.

'What's your secret?' a deep male voice asked.

There was no doubt he was talking to me, since his mouth was so close to my ear that he could have whispered the question. And as if that wasn't enough, he touched my shoulder at the same time. I almost jumped out of my skin.

'Sorry?' I said, fighting not to look too shocked as I turned around to see a gorgeous man – six foot, athletic, with dreamy chestnut eyes – beaming a perfect grin at me. Then came this deep, infectious laugh.

'Don't look so startled,' he said. 'You were behind me on the road. Black Golf, right? I was wondering how you were able to park so quickly. One minute you were there; the next you weren't. It took me ages to find a space. Do you have a secret spot?'

It feels strange talking to you about a man this way, considering . . . well, you know. Honesty's essential, though. I wouldn't be confiding in you if I held that kind of thing back.

Once I realised what this guy was talking about, I relaxed. To be honest, I could hardly believe that such a handsome stranger had noticed me, never mind started a conversation. He looked in his late thirties, well dressed in a light-grey suit and tie; clean-shaven with cropped hair. I decided to enjoy it, not least because I could see the Queen Bs staring at us, wondering why he was talking to me and not them.

'Um, there is a spot a few streets away that I tend to use.'

6

'I knew it,' he replied. 'And let me guess, you're not going to tell me in case I nick it in future.'

I smiled. 'It's not that secret. There's room for more than one car. Did you see me turn left on to Meadow Street?'

I gave him the directions and, next thing I knew, we were shaking hands.

'I'm Rick,' he said.

'Nice to meet you. I'm Maria.'

I wondered how he'd been able to recognise me just from seeing my car behind his. When I asked him this, he laughed.

'You stopped for petrol on the way, right? Don't worry, Maria. I'm not stalking you or anything. I just happened to be doing the same thing. I noticed you at the pump and then you followed me out afterwards.'

Rick explained that he and his daughter, Anna, had recently moved to the area because his job had been relocated. He's a finance manager for a large retail firm, apparently. I didn't ask, but there was no mention of any wife or girlfriend. Today was Anna's first day at her new school, he explained, adding that she was eight, the same age as Ruby. The weird thing was when the school doors opened and Ruby ran out into the playground with Anna in tow, begging me for her new friend to come to play at the house. Coincidence or what?

Before I go on, I must say how much Ruby misses you. Please don't think for a second that she's forgotten you and moved on. I could list countless examples of how that's not the case; they'd break your heart. But again, that's not why I'm writing to you.

Where was I? Oh yes, Ruby and Anna coming out of school together, all smiles. They were both buzzing about having a new playmate, as kids do. It was lovely to see.

'Pleeease can she come, Mummy?' Ruby asked, arms squeezed tight around my legs and puppy-dog eyes peering through her long blonde curls.

I looked over at Rick. He was being accosted in a similar way by his own daughter, who was a little taller than Ruby, with shoulder-length dark hair in neat plaits. 'What do you think? I'm fine with it if you are.'

'Sure,' he replied, flashing his pearly whites at me. 'When were you thinking?'

'How about tomorrow?'

I could have invited them there and then, to be honest, but I knew the house was a mess and I didn't want that to be his or Anna's first impression of where we lived.

'Fine with me. Am I invited too?'

'Of course.' I smiled. 'I wouldn't expect you to entrust your daughter to someone you'd just met.'

He beamed back at me in a way that felt like we might be flirting with each other. 'I don't know. You look like a pretty safe bet. And you did share your parking secret with me. We'll look forward to it, won't we, Anna?'

She replied with an excited nod.

'Great. See you here tomorrow, then?'

'Fantastic.'

And that was it: play date arranged. I've been cleaning the house ever since. Tidying up is my way of dealing with the nerves.

I could have imagined the flirting thing; it's been so long, I'm not sure I even know how to do it any more. Luckily I stopped short of saying: 'It's a date.'

I'll tell you what: I can't wait to see the look on the Queen Bs' faces when we leave together. It'll be priceless.

Time to go now. It's late and my empty bed awaits. I'll write again soon.

Love as always,

M

Xx

CHAPTER 2

Roof tiles clatter, boards creak and the window rattles in its frame as an angry wind gusts outside. The sound distracts me for a moment. From my pillow I scan the bare ceiling above me as if it might contain clues to answer the questions swirling around my mind. Then I flick my eyes back to the expectant face, still glued on my own, scrutinising me.

The man, a wiry chap in his late fifties or early sixties, scratches the top of his head, his white hair so short it barely moves. He's dressed in smart navy jeans and a pressed white shirt with the sleeves neatly rolled up.

Miles: that's what he says he's called, although it rings no bells with me. As far as I'm concerned, we've never met before and this room I'm in – this bed – is unfamiliar.

He claims to be a doctor: a retired GP. What he won't tell me is anything about myself. He wants me to try to remember first, although I know there's no point. The cupboard is bare.

'Nothing at all?' he asks, finally breaking the silence.

'No.'

Panic grabs a hold of my throat and thumps me in the chest.

Where the hell am I?

Who is this guy?

Why can't I remember anything?

I try to sit up in bed, but doing so makes my head pound like before and I flop straight back down again.

'Take it easy, lad,' Miles says. 'Here, let me help. We'll do it slowly.'

He disappears from view for a moment and returns with a second pillow. Then, supporting my shoulders, he eases me up into position. Thankfully, the pain is more manageable this way and it settles again once I stay still for a few seconds.

'How's that?'

'Good,' I whisper, breathing out a long sigh of relief.

He hands me a glass of water. I take a couple of grateful sips to sprinkle the desert that is my mouth and throat, licking my swollen, crusty lips a few times to try to moisten them.

I take a deep breath, try to speak. My voice fails a few times and I cough, my throat hurting with the effort.

'So you're surprised my memory hasn't come back yet?'

'Hmm.'

'What does that mean?'

He paces the room before answering. 'This kind of memory loss, which we call retrograde amnesia, might happen a lot in films and soap operas, but it's rare in real life. A blow to the head is more likely to affect the forming of new memories. Even then, it would have to be a serious whack and, honestly, I don't think yours was that bad. I'd have taken you to the hospital if so.'

The word *hospital* sets off the panic again. I feel it rising in my chest. 'Isn't that where I need to be? What if my brain's swollen, or I have a blood clot or something? It's agony every time I move. And I don't know who I am. That's not normal – you said so yourself.'

'Calm down. Getting all riled up is only going to make things worse. I'm a qualified doctor. I have many years of experience and I've checked you over with the utmost care. If I had the slightest suspicion you were in any immediate danger, I most certainly wouldn't be dealing with this here. Trust me, you're far better resting in bed than being jostled around in a car or an ambulance.'

'How can I trust you, though? I have no memory of you. You claim to be a qualified doctor, but how do I know that's true? You also said yourself that you're retired.'

'That's right. I am retired, but I've kept up my registration with the GMC so I can do locum work once in a while. I still have a licence to practise. Would you like to see it?'

'Yes, please, I would actually.'

'Fine.'

Miles leaves the room. He's obviously annoyed that I don't believe him, but what am I supposed to do? I don't know him from Adam.

He returns a few moments later and hands me a framed certificate. It hurts my head to read it, but it looks official enough. I pass it back to him. 'Thanks.'

'I thought you might like to see this too,' Miles adds, handing me a smaller picture frame containing a local newspaper cutting. 'Popular GP hangs up his stethoscope,' reads the headline. Underneath is a photo of Miles surrounded by a bunch of his former colleagues outside the medical centre where he apparently used to work.

I read the first few lines of the article, which confirm what he's already told me, and it's all I can manage.

'I'm sorry for doubting you,' I say, handing the frame back to him, 'but put yourself in my shoes. I don't remember anything at all and it's pretty damn terrifying. Plus my head hurts like hell.'

'I understand,' he says, although his folded arms and curt reply tell another story.

'So what now? Do I need to see some kind of specialist? What do you think?'

Miles screws up his face, emphasising the wrinkles around his sea green eyes. 'Um, no, I don't think that's necessary. It's most likely a bad concussion. Take it easy for a few days and you'll soon be back to normal. I can keep an eye on you.'

'Whatever you think is best,' I say, keen to avoid riling him any further.

He nods and throws me a pursed smile, although I'm sure I spot a flicker of uncertainty in his gaze. After pouring more water into my glass and leaving me some ginger nut biscuits to nibble, he tells me to try to sleep.

'Can't you tell me my name and something about myself?' I ask. 'Are we related? Is this my home?'

'What do you think?'

13

'I don't know,' I snap, loud enough to provoke my headache. 'That's the bloody problem.'

His voice is placid. 'I'll tell you if you still can't remember by tomorrow, but I'm confident you will. Please try to keep calm. I know what I'm doing. Studies have shown that it's preferable for a patient to be given the chance to recover lost memories for themselves.'

He shuffles out of the room, pausing before closing the door behind him. 'For the record, it's not locked,' he says, as if reading my mind. 'You're free to leave here any time you like, but I definitely wouldn't recommend that in your condition.'

I have a better view of my surroundings now that I'm sitting up in bed. I see a single-glazed sash window with curtains to match the green walls; a high ceiling, white with Victorian-style coving and a light bulb on a bare ceiling rose; a wooden chair with jeans and a black T-shirt draped over it. There's also a pine bedside table that matches the wardrobe and bookcase, plus a brushed steel reading light. None of it looks familiar.

I'm tempted to get up and peer out of the window. From my current position, I can only see the overcast sky and I wonder whether a full view of the outside world might jog my memory. However, a jerk forward and another dagger between the temples puts paid to that idea. Instead, I squeeze my eyes shut. I wait for a few moments until the pain has subsided

My phone! I think suddenly. Where's my mobile? There must be some answers on there. There will be numbers to call, photos, videos, all sorts. I'll be able to work out the last person I spoke to and see who I dial regularly. Someone will be able to tell me who I am. I feel a rush of relief at the thought of this solution and look wildly around the room. My gaze falls on blank surfaces; I can't see a mobile anywhere. There's not even a charger in any of the plug sockets. I sit forward, slowly this time, and consider getting out of bed to look for it, but as I try the pain kicks in again and, reluctantly, I accept that it's not going to happen.

'Hello?' I call out. 'Miles, are you there?'

I try a few more times, but he doesn't reply, so I scour the room again from the bed, in the vague hope I might have missed it. All I manage to do is wear myself out.

I close my eyes.

Who am I? Who am I? Who am I?

I ask myself this simplest of questions over and over, scouring the darkness of my mind for an answer. But it's not there. All I can picture is the room on the other side of my eyelids. There is nothing else. It terrifies me. I'm seized by a gut feeling that Miles is wrong and my memory won't come back any time soon, if ever. The tears start flowing down my cheeks. I feel pathetic but can't stop them coming. I cry myself to sleep.

'Wake up, sleepyhead,' a girl's voice whispers into my ear, so close that it tickles; makes me shiver. The voice is familiar and fills me with happiness. I snap open my eyes.

'Oh, it's you.'

'Morning. Expecting someone else?'

Miles has pulled the wooden chair up to the foot of

the bed. His eyes are fixed on mine, which are gungy with sleep, although it feels like barely any time has passed since we last spoke.

Whoever it was I thought had woken me, whatever brief memory I had of them, is gone. And yet something – a feeling that I should be somewhere else, with someone else – lingers. 'I, um. I'm not sure. Morning? What do you mean? How long was I out?'

'You slept right through after we spoke yesterday. That was late afternoon. I looked in on you a couple of times before I went to bed and you were out for the count.'

'Bloody hell,' I groan. 'That would explain why my bladder feels ready to explode.'

I lever myself upright, ready for a fresh burst of pain that turns out to be much less than yesterday.

'How's the head?'

'Better, thanks.'

'Do you remember my name?'

'Miles, right?'

'Good. And the rest?'

I pause to think and then shake my head. 'Only what we discussed yesterday.'

'You remember that?'

'Yes.'

'But nothing else?'

'No.'

The void – the absence of crucial memories I know should be there – triggers a bout of anxiety. I feel my heart start to pound; there's a tightening in my chest and my throat feels like it's closing up.

16

'Are you all right?' Miles asks, clocking my discomfort. 'Stay calm and don't panic. Everything's going to be fine. You're in safe hands. I want you to take slow, deep breaths through your nose, into your abdomen, and hold. Then breathe out through your mouth.'

He demonstrates and gets me to breathe in time with him. We do this for several minutes and, gradually, the panic dissipates.

'Calmer?' he asks.

I nod. 'Thank you.'

Gingerly, I shift myself into a seated position on the side of the bed. The varnished floorboards feel cool under my feet. Miles stands at my side, ready to help if necessary, but I'm keen to do this alone. I rise gradually, testing my legs as I go. They're a little shaky to start, but it soon passes and they strengthen up. My head throbs a little and I feel somewhat dizzy at first, but once I'm fully upright, with an arm on the wall to steady myself, the sensations ease.

'Okay?' Miles asks.

'Yes, I think so.'

I need him to tell me where the bathroom is. It turns out to be right next door, but I manage to get there by myself, which is a relief. There is still a dull pain in my head when I make certain movements. The rest of my body feels fine, albeit a little stiff.

There's not much to see outside the bedroom: a small corridor with more varnished floorboards, bare cream walls and three other doors. I open the one to the right of me and enter a glistening, modern bathroom with dark

17

tiles floor to ceiling, a walk-in shower and a separate bath. It's much nicer than I expected. There's a neat pile of white towels under the sink and a shower gel dispenser on the wall, like something out of a five-star hotel. That starts me wondering whether I've spent a lot of time in posh hotels. Or perhaps I've never been in one and that's why I'm so impressed by it. It's awful not knowing myself, my own experiences up to this point. What kind of life have I had?

The drops of water lingering on the shower screen are the only giveaway that the room has been used. It's not until I have a nose around the cabinet under the sink that I find things like a toothbrush and razor.

I stand at the toilet and do my best impression of a racehorse. Then, as I wash my hands and slap cold water on my face, I pause. Above me is a mirror. I've deliberately avoided looking in it so far. What will it feel like to see my reflection? Will it send my memories flooding back? Or will it be like looking at a stranger? I take a deep breath and straighten up.

None of the above, as it turns out. I recognise myself – tired eyes, thick stubble and ears that stick out more than I'd like – but that's it. I don't know how I know it's me; I just do. No name, no age, no identity, but a face I accept as my own. The same goes for my body. I'm tall, probably a little over six foot, and in decent shape. I'm not gym-toned, but I'm about the right place between fat and thin and I seem fit enough. I look to be in my early forties, although I feel younger. There's no obvious sign of my head injury, but it feels tender to the touch in places.

'Better?' Miles asks when I return to the bedroom, noting that the door isn't even fitted with a lock. He's wearing a navy polo shirt today, with jeans again, but I'm guessing a fresh pair. It's the fact that he's tucked the shirt into them that gives me this impression. Too neat to wear something for more than one day, I'd wager.

'Yes, much better.'

I perch myself on the edge of the bed so we're eye to eye. I'm still not sure I trust him. I'm not sure about anything. But he helped me just now and it feels like I need to build bridges between us. 'Sorry for what I said yesterday: you know, suggesting that you might have attacked me and—'

'Don't worry about it.'

'It's hard when I can't remember anything. I feel so confused.'

'Seriously, I understand. There's no need to explain. What did you think of the bathroom, by the way?'

'Um, yeah. It was really nice. Very modern.'

'Ring any bells?'

'What do you mean?'

He stands up. 'Never mind.'

'Hang on,' I say, also rising to my feet. 'Do you know where my mobile is?'

Miles hesitates for a moment before replying. 'Um, I do. Yes.'

'Great. Where is it?'

'In the sea.'

'Sorry? I don't understand. What do you mean, in the sea?'

'You dropped it just after you arrived here, lad.'

19

'Hang on. What sea?'

Miles nods towards the window. I look outside for the first time and there, sure enough, is the blue-green swell of the sea.

'Right,' I reply, my head swimming. 'I didn't realise. And I haven't bought a replacement phone?'

'No.'

He starts to head out of the room again, mumbling something about making us a cup of tea.

I grab hold of his arm. 'Wait. You told me you'd give me some answers today if I needed them – and I do, especially now I don't have my phone to consult.'

Miles lets out a gentle sigh and sits back down on the chair. 'Very well, although I still think you'll remember everything by yourself soon enough.'

'So what's my name?'

'It's Jack.'

'Jack what?'

'Um, I can't tell you that.'

'Why the hell not?'

He smiles at me. 'Because you haven't told me. The truth is, Jack, I know very little about you.'

'What?' I ask, more confused than ever. 'I don't get it. I thought we knew each other. I thought we were maybe even family. I didn't have you pegged as my dad, but perhaps an uncle or something.'

Miles shakes his head. 'Sorry.'

'Who are you, then? What am I doing here? How about you tell me what you do know?'

'You're my lodger. I bought this place after I retired

and I'm in the middle of doing it up. You're helping me in return for bed and board. The reason I thought the bathroom might ring a bell is that we fitted it together. Not long ago.'

I stare at him for a moment. That wasn't what I expected. 'How long have I been here?'

He explains that I've been staying with him for a couple of months. Apparently we met one night in a local pub and got talking. He was looking for a hand with the renovation and I needed somewhere discreet to stay – a place where I wouldn't face too many questions.

'Questions like my surname?'

'Exactly. You never told me and I never asked.'

'Didn't you think you ought to know?'

'Why? What's the difference?'

He says it was obvious I was in some kind of trouble, but he didn't need or want to know the details. Considering himself a good judge of character, he decided it was worth taking a chance on me, particularly since I seemed to know a thing or two about DIY.

'Turns out I was right. You've been a big help. I wouldn't be anywhere near as far on without you. There's still a long way to go, mind.'

'Oh? This all seems finished.'

Miles chuckles. 'You really don't remember, do you? Wait until you see the rest.'

He's not kidding. I find that out soon enough when I follow him to breakfast. I want to see as much as I can of my surroundings, hopeful that they'll trigger some memories.

We pass through the door opposite my bedroom and I'm stunned by what's on the other side. 'Wow. This place is huge.'

'A huge wreck, for the most part. Careful where you walk. Follow my lead or you might find yourself knee-deep in the ceiling below.'

He guides me along a broad landing, lined on each side by door after door, until we reach an imposing curved staircase wide enough for the two of us to descend together. As grand as the place is – or once was – it's dilapidated: a dirty, mildew-flecked, musty mess of ramshackle floorboards and part-stripped walls.

I spot the sea again through a grimy window with a rotten frame I could poke my finger through. 'Where exactly are we? By the beach?'

Miles glances back at me as he swings away from the bottom of the stairs and heads for the belly of the building. 'I'm not going to tell you everything, lad. I want you to try to remember things by yourself. Seriously, it's no good me feeding it all to you. How are you to know it's not a pack of lies? Tell me, where do you think we are?'

I'm tempted to say 'in the kitchen' as we reach our destination and he offers me a seat at a large oak dining table, pouring me a glass of orange juice from a jug. But I bite my tongue. This room has been renovated to a similarly high spec as the upstairs bathroom: granite surfaces, floor tiles and fancy appliances. There's even a built-in coffee machine above the oven.

'Well?' Miles asks again. 'Any ideas?'

I shake my head, taking a big swig of the juice in a bid to calm my anxiety.

'Okay, I'll help you out a little, lad. We're on the North Wales coast.'

'Really?'

He nods. 'Does that sound familiar?'

'Um, I'm not sure. Maybe. I guess it wasn't what I was expecting because, well, you don't sound Welsh. Come to think of it, I can't put my finger on where your accent is from.'

Miles laughs. 'I'm from Yorkshire originally, but I've not lived there for a very long time. I spent most of my working life in Cheshire and moved here after I retired.'

'What about me? What accent do I have?'

'I don't know where you're from, if that's what you're asking. You never told me. Somewhere in Northern England, I'd say, but it's not a strong accent. The answer is locked away in your head somewhere, which is why I want you to try to remember things yourself. That's all I'm telling you for now.'

Before I can argue, Miles changes the subject and starts talking about the kitchen.

'This was my first project,' he says. 'Did it before I even moved in. A man can't live without a good kitchen – not me, anyhow. You should have seen the state it was in before, John. Shocking. Made the rest look delightful.'

I pause. 'What did you say?'

'That the original kitchen was in a shocking state.'

'No, after that. What did you call me?'

'What do you think I called you?'

23

'You called me John.'

He raises one eyebrow. 'And?'

'My name's Jack. At least that's what you said before.'

'Good. You see now why I need you to remember things for yourself. What's your name?'

'Jack.'

'You're sure?'

The panic bubbles over again. As I stare at him, Miles's face begins to look strange. Kind of warped, as though I'm seeing it through a fairground mirror. I can't tell if he's leering at me or smiling; his features are morphing before my eyes. He reminds me of a wolf: a snarling, smiling wolf. 'What if it is John? Or maybe it's Nigel, or Sam, or Rick, or Ross. What is it? Tell me. Be sure. What is it?' His face moves closer to mine.

'What are you . . .' A fog descends and the room starts to spin. I try to get up from the table, only to stumble.

The world around me disappears.

CHAPTER 3

Thursday, 4 May 2017

The phone on Dan's desk rang.

He looked at the clock; ten past two already. Shit.

'Yes?'

'Hello, Dan. It's Susan on reception. I've got a bit of an angry man on the phone: a Mr Doyle. He's demanding to speak to you. I tried to put him through to one of the reporters, but he was having none of it. He insisted it had to be you.'

'Right. What's it regarding?'

'I'm sorry. I did ask him, but all he would say was that it was about a serious mistake in this week's *Herald*.'

A complaint, as he'd feared. They always came through about this time on a Thursday. Dan paused, thinking back through the many pages he'd checked the previous day. The name Doyle didn't ring any bells.

'Can I put him through?'

Dan thought back to the good old days when he had a deputy and a news editor to filter out complaint calls.

When he had the peace and quiet of a private office to deal with awkward issues, rather than the noisy open-plan space in which he now found himself. He'd been captain of his own ship. He'd been a somebody, at least to his readers in the Northern England towns and villages where the paper was distributed. He'd deliberately avoided living in the *Herald's* reporting patch in order to escape work during his free time. But now the office wasn't even based there, having been centralised to a hunk of concrete fifteen miles down the motorway, on the edge of the city. It was a ridiculous situation, but one he'd had to accept.

Technically he'd been promoted after the move: made editor of two other titles on top of the *Herald*, his original newspaper. But in reality he'd become a glorified middle manager, a cog in the wheel. The title of editor had only been retained to appease the public. To pretend their beloved local papers were the same as ever, which couldn't be further from the truth.

'Dan? Are you still there?'

'Yes, sorry. Put him through.'

He'd always hated dealing with complaints: the one thing that had risen in number – unlike ad revenues and circulation – since the centralisation two and a half years earlier. It was only to be expected when you considered the cull of experienced journalists that had taken place.

Dan was lucky to still be there. He was one of only a few senior staff from the group's weekly papers who were still standing. He didn't feel lucky, though; in fact lucky was a million miles from how he would describe his life right now. He was waiting for the roof to come crashing down on his career as it had on everything else.

'Hello?'

'Mr Doyle?'

'Who's this?'

'This is Daniel Evans, the editor.'

'So I've finally reached the organ grinder, have I?'

Not really, Dan thought. Not any more. 'How can I help you, Mr Doyle?'

'It's a bit bloody late for that. The damage is done.'

'Could you be a little more specific?'

'You called me a paedophile, Mr Evans. Used the wrong photo – my photo – with a story about some sick kiddie fiddler. I'm going to sue you for every last penny your poxy rag is worth.'

Shit. Dan's mind raced back to the only article about a paedophile in that week's *Herald*. It was a court case on page seven. Jane, one of the few original reporters still working for the paper, had been to court and emailed the piece over. So how the hell could the wrong picture have been run alongside it? He doubted it was her fault. She was one of the good ones – always so thorough.

He opened his copy of the paper and flicked to page seven, his fingers catching on the pages as he rushed to find the article. There it was, with a photo of a suited bald man standing on the court steps.

'Hello? Are you there?' Mr Doyle asked.

'Yes. Sorry, I—'

'You can shove your apologies. I want to know how the hell this happened and what you're going to do to fix it.'

Dan racked his brains. There were so many ways things could go wrong these days. He'd not had any direct involvement in placing the story or picture. He'd never even seen Jane's email: only the finished story on the page. Not that any of this would protect him. He'd be the one held to account, blamed for not picking up on it while reviewing the pages.

The paedophile's name, captioned underneath the photo, was Steven Ross. How on earth had that got confused with Mr Doyle? And why was his picture on the photo system in the first place?

'Hello? How are you going to fix this? There could be a lynch mob outside my house tonight!'

His tone was pure aggression. Understandable in the circumstances, Dan thought, doing his utmost to stay calm in response. But he could feel himself starting to sweat. What a bloody mess.

'Hold on a minute. Let me get this straight. The picture on page seven is of you and you're not Steven Ross.'

'Are you some kind of idiot? Of course I'm not him. I've never met this freak in my life.'

'Have you any idea why your photo is on our system?'

'You tell me. It's never been used before, to my knowledge. It must have been taken by one of your lot without my permission.'

'You were at court yesterday?'

'No, it was months ago. I was appealing against a drink-driving charge.'

'And you've no connection whatsoever with Steven Ross?'

28

Mr Doyle let out a loud sigh. 'Obviously not. I'm a respected businessman. Your article is the first I've heard of this nonce. As far as I know, the only thing we have in common is the name Ross.'

'Sorry?'

'Ross – his surname – is my first name.'

Dan's heart sank. That must have been it: a wrongly selected picture due to a similar filename. A schoolboy error. The kind of thing that would never have slipped through in the old days. How was he expected to spot such mistakes when he was juggling three papers; in and out of meetings all day; constantly bombarded by emails and phone calls?

Something snapped inside. It was as though a switch had flipped in his brain, and in that instant Dan decided he just couldn't handle this any more. He couldn't take it. Not on top of everything else in his personal life, which had spiralled from bad to really bloody awful over the past month. It was too much. He was done.

Without saying another word, Dan hung up the phone, grabbed his jacket from the chair and headed for the stairs. As he moved, he felt as though his legs were disconnected from his body, making their way out of the room while his insides fought to dislodge the panic in his chest.

Maurice, another surviving editor, was leaving the lift as he reached reception.

'Coming for a smoke, mate?' he asked Dan.

'Sure,' Dan replied, using him as cover to stay out of Susan's view, certain Mr Doyle would call back at any moment if he hadn't already. He dodged behind Maurice, shoving his hands into his pockets to disguise the way they were shaking.

'Good excuse to get out in the sunshine. It's supposed to be baking today. Not that you'd know it with the air-con in here.'

'Right.'

'Did you see the email from Trent?' Maurice asked, referring to the boss of their boss.

'No.'

'Looks bad. There's an urgent meeting at three thirty. Everyone has to attend. Rumour has it there's going to be another round of job cuts. Are you all right, mate? You look a bit peaky.'

'I'm fine,' Dan lied. Job cuts? Maurice's words felt like the final nail in the coffin. As they walked through the door, the heat hit him. It reminded him of exiting a plane at the start of a holiday in the sun. He had to get out of there. 'I've not got any fags. I'm going to nip to the shop for a pack.'

'You can crash off me, if you like. I've got some for once.'

'No, it's fine. I'll be back in a minute.' Dan barely knew what he was saying. The words tumbled out, but all he could think about was getting away from the office.

Maurice started saying something about the weather, but Dan had already tuned out.

Instead of walking to the shop he went to his car, a battered silver Ford Focus with an ugly dent in the near-side front door that he'd still not got around to fixing. He sat down in the driver's seat, switched his mobile off and took deep breaths. His head was swimming; pulse racing. What was he doing? Was he really going to go through with it? Had the moment arrived?

The ground floor flat where he'd been living these past few months was a simple two-bedroom affair in one of the city's bland outer suburbs – a reasonable but not especially sought-after neighbourhood. Apart from the fact it was conveniently located just a ten-minute drive from work and a quarter of an hour from his real home, Dan hated everything about the flat. It was poky and damp with a mouldy brown bathroom and a kitchen barely big enough to cook a microwave meal. He didn't even have the freedom to improve things – to occupy his mind with DIY – thanks to an unpleasant landlord who was only interested in getting his rent on time. Dan felt too old to be renting again. He'd never get used to spending so much time alone.

He let himself into the hallway, which he shared with the occupants of five other flats. He hoped not to bump into any of them, as he doubted himself capable of small talk at that moment. The muffled sound of daytime TV was coming from the flat opposite, but the woman who lived there was in her nineties, partially deaf and walked with a frame. The chances of her coming to the door were minimal.

Dan hovered for a moment above the letterbox but didn't bother checking it. He let himself inside the flat, grabbed the two items he needed from the bedroom wardrobe plus a half bottle of vodka from the kitchen. Then he left without looking back.

There were things he'd miss, but the flat wasn't one of them. It represented everything he hated about his life. It was a daily reminder of how badly things had turned out.

He thought back to what Maurice had said about more cutbacks. Would they have got rid of him this time? It was possible. The photo cock-up and the legal action that was bound to follow wouldn't help.

Who knew?

Who cared?

He was done.

He got into the car and pulled the vodka bottle out of the inside pocket of his jacket, taking a long swig. Then he put the key in the ignition and did a six-point turn in the road.

'Goodbye, flat from hell,' Dan said, flicking the V-sign as he pulled the car away and headed for the sea. He considered calling in to see to his mum on the way, but he couldn't bring himself to do it. What would be the point?

He'd decided on his destination during one of his lowest moments: alone late at night, drunk and maudlin, looking through old photos on his computer. There was one particular picture that had caught his eye, from about four years earlier. It had been taken on a family holiday on the North Wales coast: a last-minute booking in a gem of a cottage and a rare week of scorching temperatures. Similar weather to today in fact.

They were pictured on a clifftop, framed by a glorious deep blue of merging sea and sky. It must have been taken by a passer-by, as they were all together in the shot. That was one of the reasons he liked it so much. The other thing was how happy each of them looked, all blissfully unaware of the heartache and pain biding time in the shadows, waiting to ravage them.

That night, Dan had stared at the photograph for hours, until the dark moment eventually passed. He'd seen things differently in the sober light of the next morning. And yet the location had stayed with him, rising to prominence again in recent times as his outlook grew increasingly bleak. Even so, he'd been hanging on, hoping against hope that something would change. That a chink of sunshine would break through the black cloud enveloping his world and offer some hint of a silver lining.

But it had never come.

He'd been teetering on the edge for the last few days. Now he was free-falling. The phone complaint had done it, but the prospect of yet more cutbacks had sealed the deal.

The journey would only take a couple of hours or so, as long as the traffic wasn't too heavy. That was one of the reasons they'd chosen it back then for a holiday: no long car journey, no airports, and yet still a change of country. Goodbye Northern England; hello bilingual road signs, beautiful beaches and cheery Welsh folk. It couldn't have been easier. And it hadn't felt close to home at all once they were in that blissful holiday bubble of beaches, picnics, ice creams and meals out. Flying kites. Laughing at in-jokes. Enjoying being a family.

There must have been rows. What family holiday didn't include at least one or two? And yet there were none that Dan could recall. In his mind, it was perfect.

Now he was returning to relive the highlights. He'd do a whistle-stop solo tour, soaking in the memories. When daylight started to fade, he would head up to the clifftop where that photo was taken. He'd find a secluded spot overlooking the sea to park and watch one final sunset. He'd wait until no one was around before rigging up the car with the items he'd taken from the flat: duct tape and a length of garden hose bought days earlier in anticipation of this moment. Then it would be time to slip away.

It was selfish. He knew that. Especially when you considered the family he still had. But he couldn't do it any longer. He couldn't keep going; fighting the awful pain at his core, the unrelenting agony. No, he'd reached the end. It wasn't like they wanted him around, anyway. They were already doing fine on their own. They'd be better off without him.

And yet he felt like he ought to call. To say goodbye at least.

Dan looked over at the glovebox, where he'd put his mobile after turning it off. He thought about it for a few minutes as he made his way on to the motorway. He kept on thinking about it for the rest of the journey, unable to decide.

What if hearing one of their voices made him change his mind? What if he broke down while speaking to them and they realised something was wrong? Also, if he turned his phone on, there were bound to be loads of messages from work. Mind you, those he could ignore.

He decided to call the house once and let fate decide.

If they answered, then so be it. He'd speak to them and see where that led him. But if they didn't answer, he'd take that as a signal to carry on without hesitation.

It was 4.45 p.m. when he parked in a lay-by. He was already well over the border into Wales. After three more gulps of vodka, Dan made the call.

Sweating in the heat now the car's air-con was off, he let it ring for more than a minute.

No answer.

He lit a cigarette, smoked it to the butt and, despite what he'd told himself, tried again.

Still no one there.

'That's that, then,' he said aloud. Not even an answer-phone to leave a message on.

He switched the phone off, ignoring the eight voicemails and six texts from the office, and dumped it in a rubbish bin before getting back into the car and starting the engine.

He was nearly there. The agony was almost over. He'd been living with it for the best part of two years now. But his ability to cope, or at least to carry on despite the pain, had been eroded by the events of the last few months. He could have done so many things differently. He wished that he had, but there was no going back. The past was the past, whatever his regrets. And yet that didn't stop everything that had led him to this moment churning around and around in his thoughts.

CHAPTER 4

Thursday, 6 April 2017

Dear Sam,

Here we are: letter number two. I really wanted to write this yesterday, believe me, but it didn't happen. Things got hectic. There were a couple of incidents, as I'll explain later. There just wasn't time.

Getting going with that first letter was hard, but once I got into the process, it felt good. By the end I had a real sense of achievement. You probably think that's silly: to be patting myself on the back about something as simple as writing a letter. But it wasn't simple. Not for me. Nothing's been simple for a while. Not since, well, you know what.

I said I wasn't going to dwell on the past, so I'm not. Writing to you is supposed to be a way of moving forward. But in order for me to properly confide in you, I need you to be able to understand where I'm coming from. I'm not the same person I used to be. I've changed a lot since you last saw me.

You could say I've had a breakdown.

There, I've said it. It wasn't as hard as I expected. It's been my big secret, you see. It's not been a breakdown in the traditional sense. I've done it quietly, behind closed doors, keeping up a front in public; looking strong on the outside when I'm going to pieces inside.

You hear about functional alcoholics: people who maintain their jobs, homes and families despite a huge dependence on drink. I'm a bit like that. A functional fruitcake, you might say. I don't have my job any more – I'm not that functional – but most people I know haven't got a clue how messed up I am inside.

The official reason I stopped working was to be a full-time mum to Ruby. No one questioned that after what we'd been through. But actually I couldn't hack it any more. I tried going back for a few days after the dust had settled and realised that if I stayed, I'd end up having a very public meltdown. At that point I could barely handle the commute to and from the city, never mind the job itself. So I handed in my notice. Thankfully, they let me go straight away.

The rest was manageable. I had enough time to make it look that way, at least. I fell apart in private and stood tall in public. Mainly for Ruby, if I'm honest. She needed me to be okay. Without her, I'd have probably been sectioned.

I never sought any help. Not until recently. That's what led to these letters. But I'll save that story for another day.

I'm worried that learning about this will make you feel bad, which is definitely not my intention. I don't blame you for what happened, nor for the repercussions. It's important you know that. But if I don't give you the full picture, you'll never understand. You won't grasp how a basic task like writing a letter could be difficult for someone like me.

It's safe to say I'm not the high-flyer I used to be. Far from it. Simple tasks have the power to confound me nowadays. My overactive brain, once the key to my success, has become my Achilles heel.

Anyway, Sam, on to other topics. I bet you're wondering what happened with Rick, my new friend from Ruby's school. That was what I promised last time.

Things went well to start with. We bumped into each other at the parking spot that had sparked our first conversation. He was looking every bit as handsome as I remembered, dressed in a navy suit and an open-collar sky-blue shirt. He said he'd come straight from work, but you'd never have guessed it. He looked as fresh and unruffled as if he'd dressed moments earlier.

I'd only settled on an outfit ten minutes before leaving the house: black slim leg trousers with a cream tunic top; smart casual, with my hair tied back and a dash of make-up. I wanted to look like I'd made an effort, but not as though I'd spent ages in front of the mirror. I had done, but that wasn't something he needed to know.

The conversation flowed as we walked together to the schoolyard. He was quite the chatterbox, but in a good way. He wasn't one of those guys who rabbit on about themselves. He seemed genuinely interested in me and my opinions, but without being intrusive. I know what you're thinking, Sam: too good to be true. What's the catch? Well, I was wondering the same. But every time he smiled at me with that perfect grin, daring me not to imagine his lips on mine, my wariness fizzled away.

And, yes, it felt great to see the Queen Bs' eyes on us again. Were they as green with envy as I imagined or was I too busy enjoying the unique situation of getting one up on them? It's hard to say.

It's not that unusual for a dad to be at the school gates. You see quite a few, but they're not normally as good-looking as Rick. He also happens to be new to the school and potentially single, which makes him hot property. Certainly not the kind of person the Queen Bs would expect to talk to a pariah like me. Seeing them sneering at me while muttering to one another was nothing new, but this time I felt like sticking my tongue out at them. Hardly a sure-fire way to impress Rick, though, so I settled for a smug grin or two in their direction, particularly towards Horsey and WAG. Then the girls came out of school and we all headed off together.

I must stop there, although there's plenty still to tell you, believe me. I've not even got to the incidents I mentioned at the start yet. I'll write again later

CHAPTER 5

'Jack? Are you still with me? Come on, lad.'

I open my eyes and see Miles's face hanging a couple of inches above me. We're both on the floor in the kitchen. He's sitting against the wall and I'm slumped against him. The tiles feel cold and hard under my legs. My head's throbbing again.

'Wha—'

I try to speak but only a croak comes out. I clear my throat, causing my head to spin even more, before trying again.

'What happened?'

'You fainted. Luckily I managed to catch you before you went banging your head again. Floor tiles aren't exactly a forgiving surface to fall on.'

The last thing I can recall is Miles leering at me like a wolf. Was that real or did I imagine it? I search for an answer in the creases running across his forehead; I probe

41

the depths of his eyes. But all I find there is concern. I see nothing to fear.

'Why were you trying to confuse me about my name?' I ask.

'What do you mean?'

'Trying to trick me by calling me John. Reeling off all those other names at me.'

He frowns. 'I'm not sure what you mean. Perhaps it might be wise for you to get some more rest.'

I'm confused. Is he playing games with me? I consider having it out with him, a full-blown row if necessary, but I don't have the energy. I decide that either I had some kind of hallucination – a genuine possibility with my mind in such poor shape – or that Miles is using some textbook technique geared towards triggering my memories. I do hope it's the latter. I'd give anything to get them back.

'Why did I faint?'

'You didn't take it easy enough; we need to get some food down you. You'd have been better staying in bed rather than coming down here.'

I try to get up and he helps me back on to a chair at the kitchen table. 'How's that?'

I nod. 'Better. I think I'm all right now. Thanks for catching me.'

'No problem. Tell me if you start feeling faint again. Scrambled eggs?'

'Yes, please.'

'Coming up.'

He hands me a pint glass of water, telling me to drink it all, and busies himself making breakfast.

When it arrives it's delicious. The eggs are luscious and buttery, served on two lightly-toasted wedges of white farmhouse loaf. There's orange juice to drink, plus freshly ground coffee from the fancy machine I spotted earlier.

'Thank you. This is great,' I say, in between mouthfuls.

Miles, who's sitting opposite me, nods in response but continues to eat in silence.

When we've both finished the food and are sipping our coffees, he asks if I'd like some more toast.

'That would be great.'

'I need to feed you up. Get you back to health. I'll never get anywhere with these renovations on my own.'

He goes to the fridge, pulls out a glass jar and places it on the table. 'Try this if you like. Homemade marmalade. I picked it up in the village the other day. There was a fete on at the church hall. Raising money for roof repairs or something. I've no idea how it will taste.'

My eyes fall on the pot and I'm transported back to my youth.

I'm eight years old in a cool larder with my grandmother. She's tiny – only a little taller than I am – standing on tiptoes on a footstool, stretching up to a high shelf.

'Careful, Gangy,' I say, worried she might fall.

She turns and hands me the jar. Orange Marmalade, her neat handwriting reads on a small white label. There's no metal lid, like you get in the shops, but a special waxy disc and some see-through stuff held on with an elastic band.

'Isn't all marmalade made of oranges?' I ask her in my high-pitched little boy's voice.

'Sometimes I put ginger in it too,' she says, beaming that huge smile of hers at me like I'm the most important person in the world. 'I've even made it with lemon and lime,' she adds. 'But I'm not sure you'd like that.'

'I don't like any marmalade apart from yours,' I tell her.

She winks at me. 'That's my boy.'

Miles is on his feet. He looks concerned. 'What happened?'

I'm breathing fast. 'A memory. Something from my childhood. It was the marmalade. It looks like the stuff my grandmother used to make. Gangy, I called her. That's how I said it when I was tiny and it kind of stuck.'

'That all came back to you?'

I nod.

He looks pleased. 'Fantastic. That's a great sign. How much do you recall about her? Anything else about your childhood?'

'I can only remember her as she was in that moment. Nothing else, I'm afraid, although I do have a feeling she died.'

'A feeling? No actual memories of that?'

'No. I can't remember a funeral or anything. She looked so fit and healthy in that memory, and it felt nice to see her that way, as if I knew it wasn't going to last. The memory was so vivid, like I was actually there. Is that normal?'

Miles shrugged. 'Memory is complicated.'

A wave of tiredness washes over me. It makes no sense when the main thing I've done, for as far back as I can remember, is sleep. Must be to do with the head injury, although the throbbing has subsided again now.

44

'How are you feeling?' Miles asks.

'A bit tired, to be honest. Is that normal?'

'Yes. You still need lots of rest. You should go back to bed for a while.'

'Will it bring back my memories?'

'Let's hope so.'

'You don't sound confident. You're surprised they've not come back already, aren't you?'

His face remains blank, unreadable. 'You just had a memory.'

'Sure, but only a fragment: one moment from years ago. It's useless without the rest. And who knows if it was even real? Maybe I was remembering something I once saw rather than a memory of my own.'

'Is that how it felt?' Miles asks.

'No, I don't think so. But who am I to say? I can tell you what a film is, but I can't remember an occasion when I actually watched one. None of this makes any sense.'

'Like I said, memory is complicated.'

'Can't you at least tell me exactly where we are?' I ask him. 'I'd really like to know.'

Miles hesitates for a moment and then his face softens, like he's taking pity on me. 'Fine.' He walks over to a drawer and pulls out a map of Wales. He unfolds it on the kitchen table and shows me our exact location.

The information doesn't help like I hoped it would, though. It means nothing to me at all.

*

I'm trapped. I was walking through a tunnel when there was some kind of earthquake and the ceiling collapsed. I'm pinned to the ground, covered in pieces of rubble. I can't see them because it's pitch black, but I can feel their rough edges all around me, digging into my skin, holding me down. There's sensation in my arms, but I'm unable to shift them. They're wedged into place. I can't feel my legs at all.

'Help,' I shout, but it's pitiful. The sound dies as it leaves my lips, the rocks all around me sucking it in like sponges. Then I feel water creeping along my back; rising from below. Terror rips through me. I'm going to die here: alone in the dark.

I wake with a start and throw the quilt off me in disgust. It's soaking wet, as is the sheet below. My whole body is drenched in sweat. I jump out of the bed, shivering, only for a jolt of pain to run through my head, stopping me in my tracks. I stand as still as I can, my right hand squeezing my temples, and gradually the sensation fades.

The cave, the rocks: a dream, thank God. A nightmare.

I still feel so anxious, though. I have that feeling again that I should be somewhere else – somewhere I'm needed – rather than here. Someone somewhere needs me. The problem is, I don't know who. I take deep breaths, like Miles showed me, trying to calm myself down.

I'm Jack. This is Miles's house. I have a head injury.

The green curtains are closed, but it's clearly still light outside. I remember Miles leading me back upstairs after breakfast; advising me to rest. I must have dozed off

46

straight away. Goodness knows for how long. There's no clock in here.

The cold sweat is still clinging to me, so I head next door to the bathroom for a shower. It's pleasant: hot and powerful. It seems Miles and I have done a good job with this part of the renovation. Afterwards, helping myself to one of the white towels under the sink, I look around the steam-filled room and try to picture myself in here fitting all the bits and pieces. It's useless. I can't remember that at all. And yet the idea of fitting a bathroom doesn't seem entirely alien to me. It's not that I suddenly recall the correct technique for plumbing in a toilet, but I get the feeling I'd be able to work my way through it.

Back in the bedroom, I put on the clothes I wore earlier – jeans and T-shirt, sweater and trainers – and look in the wardrobe at the rest of my belongings. There's not much to see: a couple more pairs of jeans; a few shirts, T-shirts and jumpers; a well-worn black leather jacket; a week's supply of boxer shorts and socks; a pair of black leather shoes. None of it looks new, but it all seems in reasonable condition. The quality is decent, but there are no designer brands. There's an empty medium-sized navy rucksack shoved underneath the wardrobe, which is presumably how I carried everything here.

Apparently I'm a man of few possessions, although it strikes me as odd that I don't at least have a watch or a wallet. Maybe I do and I've left them somewhere else. The whole "dropping my mobile in the sea" thing is weird too. I make a mental note to bring up all of this with Miles later on.

I pull open the curtains and look out through the salt-flecked sash window. I like being able to see the sea from here. There's something captivating about it. Not that it looks very appealing. It's dull and drizzly outside; the choppy water looks more grey than blue. It's close to the house but some way down. We're on a cliff: an isolated one by the looks of things, as there are no other properties or signs of habitation in sight. Our only neighbours appear to be windswept fields, weather-beaten rocks and a rickety fence to keep people away from the steep drop.

I consider the village Miles mentioned earlier; the local pub in which he said we met. I don't think it can be that close to the house; a drive rather than a walk away, from what I gather, so little chance of company other than my host. An ideal place to hide away from the world, you might say. Perfect for a man with no known surname and next to no worldly belongings.

So what, or who, am I hiding from?

As I'm musing on this question, and failing to come up with anything in response, Miles walks past the window into my view. He's wearing a navy fleece and carrying several long pieces of wood under his right arm: floorboards, at a guess. I'm not sure where he got them from, but he looks to be bringing them into the house.

I'm about to knock on the windowpane to get his attention when I see his head snap around as if he's heard something behind him. I follow his gaze and, to my surprise, see another figure standing about a hundred metres away, close to the clifftop fence. It's a woman: long black hair, blowing all over the place in the wind; slender figure in jeans and a knee-length red coat. She's looking out to sea, so I can't see her face and I'm not sure what she did to attract Miles's attention. She stands there, hands in her pockets, the stillness of her body in sharp contrast to the constant flapping of her hair, which she makes no effort to restrain.

It's a mystery where she came from, as there was no sign of her a moment ago.

When I look back to see what Miles is doing, he's gone. I decide to head down to find him and to get a closer look at the woman. There's something about her. I can't put my finger on what it is, but my gut tells me to get out there. Perhaps she and I already know each other. If I could speak to her, maybe she could help me remember something. At the very least, it would be nice to have a conversation with someone other than Miles.

I reach the top of the wide staircase and see Miles unloading the wood in the hallway below.

'Keeping busy?' I call before descending.

He looks up at me with a smile. 'Jack. You're awake.'

'Sure am. What time is it?'

'Mid-afternoon.'

'I slept for a while, then. It's becoming a habit.'

'Be glad of the rest. Your body will take what it needs. Feeling better?'

I nod, standing in front of him now, expecting him to ask about my memory, but the question never comes. Instead he comments that I look steadier on my feet than I did this morning.

49

'What's the actual time?' I ask him.

He grins. 'Who knows?'

'Don't you believe in clocks?'

'That's the second time you've asked me that,' he replies, chuckling. 'You said the very same thing when you first arrived. As I told you then, I've spent enough of my life as a servant to the clock. Now I'm retired, I've liberated myself from it. I do things as and when I want to. Live my days and nights by light and dark, enjoying the shades in between; not worrying about exactitudes.'

'Does that mean there are no clocks at all here?'

'Only those I couldn't remove. There are two in the kitchen, for example: on the microwave and the oven, but they've never been set.'

I want to quiz him further about this bizarre arrangement, but then I remember the woman in red.

'Who was that I saw outside?' I ask.

'Outside? When?'

'A moment ago. The woman in the red coat. I saw her from my bedroom window.'

'Really? I didn't notice anyone out there. Are you sure?'

I don't know what to say. Moments ago I saw Miles looking straight at her. I'm convinced of this fact. But rather than accuse him of lying, with no evidence to back it up, I brush past him and through the front door. 'Follow me. I'll show you.'

I stride out of the house, trying to ignore the biting wind. I'm expecting to spot the woman right away, but she's nowhere to be seen. I pace up and down, scanning

50

the clifftop in all directions. There's no sign of her what-soever, which is weird. It makes me panic that she might have fallen over the edge. I run forward, scouring the line of the rickety fence and the sea below, focusing on the area where I last spotted her. But there's no sign of anything untoward. It's like she was never there.

A concerned Miles catches up to me and clamps a firm hand on my shoulder. 'Are you all right, Jack? What's going on?'

'I definitely saw her from my bedroom window. She was over there. I don't know why you're pretending she wasn't. I saw you look straight at her.'

'I'm sorry, Jack, but I didn't see any woman. I promise you that. Hardly anyone ever comes up here. I'm not sure what's going on. Maybe your mind's playing tricks on you. It could be something to do with the head injury. Come on. Let's get you away from the edge.'

'You don't even have a watch?' I ask Miles later, once he's talked me back inside and plonked me down in front of a cup of coffee in the kitchen.

He shakes his head. 'No need.'

'What about your mobile phone? There must be a clock on there.'

'I don't have one. You'll notice very little technology around here. Only essential appliances: a couple of radios and CD players. There are no televisions or computers.'

'You're joking, right?'

'I'm not. I don't want them. It's liberating to be free from their grasp. I can't believe how much time I used to

51

spend staring at a screen. TVs, computers, they're all the same: soul vacuums. I don't miss them one bit.'

'What about me? Don't I have a watch?'

Miles wrinkles his nose and sucks air in through his teeth. 'Um, no. Not any more. That was one of the conditions of you moving in here.'

'What do you mean?'

'I didn't force it upon you. You agreed.'

'Agreed to what?'

'To drop it over the cliff into the sea. We made a bit of a ceremony of it on the night you moved in. We had had a lot to drink. Don't worry, it wasn't a Rolex or anything. It was just a basic digital watch.'

'Hang on a minute. Is that what also happened to my mobile?'

Miles nods. 'Sorry. I probably should have made that clear last time, but I didn't want to overwhelm you with too much information at that stage.'

'So I willingly dropped them both into the sea? You have to be kidding.'

He shrugs. 'House rules.'

'And my wallet?'

'What about it?'

'I don't seem to have one of those either.'

'Oh, right. I see. Really? I'm sorry, but I don't know anything about that. It's not something we ever discussed.'

He looks genuinely puzzled, but it's not like I know him well enough to read him.

'I must have had to spend money at some point while I've been here.'

Miles shakes his head. 'Like I told you before, you work for your bed and board. There's no money involved in our arrangement. Never has been.'

'What about in the pub? You said we met there.'

'That's right.'

'And? How do I buy drinks?'

'You don't. We only go occasionally and, when we do, I pay. That's also part of the deal.'

'Really. What about the first time?'

'Yes, you probably bought some drinks then. It was a while ago. I can't remember the ins and outs. Listen, what are you getting at? Are you trying to suggest I've stolen your wallet?'

The thought has crossed my mind, but I don't want him to know that. Not at this stage. 'No, don't be stupid. It seems strange I don't have one, that's all. I thought it might give me some more information about myself.'

'You seem very suspicious today, Jack. I appreciate how frustrating your amnesia must be, but remember, I'm not your enemy. All I'm trying to do is help you.'

I nod, as if in agreement, but the truth is I don't know what to believe. How can I when my whole life is a void? I've no frame of reference for anything.

Did I imagine the woman in red? That's certainly the simplest explanation. And yet she seemed so real. My head's a mess. Nothing makes any sense. I need help – and I'm not sure Miles is the best person to provide it.

CHAPTER 6

Thursday, 6 April 2017

Dear Sam,

Back again, as promised. So I was telling you how Rick and I had picked up the girls from school together, wasn't I?

We agreed that Rick would follow me back home in his car – a white Mercedes. Ruby and Anna wanted to travel together, so I said they could ride in the back with me. Bad decision, as it turned out. Their chatter combined with my giddy feelings about Rick meant I wasn't paying as much attention as I should have been. Next thing I knew, I was slamming my foot on the brake to avoid a boy who darted into the road after his football. Luckily I didn't hit him and Rick stopped short of rear-ending me, thus avoiding a total disaster. But it was a close call and Anna started crying.

'Are you all right, love?' I asked her, after taking a deep breath to stop myself from swearing. 'I'm really sorry about that.'

She shook her head and pointed to her tongue.

'Eww, it's bleeding,' Ruby said, helpfully, causing Anna to cry even more.

'Oh dear,' I said, leaning into the back of the car. 'Let's have a look.'

Anna pushed her tongue out like it was the most painful thing in the world; as if it might fall off at any minute.

'Yes, it is bleeding a little,' I told her. 'You must have caught it with your teeth. Don't worry. It'll be all right in no time. Things heal really quickly inside your mouth.'

She stared at me in disbelief through her red, tear-soaked eyes. I guessed she wanted her dad, but knowing we'd be at the house in a couple of minutes, I thought it best to keep on going. I ran my right forefinger under her chin and gave her a reassuring smile. 'When we get home, I'll give you a special drink to make it better.'

I could see Rick in his car behind us, wondering what was going on, so I gave him a wave and mouthed that it was okay. He nodded back at me and then, all of a sudden, he jerked violently in his seat and his car bunny-hopped forward, stopping just short of my bumper. He was out of there in a flash, racing towards the rear of his Mercedes to see the damage. Some idiot had gone into the back of him. Goodness knows how, when he'd been at a standstill for the last couple of minutes.

I pulled my Golf into the side of the road.

Instructing Ruby to look after Anna, who was still too upset about her tongue to work out what had happened, I waited until Rick was done talking to the other driver. Then I locked the girls in the car for a minute and walked across to see if I could help.

'Are you all right?' I asked Rick. He nodded, explaining that the other driver – a woman picking up her grandchild from school in a small Citroen – had been profusely apologetic. Both cars were visibly damaged but still drivable; he wasn't unduly concerned.

'Give me a second to write down my details for her,' he said.

'I feel awful,' I replied. 'If I'd not had to stop like I did, none of this would have happened. A boy ran out into the road and I almost hit him. Not that you'd have thought it from his reaction. He raced off like it was nothing.'

'I know. I saw. Don't worry about it. What else could you have done? Listen, I'm not bothered about the damage to the car. It's nothing that can't be fixed and the insurance will be straightforward because she went into the back of me. I wasn't even moving. How are the girls?'

'Anna's a little upset. She bit her tongue when I braked, but it's only a small cut. It'll heal in no time. Ruby's watching over her.'

'Really? Oh dear. Do you mind waiting with my car for a minute while I check on her?'

'No, of course not.'

I handed him my keys and he nipped over to have a few words and a quick cuddle with Anna.

'Thanks,' he said, flashing me a grin on his return. 'It looks like she'll live.'

I offered to make Anna a saltwater rinse when we got home, but she declined. Her injury was soon forgotten once she and Ruby disappeared upstairs to play.

'Cup of tea?' I asked Rick. 'Or do you need something stronger?'

He laughed. 'Tea would be great. Nice place you have here, by the way.'

Honestly, Sam, I couldn't believe how relaxed he was about the whole thing with his car. I'd have been in a right state if it was me. After I apologised again and he brushed it off, we barely talked about that any more. Despite it all, we ended up having a really good chat. It was the first time in ages I'd had a proper one-to-one with anyone, never mind a gorgeous man. He had this intense way of talking to me with his eyes fixed on mine the whole time, like he really cared about what I had to say. It's been a while since I've felt as though anyone cared.

Not that I told him much. Certainly nothing about you. It didn't feel right at this stage. That was probably why his intensity surprised me, as neither of us went that deep into our lives. It was all superficial stuff about the school and what it's like bringing up a daughter; bits and bobs about the neighbourhood and TV programmes we've enjoyed. It was clear that we both live on our own with our kids, but for some reason neither of us went into specifics. Maybe we'd have got there eventually. But then Ruby broke her arm.

Yes, you heard me right. She and Anna were playing some game that involved them sliding down the stairs and Ruby ended up tripping and falling from top to bottom. I'd not realised what they were doing until then. Otherwise I'd have stopped them. But there was no ignoring the awful thumping sound she made on the way down. Nor the piercing scream that followed once her bone snapped.

She was lying in a heap in the hallway when I found her, Rick and I having raced through from the kitchen. Her skin had turned a deathly pallor somewhere between grey and white and she was shaking. I'm glad it turned out just to be her arm, to be honest. My first impression was that it could be much worse.

'Oh my God,' I found myself shouting, panic rising in my chest. 'What on earth's going on?'

Anna, who was looking down from the top of the stairs in terror, burst into tears again. Then I snapped into action and focused on how best to help my daughter.

Rick, I have to say, was useless at this point, which surprised me. Rather than helping, he beckoned Anna downstairs and pulled her to one side, looking queasy. Some people aren't good with that kind of thing, I suppose. It wasn't like there was blood all over the place, but Ruby's right arm – thank goodness she's left-handed – was very obviously broken. It was bent all out of shape between the wrist and the elbow. I was going to pieces inside, believe me, but somehow I found the strength to keep on going. There was no time to be squeamish. No time to over-think things and let that hyperactive brain of mine find some way to cripple me. My daughter needed me. Your maternal instinct kicks in at these moments and you do whatever's required.

I knew I had to get her to A&E as soon as possible. Rick offered to come, but I could tell he didn't really want to. Squeamish folk don't tend to be big hospital fans. 'No, no,' I told him as I tried to calm Ruby down and get her into the car. 'There's really no need. We'll be stuck there for hours. You've already had enough hassle today.'

'Are you sure?'

'Yes. You get Anna home.'

'We've not had the best afternoon, have we?'

I gave him a pursed smile, willing him to go, so I could concentrate on my daughter. 'Not really.'

'Never mind. There's always next time.'

'Sure.'

Anyhow, we went to hospital and, as predicted, it took ages. You can understand now, Sam, why I didn't find time to write to you yesterday. I—

Got to go. Ruby's calling. Write tomorrow.

Love as always,

M

Xx

CHAPTER 7

BEFORE

Wednesday, 5 April 2017

The phone on Dan's desk rang, jangling loudly through the newsroom.

He looked at the clock: 5.45 p.m. Shit.

'Yes?'

'Hello, Dan. It's Susan on reception. I'm sorry to bother you when you're on deadline. It's your wife. She says it's urgent.'

He felt like correcting her and saying 'ex-wife', although technically that wasn't the case. They were still married, but only on paper. Why was she calling him now? Better than a last-minute story coming through, which was what he'd feared, but not by much. It was never good news when she called these days.

'You'd better put her through,' he told Susan.

'Right. Here she is.'

'Hello?'

'It's Maria.'

'I know. What can I do for you?'

'There's been an accident. I'm at A&E with Ruby.'

That got his attention. 'What? Is she all right?'

'Not really. She's broken her arm.'

'You're joking. How?'

'She fell down the stairs. She was playing with a friend.'

'Bloody hell, Maria. How bad is it?'

'I'm not a doctor, Dan. All I know so far is that the arm's broken.'

Why did she always have to be so offhand with him? Dan wondered. His eyes drifted from the keypad of the desk phone to a half-finished mug of coffee that had long since gone cold. 'Trust me, I'm a journalist!' was printed on the side – a gift from Maria back in the good old days.

'Which hospital are you at?' he asked.

'St Joseph's. We only got here about half an hour ago. We'll be ages yet.'

'Can I talk to her?'

'Hold on.'

There was a pause as Maria spoke to Ruby. All Dan could hear was a hospital announcement in the background.

'She doesn't want to,' Maria said a moment later. 'She's in a lot of pain.'

'Oh. Listen, I'd come to the hospital, but—'

'But what?'

'It's Wednesday, Maria.'

She knew full well what that meant: deadline night for

61

all three of his papers. But she was clearly in no mood for cutting him any slack.

'Of course. Work comes first. What was I thinking?'

'Don't be like that. I'll get out of here as soon as I can, but you know how it is. You said yourself there's nothing to do but wait.'

'Right.'

'Thanks for letting me know.'

'You're her father.'

'What's that supposed to mean?' Dan sighed. 'Listen, I'll call you in a bit when I'm done. See where you're up to.'

'Whatever.'

'Come on, Maria. Don't be like that. Are you sure she won't speak to me?'

'I have to go. Someone's coming over.'

'Wait . . . Hello?' Damn. She'd hung up on him. Most of their phone calls seemed to end that way nowadays. Being separated was hard work – especially when a child was involved.

Was it unreasonable of him not to down tools and race over to the hospital immediately? Was that what most fathers would do? Probably, but he was so bloody busy. He found it so tough to strike the right balance with Ruby. The temptation, of course, was to wrap her up in cotton wool; do everything to keep her safe; pander to her every need. That was Maria's way, but Dan knew it would only make Ruby more vulnerable in the long run. Wouldn't they be better preparing her for the harsh realities she'd face later in life? Wasn't that the best way to—

'Smoke?'

He looked up to see Maurice standing next to his desk, a freshly rolled cigarette tucked behind one ear. There was a smile stretched across his ruddy face and he looked as laid-back as ever.

'I've even got my own today,' he said.

'So I see.'

'I can roll one for you too, if you like. Might as well take advantage while I have some baccy.'

'No, thanks. I'll stick to my Marlboro Lights. I will join you, though. I could do with a break.'

'Good stuff.'

Maurice, who was in his late forties, had wavy salt and pepper hair that got increasingly messy the longer he spent at work. He was great company: a magnetic character, liked by everyone in the office. He was good at his job and fazed by nothing. Mostly, though, it was his easy manner that people warmed to; his ability to focus on whoever he was talking to and make them feel important. He'd listen and empathise in a way that made them want to confide in him, like they had a special relationship. It was quite the gift and especially useful as a bachelor. Despite his average looks, he always seemed to have several girlfriends on the go at once. Not that he'd ever boast about the fact; that wasn't his style. He was more likely to look embarrassed than proud if someone brought it up.

'Are you all right, mate?' he asked Dan as they took the lift downstairs. 'You look troubled.'

'I had my wife on the phone. Ruby's at A&E. She fell down the stairs and broke her arm.'

'Oh, no. That's awful. How's she doing?'

'Well, she'll be there a while, by the sound of things.'

'Are you getting out of here, then?'

'I doubt it. Not for a few hours, anyway. I've still got loads to tie up. These things always happen on deadline day, don't they?'

'I can help, if you like. I'm not too busy.'

'Thanks, but it's not like I'd be able to do anything for her at the hospital.'

'No, but you're her dad. She'll want you there. Trust me.'

Maurice had a daughter of his own – a nineteen-year-old from a short-lived relationship in his younger days – so he did know what he was talking about. However, he didn't know how tricky things had been with Ruby recently. She hadn't taken well to Dan moving out of the family home. He'd always suspected that she blamed him for the split with Maria and a few weeks ago she'd said as much. It was blurted out in anger and she'd apologised later on, claiming not to have meant it, but the words had stuck with Dan. Wasn't it supposed to be the other way around? Weren't the weekends with him supposed to be the fun time? Weren't daughters supposed to be daddy's girls? Welcome to reality, he thought.

By the time they went back inside, Dan had agreed to accept Maurice's kind offer to stand in and finish his papers off for him.

'You're sure?' he asked one more time before leaving for the hospital.

'Go. Be with your daughter.'

'Thanks, mate. I owe you.'

Half an hour later he was at St Joseph's, where Ruby was slumped in a chair, her arm in a sling, waiting to have an X-ray.

'Hello, darling,' he said, crouching down next to her and kissing her pale cheek, careful not to brush against her arm.

She gave her best attempt at a smile, although it barely registered on her drawn face. 'Hi, Daddy,' she whispered.

'You look wiped out, little one. How are you doing?'

'Not good.'

'Poor thing.'

He looked over at Maria, who was sitting on the next seat along. 'Hi. I managed to get away.'

'So I see.' She didn't go as far as thanking him, but she did look pleasantly surprised.

'Have they given her something for the pain?' he asked.

Maria nodded.

It was late by the time they finally got Ruby home, her arm in plaster, and they put her straight to bed. That evening was the longest time all three of them had spent together in ages, Dan noted. And there hadn't been one argument. It almost felt like they were a family again.

'Night night,' Maria said, planting a kiss on Ruby's forehead before leaving Dan to tuck her in.

He knelt at the side of her bed and stroked her hair. 'How are you feeling, darling?'

'Tired,' she whispered.

'Does your arm still hurt?'

She nodded, fresh tears trickling down her flushed cheeks.

'Better than before, though?' Dan asked, wiping the tears away with a thumb.

'A bit.'

'Don't worry: you'll be back to normal in no time. One of the best things about being a child is that you heal quickly. Anyway, I'd better let you sleep, hadn't I?'

She reached out with her good arm, eyes anxious. 'No. Stay.'

'Okay, love, I will.' Taking her hand, he leaned over and kissed her on each cheek. 'But you close your eyes. It's late and sleep is really important when your body needs to fix itself.'

Moving into a more comfortable seated position, Dan leaned against the side of Ruby's bed and promised not to leave until she'd nodded off.

Thank goodness she's all right, he thought, his heart swelling with the love he felt for his precious daughter.

As he sat there, silent in the dark bedroom, Dan's eyes grew heavy.

Next thing he knew, he was woken by a gentle tap on his shoulder. He turned to see Maria holding a finger to her lips. 'Come on,' she whispered, signalling for him to follow her out of the room.

Once on the landing, he asked: 'How long was I—'

'Only a few minutes.'

'Sorry. She wanted me to stay until she fell asleep.'

'Don't worry. Listen, I'm going to get changed. Fancy a drink before you go? If you're not too tired.'

Pleasantly surprised, Dan stifled a yawn. 'Um, sure.'

'I've no beer, but there's a bottle of white in the fridge.'

'Great.'

'Help yourself. I'm going to freshen up.'

'No problem. Would you like a glass too?'

'Are you kidding? I could down the bottle in one.'

'I'll make it a large, then.'

She joined him in the kitchen a few minutes later, make-up free, wearing jogging bottoms and a hoodie. It was quite a comedown from the outfit she'd been wearing before, which had been the most dressy he'd seen her in ages.

'Comfy?' he asked with a grin, fully awake again now.

'What?'

'Nothing.'

He was thinking back to when she used to dress up, not down, for him. But he stopped himself from saying so. Things between them right now were the most amicable they'd been in ages. Showing up at the hospital had earned him precious brownie points. No point ruining it.

'The outfit you had on earlier was really nice,' he added. 'That's all.'

She squinted at him over the kitchen table. 'And now I look a mess.'

'That's not what I said. I was paying you a compliment.'

He stopped short of accusing her of twisting his words. That would definitely lead to an argument.

She stared at him for a moment. He imagined the cogs of her mind whirring behind her beautiful hazel eyes. They'd once beamed pure love at him. Now they were more often than not a tool of accusation; of anger and frustration. Maybe even hate, although he hoped not. He couldn't bear to think that things between them had veered so far off course. They'd been so good together. Under normal circumstances, he was sure they'd still be happily married. But what they'd been through was enough to tear apart even the strongest of unions.

She sighed. 'I'm tired. It's been a long day.'

'No problem,' he replied, pleasantly surprised. He couldn't recall the last time Maria had backed down like that.

They'd not discussed the accident in front of Ruby for fear of upsetting her. But now she was out of earshot, Dan was keen to know what had happened.

'I didn't see it,' Maria explained. 'She was playing on the stairs, which she knows she shouldn't have been doing. I was in the kitchen.'

Dan knew that had their roles been reversed, Maria would have made a big issue of the whole "playing on the stairs" thing. He'd have been blamed for letting Ruby do it and accused of not paying enough attention. But he knew the reality: Ruby was eight and didn't always do as she was told. You couldn't watch children constantly at that age. You had to give them space to learn through making mistakes.

'Which friend was she playing with?' he asked. 'Anyone I know?'

'Um, no. A girl called Anna. She's new in Ruby's class. Recently moved to the area.'

'Really? Great. What's she like?'

'Nice.'

'Did she come by herself or with her mum?'

Maria looked to the floor and scratched her forehead in that way Dan knew she did when she was uncomfortable. 'Um. With her dad, actually. Rick.'

'Oh, right. I see.'

Dan did his best not to look surprised, irritated even. But he could see from Maria's expression that he'd failed. He'd never had much of a poker face.

'What?' she asked defensively. 'It's not that unusual these days for a father to pick his kids up from school, you know.'

'I never said it was. If you remember, I did it more than you when we were both working.'

'You're having a go at me for staying at home now?'

'What are you on about?'

'I heard the tone in your voice: derogatory, like I'm not as good as you, because I choose to be a full-time mum. You can jump off that high horse right now. Your earnings don't come close to what mine used to be. And if it wasn't for the money from my parents—'

'Yes, yes, I know. Heard it all before. We wouldn't be in this dream house of ours, if it wasn't for them. Well, I'm not, am I? Not any more. I'm in my lovely damp flat instead. And as much as I hate it there, do you know what? It beats being here with you. You can shove your family money up your arse, Maria.'

He slammed his half-full glass of wine on to the table, somehow not breaking it, and got up to leave. But now he couldn't stop himself. She'd popped his cork, like a shaken bottle of fizz; the words came out by themselves. 'It's not possible for us to have a normal conversation any more, is it? Whatever I say, you always find a way to turn it into a bloody argument. Why the hell do I bother? You're not the woman I married. You're not even a shadow of her. There's no going back for us, I can see that now. We're done. We might as well get on with the divorce. Get it out of the way. Then I can be free of you. Maybe you can run off with your new friend Rick. It makes sense now why you were so dressed up today. Trying to impress him, were you? Well, good luck with that. Best not let him see how twisted you are, or he'll run a mile.'

Dan had expected Maria to fire back at him with a verbal assault of her own, but it didn't come. Instead she burst into tears, which stopped him in his tracks, instantly cooling his anger and turning on the tap of regret. He took a deep breath, resisted the urge to apologise for his outburst, and left without another word.

'Idiot,' he said to himself, getting into his car and slamming the door. He couldn't believe he'd let himself say all that stuff. No one knew the right buttons to press to upset her better than he did. She'd done the same to him on enough occasions, but he tried not to get sucked into that kind of thing. Epic fail this time, he thought. The worst bit was what he'd said about getting a divorce. In truth, that was the last thing he wanted, so why on earth had he said it? The one consolation was that he hadn't gone further. He hadn't mentioned her mental health, which would have been a tough one to come back from. And he'd not brought Sam into it, thank goodness.

He considered returning to apologise, but he knew what Maria's reaction would be if he did. She'd throw it straight back at him. She hated it when people said sorry for things, especially just after they'd said or done them.

'You can keep your apology. I don't want it.'

How many times had she said that to him over the years? Countless, especially at the start of their relationship, before he got wise to it. She felt an apology was the easy option, favouring actions rather than words. Mind you, that opinion was forged in different times: days when she rarely got angry herself; when judging others for speaking in haste wouldn't have been hypocritical. Things were different now. She was different.

All the same, going back to say sorry didn't feel like the right move, so Dan drove home. Well, he went back to the flat, which was the closest thing he had at the moment. He'd never think of it as home, because it wasn't. He hated it too much for that. It felt more like a prison. Ironically, the place he thought of as home was the house he'd just left, having done a good job of making sure he wouldn't be invited back any time soon.

He opened a bottle of vodka and necked three shots in quick succession. He hoped the booze would raise rather than lower his spirits. Experience told him it could go either way. Looking for a distraction, he decided he ought to text Maurice to make sure everything had gone well with the papers.

He'd downed several more shots and two bottles of beer by the time Maurice's reply eventually arrived.

All good. How's Ruby? She was glad to see you, right?

Yes. Tucked up in best not, ATM on plate.

What? Bloody predictive text. Realising he was already quite drunk, Dan deleted the message and started again, concentrating to make sure he got it right this time.

Yes. Tucked up in bed now, arm in plaster. Thanks again. See you tomorrow.

Maurice's question got Dan thinking. Had Ruby been pleased to see him at the hospital? He'd thought so at the time, but maybe he'd seen what he wanted to see. Her reaction had actually been quite muted. He'd put that down to the pain she was in, but now he wasn't so sure.

He could feel himself sinking into one of his moods, but it was too late to change anything now. He took another gulp of vodka, no longer bothering with the shot glass.

CHAPTER 8

I wake up to find I can't move. It's getting light outside and I'm looking up at the high ceiling of my room at Miles's house. I know who I am: I'm Jack, and I have a head injury. But I can't move. It's like some invisible force is pinning me to the bed. I try again and again to raise myself up, but it's no use.

What the hell's happening? I try to stay calm and rational, but it's no good. My breathing gets faster; I can feel myself breaking out in a cold sweat. Panic is here. I can feel his bony fingers pressing down on my chest. I can smell his rotten breath.

'Miles,' I call out. 'Help me! I'm paralysed.'

I shout his name more times than I can remember. Louder and louder until my voice cracks, my throat like sandpaper. He doesn't come.

What time is it? I wonder. Impossible to know for sure in this house without clocks, but I'd guess at five or six o'clock. Miles must still be asleep. That's why he's not coming. He will in an hour or two once he wakes up. I need to calm down. Wait it out.

Easier said than done. I'm paralysed! Of course I'm panicking.

At that moment I hear the creak of the bedroom door opening. I try to look in that direction, but my head's having none of it and my eyes will only roll back so far.

'Miles? What took you so long?'

But it's not his voice that replies.

'Hello, my love. Did you call me?'

When I answer, my voice is that of a child. I'm still around – still part of the action – but not in the driving seat and no longer paralysed. 'Yes, Gangy. I had a bad dream. I woke up and—'

'And what? You can tell me.'

'I thought there was a bat in here.'

'A bat? Where?'

I point to the corner of the room and she walks over to it. She has a good look around, even kneeling down and peeking under the chest of drawers. 'No,' she says, once her search is complete. 'There's definitely no bat here. None whatsoever. I think you still had one foot in the Land of Nod.'

'What's that?'

'The Land of Nod is where we go when we're asleep. It's a tricky old place. When you're there, you think it's real life. When you're fully awake, it doesn't seem real at all. Sometimes, when you first wake up and one world blends into the other, you can get confused. Was there a bat in your dream?'

'Yes.'

'There you go. That explains it. I dreamt I was a rabbit the other night.'

I giggle as she twitches her nose at me.

'I really believed it too,' she continues. 'I led a full life. It seemed like I was there forever, hopping in and out of my warren; eating carrots and so on.'

'Mum says rabbits don't really eat carrots.'

'She's right. Carrots aren't what they naturally eat in the wild. But I bet they'd like the ones I grow in my garden, because they're super delicious, aren't they?'

I nod enthusiastically. She knows I love her home-grown veggies.

'Anyway, I ate carrots in my dream. Like Bugs Bunny. Then I woke up and laughed at myself for believing I was a rabbit.'

'What was it like?'

'Being a rabbit? Good fun, from what I can remember. But that's the other thing with dreams: the memory of them fades before you know it.'

'What colour rabbit were you?'

'Light brown with a bushy white tail.'

I smile. 'Gangy?'

'Yes, love.'

'Do I have to go back to sleep?'

'Not if you don't want to. We're both awake now. How about we go downstairs and make some breakfast?'

I jump up and throw on my dressing gown.

'I'll need a hug first,' Gangy says, and I throw my arms around her.

'I love staying here,' I tell her.

'And I love having you.'

'Come on. Time to get up.'

My eyes snap open and Miles is leaning over the bed, opening the green curtains and letting the daylight stream in.

'Morning, lad. How are you feeling today?'

'I can't—' I realise I've just turned my head. I sit up without any effort. Everything's working again. The whole paralysis thing must have been a dream.

'You can't what?'

'Um, nothing. It's fine.'

'How's the head?'

'Good. It hardly hurts at all now.'

'What's your name?'

'Jack.'

'And who am I?'

'Miles. I'm your lodger. This is your house. I'm helping you fix it up.'

'Excellent. Anything else come back to you?'

'Maybe. I'm not entirely sure. I think I dreamt a memory. Is that possible?'

Miles shrugs. 'I don't see why not. What was it about?'

'It was something from my childhood. Like last time, with the marmalade. It involved my grandmother again.'

I talk him through the scene that played out in my head. Miles sits on the wooden chair, listening to me with his head cocked to one side.

76

'What do you think?' I ask when I've finished.

'Sounds like a memory to me. What do you think? How did it feel?'

I nod. 'Like I'd been there before.'

'What did your grandmother look like?'

'Um, I don't know. I should have paid more attention. Small, I think – for an adult. She wasn't that much bigger than me. Short curly hair. Kind eyes. She was wearing a dressing gown. Light green, maybe.'

'That's good.'

'But why her? Why's she the one I remember again? Why my childhood? What about everything in between? When's that going to return?'

Miles sits back in the chair and runs one hand through his short white hair. 'Take it easy. That's a lot of questions. Memory's complicated.'

'Yes, but you also said this kind of memory loss is rare. What did you call it again?'

'Retrograde amnesia.'

'That's it. So what's going on? Why hasn't everything come back? Don't take this the wrong way; I know you have lots of experience as a GP, but don't you think I maybe ought to see a specialist or something? Go to a hospital?'

'Sure, if you're worried, we can do that. No problem. The nearest hospital is a good drive away, though. Plus the only doctor you'll get to see on a weekend is at A&E – probably some youngster who qualified five minutes ago. There's really no point going there until next week when someone senior is around.'

'What day is it today?'

'Saturday.'

'Oh, right. I didn't realise.'

He reassures me that he's perfectly well qualified to keep an eye on me for the time being. I mention the paralysis, in case it's important, although Miles is sure it was only a dream, most likely spawned by the frustration of my memory loss.

'But you will take me to the hospital next week?'

'Of course.'

'It's not that I don't have faith in you, Miles. I'm just desperate to get my memories back. It's so frustrating not knowing who I am. If there's anything that can be done—'

'Don't worry, Jack. I understand.'

'Are you sure it's not worth going today? Isn't there a chance there might be someone who can help?'

'No. It would be an utter waste of time. You'll have to trust me on that.'

'Could we go on Monday, then?'

'Yes, Monday we can do.'

After a shower and breakfast, I find Miles busy laying floorboards.

'Can I help?' I offer.

'No, I don't think you're ready to get back to work yet.'

'But that's why I'm here, isn't it?'

'It's too soon.'

'What shall I do, then? I need to get busy with something or I'll go crazy.'

Miles shrugs.

'Maybe I'll get some fresh air. The weather looks decent: the sun's out and there's no sign of any rain.'

'I'm not sure that's a good idea in your condition.'

'I'll be fine,' I insist. 'Don't worry. I won't go near the edge of the cliff. I could really do with . . .'

Miles throws me an expectant stare.

'Yeah, I was going to tell you that I need to clear my head,' I say. 'Then the irony of the expression struck me. What I really want to do is fill my head back up. But you know what I mean.'

'I'd rather you put your feet up.'

'Just a little walk. I'll stay close to the house, I promise.'

'Fine. You're a grown man and you seem steady enough on your feet now. But please don't go close to the edge, and don't push yourself too hard.'

'I won't. Thanks, Doc.'

Outside, the fresh sea air feels great on my skin. Despite what I've told Miles, I can't resist walking over to the rickety fence and peering down the jagged cliff face to the swirling sea, which looks chilly and agitated. I'm not sure what time of year it is, which is an odd feeling, yet I'm dressed for winter in a jumper and jacket. That must be right, I think. The sun might be out, but there's no warmth, especially in the coastal breeze. I take in my surroundings, noting the bare branches of the few trees nearby and the lack of any flowers. Then I look back at the house: a last outpost of civilisation in this remote spot, as worn and neglected as it is imposing. There's so much still to be done, I think, eyeing all the flaking paintwork, rotten wood and damaged roof tiles. No wonder Miles needs my help.

Wandering over to the rear of the house, I come across a mud-caked green Land Rover parked at the top of a winding dirt track. I assume this leads to a proper road. The car looks old but functional. I stare down the track; just knowing for sure that there's an actual route to civilisation comes as a relief.

I hear a thumping noise behind me and I turn to see Miles struggling to open a decrepit wooden window on the first floor. He eventually succeeds and waves to me with a smile. 'Ring a bell?'

'Sorry?' I say, cupping one ear and moving closer.

'There,' he replies, pointing to a spot of overgrown grass and a mound of earth to my left-hand side.

Despite having a good look around, I've no idea what he's talking about. I shrug, perplexed.

'That pile of soil,' he says, pointing again. 'It's where I found you unconscious after your accident.

'Really?' I look again, but still nothing comes back.

He nods to one side. 'The ladder's over there.'

I go to it, run my hands over the cold aluminium, but it's as unfamiliar as the rest.

'I think you must have been looking at the state of the roof. We'd been talking about sorting out the tiles for a while. I'm not sure why you decided to do it when I wasn't around, though; it's not wise to go up a ladder alone.'

'Clearly not.'

'And? Any recollection?'

I look around again, as if that might somehow trigger

80

my memory, but there's nothing. As far as I'm concerned, it's the first time I've ever seen this side of the house. I shake my head. 'It's not familiar at all. I was—'

I stop mid-sentence as something catches my eye: a flash of red in my peripheral vision. I turn in that direction, but there's nothing there.

'You all right?' Miles calls down to me.

'Yes, I'm fine. I'm going for a wander. See you in a bit.'

'Be careful. Make sure not to lose your way.'

'Don't worry, I won't.'

I'm convinced the red is from the woman I spotted out of the window yesterday: the slender figure looking over the cliff, who Miles claimed not to have seen. There's no logic to this other than the fact that she was wearing a red coat, but I'm gripped by the notion and I race in that direction to try to catch her.

There's no sign of her at the front of the house. I'm confused. I look all around, casting my eye up and down the coastline. I retrace my steps to the rear of the house, taking care to stay out of Miles's view, but still no luck. Eventually, after several minutes of scratching my head, I figure I must have imagined it. It's the only rational explanation. I have had a recent head trauma. Seeing flashes of colour is probably a side effect. Besides, if I'm to believe Miles, I probably imagined her in the first place. And yet somehow I'm still not convinced of that. The first time I saw her she was so realistic, so alive.

I return to the front of the house and decide to walk to the place along the clifftop where I first saw the mysterious woman in red. Miles wouldn't approve, but what he doesn't know won't hurt him. I soon reach the spot, but of course she's not there and there's no sign of her either. So I carry on, focusing on a crooked sea stack in the distance that reminds me of a witch's nose.

I take in the cool, fresh air with deep breaths – as slow as I can manage – in a bid to calm myself down. I feel all worked up; my shoulders ache. I hadn't realised how tense I was until now. Having no memory is so frustrating; how can I understand myself when my past is a mystery? My mind is like an empty library: useless without the volumes of knowledge that define it.

I'm picturing that image in my mind when it's ripped apart and set alight by the burning arrow of another memory.

It's dark and the streets are full of monsters with bags of loot.

A little ghost is gripping my hand and pulling me towards the light of a nearby front door. 'They have a pumpkin in the window,' she says. 'They should definitely answer.'

'Well spotted,' I tell her. 'You've got excellent eyes for a ghost. Would you like me to come to the door with you or to hang back?'

'I want you to come. You don't look scary though. I said you should have worn a mask.'

'Never mind. I'll pull a really creepy face instead. How's this?'

She looks up at my attempt at facial contortion and giggles while pressing the bell.

A moment later the door swings open and we both shout: 'Trick or treat!'

'Wow! You do look scary,' booms the large bald man who answers. 'I'd better give you some sweets, hadn't I?

He reaches to grab a big bowl of mini chocolates from a shelf above a coat rack standing beside the door. How strange, I think. All the jackets hanging there are red.

'Here, help yourself,' he says. 'And please don't trick me.'

As the little ghost reaches out, the man turns to me. 'Are you okay?' he asks. His voice is different now, though. It sounds female. Like that of a young woman.

What's happening? One moment I'm looking him in the eye, wondering what the hell is going on with his voice, and the next everything fades to black. I'm shouting out, but I can't hear myself, like I've been muted. I'm confused, afraid.

Then I hear that voice again.

'Can you hear me?'

It definitely sounds like a young woman; maybe a teenager. The tone reassures me somehow. It seems familiar, although I can't put my finger on why.

'You have to get up. It's not safe here. You need to open your eyes.'

Bright sky is above me: light blue with fluffy sheep clouds. I turn my head to the right, feel damp grass under my cheek and view the sea through the gaps in the rickety fence. Why am I lying on the ground? What happened?

I heave myself up. First into a sitting position and then, once I'm sure everything's working, on to my feet. I feel dizzy, especially when I look at the sea far below. There's a twinge from my head, but nothing like the pain I felt when I first woke up after the accident. I must have fainted or passed out. It didn't feel like that, though. It was more like I was in a trance – reliving a forgotten memory, as I had before.

So who was the young girl trick-or-treating with me? Was the little ghost my daughter? It felt like she was. But how can I be a father and not remember? That's not the kind of thing you ever forget, is it? I must be mistaken. Maybe she was a niece, a young sister or a friend's daughter. Perhaps it wasn't a memory at all. It could have been a scene I watched in a film, although again it felt so real.

I think back to the feeling I keep having that I should be somewhere else, with someone else. Maybe there's a good reason for that.

I shiver in the wind. What about the older girl's voice that spoke to me at the end? She told me to get up. She said I wasn't safe. Was she right? And why did she sound so familiar?

I turn 360 degrees, scanning the open space in every direction for some clue. And then I see her: far in the distance along the clifftop, in the opposite direction from which I was walking.

The woman in red. Or maybe not a woman at all. Could she be the one who just spoke to me? Could she be a girl? A teenager?

She looks identical to the last time I saw her; same jeans and knee-length coat, billowing long black hair. She's looking at me, although she's some distance away: too far to clearly make out her face. So how could she have been talking to me?

I cup both hands around my mouth and shout to her. 'Hello! Can you hear me?'

She doesn't react, so I wave my hands above my head, staring at her the whole time and shouting some more.

She stands there, hands in her pockets, looking straight at me but through me.

Then I blink and she's gone.

CHAPTER 9

Friday, 7 April 2017

Dear Sam,

Sorry about breaking off so abruptly last time. Ruby had got herself all confused, poor thing. She'd had some sort of nightmare; then she woke up and got into a panic at not being able to move her arm. It'll take her a while to get used to the plaster cast.

I'm keeping her off school for a couple of days. Yesterday she was shattered after all the time we spent at the hospital. Today it was more about giving her a chance to get used to doing everything one-handed. She should be fine to go back next week, from what the doctors said. As long as she's not in any pain and keeps her arm rested in a sling. She'll still be able to do most of her schoolwork, thanks to being left-handed, but there'll be no PE or Games for a while. She's mainly excited about all her friends signing the plaster.

I didn't have a chance last time to tell you about

the hospital visit itself. We went to A&E at St Joseph's and were there for hours. One nice – and somewhat surprising – thing was that Dan turned up.

There, I've mentioned him. You probably wondered when I was going to. It had to happen eventually; he's still in our lives and always will be, despite what happened between us. Forgive me if I'm not as impartial or diplomatic about him as I ought to be. I'm writing to your future self, Sam, not to the person you were. So these letters are making the assumption that you know all about the separation and so on. The whys and wherefores are not something I want to discuss here. I will say, though, that you mustn't feel bad about any of that – I'm not suggesting you do; there's absolutely no reason to. But just in case.

I rang him at work after the accident. He said initially that he couldn't make it, because it was deadline night, but then he turned up after all. That was unexpected and, in light of Rick's disappointing response, it actually felt refreshing. Dan was really supportive, and I think Ruby and I both appreciated it.

Things between us were really good for once. Dan stayed at the hospital the whole time and followed us home to tuck Ruby up in bed. He even stayed for a glass of wine. But then things turned sour. First he said something derisive after I changed into some casual clothes. Then he picked up on the fact that Rick had been here and got all narky with me. He didn't actually accuse me of not paying enough attention to Ruby when she had the accident, but I could tell he was thinking it. He put me on a guilt trip about giving up work and, before I knew it, he was asking for a divorce and saying all kinds of hurtful things.

After everything I'd been through that day, it was too much. I burst into tears. Pathetic, I know, but I didn't have the energy to argue back. Dan went home. I sat there, sobbing my heart out until there were no tears left.

All in all, a pretty dreadful day.

The thing is, Sam, before we had that argument, I was feeling better about our relationship than I have in ages. Dan turning up at the hospital renewed my faith in him. It felt nice the three of us being together again as a family unit. A small part of me even started to wonder . . .

No, I can't bring myself to say it. Not after how it all turned out. I guess that was why it hurt so much when he started having a go at me. The irony is I've done that to him on loads of occasions; if I've not actually used the D word at some point, then I've definitely implied it. I've shouted and screamed at him; behaved in the bitchiest way possible countless times. I even made him return the present he gave me last Christmas, because we'd agreed not to do gifts. Nasty or what?

That might not sound like how you remember me, Sam. I never used to lose my temper so easily, did I?

It's part of the personal problems I've been having: the breakdown I mentioned in my last letter.

The thing about Dan is that he usually takes whatever I say firmly on the chin. As awful as that sounds, it's true. He's not the type to shout back, even when I deserve it. He definitely hasn't asked for a divorce before. He's never been one to say much at all about his emotions. That's played a part in the problems between us. So in a way, although it sounds warped, I'm glad he shouted at me. It was good to see him being passionate, but a shame it was so horribly negative.

Gosh, just thinking about the current state of my relationship with Dan has got me welling up, especially since we used to be so good together. The way we met – in a pub with a group of friends – might not have been especially romantic. (I've told you the story before about how I knocked over his beer, spilling it all over his shirt.) But everything else about the start of our love affair was perfect. We fell head over heels for each other. I knew I wanted to marry him after we kissed at the end of that first meeting, believe it or not. I'd never got on so well with another person, male or female, before. We just clicked instantly, as if we'd known each other for years, even though I spent the first half an hour or so apologising for my clumsiness. It was like everyone else we were out with that night disappeared. Within a few weeks we were inseparable, and it remained like that for so long.

Relationships change over the years, of course, especially when you start a family. But when you're married to your best friend and soulmate, as I truly felt I was, you travel through the ups and downs of life confident that your relationship will stand the test of time, no matter what. Unfortunately, as we eventually found out, even the strongest marriages have their breaking points.

Anyway, I digress. Back to the other night. After Dan had left and I'd cried myself out, I got into a bit of a state. I'd better explain. Sorry for the heavy subject matter again, Sam, but I need to do this.

You've heard of OCD, right? Obsessive Compulsive Disorder. It's kind of a trendy mental illness these days. All sorts of people claim to have it: famous sports stars, actors, comedians, you name it. It's often mentioned in a light-hearted way. They say something like: 'I'm a bit OCD.' Then they go on, with a wry grin, to explain how they like to order things in a certain way in their kitchen cupboards or have to check the front door twice before going out.

This winds me up because from my perspective, as someone who definitely does have OCD, it isn't funny at all. It's debilitating, humiliating, infuriating; rather than tell people, I do my utmost to hide it, even from those closest to me.

On the other hand, you get films and TV documentaries taking things to the opposite extreme. They tend to portray OCD in its most acute form. You see someone housebound or unable to lead a normal life because of it. They're some kind of twitching wreck, hopping down the pavement to avoid cracks, or scrubbing all the skin off their palms for fear of germs. I understand why the producers and directors do this, as extremity makes for a more powerful story, but I just wish someone would portray the condition in a way that more closely matches my own experience.

I'm a functional fruitcake, remember, and I think the middle ground – the place where I and many other sufferers live, hiding our craziness from view – gets overlooked.

For a long time, I tried to hide it from myself by denying it was there. Now, finally, I've come to terms with it. I've sought help and I'm on the road to recovery, but it's hard enough for people to understand without it being portrayed inaccurately in popular culture.

Wow. I can't believe I told you all that, Sam. I thought it would be hard, but in fact the opposite was true. The words flowed right out of me. I wonder if this comes as a huge surprise to you, or if it kind of makes sense. With hindsight, you see, I think I've probably had a latent form of it for most of my life, which developed into full-blown OCD when I had my breakdown.

I've always liked things 'just so'. I used to keep items on my desk at work in certain positions, for instance, and I'd get annoyed if someone moved them. I suppose I did it at home too, insisting on things being neat and tidy around the house. But it rarely got in the way of my everyday life and I never thought of it as anything more than fussiness or perfectionism. Even at school I remember tearing pages out of my workbooks and starting again because what I'd written the first time wasn't neat enough. But it was only little things like that, every now and again.

Rosie, my counsellor, has been teaching me how to use cognitive behavioural techniques to overcome my OCD. It's a self-help method and, although it's not easy or a quick fix, I've been doing my best and I have been seeing good results. It's not all plain sailing, though. I said earlier that I got myself into a state after Dan left. What I meant was that I had an OCD episode and ended up back at square one.

It's a condition that affects people differently. For some it's all about hygiene: obsessive cleaning due to fear of contamination. Others can't stop themselves hoarding junk. In my case, there are two main obsessions. The first is a fear of harm occurring to me or my family, which leads to me repeatedly checking things like door locks and smoke alarms. The second is an excessive concern with exactness or order. This can emerge in a variety of situations, from tidying the house to writing a letter, but it's basically a kind of extreme perfectionism. It could mean, for example, taking an hour to do a job that should only take minutes. It's an obsession with getting small tasks 'just right' as if by doing that you'll make everything else in your life perfect too.

Sounds absurd? No doubt. Even I know it's ridiculous, but when I'm trapped in the middle of an episode, I just can't stop. Not without following the steps Rosie's been teaching me.

I hope I've not lost you, Sam, prattling on about all of this. It must be a lot to take in. Believe me when I say that I'm tempted to scrub out this whole page, screw up the paper and start over. It's like there's a voice in my head urging me to do so – begging me – with the false promise that I'll do a better job next time. But I'm fighting it. I'm fighting so hard.

You know how in cartoons a character sometimes has an angel and a devil pop up on each shoulder, one urging them to do good and the other to do evil? It feels a bit like that. The angel, in this case, is the part of me that wants to beat the OCD. But fighting it is always the harder choice. And sometimes the devil won't stop. He goes on and on and on and on and on and on. His voice bounces around my head like a rubber ball, demanding to be heard.

That's what happened after Dan left the other night, and I didn't have the strength to resist. I locked the door after him, but five minutes later I felt the urge to go and check it. Even though I knew it was locked. I tried to resist, to stay put where I was, but eventually I gave in. I checked it once and then dozens of times. I couldn't tear myself away from that bloody door. And then when I finally did, I found myself at the bottom of the stairs, worrying that the carpet wasn't properly fixed down; that Ruby could have another fall. I went up and down the stairs, over and over again on my hands and knees, checking every inch. And then I was at the back door, twisting the key in the lock like a mad woman.

It went on for hours. Somehow I managed to pull myself together before Ruby woke up. I had to. I couldn't let her see me like that, although I'd hardly slept and was shattered. In the cold light of morning, I felt ridiculous. I felt ashamed, as I always do after tearing myself free of its clutches. If only that was enough to stop it happening again.

Gosh, I'm really starting to wonder if I've gone too far with this, telling you too much in one go. Maybe I ought to start over.

Maybe.

No!

No starting over!

Move forward.

Keep moving forward.

You see? I'm fighting it right now.

You must think I'm . . .

Sorry about that, Sam. I needed a few minutes to compose myself. I made a cup of tea.

It's time to move on and tell you about something else. Lighten things up.

So Rick phoned me yesterday.

'How are you?' he asked. 'How's Ruby? Anna said she wasn't at school today. She was worried about her. Me too, of course.'

He sounded nervous. Embarrassed. Not the self-assured, relaxed person I'd first met. No doubt he felt bad about the way he'd reacted to Ruby's injury. He'd not exactly been supportive. Useless more like.

'Well, she has a broken arm,' I replied.

'Right. Oh dear. Everything went well at the hospital?'

'Yes. It took a while, but we got there in the end.'

'Ruby's arm's in plaster now?'

'That's right.'

There was a long pause. He was waiting for me to expand, but I didn't feel like making things easy, so I stayed silent; waited for him to say something else.

'Right. That's good. The plaster, I mean. Well, not good exactly, but it'll help it to heal.'

'Yes,' I said, enjoying feeling in control for once. I almost mentioned that my husband had joined us at the hospital but thought better of it. Why risk blowing things when they'd reached such an interesting phase?

'How long is Ruby likely to be off school?' he asked.

'Not long. She should be back next week.'

'Oh, good. I'll tell Anna that. She'll be pleased.'

Rick went on to apologise for 'being a little squeamish', as he put it, asking for the chance to make it up to us.

'I'm not a bad cook,' he said. 'I wondered if the two of you might like to come over for some food this weekend. Only if Ruby's up to it, of course.'

95

I said yes. I'm not a big fan of apologies, as I'm sure you remember, but he is gorgeous and I couldn't resist.

We're visiting their place tomorrow afternoon. I'll let you know how it goes in my next letter, which I promise will be more upbeat.

Love as always,

M

Xx

CHAPTER 10

BEFORE

Friday, 3 March 2017

'One for the road?' Maurice mimed smoking a cigarette at Dan, holding out his two fingers and gesturing towards the door of the newsroom.

'Go on then.'

'Can I be cheeky?'

'Sure.'

'I'll buy you a pack next week. I must owe you at least twenty by now.'

'Cool.'

'What are you working on?' Dan asked his friend as they waited for the lift.

'I'm trying to nail a good headline but not getting very far. I think my brain's fried.'

'What's the story?'

'It's about a United fan who flew to Holland alone for

the match in Eindhoven this week but had his ticket stolen and ended up watching it on TV in an Indian takeaway near the stadium.'

'What? Couldn't he get another one off a tout?'

'His wallet was stolen too. It was a pickpocket job, apparently. Luckily he'd left a couple of notes back at his hotel room, but he needed those for food and the journey home.'

'Bummer,' Dan replied as the lift finally arrived and they stepped inside. 'Funny story, though.'

'I know. It just needs a nice pun as a headline.'

'What do you have so far?'

'Not much. I looked up the meaning of the name Eindhoven on the Internet, hoping for some inspiration, but that wasn't a lot of help. Roughly translated from the Dutch, as best as I understand, it means "End Lands" or something like that.'

'End Lands? That sounds a bit ominous, like somewhere you go to die.'

'I know, right?' Maurice said. They stepped out of the lift into reception, which was already closed for the day, and headed for the door. 'I mean, I could probably do something like "Eind of the road" but it's not great. All suggestions welcome.'

'Hmm. I'll have a think. I visited Eindhoven once, years ago. Nice place.'

When they got outside, Dan produced his Marlboro Lights. He'd always think of them as such, despite the term *light* long since being outlawed as an official brand for cancer sticks. It made them sound too safe, apparently, while of course they still killed you. He wondered if the youngsters called them Marlboro Gold, as they were supposed to. Mind you, not many of them smoked these days. You were more likely to see the young ones with those e-cigarettes, which seemed like a waste of time to Dan. He had puffed on one at the pub once, at the insistence of a bloke he was chatting to, but he hadn't been impressed.

No, he was happy to stick with the devil he knew and Maurice felt the same. Idiots of habit, the pair of them, hooked long ago and too weak-willed to knock it on the head. Dan had actually managed to stop for several years after Ruby was born. And yet the desire had never truly left him. Once he'd started again – probably the stupidest move of all – that was it. Especially now he lived alone, with no one nagging him to stop on a daily basis. His only incentive to quit was the ridiculous price tag. But even that was avoidable if you knew the right people and bought in bulk, no questions asked.

'You'd never catch any of that lot working even a minute after five, would you?' he said, nodding at the empty reception desk as Maurice held the door open.

'No chance. I don't know why we do it. It must be ingrained in us. I remember my first editor giving me a lecture about not being a clock-watcher. "Journalists work long hours," he told me. "It's part of the job. That's why they pay us so well." He always fancied himself as a comedian.'

Dan laughed, stuck a cigarette in his mouth and handed Maurice another.

'Thanks. It was him who got me smoking,' Maurice went on. 'Bastard. And drinking. We might have worked long hours, but there was always time for a couple in the pub. He never seemed to find much time for washing, though. People used to joke that he looked and smelled more like a tramp than a newspaper editor.'

'The good old days,' Dan replied. 'There was this guy, Clive, I used to work with when I first started out. He'd been a reporter forever and was a total old soak. Anyway, the girls in the office were forever complaining about his lack of hygiene. One day my editor at the time – Alan Fitchie, if you remember him – took him to one side to have a word. He was a straight talker, Alan, and legend has it that he told Clive he ought to put all his clothes in a heap and burn them before taking a long shower.'

Maurice laughed. 'Yes, I remember Alan. That definitely sounds like the sort of thing he'd say. What happened? Did it work?'

Dan shook his head. 'Nope. Clive stormed out of the office in a huff, stayed away for the rest of the day and then reappeared the next morning, whiffy as ever, pretending like nothing had happened.'

'Did Alan say anything else to him?'

'I don't think so. No point.'

Dan grinned.

'What?' Maurice asked.

'Oh, I was remembering this time I gave Clive a lift to some meeting or another. He got in the car with this fancy leather briefcase, which was totally not his style, and I wondered what on earth he had in there. Then he opened it up and the only thing inside was a can of Red Bull. I guess he needed it to get through the day.'

'Hah. I think every old newspaper office used to have a reporter like him. Clive? No, I don't think I ever had the pleasure. He wouldn't like it much here, would he? I swear the lack of pubs nearby was one of the main reasons they chose to move to this bloody office. They've done all they can to knock the journalists out of us. Turn us into robots.'

'There's the Red Lion,' Dan said with a grin. 'It's only a quick drive.'

'Yeah, right. That place should have its licence revoked. I've nothing against kids' play areas, but they don't belong in pubs.' He shuddered. 'Honestly, I'd rather have a can in the park with the teenagers than drink a pint of the piss they serve there.'

'How about "naan too happy"?'

'Sorry?'

'For your United headline. It just popped into my head. You know, like naan bread.'

Maurice laughed. 'Yes, I like it. Short and snappy. Ideal. Thanks, mate. I can go home now. Where did that come from?'

'The big pun cloud in the sky, I guess. What are you up to this weekend?'

'This and that. I've got decorators fixing up my lounge and kitchen at the moment. The place is like a building site, so I'll probably steer clear.'

'Yeah, you said you were having some work done.'

'It's costing me a fortune, Dan. I wish I'd not bothered.'

'Why didn't you do it yourself?'

'You're joking, right? I'm useless at that kind of thing. I don't do DIY. I do BIY: break it yourself.'

Dan laughed. 'I'm the opposite. I hate paying someone to do something I can fix myself.'

'You mean you're tight.'

'That too. But no, I actually enjoy it – especially jobs I've not attempted before. It's like solving a puzzle.'

'If you say so. What's the biggest job you've done?'

'I refitted our upstairs bathroom.'

'By yourself?'

'Pretty much, apart from some wiring. I used an electrician for that.'

'Impressive.'

Dan shrugged. 'So what are your plans if you're avoiding the house? Visiting one of your lady friends?'

'Maybe. What about you?'

'The only date I've got is with Ruby.'

'That's nice. Is she spending the weekend?'

'Yes.'

'What have you got lined up?'

'I'm not sure yet. Depends on the weather.'

'Nothing like a bit of father-daughter time.'

'Hmm. She's a bit awkward at the moment, to be honest. I think she blames me for the split.'

'I wouldn't worry. Kids go through phases. Spoil her rotten. That's always worked for me.'

Later Dan drove to pick up Ruby. It still felt odd going there as a visitor; knocking on his own front door. A large

1960s detached property with four big bedrooms, two bathrooms and a good garden, it was a home he loved. The location was great too: a quiet spot in a nice small town surrounded by countryside, plus decent schools and good transport links to the city. Despite the awful thing that had happened there and the period of constant arguments that had preceded his split from Maria, Dan's affection for the house had never waned. It had been tired and unloved when they moved in. But after a lot of hard work, mainly on his part, it had ended up perfect. There was even a downstairs study: something he'd always wanted. He knew every inch of the place. It couldn't be more different from the grotty flat where he currently spent his nights.

Maria answered the door. 'You're late.'

'Hello to you too.'

'Well, you are.'

'Only by twenty-five minutes, Maria. I was busy at work. Is it such a problem?'

'She needs to be able to rely on you. That's more important than ever now she doesn't see you every day.'

And whose fault is that? Dan thought. Maria was the one who'd asked him to move out. He'd wanted to work on repairing the relationship.

'Is she ready?' he asked.

'She was ready half an hour ago.'

Dan sighed. 'Do you really want to do this now, Maria? For goodness' sake. Sorry I'm late, okay?'

'You can keep your apology. I hope you've got some tea sorted for her. She's normally eaten by this time.'

'I'm not an idiot, Maria.'

'I didn't say you were. It would just be nice if you were punctual for once.'

Dan didn't have the energy to argue. 'Whatever,' he said. 'I'm going to wait in the car.'

After a few minutes, he was glad to see Ruby come out of the front door with her coat on and a rucksack over her shoulder. She opened the rear door of the Focus and climbed in. 'Hi, Dad.'

She'd started calling him that, as opposed to *Daddy*, soon after he moved out. It shouldn't have bothered him, but it did. Especially since Maria was still *Mummy*. He'd never said anything to Ruby about it and had no intention of doing so. But despite telling himself it was a natural sign of her growing up, he knew it meant more than that. Whether she was doing it consciously or not, he had no idea. But it conveyed a change in their relationship – a distancing – and as inevitable as that might be, he didn't like it one bit.

'Hi, darling,' he said, leaning back to give her a kiss. 'How are you?'

'Good. I was doing a poo when you arrived.'

He smiled to himself. 'Oh, right. Sorry I'm a bit late. I got held up at work.'

'That's okay. When are you going to fix your car door? It looks weird with that hole in it.'

'It's not a hole, it's a dent. I haven't got around to it yet. I'll do it soon.'

'Good.'

Dan looked at his daughter in the rear-view mirror. Her emerald eyes twinkled back at him. Her long blonde curls were tied into a neat side ponytail with a red and white clip holding back loose strands. 'Your hair looks nice. Did your mum style it for you?'

'No,' she replied, as if the question was a crazy one. 'I did it myself.'

'Wow. I'm impressed.'

Ruby shrugged. 'It's easy.'

'How's school?' he asked her after a few minutes of driving.

'Good.'

'Have you got much homework to do this weekend?'

'A bit. I've already started it with Mummy.'

'What's it about?'

'Well, there's spellings and maths, like every week, but we also have to do some research about mountains.'

'What kind of research?'

'Oh, you know, on the Internet. We have to find ten facts about famous mountains. I've already done six. Mummy said I could do the rest when I get home.'

'I see. What did you learn so far? What were your six facts?'

She frowned. 'I don't know. I can't remember.'

This was a typical Ruby answer. She wasn't big on sharing, especially about school. He was surprised she'd even told him what she had.

Sam had been the opposite at that age. She used to tell them everything: the whole day, from start to finish, as soon as she got home. If only it had lasted. If only she'd continued confiding in them as she'd grown older. Things could have been so different.

Was it good, then, that Ruby wasn't the same? Did that mean she'd go the other way as she grew up, sharing more, rather than less? Dan hoped so. Sometimes he wanted to beg Ruby to tell him everything. To implore her never to follow in her older sister's footsteps. But he and Maria had discussed this matter at length and they'd decided – yes, they could still agree on some things – not to put that pressure on her, for fear of pushing her the other way.

She was still young. She and Sam were so different. And yet sometimes when he looked at her he caught a glimpse of his other daughter, especially around the eyes, which were the same striking green. He tried not to think about Sam when he was with Ruby, because doing so was too painful. It never led him to a good place.

He switched on the car radio to divert his attention. The news was on and Ruby groaned. 'Can we listen to something else, Dad? This is boring. Can you put Radio One on?'

'Fine.'

He did as she asked and immediately regretted it. But he knew better than to criticise the music she liked, so he suffered in silence.

'What do you think about McDonald's for tea?'

'Yay,' she replied with a smile.

Dan had been planning to cook something at home; he'd decided to go for fast food instead to get back at Maria for how she'd treated him. It was childish, but he also knew how much she disapproved of McDonald's and he couldn't resist. Especially since he and Ruby both liked it.

'Shall we use the drive-thru and take it home or would you rather eat in?'

She opted for the latter.

Less than half an hour later, they were done and heading back to the flat. The food was certainly fast, although Dan didn't feel as full as he'd expected. Ruby, on the other hand, with the film tie-in cup she'd received with her meal, was more than happy.

'Mummy never lets me go to McDonald's.'

'Oh?' Dan replied, a little ashamed.

'She's says it's rubbish, but I love it. Holly in my class goes every week.'

'Really?'

'Yeah. She has it for tea every Sunday. I wish I could.'

'Well, it's better not to have anything too often. That's never good for you.'

'What about fruit?'

'There's no harm in having too much fruit, clever clogs, but burgers and chips aren't quite the same, are they? Who's Holly again? Do I know her?'

'She sits on my table.'

'Is she your best friend?'

'No, I don't have one. Mummy says it's better to be friends with lots of people. Can we talk about something else now?'

Ruby had fallen out with her former best friend – a girl called Amelia – a couple of months earlier. Amelia had been saying nasty things to Ruby about her curly hair and the way she looked. She'd been playing mind-games with her, like only girls know how, threatening not to be her friend if she played with certain people or did certain things. Once Maria had got wind of it, she'd panicked and gone to the teacher, demanding that she took action. Amelia had been spoken to, which led to a row between the two girls, and that was the end of that. Ruby barely spoke to her any more.

Maria had probably overreacted, but it was understandable. Better safe than sorry. Ruby didn't need so-called friends like that.

'What would you like to talk about?' Dan asked.

'Oh, I love this song. Can you turn it up?'

'How about a please?'

'Please, Dad.'

He turned up the radio, wondering what it was about this particular piece of plastic pop that Ruby liked. She sounded so cute singing along with her fake American accent. He wished he could keep her this age forever: old enough to have a proper conversation, to be a genuine companion, but with her innocence still intact. It wouldn't be long now until that started to change. The fluctuations between the child she was and the woman she would become, already evident, would slowly rebalance as the tide of her life forever turned towards adulthood. It was the no-man's-land of those changing years that terrified him.

The song finished and some overzealous DJ started prattling on about his exciting weekend.

'Dad,' Ruby said. 'Please can I watch some TV when we get back?'

'Um, have you watched any yet today?'

'No. Nothing.'

'A little before bed, then.'

A short while later, Dan wished he'd said no. He walked into the lounge from the kitchen and saw Ruby, her face one big scowl, throwing the remote control on to the floor.

'What the hell's going on?' he said. The words came out more forcefully than he'd intended, causing Ruby to jump with shock and then burst into tears.

He sat down next to her, but she recoiled when he tried to give her a hug and sobbed into a cushion.

'Come on, love. There's no need to get upset. I'm sorry I raised my voice like that. I didn't mean to scare you. But what were you doing throwing the remote on the floor?'

He leaned over to pick it up and flicked through a couple of channels to make sure it still worked. 'Well, the good news is that it's not broken,' he said. 'But please don't do that again. Ruby, are you listening to me?'

He waited for a reply but got nothing. She kept her face buried in the cushion.

'I'd like you to look at me now. Otherwise, you can go to bed.'

'Fine.' She rolled over with a groan and stared at the ceiling through red, puffy eyes.

'What's the matter?'

'You shocked me.'

'I know. I've said I'm sorry about that. I didn't mean to raise my voice. But what about you? Don't you have something to say to me?'

'Sorry.'

'What for?'

'Throwing the control.'

'That's better. And would you care to explain why you did it?'

She stared at the ceiling again.

'Hello? It's polite to answer when someone asks you a question, Ruby.'

'Fine. It was because there's nothing nice on. You don't have any of the good channels here that we have at home.'

Dan started laughing. He couldn't help himself once it struck him how ridiculous it was that this whole incident had been sparked by his TV channel selection.

'Stop it,' Ruby shouted, her face gripped by fury. 'Stop laughing at me.'

'I'm not, darling, but come on. Don't you think it's a bit—'

It was too late. She got up from the couch and stormed off in the direction of the spare bedroom. 'I'm going to bed. I know that's what you want. I hate this stupid flat. Why do you make me come here?'

Ruby's words were like a slap to the face. She sounded like a teenager already, slamming her bedroom door a moment later as if to confirm the fact. The noise made Dan wince, not least because of the mottled glass panes in the door. She'd riled him, but he had no intention of letting her know that. He took a deep breath, a couple more, and then went after her.

He opened the door, glad to find it still in one piece,

and saw that she'd dived fully dressed under her quilt. 'Go away,' she shouted.

Dan walked in regardless and knelt down at the side of the bed. 'There's no need for this, Ruby. And there's definitely no need to slam the door like that. You're lucky the glass didn't smash. Do you have any idea how dangerous that would have been?'

'Stupid door. Leave me alone. I want to go to sleep.'

It was too much. He took another deep breath, knowing he had to get firm with her now but still desperate not to lose his cool.

'Ruby Evans,' he said. 'I've had quite enough of this bad behaviour. Pull yourself together. Any more and there will be no TV or treats of any kind this weekend.'

'Good. I'll go home and you can be on your own. That's why you left us and moved here, isn't it? It's all your fault. I hate you.'

CHAPTER 11

The wind catches the front door as I enter and an almighty slam echoes through the bare belly of the house.

'Hello?' Miles shouts from somewhere out of view.

'It's me,' I reply. 'Jack.'

'Back already?' he says, appearing at the top of the stairs, a hammer in one hand. 'Everything all right?'

'I had a funny turn.'

Miles frowns. 'What happened?'

'I'm not exactly sure. One minute I was walking by the front of the house. Next thing, I was reliving another memory. Well, I think that's what it was. When I came to, I was lying on the grass. I must have passed out.'

'Oh dear. Grab a seat in the kitchen. I'd best check you over. Give me a minute to wash my hands and find some equipment.'

He gives me a thorough examination: torch in the eyes, blood pressure, temperature check and so on.

'And? How do I look?'

He shrugs. 'Nothing out of the ordinary that I can see. How's the head?'

'Much better.'

'Good. It looks that way too, but I am a bit concerned about what happened. How long do you think you were out?'

'I'm not sure. It felt similar to what happened in here before. When you said I fainted.'

Miles nods, his eyes thoughtful. 'This is what I feared might happen. Just as well you weren't by the edge of the cliff.'

I nod, sticking to my story rather than admitting the truth.

'What was the memory this time?' Miles asks.

'It was, um, different. If it was an actual memory. It was Halloween and I was out trick-or-treating with a little girl in a ghost costume. I felt like she was maybe my daughter, but I'm not sure. I've never mentioned anything to you about having a child, have I?'

Miles shakes his head. 'No, never. Sorry.'

I skip the bit about the girl in red. I'm not comfortable telling him that. Apart from the fact it makes no sense – and I don't want to sound crazy – I'm thinking about the first time I spotted her and Miles claimed not to have seen anyone.

'So what's the verdict?' I ask.

'Rest, rest and more rest. Clearly you need to take it easy.'

'And go to the hospital on Monday?'

'Yes. That too.'

'The funny thing is that I feel all right. I know that

113

doesn't tally with what happened, but I do. Another memory coming back is a good thing, right? Don't ask me to sleep, because I'm not tired. And don't ask me to do nothing or I'll die of boredom. I can't believe you don't even have a TV.'

'There are books you could read.'

I shake my head. 'I need to do something active. Why can't I help you with the floorboards? You don't have to let me do much, but at least I'd feel useful. And you'd be there to watch over me. You'd be on hand if I was to faint again or whatever.'

'I'm not sure that's a good idea. But I do need to pop to the village. The nails I have aren't right for the boards. There's a hardware store where I can get some others. You can come too, if you like.'

'By car?'

Miles nods.

'That sounds good.'

'Right. Give me ten minutes. And drink some water while you're waiting. You need to keep well hydrated.'

'I'm on it, Doc.'

'And?' he asks as we head outside a short while later. 'How much water did you drink?'

'Two pint glasses.'

'Good.'

'You sound like my daughter,' I say. 'Ever since—'

Miles, who is leading the way to the car, stops in his tracks. He turns and looks at me, his eyes like saucers. 'Ever since what?'

'I, um. I don't know. The words came out without me thinking about them. I can't . . . no, it's gone. Does that mean I'm a dad? That I do have a daughter? She must be the one I was trick-or-treating with in that memory. She was only little, though. How could I have abandoned her? How could I not have mentioned her to you?' My voice is rising.

Miles shrugs. 'Maybe it wasn't a recent memory.'

'Why didn't you say something?'

'Like what, Jack? If you do have a daughter, this is the first I've heard of it.'

'I really never mentioned her before?'

He shakes his head. 'We never talked about that kind of thing. You showed no inclination to do so.'

'What did we talk about, then?'

'Other things. Working on the house has kept us busy ever since you got here.'

'Yeah, but surely that's not all we talked about. It sounds like we barely know each other.'

Miles doesn't reply, but the idea that I might have a child – maybe more than one – has unsettled me. And does that mean I have a wife or girlfriend too? If so, why the hell am I here and not with them? I'm not prepared to let this go.

'Tell me something about you,' I say, hoping such a conversation might trigger more of my own memories. 'What are you doing here in this huge place all alone? Haven't you got a family?'

As soon as I've asked those questions, something else occurs to me. It's an idea that doesn't sit comfortably in

115

my stomach, but I blurt it out regardless. 'Hang on. You and I, we're not. You know. We're not—'

'Gay?' Miles replies, saying the word I'm struggling to spit out. He laughs. 'No, no. Don't worry. We don't have, er, that kind of relationship. That's not my bag and, from the look on your face, I doubt it's yours. Whatever gave you that idea, Jack?'

'Not knowing anything about yourself messes with your mind. A minute ago I discovered I probably have a daughter, but I've never mentioned her to you, which is plain odd. I mean, what am I *doing* here? Nothing makes any sense.'

Miles turns and continues walking towards the car, gesturing for me to follow.

'I can't tell you what you're doing here, Jack,' he says. 'That's something you need to find out for yourself. It's locked away somewhere inside your mind, I'm sure of that. I can tell you about me, if it helps. I do have a family: a wife and daughter. But I don't see them much. My wife and I, we're . . . I suppose *estranged* is the word. As for my daughter, things aren't quite that bad, but let's say that she tends to side with her mother. It's been a while.'

'I'm sorry to hear that. What are their names?'

'My wife's called Sarah and my daughter is Alison. She's thirty.'

'Any grandchildren?'

'No, Alison's not even settled yet. Too busy with her career.'

'Is she also a doctor?'

Miles laughs. 'Oh, no. There was never much chance

116

of Alison following in her old dad's footsteps. She works every bit as hard, though, from dusk till dawn and then some. She's a solicitor.'

'Right. And your wife?'

'She's retired, like me, although she used to be a teacher. Primary school.'

'So why the big project? You're not planning on doing this whole place up for yourself, are you?'

Miles rolls his eyes. 'I was wondering when you'd ask me that. No, probably not. I haven't thought that far ahead, to be honest. It sounds crazy, but it's the truth. I inherited this place from an uncle several years ago. I knew what a state it was in and never got around to doing anything about it. Then I retired and suddenly had a lot of time on my hands. It seemed like an ideal project. A way to keep busy.'

'He must have been some wealthy uncle,' I say, eyeing the huge house behind us. Miles climbs into the driver's seat of the Land Rover I saw earlier and I head for the passenger side.

As I get in, Miles is reaching over and rooting around inside the glovebox. It's chock-a-block with junk: cracked CD cases, rolls of tape, empty crisp packets, a screwdriver, a couple of ballpoints and at least two pairs of sunglasses. Eventually, with a triumphant cheer, he pulls out a set of car keys. 'Bingo. I knew they were in there somewhere. Not very secure, I know, but you get complacent when you're in the middle of nowhere. Yes, he was rather well-off, Uncle Freddie, although you wouldn't guess it from how he let this place get into such a state. He was an odd chap: a recluse. I only met him a handful of times and I always thought he hated me. Then he popped his clogs and split his estate between me and a handful of animal charities. Never had any children of his own. Just lots of dogs and cats.'

'Did he live here?'

'Yes, for a long time, but not in his last few years. His health was poor and he rented a place in Spain, hoping the warmer weather would help. He had this place stripped of all his stuff, as if he was planning to sell it, but for some reason he never did. I'm not sure why. It had been empty for the best part of a decade by the time I moved in. I thought perhaps he'd struggled to find a buyer, because it was in such bad condition, but I've asked around and no local estate agents ever remember it being on the market.'

The clock on the dashboard reads 10.54 p.m. I had wondered whether Miles might have forgotten to change this one and that it might tell the actual time, but no chance of that. It's daylight outside.

He turns the key and it takes a few seconds for the engine to fire up. 'Don't worry, lad,' he says. 'She always does that, but she's never let me down yet. Have you, Gigi?'

'You have a name for your car?'

'Sure. Don't you?'

'Um, I don't know. I don't think so. Mind you, I don't even know if I have a car. Is that something we discussed?'

'No.'

'So why Gigi?'

'Because she's my Green Goddess. You know, like the old Bedford fire engines.'

I give him a blank look.

'The green ones from the 1950s – tough old things that lasted half a century. The Army used to use them when firefighters went on strike.'

I nod, finally understanding what he's talking about. 'Oh yes, I remember.'

Miles clunks the gearbox into reverse, rolls the car back a few feet and sets off down the dirt track I saw earlier. He drives fast despite the uneven surface and, as I'm jolted from side to side in my seat, I'm gripped by a sudden sense of panic.

My sharp intake of breath is loud enough for Miles to notice. 'Are you all right?' he asks.

I nod that I am. I'm not, though. My heart's working overtime. I'm breathing through a straw. The pressure inside my head is rising.

All three of them are staring at me expectantly as I look up.

The tall woman glances down at the papers on the table in front of her. Then she looks back at me, her lips twitching up on one side. 'You were saying?'

'Yes. Sorry. I, er, can't say I'm over the moon about the situation. Who is? But I'm a realist. I can understand why it's necessary. Tough times demand tough action. If you keep treading water, hoping not to get swept up in the tide of change, you run the risk of drowning.'

I look up at them and smile, but it's as much to stop me from throwing up as it is to check that my words have gained their approval. They have, of course. I'm telling them what they want to hear – a stream of cliché-ridden bullshit – and they're all beaming back at me.

'So you're on board with the changes?' the porky HR manager asks, a slug of sweat sliding down from his temple on to one cheek. The Grim Reaper disguised as that police chief from *The Simpsons*.

'Definitely,' I reply with strong eye contact. 'You can count on me.'

'And the rest of your staff?' the other man asks. He's the one in charge and I should know his name, but my mind's gone blank.

'I don't foresee any problems.'

My thoughts flick back to my own office, a couple of hours earlier, when they were all laying into the plans, begging me to voice their opposition to the 'big bosses'. I said I'd do what I could, but I already knew that resistance was futile if I wanted to keep my job. Which I do. I mean, what else is there for me? This is simple self-preservation, I think, as I pimp myself out to the suits sitting opposite me.

'Jack?' the boss man, whatever he's called, says to me in a voice that isn't his own.

Who's Jack? I wonder.

The Land Rover is stopped in the middle of the dirt track and Miles is up in my face, looking very concerned, scrutinising my eyes. He looks like he's about to slap me around the chops, so I pull back and mumble that I'm all right.

'I had another flashback – memory – whatever you want to call it. Did I pass out again?'

'Not exactly. It was more of an absence. Your eyes glazed over. You wouldn't respond to my questions.'

'What does that mean? It's not normal, is it?'

'I'd like to ask whether you've experienced anything like this before, earlier in your life, but I know that's not something you can answer. Can you tell me what just happened from your perspective?'

'Like I said, another memory. I assume that's what it was, anyway.'

'A memory of what?'

'I was in a boardroom: modern, simply furnished. I was facing a panel of three people. I knew they were my bosses. It was about some big change that was taking place at work.'

'What was your job?'

'That's the weird thing. I don't know. I did when I was there in the moment, but now it's gone. I have no idea.' My brain is fried. I rub my temples, but it provides little relief. 'What's happening to me, Miles?'

He shakes his head. 'I'm not sure. There's only so much I can see and do here. I think you definitely should have a scan at the hospital. Just as a precaution.'

'Really? Today?'

'No, it'll still have to be Monday. But I'll be keeping an extra close eye on you in the meantime. And no more solitary walks.'

121

'A brain scan? Can you arrange that?'

'I know a couple of people there.'

Miles is all for returning to the house and leaving the trip to the village until later. But I tell him to continue, as long as he takes it easy behind the wheel, especially until we reach a proper road. I haven't forgotten the panic I felt as we first started driving. I'm not sure where it came from, but thankfully it seems to have gone now.

Despite the slower speed, I'm still bounced from side to side as the car makes its way from crater to crater along the track. Eventually, after every bone in my body has been shaken, I see the welcome sight of tarmac ahead. We take a right turn.

I'd hoped that I might recognise some of the sights along the way. But other than empty fields, bushes, trees and the odd isolated house, there's little to jog my memory. Heading inland as we are, there aren't even any good views of the sea.

When we reach the village, it's not much to look at. There are a handful of small shops, a pub and a church. There's also a primary school: a tiny one that looks like it could only accommodate a handful of pupils. But from the small number of houses I see here, that's probably more than enough. None of it rings a bell, although Miles tells me I've been here plenty of times before.

So what on earth brought me here in the first place? With no apparent ties to the area, how did I end up in the village's only pub, the Red Lion, on the night Miles and I met?

We park outside the small hardware store.

'Are you sure they'll have the nails you need?' I ask.

He laughs. 'I've yet to ask for anything they don't have. It's one of those old school places where you tell them what you need and they disappear and find it for you. It might not look very impressive, but I think there must be a huge underground cavern somewhere nearby where they keep all the stock. It's brilliant, honestly.'

We both step out of the car. I'm about to follow Miles when he asks if I'd mind popping to the general store, which is immediately opposite on the other side of the road. 'We could do with some bread and milk,' he says, holding out a ten-pound note, only to pull it back a second later. 'Hang on. Maybe that's not such a good idea. Probably best we stay together.'

'Nonsense,' I reply, reaching forward to grab the note. 'I insist.'

I cross the road, aware of Miles watching me do so, and enter the shop.

I see her as soon as I'm inside. She's standing behind the counter, staring straight at me. I don't know how I know it's her. To my knowledge, I've never seen her close up before.

But there's no doubt in my mind.

I'm a hundred per cent certain.

It's the girl in red.

CHAPTER 12

Sunday, 9 April 2017

Dear Sam,

It's 2.07 p.m. and I'm sitting in the kitchen. Ruby is snoozing on the couch in the lounge, so I thought I'd take the opportunity to write again. I have plenty to tell you, but before I start with that, I want to say how much I'm getting out of doing this.

When Rosie, my counsellor, first suggested the idea, I wasn't at all sure. It seemed weird. You probably guessed as much. Initially, I stonewalled her every time she mentioned it, but as I got to know her and so much of her other advice proved useful, I started to consider it.

She says a lot of my problems stem from what happened with you. I mean, of course they do. I don't need a counsellor to tell me that. Not that I hold you in any way responsible, Sam. I'm the one to blame. I should have seen it coming. I should have been there to stop it. I know Dan feels the same. As your parents, how could we not?

I've told Rosie on countless occasions how much I miss you and how I wish I could talk to you. That's what led to her suggestion. She said writing in this way would help me reconnect with my memories of you at the same time as finding a pathway through my issues.

Even after opening up to the idea, I was sceptical.

'What will it achieve to write a letter to my dead daughter?' I asked. Two words I never thought I'd have to say side by side. They sounded horrible in my mouth.

'You won't know until you give it a try,' she replied.

'Oh, come on. You'll have to do better than that if you want me to have a go. You must have tried this with other people.'

She shrugged. 'Why do you think it might help?'

'That's the problem. I really don't see how it will. Sam's never going to read the letters.'

'Don't you think there's a certain freedom in knowing that, Maria?'

'But what's the point?'

'You could say the same about writing a diary.'

'Sam was only fourteen when she died. You want me to use these letters as a way to disclose my innermost thoughts and feelings. But I wouldn't realistically share such things with my teenage daughter, would I?'

'Fair enough. How about you imagine writing to an older version of her, then? A future version, if you like: the woman you imagine she would have become one day, if things had been different. Does that sound like something you could try? That's all I'm asking.'

So I did try – and it's working out well. I find it cathartic and, against all odds, I think it's helping me to feel close to you, Sam. As stupid as it sounds, I feel like maybe I am, somehow, getting through to you with these letters. Even though I'm not posting them anywhere and I know you're not around to read them. It's ridiculous, but sometimes I get the feeling you're reading over my shoulder as I write.

I can't believe I put that. It's as well I'm doing this in longhand, not on a computer. Otherwise, I'd have probably deleted it by now, together with all the other embarrassing things I've written. That must be why Rosie told me to do this with a pen and paper. It feels genuine and more personal. Plus it's harder to edit myself.

I'm sure Rosie also knew that doing it this way would be a greater challenge to my OCD. More messy. Less control. Less order.

'Try to make it as much of a stream of conscious-ness as you can,' she said. 'Let it all out: whatever you're thinking; whatever you want to tell Sam.'

I'll tell you about yesterday, shall I? That was when Ruby and I went for some food at Rick's place.

Ruby was grumpy because of her arm. It's going to take her a while to get used to the inconvenience of having to do everything one-handed and needing help with the things she usually does alone. Washing, in particular, is tricky. She really wanted a shower that morning, but I told her it wasn't possible and she had to have a bath instead. She was still sulking when it was time to go to Rick's for lunch.

It was the last thing I felt like doing after Ruby's palaver. I'd hardly even had a chance to spruce myself up; I almost phoned to cancel. The only reason I didn't was because I knew that Ruby was looking forward to seeing Anna. She needed brightening up and I couldn't face any more tears.

Rick wasn't lying when he said he could cook. He'd prepared a huge roast dinner for us: beef, home-made Yorkshire puddings with gravy, and possibly the best roast potatoes I've ever eaten. Honestly, the food was perfect. Even the delicious apple pie we had for dessert was homemade.

Anna took Ruby off to her bedroom after we'd finished eating, leaving the two of us alone at the dining table.

'That was superb, Rick. Thank you.'

'You're welcome. It's nice to have company and, well, I wanted to do something to make up for the other day. I know a roast is usually more of a Sunday meal than a Saturday one, but I thought what the hell – let's go for it.'

'Why not? I could eat a roast every day of the week. It's one of my favourite meals.'

'Me too. I hope Ruby liked it. She didn't eat a lot.'

'Of course she liked it. It was lovely. She's under the weather, that's all.'

Rick nodded. 'I know I wasn't very helpful when she broke her arm. Like I said on the phone, I'm a bit squeamish. Not very manly, I realise, but I've always been that way. Show me the slightest hint of blood or anything like that and I'm useless.'

Part of me wanted to agree, but in light of the amazing meal he'd cooked, I smiled and bit my tongue. He'd earned himself another chance. I'd had a little wine and as I stared at the gorgeous man across the table from me, I couldn't stop myself imagining what he might look like with his shirt off. You probably think I'm exaggerating about how good-looking he is, but really I'm not. He must spend hours in the gym every week to have such a sculpted physique. And then there's that smile; those eyes.

'Don't worry about it,' I said. 'It's in the past.'

I must just point out here, Sam, that I do feel a little guilty thinking about Rick in this way. It hasn't escaped my attention that I'm still married to Dan, although he was the one saying he wanted a divorce the other day. The situation between us feels so fragile and complicated, but Rick is a distraction from all that. I can't help but enjoy his company.

Anyway, Rick looked at me in that intense way of his, like I was the only other person in the world. 'It's important to me that you like me, Maria. I feel I let you down.'

'I do like you,' I said, the words slipping out before

I had a chance to analyse them. Next thing I knew, we were staring into each other's eyes – neither of us saying a word – and it seemed for a moment as if something was about to happen. But any illusion that we were alone was shattered an instant later by the shrill sound of Anna's voice.

'Daddy,' she bellowed from upstairs. 'Can Ruby and me watch telly?'

'You mean Ruby and I,' Rick shouted back, a grin and a raised eyebrow directed at me.

'Can we?' Anna asked. 'I was telling Ruby about that dancing film you recorded for me the other day. She really wants to see it.'

'Is that all right with you?' he asked me. 'They're always the same, aren't they? They beg for a friend to come over and then all they want to do is watch TV together. I can say no if you like. Don't worry, I won't blame you. I'll take the heat.'

I smiled. 'It's fine. Ruby can't do much with her arm like it is and she needs to rest.'

Once the girls were settled in the lounge, their film underway, Rick and I went to the kitchen to do the dishes. He was all for leaving them until after we'd gone, but I insisted; partly, I must admit, because I was keen to spend more time alone with him.

Gosh, I must sound like a teenager. It's exciting to have someone interested in you when you're not used to it, though. Especially a man like Rick.

I had visions of a movie-like scene: something straight out of a Hollywood rom com. I pictured him standing behind me, embracing me with those big arms of his as I did the washing up. Then I imagined turning around, playfully wiping soap suds on his nose before being pulled into a passionate kiss.

But it didn't go quite like that. Instead, I slipped on a patch of something greasy on the tiled kitchen floor and lost my balance. I did manage to stay upright, but only by dropping the two items I was carrying back from the dining table and catching myself on a nearby section of worktop.

You're probably wondering what those two items were. Well, unfortunately, I had a gravy boat in one hand and a bottle of red wine in the other. Both were still around half full and they each went flying. The gravy boat smashed into pieces with a loud crack on the floor and splattered its contents far and wide, including up two of the walls. The bottle went the other way, crashing into the fridge, shattering and spraying all over the place. It was like a shit storm meeting a blood bath, with me and Rick caught in the middle.

I've not mentioned yet that Rick's house, although rented, is brand-spanking new and immaculate throughout. It's part of this enormous modern estate they're still finishing off about a mile away from our place. Do you remember that field we used to walk through near the river: the one where we flew a kite a few times? It's there. Not that you'd recognise it. Apart from the tiny patches of turf they call gardens, there's no green in sight any more. Just row after row of houses: mostly finished, but some still mid-construction.

There's never a good time and place to hurl gravy and red wine everywhere, but you'd struggle to find worse.

'I'm so sorry,' I said, horrified at the sight of the mess.

Rick's eyes were on stalks as he surveyed the damage.

'Don't worry,' I told him, grabbing at a roll of kitchen towel on the window ledge and diving into the mess. 'Leave it to me. I'll sort it out. I'll clean it all up.'

His mouth was wide open, like he was about to say something. Then the phone in the hall started to ring. He looked in that direction and back at the havoc in front of him as Anna and Ruby appeared at the doorway, jaws on the floor.

'What happened?' Anna asked.

'Don't come in, you two,' Rick said quickly. 'There's broken glass everywhere. Anna, could you get the phone, please? You need to leave us to clear this mess up.'

'But, how—'

'Do what I ask, Anna. The phone.'

'We're going to need a lot more kitchen towel,' I said, throwing the soggy, stained sheets I'd already used into the sink. 'Where do you keep it?'

'I, um—'

'It's Mummy on the phone,' Anna said, reappearing

at the door with the portable receiver held to one ear.

'Tell her I'll call her back. Explain we're having a situation here.'

'We're in the middle of a crisis,' Anna said into the phone as she walked away into the hall. 'Dad's busy with Maria. He says he'll call you back.'

'Oh, bloody hell,' Rick said. 'I'd better speak to her. Can you manage here for a minute?'

'Sure. As long as you've got more kitchen towel. And some cloths maybe.'

'Under the sink. I won't be long.' He left the room quickly, frowning.

I was a little surprised he was so bothered about what his ex thought. Mind you, I know from my own experience how tricky it can be to keep the peace when there's history and emotions and children involved. So who am I to judge? I grabbed more kitchen roll and cloths and got on with the clean-up from hell.

By the time Rick returned, which must have been about ten minutes later, things were already looking much better. The walls were still wet from being wiped, but neither the gravy nor the wine seemed to have stained them, probably because I'd acted so quickly. I'd found a dustpan and brush under the sink and was busy sweeping up the shards of glass and crockery pieces.

'Wow. You've done so much already,' he said. 'I'm sorry for taking so long on the phone.'

'Don't be silly. I should be the one apologising. It's my own clumsy fault.'

He moved to kneel down next to me. 'Here, let me have a go with the dustpan and brush.'

'No, I'm fine, really. And be careful. There could still be bits of glass. It needs a good vacuum.'

'I can do that. Gosh, I can't believe you've got rid of all that gravy and wine. It looks almost back to normal. You're a miracle worker.'

'That's not exactly how I'd describe myself right now,' I said. 'Clumsy oaf would seem more apt.'

'Nonsense. You slipped. I spilled some vegetable oil on the floor earlier and, like an idiot, I didn't clean it up properly. Thankfully you didn't hurt yourself. You didn't, did you?'

I shook my head.

'Good, good. Definitely nothing for you to apologise for, anyway. Especially after all that cleaning up when you're my guest. I'm the one at fault. It could have been Ruby who slipped; she could have broken another limb! I'd never have forgiven myself.'

I stood up. 'Let's agree to stop apologising to each other. Have you got some newspaper for these broken pieces? It's safer in the bin that way.'

'Sure. I'll get that now. Then the vacuum cleaner. And if you want me to stop apologising, go and put your feet up in the lounge with the girls. I'll take care of the rest.'

I nodded, but once he'd gone, I continued with the clean-up. My OCD insisted on me giving the

133

walls another wipe to ensure there was no trace of debris. And I wasn't leaving that room until I was one hundred per cent sure there were no shards left on the floor for someone to step in. If it had been my own kitchen, I'd have been stuck in there for hours to come. But I couldn't let Rick see me like that, so I tore myself away and moved to the lounge.

Not that it was easy. The whole time he was finishing up in the kitchen, I was twisting my fingers anxiously in my lap. The girls were busy watching the movie, but I didn't take in any of it. I was too busy trying to extricate my mind from reruns of the disaster that had just played out.

Eventually, Rick appeared with a coffee for the two of us and, as he sat down, I finally felt able to relax a little. I did ask him about the phone call; he said it was fine, not volunteering any more information. Whether that was simply because of the girls being in earshot, I'm not sure, but I took the hint that he didn't want to talk about it.

We left soon afterwards. Ruby looked shattered and I wanted to get her home to bed.

Speak of the devil. She's calling me from the lounge now. Time to go.

Love as always,

M

Xx

CHAPTER 13

BEFORE

Tuesday, 14 February 2017

Dan stood at the lounge window of his crappy flat and watched the snow overwhelm the communal garden. It was coming down thick and fast: a torrent of fat flakes racing each other to the ground.

Getting into the office tomorrow – deadline day, of course – would be a nightmare, although better from here in the suburbs than it would have been from out at the house. Then, once he got to work, he'd have to squeeze in all those weather-related stories: the sledging snaps; the inevitable school closures; the traffic chaos.

Perfect weather for Valentine's Day. How romantic for all those lovebirds, he thought, envious of their happiness. There was a time, long ago, when he and Maria used to be like that: a happy young couple out on a date to celebrate Valentine's. He could even remember the two of them walking home through falling snow one year, early on in their relationship, arm in arm and stuffed with expensive restaurant food.

Back then, they had been utterly content in each other's company. It made Dan's head hurt to think how great they used to be together. It gave him hope that they could still fix things, while also frustrating the hell out of him that they'd drifted so far apart. Once upon a time people used to call them the perfect couple. With hindsight, Dan could see why: they'd had that magic combination of being in love as well as best friends. They'd enjoyed a lot of the same books, films, pubs, clubs and restaurants. They'd largely liked and disliked the same people – and realised they didn't need or want a big social group, since they were both happiest when it was just the two of them. And when their views had differed, such as on the topic of religion, each had respected the other's opinion rather than trying to change it.

That was a million miles away from where they'd ended up. And whether it was snowing or not, Dan knew for sure that neither of them would ever again view Valentine's Day the way they once had.

February the fourteenth was Sam's birthday. Everything else paled into insignificance. She should have been turning sixteen. They should have been celebrating her milestone as a family. Instead, she was gone. Absent again on her special day. Frozen in time. Fourteen forever, like the date.

Dan walked over to the coffee table and poured himself

another drink from the open bottle of vodka. He'd not even bothered to replace the lid. What was the point? He'd be drinking it all tonight. And whatever else it took.

The pain was always there. It never left him. But days like this tore at the wound; they poked and prodded at it, allowing no respite.

He'd barely done a thing at work. Even Maurice hadn't been able to keep up with all his cigarette breaks. Several people had asked if he was all right, sensing that something was wrong; he'd said he was fine, which couldn't have been further from the truth. And then at 2 p.m., unable to bear it any more, he'd left for a fictional hospital appointment.

It was 6.30 p.m. now. He'd been drinking for four hours: first in a quiet corner of a local pub and then, once the after-work crowd arrived, he'd returned here. Not home. He couldn't bring himself to call it that. He still held out hope that he'd be able to reconcile with Maria and move back to his real home. He had to believe that was possible for the sake of his own sanity.

If only Maria was on the same page. Last week she'd flown off the handle because he'd not found time to call in and fix a leaking tap in the downstairs bathroom.

'I've been really busy at work, Maria,' he'd explained on the phone. 'Sorry.'

'Forget it. I'll get a plumber in, like I wanted to do in the first place.'

'Don't be ridiculous. It's a five-minute job. I'll do it at the weekend. Surely it can wait until then.'

'The constant dripping is driving me mad!' she yelled, forcing him to move the receiver away from his ear.

Dan couldn't stop himself. 'Maybe you shouldn't have kicked me out of the house, then.'

'I knew it. I knew you were deliberately not fixing it to wind me up.'

'What? Don't be ridiculous.'

'You're ridiculous. A waste of space. The sooner we make this split official, the better.'

'What the hell does that mean?' Dan asked. 'You need to calm down.' But she'd already hung up – and he knew full well she'd been talking about divorce.

He didn't think she'd meant it. When she was angry, Maria had a habit of saying whatever nasty thing came to mind. It was something he'd learned to ignore. He'd gone over that night to fix the tap, giving in to her as usual, and the row hadn't been mentioned. But it still hurt.

Now Dan found himself picking up the phone to speak to Maria again. He hadn't planned to do so. He'd wanted to wait and see if she'd phone him. But he'd changed his mind. He needed to speak to her and to Ruby now, before the drink got the better of him. They were the only other people who could understand what he was feeling.

She picked up on the third ring. 'Hello?'

For a moment, Dan felt a burning desire to tell Maria how much he loved her, but he gulped it down with a swig of vodka rather than making a fool of himself.

'Hello? Is anyone there?'

'Hi, it's me, Dan. Sorry, I was just, um—'

'How are you?'

'Yeah,' he replied, trying to hide the waver in his voice. 'Today was never going to be a good day, was it?'

'No.'

He cleared his throat. Shook his head to pull himself together. 'What about you, Maria? How are you coping?'

'Let's just say tomorrow can't arrive soon enough.'

'And Ruby?'

'She's not said much. You know what kids are like. They get on with it. I've been trying to do the same.'

'Not easy, is it?'

'No.' After a pause, she added: 'Have you been drinking? You sound a bit—'

'I've just got in from work, Maria. I'm emotional, that's all. I thought you of all people would understand.'

'Fine. No need to shout. It was a simple question.'

'I'm not shouting. Why do you always say that? I'm talking in my normal voice.'

Maria let out a long sigh.

Dan felt a wave of anger rise up in his chest, but he took a deep breath and forced it back down. 'Let's not do this today,' he said. 'For Sam's sake. We're both hurting. There's no need to take it out on each other. Sixteen years ago—'

'Don't. I can't. Hold on.'

Dan found himself picturing the magical moment when Sam was born: the best Valentine's gift ever. He remembered holding her for the first time – this precious, fragile, noisy little bundle of life they'd created – and feeling so elated; so content that they were now a real family. He'd been brimming with optimism about their future together. How had he allowed it to go so wrong?

Ruby's voice appeared on the line. 'Hello, is that you, Dad?'

Dan swallowed down his feelings. 'Hello, love. Yes, it is. How's my girl?'

'I'm fine. What's the matter with Mummy? Why's she crying?'

'We were talking about your sister, darling. It would have been her birthday today.'

'I know.'

'It's a difficult day for all of us. How are you coping?'

'I'm all right.'

Dan could sense his daughter's discomfort, so he didn't push the subject. 'How was school today?' he asked, taking care to speak clearly and not to slur his words.

'Good.'

'Did you do anything special?'

'The usual stuff.'

'Numeracy? Literacy?'

'Yeah, that kind of thing. Hey, Dad. Guess what.'

'Go on.'

'Do you know Nathan in my class?'

'Um, yes, I think so. Does he have blond hair and glasses?'

'Yeah. Guess what pet he's got.'

'Um, I don't know. A dragon?'

'Dad, don't be silly. Dragons aren't real.'

140

'Well, actually, you can get these pets called bearded dragons. There's a man at my work who has one.'

'Really?'

'Uh-huh. They're not proper dragons like you get in films. They're much smaller and they don't breathe fire or anything. Have a look on the Internet and you'll see what I'm talking about. So what kind of pet does Nathan have?'

'A pug. A really cute little black puppy. His parents brought him with them when they picked Nathan up from school and I stroked him. He's so wrinkly and soft.'

Ruby had been a dog lover for as long as Dan could remember. Pugs were her favourite breed. She was forever looking at videos and photos of them online and wanted at least two of her own when she grew up. Dan wasn't sure from where the interest stemmed, but he suspected it was fuelled by the fact she wasn't allowed a dog of her own. The main reason for that was Maria, who couldn't bear dogs, having been bitten by one as a child. Dan could take them or leave them. Ruby had tried to convince him to get one when he moved out, but he'd told her it wasn't fair, considering he was out at work so much. Privately, he was thinking more about the prospect of moving home one day. He didn't want to do anything that might stand in the way.

'What's this pug of Nathan's called, then?'

'Doug.'

'Doug? That's an unusual name for a dog.'

'Doug the pug: it rhymes.'

He laughed. 'Oh, I see. That's funny. Maybe you should ask Nathan if you can go round to his house for a play date. Then you could get to know Doug as well.'

'Are you crazy?'

'What?'

'Why would I want to go to a boy's house after school?'

'Of course. Sorry. What was I thinking?'

The irony of this conversation, which would no doubt be playing out in reverse in a few years, did not escape Dan. He resisted the momentary urge to pull her leg about whether Nathan had sent her a Valentine's card.

'Hold on,' she said, 'Mum's calling something.' There was a pause and then she was back. 'I have to go for a shower.'

'Really?' Dan made a sniffing sound into the phone. 'Oh, yes. That makes sense.'

'What do you mean? Why are you making a rabbit noise?'

'A rabbit noise?'

'That sniffing you were doing.'

'Oh, right. I was smelling your ear to see if there were any potatoes behind it. I think there are a few, so a shower's probably a good idea.'

'Daddy! You can't smell things through the phone.'

'That's what you think.'

'You're being silly. I know you are. Anyway, I don't have any potatoes behind my ears.'

'Well, if you say so. Give them a good soaping just in case. Okay?'

'Okay.'

'I'd better let you go. See you at the weekend. Love you.'

'Bye, Dad.'

And that was it. The phone went dead. Dan was all alone again.

It bothered him how the conversation had gone with Maria. All he wanted was to resolve things with his wife. So why did it never work out as planned? Why was an argument always waiting in the wings? Could they ever get back what they'd once had? As much as Dan wanted to believe that they could, it was hard to keep the faith.

He wondered if he ought to have wished her a happy Valentine's Day or even sent her a card. That would have been weird, though, right? It wasn't the kind of thing you said or did to each other when you were separated. And yet they were still technically married. No, stuff it. What would have been the point? In Maria's eyes, everything he did these days was wrong.

Still, he couldn't remember the last time they'd been apart on February the fourteenth. Despite Sam's birthday rightly taking priority, they'd always continued to mark it with cards, flowers and chocolates. Until last year. There had been no Valentine's celebrations then.

It wasn't unusual for couples to split after losing a child. Dan was only too aware of that fact. Grief was capable of wrecking even the strongest union. He'd suggested couple's counselling some time ago, but he'd never managed to convince Maria. So he'd gone along with her request for a trial separation, buying her pitch that the time apart – and a break from the constant arguments –

might heal their wounds. There had been little sign of that so far.

'Bottoms up,' he said to the empty room, downing the rest of his glass of vodka, pouring himself another and downing that too.

The next thing he remembered was coming round on the couch to the unmistakeable growl of Tom Waits playing on the hi-fi. It was far too loud and, finding the remote control on his stomach, he turned it down. It was 9.55 p.m. He must have been out for a couple of hours at least. The vodka bottle was on its side on the floor, all but empty.

Dan felt somewhere in between drunk and hungover. He wrestled himself to his feet and stumbled to the bathroom, blurry-eyed and dizzy. Afterwards, nursing a pint of water and steadying himself with a hand along the wall, he made his way back to the sofa and flopped into its familiar embrace.

He needed to speak to someone: a friendly voice. He didn't trust himself to be alone with his thoughts.

He patted himself down and found what he was looking for – his mobile. He'd left it on silent and there was a missed call. It was from Maurice, not Maria as he'd hoped. He pressed the screen, only intending to swipe the notification away, but without meaning to, he found himself returning his colleague's call.

'Bugger,' he said, trying to stop it. 'Stupid bloody thing.'

'Hello?' a tinny version of Maurice's voice piped out of the earpiece. 'Dan? Are you there?'

Oh, well. He'd wanted to speak to someone; Maurice

was a safer option in his current state than bothering Maria again.

'Sorry. Yes, I'm here. Hi.'

'Are you okay, mate?'

'Sure. I noticed I had a missed call from you. I was actually going to leave it until the morning, but the stupid thing phoned you anyway. Sorry. I know it's, um, getting on.'

'You know you can call me any time.'

'But it's Valentine's Day. Aren't you busy with one of your—'

'It's fine, honestly. I wanted to catch you at work, but then someone told me you'd gone. Something about a hospital appointment.'

'Oh, right, yeah. That. I'm fine, honestly. Nothing to worry about.'

'Are you sure? You were smoking like a chimney at work. Listen, I don't mean to pry, but wouldn't it have been your Sam's birthday today?'

Dan felt his eyes welling up. He didn't trust himself to speak.

'I can't believe I didn't remember sooner,' Maurice continued. 'I feel awful. It came to me as I was driving home. Some friend I am. There was no hospital appointment, was there?'

Dan sighed. 'No.'

'Why didn't you take the day off?'

'I don't know. I probably should have. You won't say anything, will you?'

'Of course not. What have you been doing since you left?'

145

'Drinking mainly.'

'Alone? Haven't you seen Maria and Ruby?'

'I spoke to them on the phone earlier.'

'Bloody hell. Where are you now?'

'At the flat.'

'Would you like me to come over?'

'No, no, no. Don't be silly. I'm going to bed in a minute.'

'Are you sure? It's not a problem, honestly.'

'I'm sure.'

'What?' Maurice said. 'Hold on a minute, mate.'

Dan could hear the muffled sound of a conversation. The rise and fall of two voices – one male, one female – a disgruntled air about the latter, although Dan couldn't make out the words.

'Sorry about that,' Maurice said a moment later.

'I'm going to let you go. You've got company.'

'No, don't worry. This is more important.'

'It's Valentine's Day, Maurice. Go and have fun. There's no need for everyone to be down just because I am. I'm going to bed now. I'm fine.'

After saying goodbye, Dan picked up the vodka bottle from the floor and drained the last few drops before heading to the kitchen to find another.

He had no intention of going to bed yet. He'd only said that to stop Maurice from coming around. No, he didn't fancy hours of lying awake with his demons whispering at his ear. So the only option was more drinking. He'd obviously not done a good enough job the first time around. Time to try harder.

He added ice and a dash of Coke to the next stiff

measure he poured himself, plus two ibuprofen to numb the swelling beat of a headache.

He took the drink to the kitchen and smoked a fag out of the window, using a cereal bowl as an ashtray. It was a non-smoking flat. Weren't they all these days? But he'd got used to doing it this way, spraying a bit of air freshener after every cigarette. It was easier than going outside.

Head spinning with a nicotine rush, he picked up his drink and the bottle and headed to the second bedroom: the one Ruby stayed in when she came to visit, which doubled up as a computer room. He turned on the ageing Windows desktop. The Wi-Fi card had packed up a couple of days earlier, so it wasn't connected to the Internet. That didn't matter. He'd long since given up looking at Sam's old social media accounts. Doing so had always felt intrusive, and he much preferred the personal, family stuff anyway. The real Sam without all that pouting. After the PC had creaked its way through the lengthy process of booting up, he found the relevant folder on the hard drive.

It was mainly photos he had of her, plus a few short video clips. It wasn't nearly enough. Why hadn't he taken more while he'd had the chance? Still, at least there were some. Something to hold on to. He cherished the videos in particular, which had the power to bring his daughter back to life in those precious captured moments. Seeing her running along the beach, chasing Ruby; pulling the cap from her younger sister's head and then racing towards the sea; pretending she was going to throw it in as Ruby fought to catch up with her. Dan had watched those three minutes and thirty-two seconds over and over again, as he had all the other clips.

Sam as a fairy in the school production of *A Midsummer Night's Dream*.

Sam diving into an outdoor pool in a green and black swimming costume.

Sam getting a make-up lesson from Maria – all pink lips and blue eyeshadow.

Sam dressed in her navy blazer and red tie on her first day at secondary school.

Sam giving Ruby a piggyback on the beach.

Watching them was like experiencing a terrible pain and a warm pleasure all at once. He loved hearing his daughter's voice again: something he was terrified he might forget without the videos. He adored seeing her. But he hated the fact that this was all he had left.

His elder daughter, gone forever; the whole family torn to shreds in the process.

Sitting there in the dark room, the only light coming from the monitor, Dan upped the pace on the drinking, numbing himself the only way he knew how.

When he came to, slumped on the desk chair, the monitor had gone into standby, although the computer was still whirring away. He felt a sudden sense of panic, remembering the idiotic thing he'd done. He'd permanently deleted it, hadn't he? The whole folder – all those precious memories – gone in a moment of drunken madness.

Shit. He had to get the folder back. Had to retrieve it.

Why the hell would he do that? Why would he delete the only links he had to her?

He shook the mouse to wake the screen. The light was enough to see the keyboard but not his address book. He switched on the desk lamp and flicked through the pages with clammy fingers. Until he found him: Ant, the IT guy who used to cover his office before the centralisation. He'd been one of the casualties of the cutbacks. Now he worked for himself as a mobile tech repairman. Dan had used him a couple of times before to fix problems on his home PC.

He glanced at his watch before calling: 11.55 p.m. Far too late, but he couldn't stop himself. He had to do something.

He used the landline, not sure where he'd left his mobile. It rang for ages. He dreaded hearing voicemail; then Ant picked up.

'Hello?'

He didn't sound happy. Dan reeled off the words, trying not to sound drunk.

'Sorry to call so late. It's an emergency. I've deleted some files by accident. Not into the recycle bin: properly deleted. I need to retrieve them. There are no other copies. I've never done this before. Is it even possible?'

'Whoa. Slow down. Who is this?'

'It's, um—'

As he was talking, Dan had been clicking his way through to where the deleted folder should have been on the computer. The thing was, he'd just realised that it was still there, as were all the pictures and video clips, at least as far as he could see. Nothing looked to be missing at all.

What was going on? A minute ago he'd been certain he'd deleted the lot. Unless . . .

It dawned on him that it must have been a dream, an alcohol-fuelled nightmare. And yet it had felt so real. What an idiot. Why on earth hadn't he checked before phoning Ant, rather than being led by panic?

'Hello? Are you going to tell me who you are? Or is this some kind of prank call?'

Dan's mind was whirring. He had a withheld number on his landline. Short of recognising his voice, there was no way Ant could know it was him. So although he felt bad about it, he did the only thing that made sense at that moment: he hung up.

Before going to bed he checked through the computer folder, which – to his considerable relief – definitely appeared intact. He found a USB stick and copied everything across to it, as he'd intended to do ages ago.

The last file he copied was a photo taken in summer 2013. It was one of his favourites: so beautiful. All four of them together – him, Maria, Sam and Ruby – on a North Wales clifftop, framed by a glorious deep blue of merging sea and sky.

He'd been meaning to order decent prints of that and some of the other pictures to put up around the flat. At least he had the freedom to do so now. At the house, Maria still insisted on keeping all the photos of Sam shut away in her old bedroom. She'd had a wobbler one day and removed them from the lounge and so on. It was something to do with them getting in the way of her accepting Sam's death. Dan hadn't been happy about it, but there was no arguing with her when she got like that.

He took one last lingering look at that beautiful image before shutting down the computer.

The four of them all looked so happy then. If only he could go back to that moment. If only it had never ended.

CHAPTER 14

'Can I help you?'

The girl's words snap me out of my daze. I realise I can't keep on standing here in the doorway of the shop, gawping at her. I look down at the ten-pound note in my hand, which Miles gave me for a reason.

'Um, sorry, yes,' I reply, easing off my grip on the handle and hearing the door swing shut behind me. 'I, er, I'm just after some milk and bread.'

She points towards the far corner of the store. 'Over there.'

'Lovely. Thanks.'

She gives me a lethargic nod and returns to a magazine she's reading. Apparently I'm no longer of interest.

I wander in the direction she's indicated and find a good selection of both items. I pick up the largest carton of milk I see. Then I choose two medium-sliced wholemeal loaves – a brand I've seen in the kitchen before. People can be picky about bread, I think. Best stick to what I know Miles likes.

But what I'm really thinking about is the girl and what I might say to her. It leads me to wonder again about my suspicions that I might be a father and to curse my damn memory loss for keeping me in the dark. Wouldn't having a daughter of my own mean I'd find it easier to talk to this girl? Not necessarily, I tell myself, in a bid to shelve my ongoing frustration. Not if they were totally different ages. And teenagers are supposed to be tricky anyway, aren't they? Do any parents really know how to talk to adolescent kids?

As I make my way back to the counter, she continues reading the magazine. Her long black hair is tied in a side plait, which hangs down the front of her right shoulder. She's wearing a navy polo shirt with a green apron on top. Fresh-faced and make-up free, she looks around fourteen or fifteen years old. How am I so sure that it's her – the girl in red – when I've only ever seen her from a distance? My certainty starts to wane and then, as I put my items on the counter, she flicks her emerald eyes up to look at me and I'm confident again that it's her. It's not the striking colour: I've never been close enough to notice that before. It's something deeper. I can't put my finger on it.

What about her voice? I wonder. I try to recall the sound of the girl I heard on the clifftop. Was it the same as the voice that spoke to me a moment ago? Possibly, but I can't say with any degree of certainty. Perhaps talking to her some more will help.

'Hello,' I say with a grin, hoping it comes across as friendly rather than creepy. I'm aware of the need to tread carefully talking to a girl of her age, especially after the staring incident when I first entered the shop. I have to find a way to engage with her without coming across as a weirdo.

'Is that everything?' she asks, the shadow of an enforced smile crossing her lips, her eyes looking to the door.

'Yes, thank you.'

I pass her Miles's ten-pound note and scour her face for some sign that she recognises me. It doesn't come. She places my change on the counter and looks back down at her magazine.

'Perk of the job?' I ask.

'Sorry?'

'Magazines: you must get to read them for free.'

'Oh, I see. Yeah.'

'Helps pass the time?'

'Sure.'

This couldn't be going worse. She's willing me to leave. I can see it in the strain on her face. I must be wrong. I've got my wires crossed. It's hardly a surprise, considering the state of my memory. My mind must be playing tricks on me. It can't be the same girl.

And yet I find myself looking behind the counter, wondering if I might see a knee-length red coat hanging somewhere.

What's wrong with me? Apart from the obvious. Forcing myself to be normal, I pick up the bread and milk and start to walk towards the door. But before I reach it, I can't resist turning back to her and opening my mouth again, just one more time.

'Did I see you walking along the clifftop earlier?'

She looks up again from her magazine, eyebrows and forehead clenched in a frown. 'Pardon?'

'I'm staying up there – in the big old house. I'm sure I've seen you pass by. This might sound weird, but I had a fall this morning. Someone helped me and, well, I'm keen to say thank you to whoever it was. I wondered if, er, it might have been you.'

'I've been working here since eight o'clock this morning.'

'Really? That's odd. I could have sworn—'

The sound of the door being thrust open behind me grabs my attention. I turn and see Miles.

'Oh, there you are, lad,' he says. 'I'm done. I was wondering where you'd got to. Are you ready?'

'Yes, I'm coming.' I hold up the two loaves of bread and the milk carton. 'Is this enough?'

'Plenty.'

I glance back at the shop assistant, who's now picked up a mobile phone and is tapping the touch screen.

'Sorry about that,' I say, doing my best to throw my voice in her direction. 'Must have confused you with someone else. Goodbye now.'

'Bye,' she replies, without looking up.

I follow Miles outside, feeling confused and stupid.

'What was that all about?' he asks.

'Oh, nothing. I was trying to make conversation, that's all. I don't know why I bothered. You know what teenagers are like.'

155

'I do indeed,' Miles replies. 'I remember going through all that with Alison. Once was enough. I don't know how people with several kids manage. Must be a nightmare.'

Once we're in the car and heading back to the house, I can't stop myself from asking Miles whether or not he knows the girl.

'Not really,' he says. 'I might have seen her in there before, but I couldn't say for sure. They seem to have several young people on their books. Cheap labour probably.' There's a pause. 'Why do you ask?'

'She seems familiar. I wondered if I knew her from, you know, before my accident.'

'Not to my knowledge.'

'She's not a neighbour: someone I might have seen at the house?'

Miles shakes his head. 'We don't really have any neighbours. You get the odd rambler passing by, but they're usually closer to my age than hers.'

I'm not getting anywhere. I change the subject. 'So you got the nails you needed?'

'In a flash. How are you feeling?'

'Not bad.'

'Good. Do you want to head straight back or are you up for a detour?'

'A detour? That sounds intriguing. What did you have in mind?'

I'm looking out of the window as I ask this, scanning the side of the road for something I might remember. When Miles doesn't answer, I turn to look at him only to see – to my horror and utter confusion – that he's no longer there. The driver's seat is empty.

'What the hell?' I shout, diving over to grab the steering wheel as instinct kicks in.

Words and rational thoughts escape me as I try to get my head around this impossible situation. The road is on a downward slope and there's a sharp corner coming up, from which – as if things weren't bad enough already – an angry red truck emerges at speed.

I gasp.

'Everything all right?'

'Sorry?'

'You seem a bit lost.'

'I, er—' I look around and can't understand what's going on. There are people everywhere. Travellers wheeling cases, studying information screens, queuing, using their phones.

The woman who spoke to me is wearing a hi-vis vest over a navy jacket and a sky-blue blouse; a photo ID pass around her neck says her name is Diane and she's a customer service assistant.

I'm in an airport? I think, perplexed. Wasn't I . . . ? But whatever it was I was questioning slips from my mind before I have a chance to grab on to it.

'Sir, have you already checked in? Do you have a boarding card I could look at? That way I can point you in the right direction.'

'Hang on,' I reply, patting the pockets of my suit trousers and then my jacket.

'What about your bag?' she offers, eyes pointing at my feet where I notice for the first time a small shoulder bag – the kind that usually holds a laptop.

'Actually,' I say, pulling a folded piece of paper and a passport out of the inside pocket of my jacket, 'I think this must be it.'

'Where are you headed today?' she asks as I open it up.

I hand her the sheet and reply at the same time. 'Eindhoven.' I can't work out whether I knew that before reading it or not. Now that I've said it, I feel like I've always known that to be my destination, although a moment ago I could have sworn . . . well, I'm not exactly sure. I was a bit confused. It's like there was a mist obscuring my thoughts, but now it's lifting.

'Very nice,' she replies. 'I love Holland. We're not supposed to call it that any more, though, are we? The proper name is the Netherlands. My daughter-in-law is Dutch; she's lived here for years now. She'd tell me off if she heard me calling it Holland. I think that's only a small part of the country – a couple of provinces or something. She has told me, but I don't remember exactly. Anyhow, now we know where you're going, let's have a look how your flight's doing.'

She gestures for me to follow her and heads towards a nearby information screen. I pick up my bag, throw it over one shoulder and walk at her heel like an obedient dog.

Once we're within viewing distance, Diane stops. I do the same and wait as she squints up at the large monitor.

I probably should be looking at it too, but instead I find myself watching all the people around me, wondering where they've come from and what their destinations might be.

After a long few seconds, she turns back to me with a practised smile. 'Well, the good news is that you've still got plenty of time until you need to be at the gate for boarding. Unfortunately, there is a delay to your flight. It's only showing as forty minutes, so hopefully that'll be it, but I can make an enquiry for you; check if it's likely to change.'

'That would be great. Thanks.'

'Bear with me. I won't be two ticks.'

Diane trots to a desk in the nearest check-in zone and, after a quick word with a colleague, she picks up a phone.

As I'm waiting for her, a huge man in a leather trench coat rushes by, running over my foot with the wheels of his case. I notice that – bizarrely – he's holding one of those retractable dog leads in his left hand. It stands out because of its fluorescent yellow colour. 'Hey!' I shout after him. 'Watch where you're going.' But he continues without a backward glance, like an articulated truck that has just flattened a mouse.

Why does the word *truck* make me feel so strange?

I picture it in my mind's eye as a blood-red mechanical beast, racing around a sharp corner, engine roaring. And then—

A tap on my shoulder. Diane again.

'Sorry, sir. Did I startle you?'

'Yes. I mean no. It's fine. I was lost in my thoughts for a moment.'

She frowns at me. 'Are you sure that's all? You look pale. Would you like to sit down? Or perhaps I could get you some water.'

'No, thank you. Please could I have my boarding pass back?'

'Of course.' She hands me the piece of paper. 'The flight's fine, by the way. I mean, it's still late, but the delay isn't expected to increase. The departure lounge is straight up the escalator.'

I thank her and head on my way. Eindhoven, here I come.

I travel up the escalator feeling relaxed and happy. Not a care in the world. I enjoy spending time in airports. There's always something to do, even if it's just people watching. My favourite part is once you've passed through all the security checks. Then you're in the bubble: the restricted no-man's-land that's neither one place nor another. There's something special about that.

I'm almost at the top of the escalator when my eyes wander across the crowd below and something – or I should say someone – catches my attention. It's a slender figure in jeans and a knee-length red coat. A girl, maybe a teenager. It's hard to tell at this distance. She seems to be looking straight at me, mouthing something I can't work out, and waving. I look around to see if she could be signalling at someone else, but there's no one nearby. Then I reach the summit, slide on to static ground again and she's out of view.

Who is she? There's something familiar about her, but I can't put my finger on what.

I'm standing at the top of the escalator, pondering this and wondering what to do about it, when something heavy crashes into me from behind and sends me tumbling.

CHAPTER 15

Monday, 10 April 2017

Dear Sam,

How my life has changed since the days when I worked all the time. Do you remember the crazy amount of hours I used to spend in the office? Sorry, that's a stupid question. Of course you do. You wouldn't believe how much I regret that. All that time we could have spent together instead.

As a young woman I remember going around telling people that I had no regrets about anything. 'What's the point?' I used to say. 'The past is done. Move forward. It's not like you can go back and change anything. Regrets feed misery.'

How ironic is that, considering all the time I've wasted giving in to my OCD? Naive or what? It was easy to have no regrets when nothing major had gone wrong in my life. Then I lost you – my daughter, my firstborn, my flesh and blood – and my world collapsed. How could it not? I carried you inside me for nine months. No parent should ever have to bury their child. It's unnatural.

There I go again getting all worked up about the past when I said I wouldn't. Sorry, but it's hard not to, as it feels like I'm finally able to talk to you, and there's just so much I want to say.

The point is that my life is very different now from my days as a solicitor in the city. Back then, I used to think that building my career was so important. I'd justify being away from you and Ruby so much by telling myself it was only for the time being. That I'd make it up to you later, once I was established. That I was doing it for our family, to give us a better life. But in truth I was doing it for myself, to prove that I could have a successful career alongside a husband and two children. I put my own wants and needs above those of you and your sister, living to work when I should have been working to live, which was unforgivable. I know that, believe me. I've lived with it every day since you left us and I always will.

It's 10 a.m. In the old days that would have meant I was two or three hours into a shift at the office that might not finish until 8 p.m. In the new world order, I'm sitting at the kitchen table with a coffee, writing to you and looking forward to picking up Ruby after school. I hope she manages with her arm. I spoke to her teacher this morning when I dropped her off and she promised to keep a close eye on her. I spent the journey home from school worrying about how she'd manage and then, as soon as I walked through the front door, I started thinking again about how she fell in the first place. That's the only problem with having all this time on my hands nowadays and being alone so frequently. It means there are a lot more windows of opportunity for my OCD to strike.

I was on my hands and knees again, checking that the carpet was properly fixed down. Then I noticed it was worn in a few places and decided the safest course of action was to replace it. This would also mean changing the landing carpet, at considerable cost, but nonetheless I found myself taking measurements and browsing carpets online.

I was on the cusp of jumping in the car to go and visit some carpet showrooms when I heard the voice of Rosie, my counsellor, urging me to question what I was doing.

Don't worry, Sam, I didn't literally hear her voice in my head. I'm not that far gone. I imagined what she might say to me if she was there. 'Is this a real problem or is it OCD?'

'It's OCD,' I said to the empty house. I walked to the stairs and stared at the carpet as I told myself: 'It doesn't need replacing. Ruby breaking her arm was an accident. You can't control everything.'

Then I switched off the computer and sat down with my notepad to write this letter. You wouldn't believe how difficult it was to tear myself away, but I was determined and, eventually, the pangs subsided. I think it's the combination of the physical act of putting pen to paper and the mental process of stringing together my thoughts. Whatever, it helps.

Being in the clutches of an OCD episode must be hard to understand for someone without the condition. Once it has you under its spell, you do things that defy logic, like a junkie chasing a fix to a problem that doesn't exist; usually in a bid to avoid a larger issue that does. Giving in to the urges it presents only makes things worse. You scratch the itch and it becomes a rash; you scratch the rash and it gets infected, and so on. But it's so easy to give in. Like I did with the carpet this morning. And look how that snowballed.

I'll give you another example – and it's a hard one for me to admit to you, Sam. A few months after you died, I had what I now understand was an OCD episode regarding all the photos of you on display around the house. It was New Year's Eve and I was home alone for a few hours. We'd just got through our first Christmas without you, which had been incredibly tough.

Left alone with my thoughts, I decided that I'd never be able to come to terms with your death when there were reminders of your life everywhere I looked. So I went around the house, obsessively removing every photo of you. I didn't destroy them or anything. I could never do that, darling. I just moved them all to your bedroom, so I could look at them when I chose to. Neither Dan nor Ruby was happy with the arrangement, but I was insistent to the point of shouting and screaming, so I got my way.

Eventually, Dan convinced me to let poor Ruby have one photo in her bedroom: a lovely snap of the two of you with your arms around each other. It was taken on that fabulous holiday we had in North Wales. However, I'm embarrassed to admit that it's still the only exception. I do always carry a photo of you in my purse and I often look at the ones I moved to your room, but I've not yet got to the stage when I can put them back around the house. That'll be a big step for me. And yet I do hope it will happen one day soon. Writing these letters and working with Rosie is all about overcoming such challenges.

I'm definitely making progress. Look how I've managed to deal with my nutty notion of replacing the carpet. I've just about beaten that now. And yet, frustratingly, I know that another inspection of the stairs is all it would take for me to get back there. Sometimes, to overcome it, you're supposed to do that: deliberately spark an urge but not respond. Take the pain until it subsides, thereby reducing its impact next time. Maybe I'll try that after I finish this letter, although the idea scares me.

Now I hope you're still with me, Sam, as I've something significant to tell you about your sister. We had a big discussion last night, you see. It all started because she lost a baby tooth earlier in the day. Not long after I finished my last letter, actually. It was late afternoon and I gave her an apple as a snack. The tooth had been loose for a couple of weeks and eating that piece of fruit was what finally shifted it.

When it came to bedtime, she put it in the special purse she has for leaving her teeth for the tooth fairy. She placed it on the end of the bed before giving me a serious look. 'Mummy, can I ask you something?' she said, at which point I realised what was coming and took a deep breath.

'Yes, of course, darling,' I replied. 'What is it?'

'Um, is the tooth fairy real?'

I felt an inane smile trying to form itself on my lips – embarrassment, I suppose – but I squeezed them together; forced myself to keep a straight face, for her sake.

'Why do you ask?' I hedged, in two minds as to what to do. I knew I could keep the magic going a bit longer if I chose to, but eight seemed about the right age to tell her the truth. I was surprised she'd believed for so long in this modern age of scepticism and constantly flowing information. But part of me didn't want to let go of the innocence that stayed alive within her while she did.

'I don't know,' she said. 'We were talking about it at school and some of my friends said they don't believe any more.'

'I see. Well, what do you think?'

As those words came out of my mouth, I knew they could only take the conversation one way. But what the hell, I thought: it's just the tooth fairy.

Only it wasn't. Once we'd talked through the ins and outs of what actually happened to her teeth and who left the money, she fired another question at

167

me. 'What about Father Christmas, Mummy? Is he real?'

I hesitated, realising this had now become a more significant moment.

Do you remember how you found out, Sam? It wasn't all in one go. I told you about the tooth fairy when you were seven. We'd been to the dentist and he'd made some comment about it being an expensive time for me, because you'd lost several teeth. Later you asked me what he meant, so I had no choice but to explain. But that was that. No further questions. You didn't stop believing in Father Christmas until a couple of years later. Yes, I'm pretty sure you were nine. I didn't tell you, did I? It was your father. I remember coming in from a late night at work and hearing about it. You'd watched some Christmas movie together, hadn't you? Something had sparked the question and Dan told you the truth, making you swear not to spoil it for your sister. I don't think you got too upset. You'd guessed as much already.

Ruby wasn't so well prepared.

'What do you think?' was my eventual response to her question. Instead of replying, she covered her face with one of her teddy bears.

After a long, uncomfortable silence, I asked her if she was all right. She nodded but I could see the tears swelling in the corners of her eyes. I did consider backing down and sustaining the illusion in this case, but it felt dishonest. They say children don't ask until they're ready for the truth, so although my heart felt like bursting, I held firm and left the direction of the conversation in her hands. There was more uncomfortable silence, but eventually she spoke again. 'He's not real either, is he?'

'No, darling, he isn't.'

'So who brings the presents? And who drinks the sherry and eats the mince pie that we leave by the fireplace?'

'Your father and I do,' I said, looking away from her to hide the tears flowing down my own face.

When I'd composed myself enough to turn to her again, she looked embarrassed. Her eyes seemed to be saying: 'What an idiot I am. What a silly little kid.'

That was probably the most heartbreaking thing of all. I took her into my arms and gave her a huge hug.

'Are you all right, love?' I asked. She nodded, but her eyes were still red and I could see fresh tears waiting in the wings.

'It's a bit disappointing, isn't it?' I added, scrabbling to say something meaningful and failing miserably. 'But it doesn't mean you can't still enjoy Christmas. Everyone believes as a child, but you get to a certain age and start to wonder. You ask questions and then, well, you have a conversation like the one we're having now. I had the same conversation with my mummy too.'

'Did Sam know?'

I nodded. 'She agreed to keep quiet, so as not to

spoil it for you. But she believed when she was younger, of course. It's nothing to be embarrassed about. Finding out is part of growing up. You're getting to be a big girl now and I'm very proud of you.'

She didn't want to talk about it after that. I think she needed time to process the—

Sorry about that. I had to get the phone. Normally I'd have let it go to voicemail, as you get so many of those annoying call centres ringing up, but I was worried it might be Ruby's school. In fact it was Dan.

'How's the wounded soldier?' he asked. 'Has she gone to school?'

'Yes. I spoke to her teacher when I dropped her off. She's going to watch over her. Hopefully she'll be fine.'

It wasn't the first time we'd spoken – or seen each other – since having that awful row last week. He'd phoned up and popped in a couple of times in the interim, but Ruby being around meant we'd hardly had to talk to each other. We'd been civil for her sake, but there was definite tension. This time there was no way of avoiding the subject.

After an awkward gap in the conversation, Dan spoke. 'I, um, I know you're not a fan of apologies, which is why I've not said anything already. But I feel like I have to because, well, it's awkward between us now, isn't it?'

I said nothing, waiting for him to continue. 'The

thing is, Maria, I am sorry for what I said. I don't know why I got so worked up.'

'Which part are you sorry for: calling me twisted or asking for a divorce?'

I heard him sigh. Or he could have been exhaling a lungful of smoke. I pictured him outside having a cigarette break. He's like a chimney nowadays. I wish he wouldn't do it, for Ruby's sake if not his own, but there's no telling him.

I was tempted to tell him to shove his apology, but I stayed quiet instead. What he said had hurt me, but I know from personal experience that you don't always mean what comes out in anger.

'I'm sorry for it all, Maria,' he went on. 'The whole rant. I was tired after work and then the long wait at the hospital. I didn't mean it.' He paused, his voice softening. 'You know I never wanted us to split up in the first place.'

'You sounded pretty happy with the arrangement the other night.'

Dan sighed – or exhaled – again. 'I'm a million miles from happy, Maria. That's probably why I said what I did, because I'm so frustrated. I miss being with my family. I miss living in my home. I want things to be like they used to be. I know that's impossible without Sam, but maybe we could get part of the way there. I think the three of us could still be happy together.'

'Stop. This is too much. I can't handle it, Dan. A few days ago you were pushing for a divorce.'

171

'I never really wanted a divorce, Maria! I was just trying to get a rise out of you. I don't know what else to say.'

I didn't either. My feelings were all over the place. They still are. So instead I told him about last night's conversation with Ruby, which was enough of a revelation to divert his attention.

'Wow,' he said. 'Our little girl's growing up. How did it go?'

'What do you mean?'

'The conversation. Was it all right?'

'Of course. Why not?'

'So what did you tell her?'

'The truth. What do you think?'

I'm not sure why I was so offhand with him. I suppose I was still feeling sore about the last row. I also had the feeling he was about to accuse me of not doing it properly. The problem is I'm so used to arguing with Dan these days, I slip into rows by default. I see quarrels where there are none.

'That's very informative, Maria,' he replied. 'Thanks for sharing. I was only trying to make sure we're both singing from the same hymn sheet. I don't want her to hear something from me that doesn't tally with what you've said.'

He hung up before I had a chance to say anything else, leaving me feeling bad. I do still love your dad, Sam. But things have got so complicated. At times I still think there might be a chance for us. Then we fall out. It's always one step forward, two steps back.

Part of me wants us to be able to fix things – for Ruby's sake, especially – although they say you shouldn't do it for that reason alone. A bad marriage can be worse for a child than a split, apparently. Another part of me wants to call it a day; to move on. Hence the attraction to Rick and the allure of something new.

Speaking of Rick, he texted me earlier. He asked if I fancied having lunch with him one day this week, just the two of us. He even ended the message with a kiss. He's asking me on a date, right? What else could it be? Somehow, despite the whole gravy and red wine incident, he's still interested. I was going to say yes, but after speaking to Dan I'm not sure. I know we're not together, but I've suddenly got the feeling I'd be betraying him if I went. I'm going to have to give it some thought. If only you could write back. It would be amazing to know your opinion.

Love as always,

M

Xx

CHAPTER 16

BEFORE

Sunday, 25 December 2016

Dan's alarm sounded. He thumped it off and stared, blurry-eyed, at the red LED lines telling him it was 8 a.m.

It took him a moment to remember where he was. Not the spare room. No, the master bedroom in his fantastic new apartment. Otherwise known as the room he slept in at his crappy new flat in the suburbs. Him and his two 'flatmates': damp and depressing.

What on earth had he been thinking when he agreed to rent this place? That it was cheap and in a location that suited him. Not much else. If he'd been able to jump forward in time to this awful moment – waking up here, alone on Christmas morning – would he have still signed the rental agreement? Probably, if he was honest. That was actually one of the things that had appealed most about the flat: the fact it only tied him in for three months. He still hoped he wouldn't need any longer than that.

Also, it wasn't like he could afford much else while he was still paying the bills at his real house, where Ruby had probably already opened her stocking by now with Maria.

How was this fair: him going out to work five days a week, supporting the family, but having to live here? It wasn't. He stared up at the ceiling, at the unsightly cracks meandering across the white paint. If he wanted a chance of getting back with Maria, what choice did he have?

She'd pushed him further and further away since Sam's death and this was where he'd ended up. He feared she blamed him for what had happened to Sam. He blamed himself, so why not? That would at least explain why she'd grown so cold towards him. It was more than that, though. More even than the horrific, never-ending grief he'd felt since that horrendous day.

It was like something had broken within his wife's mind. As if she could no longer function properly. She did her best to hide it, but he'd seen the way she would repeat things over and over again when she thought no-one was watching, as though it was some kind of weird ritual. On the few occasions when he'd interrupted her or tried to help in some way, her response had been one of ferocious denial, pushing him yet further away.

The first time he'd tried to talk to her about it, he'd ended up banished to the spare room, never to return. They'd explained this to Ruby by saying that his snoring had been keeping Maria awake, but Dan suspected that Ruby knew it was more significant than that.

He hadn't dared say anything more for a long time afterwards, hoping it was part of his wife's grieving process and that she would gradually improve. But of course she didn't. Eventually, after skirting around the issue for far too long, he'd tried again to broach the matter. He'd suggested, as tactfully as he could, that she might want to seek help. He'd even been on the Internet and found her the name of a local counsellor.

Bad move. That had led to an even worse row than the last and, a couple of days later, to Maria's suggestion of the trial separation.

Now here he was: hungover and alone in this godforsaken place.

The alarm sounded again – good old snooze function – snapping Dan out of his half-doze and alerting him to the fact it was now 8.10 a.m. He turned it off, properly this time, and levered himself upright.

'Merry Christmas,' he said to his reflection in the mirrored doors of the cheap wardrobe.

He walked through to the lounge and spent a few minutes tidying up his mess from the night before: bottles of beer, a shot glass. He didn't know why he was bothering. It wasn't like he was expecting guests any time soon. Force of habit, he supposed, still not used to being a bachelor. He didn't want to get used to it. Hopefully it would be short-lived: a brief chapter in his life that one day he'd look back on and smile about.

In the kitchen, his gaze fell on the vodka bottle he'd been drinking from the night before. For a moment he thought about picking it up and having another go, but he stopped himself. His boozing had accelerated enough since moving in here. At least it was still mostly contained to acceptable hours. Necking vodka at this time of the day would be crossing a line. Next thing he'd have a bottle in the inside pocket of his jacket, swigging from it at the wheel of his car. No, he didn't want to go down that route. Plus, the police were always on the lookout for drink-drivers over the festive period. No point in risking his licence.

Instead he found his pack of cigarettes, opened the window and, enjoying the feel of the cold winter air on his skin, lit one up.

Dan found himself thinking about the first Christmas he and Maria had ever spent together. He remembered it like it was yesterday. They'd been a couple for less than six months and were madly, passionately in love. Neither could bear to spend a night alone, so although they still had separate places, they were always together at one or the other. Although they'd received various invites from family and friends, they decided to spend Christmas day alone at Maria's flat.

They'd filled stockings with little treats for each other, which they opened in bed. Later that morning, still in their dressing gowns, they opened the rest of their presents under the tree they'd chosen together, drinking Buck's Fizz. After returning to the bedroom for a while, they shared the cooking duties. Neither had prepared a turkey roast before, but they had great fun working out what to do. They spent most of the time in the kitchen laughing as they took it in turns to mess things up. Surprisingly, the end result was edible, although it definitely wouldn't have won them any awards.

'I'm going to get the Christmas pudding,' Dan said after polishing off the rest of his red wine in a bid to numb the nerves he was feeling.

'I don't think I've got any room,' Maria replied.

Dan grinned and, as he stood up with their plates, gave her a quick kiss. 'Sorry, but it's obligatory. I'll take care of it while you chill out for a few minutes.'

He'd been planning this for some time and was anxious to get it right.

'Are you sure you don't need any help?' she shouted through to him a short while later.

'Nope, I'm almost done.' He poured the warmed brandy over the top, steadying his shaky hands as he did so, and held a light to it. Then he grabbed the plate and carried the fiery blue pudding straight through to the lounge. 'Da dah!'

Maria's face was a picture. 'Wow! That looks amazing. How did you know what to do?'

'I have my ways, gorgeous,' he said, hoping his face didn't give away the butterflies in his stomach.

Once the flame had died, he carefully cut them both a piece and handed one to Maria. 'Enjoy, but be careful. You never know what you might find in there.'

'Ooh, that sounds fun.' A moment later she came across her silver prize and pulled it out. 'Hmm, now what do we have here? Could it be a sixpence?'

Dan felt his heart pounding in his chest. 'You'll have

to open it and see. I wrapped it in tin foil. I didn't think it would be very hygienic otherwise.'

'Good plan, Batman.' She took it in her hands and made them quiver with mock anticipation as she opened it up. 'Exciting!'

As the silver coin was unveiled, Dan's tiny folded note fell out, as planned.

'Yes! Twenty pence,' she said, 'but hold on. What's this little piece of paper I see?'

Dan shrugged, feigning ignorance.

It seemed to take forever for her to unfold it. Then she started reading and tears – happy ones, he hoped – started to form in her eyes.

He knew the words, penned in his tiniest handwriting, off by heart:

Maria,
I've never been so happy as I have with you these past few months. You're amazing and I love you. Let's live together?
Dan
X

She looked up and, wiping the corners of her eyes, beamed at him. 'Let's do it,' she said, voice wavering with emotion. 'Let's live together. I love you too, Daniel Evans. Now get over here and kiss me.'

Back in the present, a couple of hours later, Dan found himself standing in front of what he still considered to be his own front door. He was wondering whether to ring the bell or to let himself in. He had his key but decided against using it, in case doing so sparked Maria to ask for it back.

It was Ruby who answered the door. 'Hi, Dad. Can you guess what Father Christmas brought me?'

'Hang on. First I need a Christmas hug.'

As Dan embraced his daughter, Maria appeared. 'Hello. Merry Christmas,' he said before greeting his wife with a chaste kiss on the cheek.

'Merry Christmas. How were the roads? Not too icy, I hope?'

'No. They were fine.'

Dan wished he could say the same about Maria, but she didn't seem the slightest bit happy to see him. The frosty reception she gave him made it clear that he'd been invited purely for their daughter's sake. How had the two of them become so distant? Their relationship had drifted so far off course now; part of Dan feared they'd never work things out.

He took a deep breath and tried not to feel too sad. Maria had at least made an effort to look nice, wearing make-up and a long black dress, her hair up in a bun. But he could tell straight away how tired she was from the thin red veins snaking their way across the whites of her hazel eyes: usually one of her most beautiful features.

'Are you all right?' Dan asked. He almost added that she looked tired but thought better of it. It didn't take much to spark an argument these days and he was aiming for a row-free visit.

'Fine. I need to get back to the kitchen.'

'Can I help at all?'

'No, thanks.'

'Your job is to play with me,' Ruby said.

'Great. Let's see what Santa brought for you, then.'

Dan followed Ruby through into the lounge where the various presents she'd received so far were arranged in a neat pile on the coffee table. As expected, the one she was most excited about was the tablet he'd ordered online about six weeks earlier, when he'd still been living at home. Maria hadn't been keen at first, arguing that she was too young to have her own device, but somehow he'd managed to persuade her.

'Look, Dad,' she said, holding it up. 'I got my own tablet. And there are loads of games on it already. It's not an iPad, but it's still really good. It looks almost the same, doesn't it?'

'Wow,' Dan replied, feigning surprise despite being the one who'd put all the games on there. He brushed off the iPad comment, realising Ruby didn't mean it in an ungrateful way. Kids her age didn't do tact. Besides, there was no way he was paying Apple prices. 'You're a lucky girl. And what's all this other stuff?'

She gestured towards the pile before turning her attention back to the tablet. 'Have a look.'

'Is all this from Father Christmas?'

'Yep. Some of it was in my stocking and the rest was under the tree.'

'Cool. And what time did you wake up?'

'Six forty-three. Then I went into Mummy's room at seven o'clock.'

Dan felt a stab of jealousy. It was the first time he'd missed seeing that look of joy on her face when she got up on Christmas morning and tore open her gifts. And why was Maria still Mummy when he'd become Dad all of a sudden?

He wondered if this would be the last time Ruby believed in Father Christmas, remembering the conversation he'd once had with Sam. That had been after watching one of those American Santa movies where there's a naughty kid who doesn't believe but by the end he's back on board. It had had the opposite effect on Sam, sparking her to ask the question. Reluctantly, he'd told her the truth, ending the magic for her. He could still picture the look of disappointment on her face now. He hoped it would fall to Maria to break the news this time around.

'So what are all those other presents under the tree?' he asked. 'Are they for you too?'

'Most of them are; there are a few for you and Mummy.'

'Really? I'd better have a look, then.'

Dan pretended to inspect the pile while sneaking a couple of extra gifts in among them. There was little need for subterfuge, though, with Ruby busy playing on her tablet.

'Hey. What's this?' he said. 'I think you missed one from Father Christmas.'

That got his daughter's attention. 'Really? Where?'

'Here.' He handed her the small present. He knew she didn't need any more gifts. She was spoiled enough as it was. But he wanted to see her open at least something he'd chosen for her.

'To Ruby, love from Father Christmas,' she read aloud.

Dan had disguised his handwriting on the label and matched the wrapping paper Maria had used on the other gifts.

'What do you think it is, Dad?'

He shrugged. 'I don't know any more than you do, sweetheart.'

She turned the present around in her hands, enjoying the mystery for a moment. 'I think it's a book.'

'Well, darling, there's only one way to find out for sure.'

Maria walked in from the kitchen, a glass in each hand, as Ruby was halfway through tearing off the paper. 'There's some orange juice for you both here. I assumed you wouldn't want anything alcoholic, Dan, seeing as you're driving.'

He wondered whether that was meant as a dig at him – a hint that he stank of booze from the night before, which he probably did – but he chose to ignore it. 'Thanks. That's perfect.'

'Look, Mummy,' Ruby said. 'There was another present from Father Christmas under the tree. We missed it before. Oh, cool, it is a book and there's a rabbit on the front. He's so cute.'

'Another gift?' Maria said. 'Someone has done well this year. You must have been very good.'

'What's it called?' Dan asked, trying his best to ignore the look of disapproval that Maria was sending him.

'Um, *Watership Down*, it says. I've not seen it before. It must be about a rabbit.'

'Let's see. Oh, wow. That looks good, doesn't it?'

What Dan wanted to say was that it was a book he'd

adored as a child and hoped that she would too, but he knew better than that. He understood the benefit of letting her discover it for herself. Ruby was quite the bookworm, like her sister had been. It was something Dan, a booklover himself, liked to think he'd engendered in them both through regular bedtime stories. *Watership Down* was, perhaps, a little advanced for an eight-year-old, but it was important to keep challenging her and he was confident she was up to the task.

The book was soon discarded, with the tablet taking centre stage again, but that was fine. Dan could tell she was pleased with it.

Maria, wearing a pink Yummy Mummy apron he'd bought for her years earlier, disappeared into the kitchen.

'Back in a minute, love. I'm going to see if I can help your mum with the food.'

Ruby didn't look up from her tablet screen.

'Smells delicious,' Dan said as he entered the kitchen.

Maria was tending the oven. She glanced in his direction and then continued with the job at hand: turning the roast potatoes around in the hot oil. 'Thanks. Not sure if it will taste that way.'

'Problem?'

'It's hard trying to juggle everything.'

'I'm here to help. Whatever you need.'

She shut the oven door and turned to face him. 'No. I want to do it myself. Please, Dan.'

He held up his hands. 'It was only an offer. Chill.'

'I am chilled, thank you very much. But I need to be left alone.'

'Message received. If you change your mind, give me a shout.'

'Fine.'

'At least it's just us this year,' he said.

'Are you suggesting I wouldn't be able to cope with more?'

'Not at all. Only that it's easier without visitors. I realise I'm technically a visitor this time, but—'

'There's still plenty to do, trust me.'

'I know. That's why I—'

'Daaad,' Ruby's voice bellowed from the lounge. 'Please can you help me with something?'

'Coming,' he called back. He shrugged at his estranged wife, wondering what he could possibly do to get things back on track between them. 'I'd better see what she wants.'

Last year Maria's parents had come to stay and he'd been the one to take charge in the kitchen. He wasn't a fantastic cook. Maria was the more naturally gifted out of the two of them, but he was capable enough – and less flappable. He'd accepted very little help and had somehow managed to get by and produce a decent meal.

In truth, the main reason that he'd done all the work then had been to stay out of the way of Maria's mother. He and Helen rarely saw eye to eye. The two of them had clashed for as long as he could remember. It was like he'd found himself in a real life version of a Les Dawson gag. Only it wasn't funny.

Helen had an opinion on everything – and it was invariably at odds with his own. He'd never been able to do

185

or say the right thing; to be good enough for her daughter. She blamed him for what had happened to Sam too. That much was clear without her ever actually vocalising it. No doubt she was glad that Maria had turfed him out of the house. Not that he'd seen her or heard from her since then.

His father-in-law, Geoff, couldn't have been more different. A placid chap, he loved and lived to play bowls and watch sport; to sup on a good single malt whisky. He'd always been very welcoming to his son-in-law. But in all the time they'd known each other, Dan had never once seen Geoff stand up to or contradict his wife. He rarely spoke when they were together, leaving her to do the talking. So as nice as he was, he didn't amount to much of an ally. Dan couldn't imagine for the life of him what had drawn the two of them together. Talk about opposites attract.

'What's up, darling?' he asked Ruby, walking back into the lounge.

'Oh, could you help me with this game? I'm stuck.'

'What game is it?'

'*Wiggly Worm*.'

Dan smiled to himself and ruffled Ruby's hair. 'It's actually *Wriggly Worm*. What are you stuck on?'

'I can't get past this mean bird. It keeps eating me.'

'Okay, let me have a look.'

Dan enjoyed helping Ruby with computer games and the like. It made him feel useful and less over the hill than usual. He didn't want to be one of those adults who let technology pass them by. Playing simple, fun games like this reminded him of his own childhood in the 1980s, when he was a dab hand at titles like *Horace Goes Skiing* and *Daley Thompson's Decathlon*, loaded from cassette tapes. That said, he knew from his experience with Sam that Ruby would soon be running rings around him. It was amazing how much she already knew her way around her new tablet. In a day or so, she'd be showing him things.

Luckily the game in question was one he'd also installed on his phone. Although he rarely found time to actually play it, he was at least able to help.

'Like this,' he said, tilting the screen so she could watch how he did it and then handing it back to her. 'Now you have a go.'

'Great. Thanks, Dad,' she said, planting an unexpected kiss on his cheek. 'But can you stay and help, in case I get stuck again?'

'Of course. Team Evans to the rescue, right? Give me an E.'

Ruby threw him a side-glance that made it clear she wouldn't be doing any such thing. 'Don't be weird, Dad.'

'Okay,' he replied, feeling far less like a cool father than he had a moment earlier. 'Only joking.'

Maria did a good job with the dinner, which Dan found delicious. Not that you'd have thought so from the way she talked about it. Nothing was quite right in her mind, from the turkey being 'a little dry', to the cranberry sauce being too runny. And she was up and down from the table throughout the meal, getting this and checking that, which made it hard to relax.

In days gone by Dan would have told her to stop flapping.

However, their relationship was no longer up to such comments. So he ate his food, paid Maria and her cooking as many compliments as he could without fawning, and tried to maintain jolly conversation.

After they'd finished, he insisted on doing the dishes, which Maria eventually accepted. Then he brought out a pot of tea and suggested that they open the rest of the presents together.

Ruby was under the tree in a flash. She knew most of the remaining presents were for her. There were two joint gifts for Dan and Maria – a box of chocolates from his cousin Alex and a tablecloth from Maria's aunt Emily – both apparently unaware of their separation.

'You can have the chocolates,' Maria offered. 'Unless you need—'

'No, that's fine. Tablecloths aren't my thing.'

Then Ruby handed her mother the present Dan had placed under the tree earlier.

'Another one?' Maria said. 'Who's this from?'

She read the label and threw Dan a confused look. At her suggestion, they'd agreed not to get each other a gift this year. But then he'd seen a bracelet matching the necklace he'd given her last birthday and he'd gone ahead and bought it for her anyway. He wanted to show her that he still cared. That he considered the current state of affairs a temporary setback and hoped to be home soon.

He shrugged. 'It's nothing much. I saw it and couldn't resist.'

'But I haven't got you a present.'

188

'That's fine. I wasn't expecting anything. Being here and sharing the day with the two of you is more than enough.'

She opened it and Dan thought he glimpsed a flash of appreciation on her face. But it was gone before he could be sure. A moment later, she shut the box without trying on the bracelet and placed it on the arm of her seat. She turned to him and said: 'Thank you, Dan. That's lovely.' But her steely eyes told another story.

Later, when Ruby went to the toilet, she scowled at him. 'Why did you do that?'

'I thought you'd like it.'

'I do, but we're supposed to be having a break from each other, Dan. This is the kind of gift a man buys his wife.'

'You are my wife.'

'But we're not together. I invited you today for Ruby's sake, not as a reconciliation. A gift like this comes with expectations.'

'You're being ridiculous. My only expectation was that you might like the bracelet and wear it together with the necklace. I'm sorry I bothered.'

'Why are you sorry, Dad?' Ruby said, walking back into the lounge.

'Oh, it's nothing, darling. I was talking about work.'

'What about?'

'Nothing interesting.'

'You never tell me anything.'

'Don't be silly. How about we all play a board game?'

A little while later, when Dan could no longer bear Maria's frostiness – even for Ruby's sake – he announced that it was time for him to leave.

189

'Not yet,' Ruby said. 'Why can't you stay a bit longer? We don't want him to leave now, do we, Mummy?'

'Your dad's got things to do, love,' Maria replied.

'On Christmas Day? Like what?'

'I, um, arranged to meet up with a friend from work. He was going to be spending Christmas alone otherwise.'

'Who?'

'Maurice. You've probably heard me mention him.'

'Why don't you invite him here?'

'Come on now, Ruby,' Maria said. 'Stop giving your dad a hard time. We've had a nice day, but he has to leave.'

After saying his goodbyes and heading outside into the chilly evening air, Dan reached into his coat pocket for his keys and found the boxed bracelet he'd given Maria. There was a handwritten sticky note attached.

Dan,
Sorry, but please return.
Maria

He couldn't believe it. Who the hell did that: rejected a present on Christmas Day? He was torn between rage and sorrow. So he couldn't even give his wife a gift any more? What hope was there for them?

He opened the door of the car, sat down, threw his chocolates into the passenger seat and thumped the steering wheel three times. He fired the Focus up and reversed it out of the drive at speed, causing it to skid on a patch of ice and connect with the garden wall.

Wincing at the scraping sound, he put the handbrake on, got out and walked around to the passenger side to survey the damage. There was an ugly dent in the front door from where it had connected with the sharp corner of a concrete pillar cap.

'Bugger,' he said under his breath.

Other than a couple of paint marks, which he was able to brush away by hand, there was at least no damage to the wall, so no need to tell Maria.

He got into the car and headed back to the flat. The line he'd spun to Ruby about meeting up with Maurice was pure fiction. He'd be seeing out the rest of the night alone. His only plan was to drink himself into a happier place.

CHAPTER 17

Fingers click.

A voice calling down an empty corridor. 'Hello? Can you hear me?'

Fingers click again. The voice is closer. 'Sir?'

Silence.

Then the world rushes back to life with a gasp. Bright lights and noise and movement all around. There's a woman's face about an inch in front of my own: a pungent whiff of coffee on her warm breath. 'Sir? Do you recognise me? My name's Diane. We spoke a few moments ago.'

I glance down at her hi-vis vest and ID pass. I nod and try to speak, only for a croak to come out. I clear my throat and try again. 'Diane. Yes, I remember.'

I'm sitting on the floor at the top of the airport escalator, my back against a barrier. Diane's kneeling in front of me, but she's moved back a little now. Passengers spit out one after another from the moving staircase, glancing at me with a perplexed look before continuing on their way.

'How do you feel?' Diane asks.

'Stupid.'

'You banged your head. I've called for help. Someone should be here any minute.'

I check myself as best I can from my position on the floor. My head does hurt, as well as my knees and right elbow, but everything still seems to work. 'I think I'm all right.'

'I saw what happened,' Diane says. 'I was watching you from the foot of the escalator and I couldn't believe it when that big idiot in the leather coat barged his way past and knocked you to the floor. He didn't even stop. I'm sure we'll be able to track him down. His details will be on the computer and there are cameras everywhere. He should be made to apologise, at the very least.'

I think back to the giant in the leather trench coat who ran over my foot with his case earlier. It must be the same guy. No wonder he sent me sprawling. He looked at least six foot six and chunky with it.

A lad with a green first-aid kit appears. I can't be doing with the hassle of being checked over by him. He looks like a teenager with his blond hair and Tintin quiff. His only medical qualification is probably a two-hour course in an airport conference room.

'Hello,' he says in a voice too deep for his body. He flashes a nervous smile at me and then looks to Diane for direction.

'He banged his head,' she says. 'Someone pushed him over. He was out of it for a minute.'

'Unconscious?'

'No,' I say. 'I'm fine. No need for a fuss.'

I plant my palms on the cool, smooth floor beneath me and start to get to my feet.

'Wait,' Diane says, placing a firm hand on my shoulder. 'You need to take it easy.'

I scowl at her, jerk her hand away and continue to push myself upwards, doing my best to ignore the shooting pains from my joints. 'I said I'm fine.'

Once I'm standing again, head pounding, I grab hold of the barrier behind me and wait for the dizziness to pass. Then I look Diane in the eye.

'Thank you for helping me. I appreciate it. But I'll be all right from here.' I turn my gaze to Tintin, whose face is knotted with anxiety. 'Relax. I'm sorry you had to come out. It's a false alarm.'

He takes a step towards me, his green box held out like a peace offering. 'It's no trouble. I'm trained—'

'I said no.'

He jerks back in response, his wide eyes looking again to Diane for instruction. But she's equally confused.

'Sorry,' I say to them both. 'I don't mean to sound aggressive or ungrateful. I just want to get on my way.'

I look down at my bag, which is on the floor near to Diane. Maintaining eye contact with her, I lean forward to grab the strap and lift it on to my shoulder.

'I'm going to continue on my way now,' I say, wondering how this has ended up feeling like that point in a film when the hero has pulled a gun and is backing away from his enemies.

Am I the hero, though, or am I the bad guy? Diane and

Tintin are only trying to help. Why don't I let them? What am I afraid of?

Diane opens her mouth to speak, but no words emerge. She stops. Literally freezes. And everything – everyone else – does the same. The escalator has halted. The information screens are frozen. The hubbub in the background has become a deafening silence.

'What the hell's going on?' I say, my voice echoing like I'm in an empty cavern.

I click my fingers in front of Diane's face, like she did to me a few moments ago, but she doesn't react. Gingerly, I reach forward again and prod her shoulder, but I might as well be touching a lead statue. The same goes for Tintin and every other person I approach. They're all frozen to the spot, exactly as they were when this – whatever it is – happened.

I spot a skinny businessman down on one knee, tying a shoelace. I walk up to his side and push with all my might, keen to see if I can knock him over. He doesn't shift a millimetre. I kick his small wheeled case, thinking that at least will move, but it's as solid as a wall and I yelp in pain.

'What is this?' I shout. 'Hello? Can anyone hear me?'

There's no answer, so I bellow it out over and over again as I weave in between frozen people and luggage. I only stop shouting when my throat starts to hurt. Then I feel the silence closing in on me. It's oppressive – more than I can bear – and I find myself starting to vocalise my thoughts so there's at least some noise.

'Better the sound of a crazy man talking to himself than nothing at all,' I say.

After a few minutes of aimless wandering, I decide to continue on my original course towards the departure lounge. 'I might as well,' I tell a little girl frozen in the act of picking her nose.

'This can't be real, can it?' I ask the next frozen figure I pass. 'I must be dreaming. What other logical explanation is there? I bet I'm still sprawled on the floor at the top of the escalator and my mind's making this up.'

I pinch a small piece of skin on my neck and slap both cheeks.

'The crazy man's hitting himself now,' I say to a frozen official.

I walk past him, skipping the queue of people lined up in front of his podium. Rounding the corner, I enter a large security control area where there's a long line of frozen folk waiting to go through the scanners. But it's neither the sight of them nor the halted machinery that stops me in my tracks. It's the large shape I can see making his way awkwardly through them: my friend in the leather trench coat.

'Hey,' I shout in his direction. He has shoulder-length grey hair tied back in a ponytail, which flaps about as he turns his head in response.

I wave, in case it's not clear that I'm the person who called out. 'Over here. I thought I was the only one. What the hell is happening?'

He stares at me for a moment, stony-faced, before continuing on his way. Inexplicably, he's still holding that fluorescent dog lead in his left hand.

'Hey,' I shout again, starting after him. 'Why are you

ignoring me? First you run over my foot with your case. Then you knock me over by the escalator. Now you're pretending I'm not here, despite all this freakiness going on. Wait!'

It's hard to catch up to him with all the queuing people and their hand luggage in the way. Especially as he's so far ahead.

'Hold up,' I call. 'Please wait. I don't understand what's going on. You're the only other person I've seen who's not affected by this. Plea—'

He's at the front now. Standing before one of those gateway-type body scanners, he turns to face me, still way behind.

'At last,' I say. 'Please wait for me. I need to know what's going on.'

He frowns. Scratches his nose. 'What's your name?'

'My name? It's . . .'

I don't understand. My mind's blank. I can't think of it – my own name. How's that possible?

The man shakes his head and turns to leave.

'No, don't go,' I plead. 'Wait.'

I have an idea. I halt my struggle forward and reach into my pocket. My boarding card is the first thing I find, but when I pull it out and look to the section where my name should be, it's blank. I'm even more confused now. How can it be blank? Diane would have noticed if that was the case when I handed it to her. She would have said something.

I pull out my passport next, only to find the same thing: no name, not even a photo.

I look back in the man's direction, more desperate than ever for answers, only to discover he's gone.

'You can't leave me here,' I shout. 'Come back! I need your help.'

The only reply I get is a fresh echo of my own voice, but before I can call after him again, I feel a tap on my shoulder.

I turn and see Miles in the driver's seat – a concerned look on his face. He's pulled the Land Rover over into a stopping place at the side of the road.

'Jack?' he says. 'Is everything all right?'

I blink. Confused. 'Um. Yeah. Sure. Why? I didn't black out again, did I?'

'Is that what it felt like?'

'What? No, I don't think so. What did I do?'

'Nothing as such. You stopped responding for a minute. You seemed to be looking out of the window into the distance. I suggested a detour and then, well, you didn't answer. I thought you hadn't heard me at first, but I asked you several times and still nothing. It was very strange. I stopped the car as soon as I could.'

An angry red truck races by in the opposite direction, causing the Land Rover to rock from side to side as it passes.

Miles shakes his head. 'Someone's in a rush. He should take it easy before he causes an accident.'

'I think I, um, must have slipped into some kind of daydream.'

'Was it another memory?'

I rack my brains, but I can't recall for the life of me what it was. 'It sounds weird, but I don't know. I could have sworn I did a moment ago, when you first asked. Now it's gone. Sorry.'

Miles appears sceptical. 'Really?'

'Yes, I'm not making it up.'

'No, no. I wasn't suggesting you were. I'm puzzled, that's all. We could really do with getting hold of your medical history. That might shed some light on what's going on.'

'How do we go about that without knowing who I am?'

He stares at me for a second longer and then shrugs. 'That's the problem.'

CHAPTER 18

Friday, 14 April 2017

Dear Sam,

I know it's been a little while since my last letter. Each morning for the past few days I've been waking up full of good intentions and then one thing or another has stopped me from putting pen to paper. At least I'm writing now.

I'm always talking about myself and it seems wrong that I don't put questions to you. I know I won't get an answer. I'm not delusional. But I have to believe that you're still out there somewhere, Sam. You grew inside me. If I still exist, how can you not?

So where are you? I hope it's somewhere wonderful, where you wake up each day looking forward to what's ahead; where you are surrounded by people you love and who love you back.

Have you changed in the time since we were last together? Do you still look as I remember? Or have you continued to age like the rest of us? I'm not sure which I'd prefer. Whatever suits you best, I suppose. That's what matters.

It's Good Friday today: one of the holiest days in the Christian calendar. You know I'm not a church person, although I often used to go as a child with Mum and Dad. They've always been regular Church of England worshippers, as you'll remember. I stopped after leaving home. That's not to say I don't believe in some kind of God and an afterlife. I just don't feel a desire to express it in public every Sunday. I don't like to be told that certain days, like this one, are more important than others. I agree with the core morality of Christianity, but not with the archaic rules and regulations that ignore the realities of our modern world. I prefer to go my own way.

It's part of the reason why your father and I didn't have you or Ruby christened. I didn't want to be hypocritical. I thought it was important for you to be able to choose for yourselves once you were old enough to do so. There's also the fact that Dan is an atheist, but I know he'd have let me christen you if I'd insisted. Like he let me have your funeral in a church, which somehow felt like the only option to me. I had to make the choice for you that time and, despite my usual stance, nothing else felt right.

It may surprise you to know that I pray most nights. That was one habit I developed as a child that I didn't grow out of as an adult. Mainly because it was the part of religion I got on with: the private part, carried out on my own terms. I don't kneel at the end of the bed or anything. It's far less formal than that: more of an internal monologue followed by a period of silent reflection. It's often the last thing I do before falling asleep.

I believe in something – some greater being or purpose behind our existence – but I don't see the need to explain it any further than that. Why do I believe? I can't imagine how all of this could exist otherwise. But the rest is pure speculation. The fact is there's no way to know the truth until you die, which is fine with me. I'm happy to wait for my time to find out.

This leads me on to my next question, Sam.

Was it really your time to go when you did?

I struggled to believe so when it happened. It's such an awful thing as a parent to outlive your child. I stopped praying for a long time, until I could no longer bear the hopelessness. And when I did eventually start up a new dialogue, it was that question I asked over and over again.

I thought I'd almost come to accept that it was your time, but now I can't stop myself asking you the question. You were so young. You still had so much ahead of you.

Have you accepted it? Or do you wish you were still here with us? I pray that you're happy and in a better place: somewhere that makes this old world of ours look dull and lifeless.

I have to believe that. It's why I returned to praying. The idea of you not existing any more – of us never meeting again one day – is unbearable. That's what belief is all about. It's comforting.

We will meet again, won't we? I hope so, my darling girl, with all my heart.

I had to stop writing for a moment then. Sometimes the pain of missing you is so strong it's like I can't breathe, as though I've been winded. I can feel myself getting melancholy; you'd think it was three in the morning and I was sipping on a stiff drink, staring into the darkness. It's actually 11.36 a.m. Ruby's spending the first day of her Easter holidays with Dan, so I'm alone, sitting at the kitchen table next to a mug of half-drunk cold coffee. The weather's lovely: one of those gorgeous April mornings that tricks you into thinking there might be a red hot summer ahead.

I'm looking into the garden and the grass badly needs a mow. I never thought I'd catch myself thinking that. I used to berate Dan for doing it too often. I even accused him a couple of times of using it as a way to avoid spending time with us. Now I wish he was here to do it for me. He probably would if I asked him, but let's be honest – he does enough already. It wouldn't be fair of me to take advantage of him like that.

I can't help but think of mowing as a man's job, like checking the oil and water levels in my car. Not very feminist of me, I know, but Dan always used to do those things for me. It's not like they're difficult. I'm managing all right, apart from the flat tyre I had a few weeks ago after not checking the air pressure for ages. They're just not jobs I enjoy doing or want to have tagged on to my household routine.

The grass can wait a little longer. At least until I've finished writing this letter. There's no way I can end now without telling you about yesterday and my lunch date with Rick. I told you last time that he'd sent me a text about it. I wasn't sure whether or not to go, so I didn't reply straight away. But the next morning, as I was still umming and ahhing about it, I bumped into him on the school run. He and Anna were getting out of a small lime green car as Ruby and I pulled up.

'Morning, Maria,' he said with a wide grin. 'What do you think of my new wheels?'

'Um—'

'Don't worry. I won't be offended. I know it's awful. Anna and I are calling it the Snotmobile. It's a hire car. They dropped it off last night and I'm landed with it until mine's back from being repaired. Not exactly like for like, is it?'

'No, I suppose not. How's it going with the insurance?'

'Fine. They're confident it'll be a straightforward claim against the other driver.'

'That's good. I still feel bad about what happened.'

'Don't. It's fine. Hello there, Ruby. How's the arm?'

'Good,' she replied, having spent the entire car journey moaning to me about how much it annoyed her. The novelty of having a cast for everyone to sign had worn off, replaced by the irritation of not being able to do games or PE and struggling with everyday tasks. I'd done my best to reassure her that the plaster would be removed in no time, but my words hadn't seemed to help.

We walked the girls to the front gate. Or I should say we followed them as they ran ahead.

'Ruby's doing well, isn't she?' Rick said. 'It's amazing how kids bounce back. I remember on holiday in Turkey one time when Anna and I both got this sickness bug. It took me days to get over it, but not her. After being up all night, head in the toilet, she was back playing in the pool the next afternoon. Probably shouldn't have been, for the other kids' sake, but there was no stopping her.'

I smiled. 'You should have heard Ruby in the car a minute ago. She was moaning like it was a life sentence.'

'It can't be much fun. No swimming for her, I suppose.'

I shook my head. 'Definitely not. Washing's hard enough. She has to go in the bath now rather than the shower, which causes an argument most nights. And she hates that I have to help her.'

'I can imagine.'

After we'd waved goodbye to the girls and were walking back to our cars, I knew I ought to say something about Rick's text. I have to admit, I'd noticed some of the looks he was getting from the other mums that morning and I'm pretty sure he'd noticed too. It served as a reminder that if I messed him around, there'd be no shortage of other women happy to take my place. God forbid one of the Queen Bs should get their claws into him.

Do it, I told myself. What is there to lose? It's only lunch. I shoved my guilty feelings about betraying Dan to the back of my mind; I thought about his drinking, his smoking, his moods; the endless rows we'd had and his nasty rant the other night.

So I went for it. Well, I attempted to, but it didn't quite work out. Rick and I tried to speak at the same time. Then each of us stopped speaking at the same time, to allow the other to continue. Then we both blurted out 'you first' in sync and broke into a fit of giggles.

'Seriously, you first,' I said eventually. I could feel my cheeks flushing.

'I was going to ask you about my text,' he replied, still smiling. 'You did get it, right?'

'Yes. Sorry. I meant to reply but—'

'It's fine if you don't want to. I understand.'

'No, that's not it.' I was gabbling a bit and I took a deep breath, forcing myself to slow my words down. 'I'd love to have lunch with you. I wanted to reply in person, that's all. When were you thinking?'

We settled on Thursday – yesterday – as Rick was working from home. He suggested an Italian restaurant that opened recently in what used to be the Derby Arms pub. You remember the place, don't you, Sam? It's down that windy lane that runs behind the swimming baths. We had dinner there that time when there was a power cut and the staff brought out loads of candles so we could still see one another. Ruby was scared and you were great with her, sitting her on your knee and singing songs into her ear until she was calm again. It closed about a year ago and lay empty for a while until this Sardinian family came along and gutted it. I'd not been before yesterday, but I'd heard good things and wasn't disappointed.

Rick looked as gorgeous as ever, dressed in a pair of cream chinos and a red polo shirt that showed off his powerful arms, broad shoulders and generally perfect body. I'd gone for subtle make-up with a demure maxi skirt and blouse. I wanted to look like I'd made an effort, Sam, but not overly so.

There were only a handful of other people in the restaurant. I had a delicious prawn linguine dish with a glass of white wine and raspberry cheesecake for dessert. You always liked cheesecake, didn't you, Sam? Well, you'd have loved this one, trust me. It was so creamy and delicious. Rick had a spicy pizza and profiteroles with mineral water.

'You're not going to make me drink alone, are you?' I asked after the voluptuous Italian waitress, mid-forties but dressed twenty years younger, had taken our order.

'You go ahead. I could kill a glass of red, but I've got a report to finish this afternoon. Lunchtime drinking makes me sleepy.'

'How conscientious.'

Rick laughed. 'You haven't met my boss.'

'That bad?'

'Not really. I'm just joking. I've definitely had worse.'

'How's it all going at work?' I asked him. 'Have you settled into the new office okay?'

'Well, you know how it is with these things. There are always teething troubles. We're getting there.'

'What does it entail exactly, being a finance manager?'

'Nothing very exciting, trust me. Lots of number crunching and strategic analysis. I won't bore you with the details. It pays the bills, though.'

He nodded in the direction of the waitress, who was chatting with a young beefcake of a barman, and lowered his voice. 'Not leaving much to the imagination, is she?'

I smiled.

'Have you seen the way those two are looking at each other?' he added.

'No, what do you mean?'

Rick raised an eyebrow. 'Don't make it too obvious that you're watching, but there's something going on there, I reckon.'

I stole a furtive glance at the bar. 'Do you think so? She's old enough to be his mother. Besides, doesn't she run the place with her husband?'

Rick shrugged, flashing those perfect white teeth at me. 'All the same.'

Their potential affair became an ongoing joke

between us, filling in gaps in the conversation and, somehow, making our own interactions more intimate.

Don't get me wrong, we talked about lots of other things too. The conversation flowed, from the familiar topic of our respective daughters, to films, music, favourite holiday destinations, food and drink. Typical first date chat, I suppose, although I'm no expert. Prior to that, I'd not been on a date with anyone other than Dan for years.

There was an awkward moment when Rick asked if I'd ever wanted to have more than one child. The question totally blindsided me. I had no idea what to say. My throat closed up, which he mistook for me choking on a prawn from my pasta dish. He was very concerned, even dashing around to my side of the table to see if he could help in any way. It was refreshing in light of his previous behaviour when Ruby broke her arm, but – unbeknown to him – totally unnecessary. Anyhow, I let him think that it was because of the food and, luckily, it caused enough of a distraction so his question got forgotten. Not that I've forgotten about you, Sam. How could I? I just didn't know how to tell him about you yet. I didn't think I'd be able to make it through the sentence without crying.

As for the rest of the chat, I had planned to make some subtle enquiries about how Rick had ended up as a single dad, but he suggested early on that we should avoid talking about each other's past relationships. 'Plenty of time for all that miserable stuff later,' was how he put it. 'Let's concentrate on getting to know each other today.'

Rick was flirtatious: offering me compliments, maintaining eye contact and occasionally brushing his hand against mine or touching my arm. Nothing full on. He kept it light-hearted, like our banter about the two staff members.

Afterwards, the killjoy in me questioned whether his performance was perhaps too polished, as if he'd done this a lot before. He was such a gentleman from start to finish. He opened doors for me, took my coat, and insisting on paying for everything, despite my objections. He made the whole experience feel special.

We'd greeted each other with a kiss at the start of the date. Just a peck on the cheek. In the car on the way home, I was wondering how we'd say goodbye.

'I've had a lot of fun,' Rick said as we pulled up outside my house.

'Me too. Especially getting a lift in the Snotmobile. That has to be the highlight.' I was doing my utmost to sound relaxed and confident, but in truth I was a bundle of nerves at that point. It was as if I was a teenager again, getting a ride home with a new boyfriend in his parents' car; wondering what was going through his mind and whether he was about to lean over and snog me.

Rick rolled his eyes. 'Charming. What about my scintillating company?'

'A close second.'

'I can live with that. No point trying to compete with a supercar. So are we going to do this again?'

'That depends. How long have you got the Snotmobile?'

'A little while yet, I reckon.'

'You're on.'

'Excellent. But no choking episodes next time, please. You gave me a fright there.'

'I'll do my best.'

'Glad to hear it,' he replied with a grin. 'Oh, wait a second. I have to get something.'

He jumped out of the car and ran to the boot, appearing at my door a moment later with two Easter eggs. 'These are for you and Ruby.'

'Oh, Rick,' I said, climbing out of the car. 'You shouldn't have. I feel bad now. I haven't got anything for you.'

He shrugged. 'Not at all. I didn't expect it. Have a great Easter.'

'You too. You're in Brighton, right, with family?'

He pulled a face. 'Unfortunately. I'd rather be at home, like you. Catch up soon?'

'Definitely. Thanks so much. I had a lot of fun.'

He grinned. 'Me too.' Then, before I knew it, he was giving me another peck on the cheek. Buoyed by the wine, I considered throwing my arms around him and giving him a proper kiss, but I chickened out. All I managed was a little hug. Next thing I knew, he was walking back to the driver's side of the car and my chance was gone.

Afterwards, I was like a besotted schoolgirl. I found myself skipping from room to room, too excited to do anything other than laugh at my reflection in the mirror and relive each moment of the date in my mind. I wanted to talk it through with someone. I almost wrote to you then, Sam, but I found myself too hyper to sit down and put pen to paper.

Instead, I daydreamed of what might have happened if I'd been more daring and gone for that kiss. Or what if I'd taken it a step further and invited him inside? It's probably as well I didn't. I doubt I'd be able to handle that much at this early stage.

Maybe next time.

I'll write again soon, Sam.

Love as always,

M

Xx

CHAPTER 19

BEFORE

Friday, 28 October 2016

'Hello. Anyone home?'

'Hi, Daddy. I'm in the lounge.'

'Where's Mummy?'

'I'm not sure. Upstairs, I think.'

'Maria?' Dan called up the stairs. 'I'm home.'

There was no reply, so he hung his coat up and headed for the fridge. He pulled out a cold bottle of beer, flipped the cap off with the opener on the door and took a long swig.

He was about to head to the lounge when he thought of Ruby. 'Would you like a drink, love?' he called.

'Yes. Water, please.'

He smiled at this. Ruby's class teacher had made a big thing this term about the importance of drinking lots of water and his daughter had really taken it to heart. Good on her, he thought, wondering how long it would last until she was asking for cordial or Coke again.

He carried the water through to the lounge with his beer. 'Here you go, darling,' he said, placing the plastic beaker on to the coffee table and planting a kiss on Ruby's forehead.

'Thanks, Daddy,' she replied, eyes staying glued on the TV.

'How was school?'

'Good.'

'What did you get up to?'

'The usual stuff.'

'Who did you play with?'

'Amelia.'

'Got any homework?'

'A bit.'

'Such as?'

Ruby sighed.

'Oh, come on, grumpy head,' Dan said, ruffling her curls. 'Is it really that hard to say a few words to me when I get in from work?'

'I'm not grumpy. I'm just watching this programme.'

Dan looked at the screen, awash with precocious, over-eager American kids, and resisted the urge to say something disparaging. 'Well, I'd still like to know what you've got to do for homework this week, Ruby. Maybe we'd better turn the television off if it's so distracting you can't tell me.'

'Fine,' she puffed, wriggling with frustration in her seat. 'I have to practise my seven and eight times tables, I've got my spellings to do – like every week – and I have to write a review of the last book I finished.'

'Thank you. That wasn't so hard, was it? And have you done any of it yet?'

'Daaadddy!'

'It's a simple question, Ruby. Shall I turn this off?'

'No! Please don't. I've done most of my spellings and Mummy said I could do the rest tomorrow and Sunday.'

'Right.'

'I bet you're going to turn the telly off anyway, aren't you?'

'I will do if you take that tone with me. Why are you so moody today? Did something happen at school?'

'No. I'm tired, that's all.'

'I'm tired too, darling, but we don't have to take it out on each other.'

Dan took a long swig on his bottle and watched a few minutes of the TV show, which only served to confirm his suspicion that it was mindless nonsense. Mind you, that was probably what his parents had thought of the things he watched as a child, which he now considered classics.

'Did Mummy say what was for tea tonight?'

'No.'

'Are you getting hungry?'

'A bit.'

'Right, I'll see if I can find out. Did you say she was upstairs?'

'I think so.'

Dan necked the last few drops of his beer and went to look for his wife.

'Maria,' he called as he got to the top of the stairs.

'What?' a muffled voice replied from the other side of their bedroom door, which was closed.

Dan still thought of it as their bedroom, but he hadn't slept in there for ages, thanks to his banishment to the spare room.

'Everything all right?' he asked, tapping gently on the door, knowing better than to barge in.

'Yes. Fine. But don't come in. I'm in the middle of something.'

'I was wondering what was for tea. Ruby's getting hungry.'

'Do I have to do everything?'

'I can do it,' Dan replied, keen to avoid starting the weekend with an argument. 'But it would be helpful to know what you had planned.'

'Why don't you have a look in the fridge? Oh, bloody hell. I've lost my place now. Why can no one leave me alone?'

'Fine, fine. Never mind. I'll sort something out.'

Dan headed back down the stairs. He dreaded to think what she was doing in the bedroom. It wouldn't have surprised him if it involved her obsessively poring over the photos of Sam she insisted on keeping hidden away. He'd caught her doing that before. Whatever it was, he could tell from the answers he'd received that there would be no reasoning with her. She was having one of her episodes. Trying to talk to her about it was only likely to make things worse. That was how he'd got himself moved into the spare room, after all. No, she'd end up shouting and screaming at him; Ruby would get upset too. It wasn't worth it.

Maria had never been like this before Sam died. Sure, she'd been a bit fussy: liking her clothes to be hung up in a certain way, for instance, and getting cross if he didn't stick to the way she'd ordered things in the kitchen or bathroom. She'd always been a bit of a perfectionist, especially when it came to her job. But lots of people were like that. And she hadn't ever let it get the better of her back then. Not like it did now, on what seemed to be an ever-increasing scale.

Maria needed help. Dan knew that. But she wouldn't listen to reason. She did her utmost to hide what she was doing from him – including kicking him out of their bedroom – and she refused to admit there was any problem.

As he walked into the kitchen, Dan decided enough was enough. He'd have to speak to her, regardless of the consequences. What was the worst thing that could happen? They were arguing all the time anyway. What did one more blazing row matter if it led to Maria facing up to her problem? She needed professional help to get past this. Maybe even some kind of medication. Clearly it all stemmed from her grief, but it had gone way beyond that now. Why on earth had he let it linger on for so long?

He'd looked into it a bit on the Internet – mainly at work, to avoid any chance of Maria finding out. What he'd read had backed up his initial suspicions that she had some kind of Obsessive Compulsive Disorder. It wasn't something he'd ever experienced outside films, books and newspaper articles. As a result, he did struggle to understand why sufferers couldn't pull themselves together and stop whatever behaviour they were repeating. And yet the same was often said about people suffering from depression. This was something he had experienced, albeit on a limited scale, and he'd needed therapy to get through it. He'd even read that there was a significant relationship between the two conditions and they were often treated in similar ways.

He decided to look up the name of a local specialist, which he could pass on to Maria when he spoke to her about it. That would be more positive than simply telling her she needed help, wouldn't it? He'd do that when he got a quiet moment sometime this weekend, with a view to having the chat after Ruby had gone to bed on Sunday night. That way they might be able to have a nice couple of family days together first. He wasn't holding his breath, though. Look how she'd reacted to his earlier suggestion of couple counselling.

'I'm going to sort tea out,' Dan told Ruby. 'Mummy's busy.'

'What are we having?'

'Not sure yet. I need to see what's in the fridge.'

The front doorbell rang, followed immediately by a knock.

'Who's that?' Ruby asked.

'I've no idea. Are we expecting anyone?'

'No, I don't think so.'

Ruby turned her attention back to the television and Dan trudged towards the door.

He opened it to find a pair of bored-looking girls in

218

winter coats chewing gum. He didn't recognise them; they looked to be around thirteen or fourteen, the taller of the two with braces on her teeth. About the same age Sam had been when she left this world . . . halfway between a girl and a woman. Not yet comfortable in her own skin.

'Hello. Can I help you?'

'Trick or treat!' the smaller one said without looking him in the eye.

'What?'

'Trick or treat,' she said again.

'Yes, I heard you the first time. But it's not Halloween yet.'

The youngsters looked at each other, shrugged, and then looked back at Dan with blank faces.

'Sorry, girls. We don't have any sweets or anything in yet. You'll have to come back on Monday.'

He almost said something about how they ought to dress up next time, but he held back. No point antagonising them. It didn't take much to wind kids up at that age.

'Sorry to bother you,' the taller girl said.

She looked so dejected that Dan almost caved in, but he really didn't have a clue what he could give them. Other than money, of course. But if he did that and word got around, he'd be inundated with callers. Plus he hated the whole concept of trick-or-treating. It was glorified begging, at the end of the day, with a little extortion thrown in for good measure. Mind you, he'd promised Ruby he'd take her out this year, having avoided it the last few times due to work commitments. She wanted to dress as a ghost in a white sheet: a nice easy costume at least.

Back in the house, Dan finally got to the fridge and, after taking out another beer, he weighed up what to cook. There wasn't much to choose from. However, there were a couple of packs of fresh pasta and enough bits and bobs to drum up a half decent tomato sauce.

'I'm going to make some pasta,' he shouted through to Ruby. 'It won't take long. Can you let Mummy know? Tell her about twenty minutes.'

He waited for a reply, but none came. 'Hello? Ruby?'

'Yes,' she called back eventually. 'What kind of pasta?'

'The tasty kind. Did you hear what I asked you?'

'Ye-es.'

He stuck his head through the door into the lounge. 'Less of the attitude, please. Just do it.'

'I will.'

'Good. And after you've done that, I'd like you to come and lay the kitchen table, please.'

'Do I have to?'

'Ruby.'

'Fine.'

About twenty minutes and two more beers later, Dan called out that the food was ready.

Ruby appeared first.

'Have you turned the television off and washed your hands?'

'Yes.'

'Good girl. Is Mummy coming?'

She shrugged. 'I did tell her, but she was doing something in her room.'

'Right. I'll go and find her. You grab a seat. Here's your food. Help yourself to grated cheese.'

'Goodie. Smells yum. Can I start or do I have to wait?'

'Dig in. I'll be back in a second.'

He walked over to the foot of the stairs. 'Maria. Tea's re—'

'Yes, I know,' his wife replied, appearing from the bedroom and shutting the door behind her. 'I'm coming.'

'Everything all right?' he asked her a few minutes later when they were all at the table.

'Fine. But don't go in the bedroom, please. The same goes for you, Ruby. I'm in the middle of something and I don't want to have to start all over again.'

'What are you doing, Mummy?' Ruby asked. 'Can I help?'

Maria took a deep breath. 'No, thank you, darling. I'm sorting a few things out. Having a bit of a tidy up: like we do in your bedroom sometimes.'

'Are we doing a car boot sale?'

'Um, no. Why do you say that?'

'Holly in my class did one a few weeks ago. She was allowed to have her own stall and to keep all the money she made from selling her old toys.'

'Really?' Dan replied. 'That sounds like a good idea.'

'Maybe we should sell some of Sam's things,' Ruby said, shocking Dan and causing Maria to almost choke on her food.

After making sure his wife was okay, Dan ventured: 'Perhaps Ruby's right. It could be time to sort through some of her things.'

He'd been thinking they ought to tackle Sam's room for a while now. It was a job he knew they'd have to do one day, but he'd never found a good moment to bring it up before.

Apparently it was still too soon for Maria. The colour had drained from her face and she was staring into the distance, not saying a word.

'We don't have to if you don't want to, Mummy,' Ruby said, her face creased with concern.

It was then that Dan noticed the tears in Maria's eyes. 'Don't worry,' he mouthed to Ruby before changing the subject and telling her how nice her hair looked. 'Did Mummy style it for you?'

She nodded.

'She's done a good job. Your curls look gorgeous.'

Dan would have liked nothing more than to been able to put his arms around his wife to comfort her. That's what he would have done in the old days, without hesitation. But their relationship wasn't like that any more. He knew Maria would react negatively – probably pushing him away and snarling something violent at him – and he didn't want Ruby getting any more upset. So instead he blabbed unimportant pleasantries to his daughter as if nothing was wrong, hoping Maria would eventually join in too. She didn't. She remained silent for the rest of the meal, standing up to leave the table as soon as they'd all finished.

'I'm going back upstairs. Please can you put Ruby in the shower and read her a book tonight?' It wasn't really a question.

'Sure,' Dan replied. 'No problem.'

It pained him to see how bad things had become. There was so much left unsaid between them. And without communication, Dan knew their marriage was in big trouble. It was rusting away before his eyes. He really had to speak to Maria soon. It wasn't that he was going to put it all on her or anything. She wasn't the only one to blame for how things had become. But how could they ever fix it if they weren't talking to each other and addressing their problems head on?

He'd definitely speak to her. It couldn't be delayed any longer. And hopefully the end result would be a big improvement in their relationship. They'd lost one daughter, but they were lucky enough to still have another – and each other. Christmas was only a matter of weeks away now. Could things already be improved by then? Dan hoped so. He couldn't handle the thought of a festive repeat of the meal they'd just had. He had to believe there was still hope for them. The alternative didn't bear thinking about.

CHAPTER 20

I'm trapped. Pinned down with some kind of straps. I can only lift my head a touch, but I can see what looks like a thick brown leather belt over my chest. There must be more of them holding the rest of me down, because I can't move. I can't feel my legs at all. What's going on? Where am I?

And what's that acrid smell? Burning chemicals, like a school science lab.

I think I'm in some kind of corridor – a narrow room at least – but the bare, off-white walls offer no more clues than the spotlights on the ceiling above me.

I seem to be on one of those trolleys they wheel sick people around on. That's my best guess from the little I can see. So does that mean I'm in a hospital? How did I get here? What happened? Isn't someone supposed to be looking after me?

'Hello?' I call. Well, croak would be a better description of the pathetic noise that comes out of my mouth. The sound dies as it leaves my lips, which are hard and cracked, like a dried up riverbed. It's as if I've not spoken in weeks. My tongue's no better: rough and sore, little more than an obstruction.

I take a gulp of cool, soothing air and try to remember where I am.

The only thing I can hear is the unhealthy rasp of my breathing.

There must be something wrong with me. Why else would I be here like this?

Am I dying? I'm gripped by a sudden sense of fear. Or what if I'm already dead?

In the distance I hear a creaking sound followed by a slam. Then footsteps. Moving at a measured pace. Getting louder. Closer.

'Who's there?' I ask.

The footsteps stop for a moment but there's no reply.

'Hello? Who is that? Help me!'

I wonder if whoever's there can understand what I'm saying. I strain to lift my head so I can see in that direction, but it's useless. The footsteps start up again. Come closer. Eventually they slow and then, as they stop altogether, a man's face appears above me. I don't know if it's because I'm lying down, but he looks huge, both in height and width. He has leathery, pock-marked skin with red spider veins etched across his nose and cheeks. He wears his shoulder-length, grey hair in a ponytail. He brings his head in closer to mine, examining me with bloodshot eyes. His breath smells rancid.

I want to say something to him, but my mouth won't move. No sound will come out of my throat. I can't even push against my restraints any more, as if this man's presence has paralysed my entire body. How am I still breathing? The idea that I can't – that I might be suffocating – makes me panic. I try to convey this via my paralysed stare. I will this man, whoever he is, to see my internal torment. I imagine a black cloud infusing the whites of my eyes, like ink in water, but the look he throws back at me is devoid of emotion. He might as well be staring at a blank piece of paper.

Next thing I know, the pillow has been jerked out from under my head and it's being lowered on to my face.

'No! What the hell are you doing?' I scream.

The sound of my voice is deafening, but only to me: only in my mind. I feel myself start to shake. Then everything stops . . . changes.

It's dark and I'm sitting in a small room in front of a computer screen. There's panic in my chest. I've deleted something I shouldn't have: something precious. I need to get it back. I have to retrieve it.

The light from the monitor is enough to see the keyboard but not my address book. I switch on a desk lamp and flick through the pages with my clammy fingers. Until I find him: Ant, the IT guy.

I glance at my watch before I call him: 11.55 p.m. Far too late, but I can't stop myself. I have to do something.

I use the landline, not sure where I left my mobile. It rings for ages. I dread hearing voicemail; then Ant picks up.

'Hello?'

He doesn't sound happy. I reel off the words, trying not to sound drunk.

'Sorry to call so late. It's an emergency. I've deleted some files by accident. Not into the recycle bin: properly deleted. I need to retrieve them. There are no other copies. I've never done this before. Is it even possible?'

'Whoa. Slow down. Who is this?'

'It's, um—'

My mind's gone blank.

Who is this?

Good question.

Who am I?

'Come on. Stay with me, lad. Fight it. Don't give in.'

It's not Ant's voice I can hear any more. It's someone else. Someone familiar.

My eyes snap open and Miles is leaning over me, hands on my shoulders, shaking me awake.

'Ah, there you are,' he says, stepping back. 'Good morning, Jack.'

'Miles,' I reply, looking at him and then down at my chest, which I can feel is covered in sweat. I want to throw the damp covers off, but I'm not comfortable doing so in front of him, as I'm only wearing boxer shorts. 'What's wrong? What happened?'

'Nothing to worry about. You looked to be having an unpleasant dream. That's all. I thought I'd better wake you. It took some doing, mind.'

'Eh? What was all that about staying with you and not giving in?'

He scratches his head. 'I'm not sure what you mean. Part of the dream, maybe?'

'It felt so real. Are you sure you didn't say anything like that at all?'

'Sorry, no.'

'Okay. Right. I guess I must have dreamt it, then. Weird.'

We look at each other in silence for a long moment and then I ask Miles the time.

He shrugs. 'Who knows? Late morning, I reckon. Maybe early afternoon. Too late to still be in bed, anyhow.'

'Shit. Do we need to get going?'

'Going where?'

'I thought you were going to take me to the hospital. No, sorry. That's not until tomorrow, is it? My mistake. It's Sunday today, of course.'

Miles stares blankly at me. 'The hospital?'

'To get me properly checked out: have a scan or whatever.'

'Is this a joke? Are you winding me up, Jack?'

'No, of course not. Why would you say that? I want to know what's wrong with me. I want to know who I am. I want my memories back.'

Miles takes a deep breath, opens the green curtains and, after staring out of the window for a moment, sits down on the chair that has my clothes draped over the back.

'The thing is, Jack,' he says in a slow, steady voice. 'We've already been. We did that last week. You don't remember?'

I sit up in bed and stare at Miles. He's dressed in his usual jeans and tucked-in shirt combo and looks to have been up and about for some time. I can't think what to say to him in reply. My brain's swirling from what he's told me.

'Jack, are you all right?'

'Not really, no. What do you mean, we did that last week? We were only talking about it yesterday.'

'What do you remember as yesterday?'

'Saturday. We went to the village by car. You needed some nails from the hardware store. I got bread and milk.'

Miles scratches his head. 'No, lad. That was last weekend. We went to the hospital a couple of days later – on Monday, like I promised we would. They checked you over but couldn't see anything untoward.'

'What about the scan?'

'You're booked in for one next week. Friday afternoon at three. In the meantime, I said I'd keep an eye on you. You were doing well until—' He breaks off.

'Until now?'

'Yes.'

'But it is Sunday today, right?'

'No, it's Saturday: a week on from the trip to the village you're talking about. You really don't remember anything that's happened in the meantime?'

I shake my head and it feels like I'm moving in slow motion. There's nothing – no memories at all of that period – and I can't wrap my mind around the fact. I'm utterly shell-shocked by this latest body blow.

Miles is saying something to me. I can see his lips moving, but I'm not hearing him. There's just too much to take in.

How can I have lost a week? I mean, seriously, a week? Just gone like that? It makes no sense. Previously my memory loss only applied to things that happened before the accident: all the important stuff, like who I am and where I come from. So why would that change? It's incomprehensible. Unless . . .

I'm struck by a terrifying thought, which chills me to the bone. What if I didn't skip a whole week? What if Miles is lying to me? He could be making the whole thing up. How would I know any different? And yet why would he do that? To avoid having to take me to the hospital? That's all I can think, but it makes no sense. He's a doctor. Why wouldn't he want me to have the correct treatment? And if he's lying to me now, where does that leave every other thing he's told me so far?

I tune back in to his voice, which is asking me if I'm all right, probably for the umpteenth time.

'What did we do over the last week?' I ask, looking Miles in the eye, hoping to gauge whether or not he's being honest. Aren't people supposed to look up and to their right if they're lying? Or is it their left? No, I'm fairly sure it's the right: something to do with the use of the imagination. I wonder how on earth I can remember that when everything else is a void.

Miles doesn't look to either side as he answers. He meets my gaze and holds it. 'Well, we went to the hospital on Monday, like I said. We also called at the supermarket that day for provisions. Otherwise we've been here, mainly working on the floorboards.'

'I've been helping?'

'Yes. You seemed much better. I thought you were on the mend. There were no more of those funny turns you had previously.'

'What about my memory? Did I recall anything more about having a daughter or about my background generally?'

He breaks my gaze and glances out of the window before replying. 'Sorry. No breakthroughs, I'm afraid.'

'Really? What did the doctor at the hospital say, then? Did he have any possible explanation?'

'You really don't remember, do you?'

'Obviously not. Why do you say that?'

'The doctor you saw was a woman.'

This latest revelation catches me unawares. 'A woman? What was her name?'

'Dr Quinn.'

'Dr Quinn? Seriously?'

'Yes,' Miles replies, frowning. 'Why?'

'Well, it's like that old TV show, isn't it? With the famous actress in. What's her name? I can't remember. You know the one I mean.'

'Sorry, I don't. I've never been much of a television drama fan.'

'*Dr Quinn, Medicine Woman*,' I say, wondering again if he's lying; if I caught him out and now he's trying to cover his tracks.

Miles shakes his head. 'Never heard of it. Good that you remember, though.'

'Yeah, brilliant. Why's there room for nonsense like that in my brain when all the important stuff has gone?'

231

'That's a good question, lad. Unfortunately, I don't know.'

'I can't be the first person this has ever happened to. Aren't there medical studies into this kind of thing?'

'Of course. But what you're experiencing is confusing, especially now your amnesia seems to have spread to more recent memories. It's almost as if . . .'

'What?'

'Nothing. It doesn't matter.'

'Of course it matters. Say it. Please, Miles. I'd rather know.'

'Well, don't take this the wrong way, but sometimes memory loss can be caused by a psychological trigger rather than a physical injury. It's known as psychogenic or dissociative amnesia.'

'Hold on. What are you suggesting? That it's all in my head? That I'm making it up?'

'Not at all. Don't forget that the scan may well say otherwise – that there is some clear physical cause. If not, then of course we have to look at other possibilities. Even so, what I've just described to you is still a very real disorder.'

'You said this was caused by falling off a ladder, Miles. I took your word for it. You could have told me anything. I'm in your hands here. Now you spring this on me.'

'Calm down, Jack. Please. This is why I was hesitant to say anything. I feared you'd react in such a way. Organic causes of amnesia can be hard to detect, so don't think I'm ruling that out, even if nothing shows up on the scan. However, I wasn't with you when you had your accident, remember. I found you unconscious in a pile of soil and put two and two together. Maybe I got it wrong.'

I run a hand through my hair, which is still damp with sweat. 'What else could have happened?'

Miles doesn't reply, so I carry on, determined to get a rise out of him. 'Well, something made my head hurt like hell. Maybe a mermaid climbed up the cliff face, sneaked up on me and walloped me with her pet turtle. That could leave me mentally scarred, right?'

'There's no need to be facetious,' Miles says, rising to his feet and heading for the door. 'Get yourself a shower. I'll make us some food. If you like, when you've had a chance to calm down, we can talk about this like adults.'

'Sorry,' I reply, feeling like an idiot.

'I'll see you in a few minutes.'

With that, he's gone and I'm left alone in the bedroom.

'Jane Seymour,' I say out loud as it comes to me who the famous actress was that played Dr Quinn on TV. Surely Miles must have heard of her. If only all my memories would return so easily.

As I shower away the remnants of my nightmare, now little more than a hazy blot in my mind's eye, I can't escape the idea that Miles might be lying to me. I mean, how can I not have remembered anything more after all those flashbacks previously? What about my daughter? I'm still convinced she exists and that I should be with her rather than here in this place. And how can almost a week have passed without me realising? I need to know for sure what's going on. So much hangs upon what Miles has told me. If I can't trust this latest information, how can I count on anything he's said?

I decide that I need to hear from the outside world. There might not be any computer or television in this place, thanks to Miles's aversion to technology, but I do remember him mentioning a couple of radios. If I could listen to one of them, I'd at least be able to confirm what day of the week it is today. To me it still feels like Sunday; Miles says it's Saturday, six days later, so confirming the actual day would be a step forward.

Rather than sneaking around trying to find one of these radios, which I've yet to come across, I decide to ask Miles. I may as well give him the benefit of the doubt in the first instance. If he's nothing to hide, why would he mind?

I broach the subject at the kitchen table after a few forkfuls of the impressive fry-up Miles has made.

'This is delicious,' I say. 'Thanks very much.'

'No problem.'

'Sorry about earlier. It's a struggle trying to get my head around losing a week. I was expecting things to get better. Not worse. This whole memory loss thing is driving me mad. The idea of having a daughter and yet not knowing who or where she is: it's so damn frustrating.'

'I understand.'

Do you? I think, but I say something else. 'Um, I remember you mentioned something about having a couple of radios about the house.'

'That's right.' He isn't looking at me. His eyes are focused on his plate.

'Any chance I could borrow one for a bit? To have in my room. I won't play it loud or anything. I just, er, you know, think it would be nice to have something to listen to.'

I expect him to say no and to come up with an excuse as to why not, but instead he smiles and says it's fine. He points across the kitchen. 'There's a portable one in that drawer. Help yourself.'

'Great. Thank you.'

We don't speak any more about my memory loss and potential causes. Miles appears to be waiting on my lead, but I don't have the energy. I can't think of anything apart from listening to that radio. And yet surely the fact that Miles is happy for me to use it is an answer in itself. All the same, I need to hear it with my own ears. I need a taste of the outside world.

'So what's the plan for today?' I ask, dipping my last chunk of sausage into a blob of brown sauce.

'Well, it looks nice and dry outside, so I was thinking of having a poke around the guttering. There are leaks in several places and I need to work out whether it's a patching and painting job or if it needs replacing. I suspect it might be a combination of the two.'

'I'm happy to help.'

He squints at me across the table. 'Are you sure, lad? I don't mind giving you the day off in light of—'

'No, I'd rather keep busy. And I need to pay my way.'

'Fine. But I want you at the bottom of the ladder. I'll do the climbing.'

'You're the boss.'

After tidying away and filling the dishwasher, we arrange to meet outside in half an hour.

'Can I grab that radio?' I slip in, trying to make it sound like a casual afterthought.

'Sure.'

I take it – a silver Sony about the size of my palm with a single speaker, extendable antenna and carry strap – and head back into the dilapidated core of the house. My heart's pumping fast with excitement. My footsteps echo as I climb the dirty, bare wood of the staircase. Then I tread my way carefully along the wreck of the hall, my nose wrinkling at the now familiar mildew smell, until I reach our oasis of civilised living with its solid varnished floorboards and cream walls.

I stop outside the only door I've yet to open here: the one leading into Miles's bedroom. Knowing he's still downstairs in the kitchen, I'm tempted to have a peek inside. My hand hovers over the door handle. I lower it until I can feel the cool metal on my fingers, but then I glance at the radio in my other hand and stop. No further, I tell myself. One thing at a time. First let's see if he's telling the truth.

I continue along the short corridor to my bedroom, let myself in and close the door. Sitting down on my unmade bed, I flick up the volume control that doubles as an on-off switch and take a slow, deep breath.

Time for some answers.

CHAPTER 21

Sunday, 23 April 2017

Dear Sam,

Hello, love. I've hardly had a moment to myself this past week with Ruby being off school. Holidays are always pretty full on compared to term time, but when your child has one arm in plaster and can't amuse herself in the usual ways, it's even more intense.

I've been itching to write to you for days. After what's happened this weekend, I can't wait any longer. It's been eventful. I'm feeling pretty confused right now. I hope that mulling things over with you might help me get them straight in my mind.

It's after 10 p.m. Ruby's been in bed for a while already, thank goodness. She's been a nightmare today. Really grumpy. It's because she didn't get much shut-eye last night. Anna came round for a sleepover – and you know how that goes. It was like when you used to have friends over for the night: lots of chatting and giggling rather than napping. It was late when they fell asleep and they were up again at some ungodly hour this morning. Apparently they'd agreed that whoever woke up first would wake the other. Hence the early start.

Most of what came out of Ruby's mouth today was whining and moaning. She didn't want to finish her homework, of course, and when she did, nothing made any sense and everything I told her was wrong. Then it was unfair that she had to tidy up her room. You know, because it wasn't like she'd made the mess or anything. The food I made for tea was all wrong. And finally we had a worse than usual row about the fact she had to have a bath rather than a shower because of her plaster cast.

'I hate baths,' she shouted over and over again. 'They're for babies. Why can't I put a plastic bag over my arm and have a shower? That's what Dad lets me do. He says it's fine.'

I wasn't having any of it. 'We can try that tomorrow, Ruby, but not now. I've already run the bath.'

'That's not fair. I told you before that I didn't want one.'

'If this is what happens when you have a friend over to stay, I don't think we'd better do it again. You've been a right madam all day and I've had enough. I'm going to count to ten and you won't like what happens if you're not in the bath by the end. One . . .'

She did as she was told, but there was thunder in

238

her eyes. The first thing I did after tucking her up in bed was to pour myself a large glass of well-chilled white wine, which I'm still enjoying right now. I needed something to take the edge off, not only because of Ruby, but everything else that happened this weekend too.

I find myself in something of a predicament after being wooed twice yesterday – by two separate men – in the space of a couple of hours.

Wooed is a strange word. It sounds so old fashioned. Like something in a Shakespeare play or a Jane Austen novel. To be honest, I almost went with *propositioned* instead, but that sounds too much like a sordid sexual advance. Think somewhere in between the two words, Sam, and you'll be closer to the truth.

I'll tell you what happened in both cases and you can judge for yourself. I have to remind myself here that I'm writing to a future version of you – a confidante – to stop this from feeling strange. Also, you've probably guessed that one of these men is Dan, who I'll keep referring to as such in a bid to avoid any weirdness. You're surprised? I doubt it. I'm sure you can guess who the other person is too. I might have two men fighting for my affections – wow, I like the way that sounds – but let's not get carried away.

I'm going to stop rambling now. (I blame the wine.)

So Ruby spent Friday night at Dan's place. Usually she would have spent Saturday night too, but he had a work do to attend that evening. I was in a good mood when he brought her home at about 3 p.m. It's amazing the positive effect a lie-in and a leisurely bath can have on you. I'd been taking Rosie's advice to try to enjoy the quiet moments I had to myself, rather than letting my OCD commandeer them.

'It's easy to be vulnerable in those moments,' she said during one of our sessions. 'Can you think of any recent examples of when you've had time to yourself and how that's made you feel?'

'It happens a lot.' I told her. 'I have a free moment that I've been looking forward to; maybe I'm planning to watch a film I've recorded or read a few chapters of my book, but something comes up. Gets in the way.'

'Like what?'

'It usually starts as something little, like going to check that the door is locked. I tell myself it will only take a minute, but then it develops into something bigger and far more time-consuming. While I'm there, I might notice a chip in the door, for instance. Next thing I'll be digging a paint pot out and touching it up, if not repainting the entire door.'

'Why do you think that happens?'

'It's as if I'm punishing myself. Like part of me feels I don't deserve that treat I was planning and swipes it away from me.'

'So how do you beat it?'

'By not giving in to that initial thought?'

'Exactly. Relax when you get the chance. Don't be so hard on yourself.'

It was good advice. Apparently even Dan could see it was working.

'You look nice and chilled,' he said to me at the front door.

'I'll take that as a compliment.'

'You should. Relaxed suits you. You look really well.'

'Are you staying for a drink, Dad?' Ruby asked as she pushed past him with her bags from the car.

'Um. I, er—'

'You're welcome to, if you like,' I said. You could argue it was a bit cheeky of Ruby to put us on the spot like that. But at the same time, it's not like she was inviting a strange man into the house. She promptly disappeared to her bedroom, leaving the two of us to talk. It made me wonder whether Dan had put her up to it.

'I was hoping we'd get a chance to have a chat,' he said, adding to my suspicions.

'Tea or coffee?'

'Coffee, please. Instant's fine.'

'Are you looking after yourself?' I asked as he took a seat at the kitchen table. 'You look tired.'

He shrugged.

'I can smell that you're still smoking. We're not young any more, Dan. You should knock it on the head. For Ruby's sake, if not your own.'

'What about for your sake?'

'That too, if it helps.'

'Careful. I might start thinking you still care.'

241

'Don't be silly. Of course I do.' I do care about him, Sam. I always will. But it's never as easy as that, is it?

I changed the subject. 'Actually, while I remember, Dan, there was something I wanted to ask you. Has Ruby said anything about that chat I had with her: you know, Father Christmas and so on?'

Dan shook his head. 'No. Why?'

Glad he'd taken the bait and moved away from a potentially loaded conversation, I said it was odd that she'd not brought the subject up again with either of us.

'I thought Easter might have sparked some mention of it again.'

'I wouldn't worry. It's not like she believed in the Easter Bunny or anything. She's probably digesting the information. It's a lot to take in. She'll ask us if she wants to know anything else. I mean, I can try and broach it next time she's over, if you're that bothered, but—'

'No, you're right. I shouldn't have been so offhand with you about it when I told you on the phone. It was all rather unexpected – and she was more upset than I imagined.'

'I wouldn't read too much into it. You may find she's accepted it now.'

'You think?' I looked at him. The bags under his eyes were far deeper than I remember them being.

'Sure. Kids are much better at adapting to change than adults. They're wired that way. They have to

242

be. How would they ever cope with puberty otherwise?'

'I suppose.'

'Look how quickly Ruby's got used to having her
arm in plaster. She could hardly do anything by herself
to start with. Now she's coping well.'

'I worry too much about her. I know I do, but—'

'It's only normal after what happened with Sam,
Maria. I worry too. I just hide it better. She's our
little girl. The only one we have left. But we can't
wrap her up in cotton wool. That's not the way to
protect her. We have to let her grow into her own
person. She's not Sam and the same thing is not going
to happen again.'

'You can't promise that.' I turned away from Dan
and busied myself with making the drinks as I gath-
ered my emotions.

'We should talk about Sam more, Maria,' he said,
which didn't help. I couldn't see the coffee granules
for a second as my eyes began to blur.

It must feel strange: me recounting this conversation to you, Sam. But I'm being honest. It's become
a difficult subject for your father and I to discuss,
you see. Initially, after you died, it was all we talked
about. Of course it was. Then gradually, as time
passed and our relationship grew increasingly strained,
it became almost unmentionable. Not because we
weren't thinking about you or missing you. That
never stopped. It was just too painful. And what we
were experiencing individually – the way we were

243

grieving – was so different that neither of us understood what the other was going through.

I'm not sure why, but I chose that moment to tell
Dan I'd been seeing a counsellor.

He looked stunned. 'Really? For your, um—'

'For my OCD,' I replied, finally carrying the drinks
to the table and sitting down opposite him. 'You can
say it, Dan. That's what I have and I'm dealing with
it. You were right to say I needed help. It took me
a while to catch up.'

'Are you seeing the one I found for you?'

'No. At least I don't think so. I binned the piece
of paper you gave me. Sorry. I wasn't ready for it
then.'

'What's his name?'

'*Her* name is Rosie Quinn.'

Dan laughed, taking a sip from his drink. 'Dr
Quinn, like the medicine woman from TV?'

I smiled too, but shook my head. 'She's not actually a doctor.'

'Oh, right. What is she then?'

'She's a well-qualified counsellor. Two of her speci-
alities are grief and OCD.'

'And it's helping?'

'Well, you said how relaxed I looked, so I guess
that's a yes. I feel much brighter. It's not going to
disappear overnight, though. There's lots of hard
work and discipline required to beat it. I've already
experienced my share of ups and downs. Rosie's
confident we can get there, she says.'

Dan was over the moon. I didn't understand it at first. I knew he'd be pleased, but he was beaming like a lottery winner. Then it dawned on me that he was interpreting it as a ticket to us getting back together. I can understand the logic, as it was after he suggested I needed help last year that I asked him to move out. But he was making a leap too far.

I was racking my brains for the right thing to say: something to discourage him without being too disparaging. I'm seeing things differently now the fog of OCD is lifting. I didn't want to rule out the possibility of the two of us getting back together one day. And yet, well, I was also thinking about this new relationship developing with Rick.

Anyway, it's irrelevant, as I never got the chance to say anything.

'This is great,' Dan said. 'It fits in really well with what I wanted to talk to you about.'

'Oh?' was all I could manage in reply, smiling to hide my unease.

He leaned forward across the table and stared intensely at me, which did little to reduce my discomfort. I thought for a moment that he was about to take my hand, but instead he pressed his fingers into the grain of the wood, as if fighting to hold them steady.

'Firstly, I wanted to apologise again for my rant the other week. I didn't mean any of it. It was pure anger and frustration. Especially the divorce part. That's the opposite of what I want. The truth is,

Maria, I'm still madly in love with you. I'm nothing without you in my life. You and Ruby are my world and, well, I'll do anything it takes to get our marriage back on track. I'll give up smoking; drinking too, if you like. I'll work fewer hours; shave every day; take more care over my appearance. I'll be more romantic; take you out for dinner; go to the ballet with you. Whatever you want. You name it. There must be a way for us to work this out, Maria. We can't let what happened with Sam ruin our family. We need to move forward together. We're better that way. In your heart of hearts, you must know that.'

'I, er—'

'I don't expect an answer now,' he said, jerking his hands away from the tabletop and clapping them together into a ball. 'Take some time. I've no intention of rushing you. We can move at whatever pace you like. Think about it, that's all I ask. Can you do that for me?'

'Um . . . sure.'

'Great,' he replied, standing up and planting a surprise kiss on my forehead. 'I'll get out of your hair.'

And so he did, leaving me perturbed and the cup of coffee I'd just made for him barely touched.

It was a speech from the heart, although he must have rehearsed it beforehand. I've no doubt it was carefully crafted. His pledges were all things I'd told him over the years: a selection box of the many suggestions I'd made to improve our relationship

246

before it had nosedived. I very much doubt he could ever achieve them all, but the sentiment was good. If nothing else, it showed he'd been listening and demonstrated his sincerity.

And yet I couldn't help feeling a little irritated that he'd turned my good news around into being about what he wanted. I mean, I know it was ultimately about the two of us – and Ruby, of course – but it felt like he was hijacking the agenda.

So how to respond? I hadn't got a clue then and I still don't.

'I'm really off now,' Dan said, shocking me as he flew past on his way out, having popped upstairs to say goodbye to Ruby. 'See you soon.'

And then he was gone. Or so I thought until I heard the doorbell ring a few minutes later. I walked over to answer it, apprehensive of what might be coming next, only to find Rick and Anna smiling back at me.

'Surprise,' they said in unison.

'Hello, you two,' I replied, glad to see that Dan's car was nowhere in sight. 'Wow, this is a surprise. To what do I owe the pleasure?'

'Well,' Rick said. 'We were hoping to do a deal with you.'

'A deal? That sounds intriguing. You'd better come in.'

'You haven't heard what it is yet.'

'That's true. Maybe you'd better tell me what it is, Anna. Then I'll decide whether or not to let you in.'

She looked up at her father, who nodded his encouragement, and said: 'If I can play with Ruby for a bit, Daddy will mow the lawn for you.'

I burst into laughter. 'What? Really? Wow, that sounds like an amazing deal. You definitely have to come inside. Quick. Hurry up and shake my hand before your daddy changes his mind.'

I'd still not got round to cutting the grass, believe it or not. I'd mentioned it to Rick when we went for lunch before Easter and then it had come up again when we'd last spoken on the phone a couple of days ago.

'I suggested it to Anna this morning,' he explained after she and Ruby had run off to play. 'She thought it was a great idea. I was worried you might have already cut the grass.'

'Oh, you needn't have. I always seem to find an excuse not to. It's a lovely offer, by the way, but you don't actually have to do it.'

His eyes widened in mock disbelief. 'Don't be ridiculous. We made a deal. You and Anna shook on it. There's no going back now.'

So next thing I knew, only minutes since Dan had left me pondering his proposal, I found myself watching gorgeous Rick mowing my lawn for me. Although we'd phoned and texted each other a lot since our lunch date, this was the first time we'd seen each other again in person. He was wearing figure-hugging jeans and a tight grey T-shirt that showed off every delicious pumped-up curve of his muscular frame. I couldn't stop watching him through the kitchen window. I even caught myself hoping that he might get too hot and feel the need to remove his top.

I was so distracted that when Ruby asked me if Anna could stay for a sleepover, I said yes without even thinking about it. Next thing I was inviting Rick to stay for dinner too and that's when I really started getting myself into trouble.

Do you know what, Sam? I'm going to leave it there. Don't worry, of course I'll tell you what happened, but it will have to wait until my next letter. Sorry, but I'm shattered and I really need to go to bed before my writing degenerates into gibberish. Goodnight, my darling.

Love as always,

M

Xx

CHAPTER 22

BEFORE

Sunday, 28 August 2016

It was here. That dreaded day.

Dan put a pillow over his head to block out the light, wanting to pretend it wasn't morning for a little longer. Then he heard the sound of the vacuum cleaner coming from the landing. He was going to have to face this day whether he liked it or not. And as it was a Sunday, he wasn't even going to have the office as a distraction.

He banged the pillow a couple of times with his fist before tossing it away and taking a long deep breath. It turned into a coughing fit, forcing him to sit up in bed. Not his own bed, but the one in the spare room, where Maria had forced him to sleep for nearly a month now. Surely she'd let him back in the main bedroom soon, although now wasn't the time to broach that thorny issue with her. It would be hard enough to get through the day anyway.

No, raising a difficult subject with Maria was what had got him turfed out of the main bedroom in the first place. He'd been worried about her strange behaviour for a while, but he'd been hoping it was a phase – her way of dealing with things – and would gradually improve. Then one night a few weeks back, it had got so weird he couldn't ignore it any longer.

They'd both been in bed for an hour or so when Maria tapped his shoulder to wake him up and asked if he'd locked the front door. 'Yes,' he replied. 'Like I told you before.'

'Are you sure?'

'Yes.'

Maria was silent for a moment and then he heard her get out of bed.

'What are you doing?' he asked.

'Going to the toilet.'

She returned a few minutes later.

'You went to check the door, didn't you?' he said.

'Go to sleep.'

He tried, but she must have got in and out of bed at least six more times in the next half an hour and, eventually, he could stand it no longer. 'Bloody hell, Maria. What on earth are you doing? I'm trying to sleep.'

'Nothing.'

'You're checking that door, aren't you? How many times now? What are you afraid of?'

'Shut up,' she spat. 'You'll wake Ruby.'

'I'll wake her? You're the one traipsing up and down the stairs every five minutes.'

'You don't know what you're talking about.'

Dan lowered his voice to a whisper, trying to calm things down. 'Listen, Maria. Sorry I snapped. It's late. I'm tired. But seriously, what you're doing, it's not normal. It's not the first time either. You need to tell me what's going on. I want to help.'

'You wouldn't understand.'

'Try me.'

Maria turned the light on. 'I think you'd better sleep in the spare room tonight.'

'What? Don't be ridiculous. I—'

'Go or I'll scream the house down.'

'And wake Ruby up? Brilliant. A minute ago you were the one—'

'Don't push me, Dan,' she growled, her eyes wild.

He could see there would be no reasoning with her in that state, so he did as she asked. Little did he know how long his exile would continue.

Back in the present, Dan picked up his phone from the bedside table to check the time. Bloody hell. It was only 7.15 a.m. These summer mornings were deceptive. So what on earth was Maria doing vacuuming so early?

Dan eyed the pack of fags lying next to his mobile and thought about lighting one up. Why not? It was his house and it wasn't like Maria was sharing the room with him. He couldn't bring himself to do it. It wasn't worth the grief it would cause. Maria moaned enough about his smoking already. She hated the fact he'd started again; lighting up inside would be a step too far. Especially today.

252

Thinking about smoking, Dan noted that it was twelve months since he'd fallen off the wagon. Buying a pack of cigarettes had been an instinctive response to the unbearable horror and devastation that had rained down on his life a year ago. The first couple had tasted awful, but after that it was like he'd never quit. They didn't help much – not really – but giving up again now was unthinkable.

He picked up the pack, climbed out of bed and, after slipping into his dressing gown, opened the door. Maria wasn't in sight. The vacuum was still going, but it sounded like it was coming from downstairs.

Dan went to the toilet, splashed some water on his face and then peered around the open door of Ruby's bedroom to see if she was awake. Her bed was empty, the quilt balled up at the foot end. She must have already gone downstairs.

Before doing the same, Dan walked to the door of the bedroom that used to belong to his elder daughter. It was closed as usual. The hand-drawn sign she'd once blue-tacked on to it read: 'Sam's space. Stay out!'

Dan stood there, staring at it; remembering.

No! He didn't want to think about that now.

He couldn't.

The horrific image flashed unwanted into his thoughts, but he forced himself to push it aside.

Locked it away.

Dug out another memory instead: the day Sam had put the sign up following a row with Ruby. He'd walked in on a shouting match between the two of them and had been forced to act as referee.

*

'She's always coming in here and messing with my stuff, Dad,' Sam said.

'It's not true, Daddy,' Ruby replied. 'I wanted to ask her something. And then—'

'Liar. I was in the bathroom and when I came back she was snooping around on my desk.'

'I only wanted to borrow a pencil.'

'Get your own.'

Ruby started crying and Dan instinctively went to comfort her.

Sam stomped her feet. 'That's so not fair, Dad. This is what always happens. She starts crying and you take her side.'

'Easy, Sam,' Dan replied. 'No one's taking anyone's side. All I want is for the two of you to stop fighting. I'm sure it's six of one and half a dozen of the other.'

'No it's not. It's all her fault. Little cry baby. I hate her.' Roaring with anger, Sam threw the nearest thing to hand – an old cup full of pens – against the wall.

'Hey! That's enough,' Dan said. 'Stay here. We're going to have words when I come back. And those pens had better be cleared away. I hope for your sake there are no marks on the wall.'

He took Ruby to her bedroom. 'Don't worry,' he told her. 'Big sisters get like that sometimes. It's a teenage thing. It doesn't mean she doesn't love you. But you mustn't go into her room or play with her things when she's not there.'

After making Ruby promise not to do so again, Dan wiped away her tears. Then he returned to Sam's room.

'I never want to hear you say that to your sister again, Sam,' he said with the door shut so Ruby couldn't listen. 'She's your family. We both know you don't really hate her, but she's only little and she might believe it. I want you to apologise.'

'But Dad—'

'But Dad nothing. You'll do what I ask or face the consequences. And if I ever see you throw things like that again, you'll be grounded for a month. Do you understand?'

Sam nodded.

'Is there any damage to the wall?'

'No.'

'Count yourself lucky.'

The memory faded and Dan found himself back in front of the door that stood between him and his late daughter's bedroom. On the one-year anniversary of the day she'd died. That argument between the girls had only happened a couple of months before then. It had marked the start of a difficult summer in which there had been a series of rows with Sam at the centre.

Dan wondered for the umpteenth time whether there was anything he could have done differently that might have changed what happened. He reached out for the handle, willing himself to go inside, but he couldn't do it. Then he nearly jumped through the ceiling as he felt it move in his hand and the door swung open.

'Daddy,' Ruby said in a tiny voice, her eyes wide with shock. 'I didn't know you were there.'

'Oh, it's you, darling,' Dan replied, catching his breath. 'What are you—'

'Sorry.'

Dan put his arm around his daughter, who was wearing pyjamas covered in cartoon cats and a pink and white striped dressing gown. He kissed her forehead and guided her to Sam's old bed, where they sat down next to each other. 'There's nothing to be sorry about. You can come in here any time you like. I've told you that before.'

'I miss her.'

'Me too. She loved you, you know. More than anything. She may not have always shown it, but that was more about her than it was about you. She actually saved your life once.'

'Really?'

'Sure. We were on holiday in a place called Thasos: a Greek island. You'd just had your third birthday. Goodness only knows how it happened. Your mother and I were furious at ourselves. But somehow, early one evening, you ended up at the side of the swimming pool by yourself.'

'I don't remember that.'

'You wouldn't, darling. Children don't tend to remember the first years of their lives. Anyhow, you fell in the pool when there was no one else around. Luckily, Sam noticed you were missing and went to look for you. She found you in the water, dived in and fished you out. She was already a strong swimmer, but you hadn't started lessons yet.'

'Was I still breathing?'

'Yes. You'd swallowed a bit of water, but otherwise you

were fine. She must have got there right after you'd fallen in. If she hadn't – well, it doesn't bear thinking about.'

'I'm surprised I don't remember.'

'We played it down, other than drumming it into you never to go by the pool again on your own. Not that we let you out of our sight for one second again after that.'

What Dan missed out in the version of the story he told Ruby was that Sam had been the one who was supposed to be looking after her when it happened. The two of them had gone off together and Sam had got distracted playing with some holiday friends, during which time her little sister had gone walkabout. He didn't include that information, as it would have ruined the impact of what he was trying to convey. Besides, Sam had only been ten years old then. Dan and Maria had since agreed this was too young to be entrusted with looking after Ruby; if anyone was to blame, it was them.

He noticed for the first time that Ruby was holding her left arm behind her back, as if concealing something. 'What have you got there, love?' he asked.

'Oh, nothing,' she replied, avoiding eye contact and blushing.

'Ruby Evans. You're the worst liar in the world, which is no bad thing. Come on. Show me what you've got.'

Gingerly, she revealed a small picture frame containing a photo of her and Sam.

'Oh, darling,' Dan said. 'Did you want to take that to your own room?'

She nodded, tears in her eyes. 'I was only borrowing it. I'll put it back. I just like to look at her sometimes.'

'Don't be silly. You can keep it for as long as you like. She'd want you to have it.'

'But I thought we were supposed to leave all the photos—'

'It's fine, darling. Honestly. We all miss her terribly, especially today. You take it and put it wherever you want in your room.'

'What about Mummy?'

'Don't you worry about that. I'll clear it with her. Do you mind if I have a quick look?'

'Sure.'

Dan lifted the silver frame to his eye level and felt himself start to well up. It was a great snap, taken around three years earlier on a family holiday to North Wales, which he remembered fondly. They were smiling, arms around each other and hair blowing in the wind, in front of the quaint ivy-covered cottage where they'd stayed. Both of his daughters, with their matching emerald eyes, looked gorgeous: a younger Ruby with a shorter, blonder version of her curls; Sam with her long black hair and slender figure, on the cusp of womanhood. Dan made a mental note to seek out the digital image from which the picture had been printed. It would be on the computer with the other photos and videos of Sam. He wanted to look at it some more.

'Are you all right, Daddy?' Ruby asked.

'Yes,' he replied, blinking back the tears, which he didn't want Ruby to see. It was important to stay strong for her, especially considering Maria's behaviour, which had grown increasingly erratic since Sam's death. 'Don't you worry about me, darling. How are you doing? Is there anything you'd like to discuss?'

Ruby shrugged. Dan could have left it there, but he decided to push on, hoping she might vocalise her feelings. 'What do you miss most about Sam?'

'I dunno. Everything really.'

'You loved her a lot, didn't you?'

Ruby nodded, looking away from Dan and out of the window. He reached his arm around her little shoulders and pulled her towards him, planting lots of little kisses on her head in place of the words he was too choked to utter.

They stayed there like that for several minutes and it was Ruby who eventually broke the silence. 'I really miss us all being happy together,' she said in barely more than a whisper.

This, more than anything, made Dan want to cry. He knew exactly what Ruby was talking about, and the declining state of his and Maria's relationship was at the heart of it. But instead of breaking down, which was the last thing Ruby needed to see him do, he took a different path. 'Don't move,' he said, looking down at the carpet. 'There's something—'

'What?'

'Just stay exactly—'

'What is it?'

Without warning, Dan darted for Ruby's bare feet and started tickling them.

'Hey, Daddy! What are you doing?'

Ruby collapsed into a squirming, giggling mess as Dan

ignored her jovial pleas for mercy, instead moving on to tickle her behind her knees, her sides and her armpits until she'd laughed herself into exhaustion and really had had enough.

'See,' Dan said as he watched his daughter catch her breath. 'We can still have fun. And it's important that we remember to do that as often as possible, especially when we're feeling sad. It's what Sam would have wanted. Agree?'

'Agree.'

'Good. Now let's go and find Mummy and see if she's ready for some breakfast.'

'I think she's cleaning downstairs.'

'I think you're right. I wonder if she fancies some pancakes. I know I do. What about you?'

Ruby nodded her head enthusiastically, reminding Dan of one of those nodding dogs you see in cars.

'I'll take that as a yes. I think we've got all the stuff we need. You might have to make do with honey instead of maple syrup.'

Maria didn't join them for breakfast. She turned off the vacuum, mumbled something about muddy shoes and not being hungry, and disappeared upstairs.

After leaving Ruby to whisk the pancake mix, Dan took his wife a cup of coffee. The bathroom door was locked, so he gave a gentle tap. 'Maria?'

'Jesus. Can I never get a moment's peace?' she snapped from the other side.

'I brought you a coffee. It's fresh from the pot.'

'Can you leave it outside the door? I'm on the loo.'

'Sure.' He paused before adding: 'How are you doing, love?'

'I'll be fine if everyone leaves me alone to get my head together.'

'I'll put the coffee here on the floor. Don't let it go cold.'

'Right.'

'You're welcome,' Dan mouthed in silent protest as he turned towards the stairs, wishing a bout of tickling would be enough to make his wife smile again too. Now clearly wasn't the time to tell her about Ruby and the photo, but he would do later on – and he wouldn't be taking no for an answer. For the sake of her daughter, Maria would just have to deal with this one exception to her rule.

He was gagging for a cigarette but knew he'd have to wait now until after breakfast.

He willed this horrible day to be over as soon as possible.

'I think it's ready, Daddy,' Ruby called. 'Can you make the pancakes now?'

'Coming.'

He stood still at the top of the staircase. After glancing back at the closed door of Sam's bedroom and the steaming mug on the floor outside the bathroom, he took a deep breath and shut his eyes for a moment.

Then he carried on.

CHAPTER 23

Nothing.

Zilch.

Not one radio station.

Not even the hint of something to tune into.

And I've tried the full spectrum – FM, AM, LW – several times over, from various positions in my bedroom. Nothing but static.

Dammit. I expected to find at least something, even in an isolated spot like this one.

In desperation, I try to open the window to see if sticking the aerial outside will help. Neither the bottom nor the top sash will budge. There's no sign of any lock holding them shut, but several hard shoves don't get me anywhere and I don't want to risk a breakage. The inside looks solid enough, but goodness knows what the exterior wood is like.

I decide to head outside. There's still time before Miles and I are due to meet up to look at the guttering. I exit my bedroom door and nearly collide with him.

'Jack,' he says, taking a step backwards, startled.

I wonder if he was eavesdropping outside my door.

'I, er, was going to ask if you'd finished in the bathroom,' he says, as if sensing my thoughts.

'Yes. I'm done.'

'That was quick.'

I shrug, holding the radio behind my back like a guilty secret. I'm not sure why, seeing as Miles was the one who gave it to me, but I keep it there nonetheless.

'Are you sure you're up to helping me?' he asks. 'You look pale. Take the day off if you need it.'

'I'm fine. Please, no more special treatment. Let's stick to what we've arranged.'

'Right you are.'

We both stand there for a moment in the corridor, staring at each other. Miles's eyes wander to my left arm – the one with which I'm concealing the radio behind my back – and I think he's going to ask about it. I'm debating with myself what to tell him when he looks back up and smiles. 'I'll get a move on. See you in a few minutes.'

I race through the house, only too aware that I don't have long. The front door is on the latch and I'm able to let myself out without having to find a key. I head straight for the rickety fence that runs along the clifftop. It's colder than I expected outside and rather breezy, making me regret not wearing my jacket. But everything else is secondary to my desire to try the radio again. I'm desperate to hear something from the outside world and it's become about more than simply checking the day. It's bizarre, but I feel frightened all of a sudden that maybe there is no one else out there. It's irrational. I can't explain it, but I'm unable to shift the thought.

I pull out the silver aerial as far as it will extend. Pressing one thumb against the milled edge of the black volume control – a rotating plastic disc embedded in the side of the pocket radio – I roll it upwards. Click. It's on and I keep turning until the wheel jams. Then I hold the speaker up to my ear, the only place it stands a chance against the babble of the sea and wind, and . . . more static.

I run my index finger over the twin disc on the other side of the radio – slowly, not wanting to miss the slightest hint of a signal. But still there's nothing.

Stay calm, I think, reminding myself of the two further wavelengths to check after this one. But it's no good. I know in the pit of my stomach that it's not going to happen. I'm not going to find anything.

And I'm right. There is nothing at all other than the rushing white noise. I give up eventually and, in my frustration, almost throw the damn radio over the cliff into the sea below. But common sense kicks in and, considering the awkward conversation this would lead to with Miles, I restrain myself.

It gets me thinking about my host, wondering whether he might have done something to the radio to stop it from receiving a signal. And then I get a brainwave, which sets me running back towards the house, around the side and to the Land Rover parked at the back.

It's unlocked. I jump into the driver's seat and press every button on the front of the car radio until it bursts into life with a greenish LED glow and the sound of the

Rolling Stones. Grabbing for the volume dial, I turn it down for fear of attracting Miles's attention and wait for the song to end. It's a favourite of mine, 'You Can't Always Get What You Want'. I've no idea how I know this when so little else is clear, but I'm glad to hear something other than static.

It's a long song but already more than halfway through. I imagine a middle-aged DJ in big headphones, squashed in a booth somewhere, getting ready to fade it out to tell the listening public an amusing anecdote. But as I'm thinking this, my eyes wander to the front of the stereo and I notice for the first time that there's no radio frequency or channel name displayed. All I can see is a spinning disk symbol.

Shit. It's a CD, I think, pressing the eject button and having my fear confirmed by the silver disc that slides out with a taunting grin.

Head in hands, I curse my own stupidity, before switching to the radio and renewing my search. The preset buttons turn up nothing but more static. I'm about to try the FM dial when there's a tap on the window to my side that shocks the bejesus out of me.

I look up, expecting to see Miles, and get yet another surprise. It's the girl in red. She's even wearing the coat this time, unlike when I last saw her at the shop. She's standing at the side of the car, leaning forward so her face is nearly touching the window. With one hand she's holding back her long black hair, stopping it from blowing in her face; the other hand is waving. She's waving at me.

I reach for the window handle and wind it down a few

inches. My hand's shaking slightly as I do so, but I try to hold my voice steady when I greet her. 'Hello.'

'Morning,' she replies. 'Sorry to bother you. I was passing when I saw you and, well, I wondered if you might be able to give me a lift. A friend was supposed to pick me up, but they've let me down.'

'Um, right. The car. Yeah, it's not actually mine. I was just listening to the radio.'

'Oh. I'm sorry. I thought—'

'Is it a lift back to the village you're after? I mean, I could ask Miles. He's the one who owns the car.'

'No, no. I don't want to inconvenience anyone. I thought you might be heading that way.'

'How will you get there otherwise?'

She shrugs. 'I'll walk. Maybe hitch a lift when I get to the road.'

'That doesn't sound very sensible.'

She raises one eyebrow. 'It's pretty safe around here. There's a good chance the person giving me a lift would be someone I know.'

'No, wait,' I say. 'Seriously. If you hang around for a minute I can speak to Miles. I'm sure he won't mind giving you a lift. You must know him. He owns this place. He was there too when you served me in the shop.'

She frowns, throwing me a look I can't read, and continues to the dirt track that leads to the road. 'Don't worry.'

I switch off the stereo and get out of the car. 'I'll find him now,' I call after her, but she walks on without looking back.

I run to the house, the lack of radio reception temporarily forgotten, and find Miles halfway out of the front door in an expensive-looking brown waxed jacket.

'Ah, there you are,' he says. 'Not wearing a coat?'

'No. I was going to ask you something, actually.'

'What's up, lad?'

'I was approached by this girl. You probably know her. She, um, works at the general store in the village. She was after a lift back there. I hope you don't mind, but I told her you might be able to help. I'd do it myself, but I don't know if I even have a driver's licence. And it's your car, of course.'

'Sorry, sorry, I'm confused. What girl?'

I run through the story again and, although Miles seems perplexed by the girl's presence, he agrees that her hitch-hiking isn't a good idea. 'Apart from anything else, there aren't any pavements,' he says. 'I wouldn't want my daughter walking along there. So where is she?'

There's no sign of her, so we jump into the Land Rover. Miles can't get it started at first. As he's trying, I spot the portable radio in the passenger footwell and discreetly tuck it into the pocket of my seatback.

'Come on, Gigi,' Miles says. 'A damsel in distress needs your help. You're not going to let her down, are you?'

I don't believe for a moment that Miles's words have anything to do with it, but a few seconds later the car roars into life. 'Good girl,' he says, stroking the steering wheel as if it's a pet. And off we go down the dirt track.

The weird thing is that there's no sign of the girl before we reach the road. I tell Miles that she got a good head start on us, but in truth I don't see how she could have made it that far so fast.

'What now?' Miles asks.

'Can we carry on a little further along the road? She can't be far ahead.'

He crawls along in the direction of the village as I desperately scour the vicinity. Soon he suggests turning back, but I ask if we can continue all the way to the general store.

'Is that where she said she was heading?'

'Not specifically, but I'd like to check. We're almost there now. All I can think is that she got a lift from someone else. I'd like to make sure she got back in one piece.'

'Are you definite she works at the shop? I can't say I've ever seen a teenage girl serving.'

'Yes. She was there last time,' I reply, straining not to sound as irritated as I feel. 'When I got the bread and milk.'

I do want to make sure she's all right, but I also have another agenda. Inside the shop will be newspapers and a definite confirmation of today's day and date. I realise now – too late – that I could have asked the girl these things when we were chatting.

'Is there anything we need?' I ask Miles as we enter the village, passing the pub and church.

'Sorry?'

'Do you want any provisions from the shop?'

'Oh, right. I see. No, I don't think so.'

He seems distracted. No doubt he's annoyed by this unexpected and, apparently, unnecessary journey. He

268

probably thinks I'm losing it; that I've imagined the whole thing.

'Sorry about this,' I say. 'I'll only be a minute. Then we can get back to looking at the gutters.'

He nods, pulling the car into the same parking spot outside the hardware store that we used before. 'It doesn't even look open,' he says, squinting into the rear-view mirror.

I turn my head to look and he's right. There are no A-boards outside advertising the latest news stories; no lights on inside; no sign of life whatsoever.

'That can't be right,' I say. 'What time is it?'

Instinctively, I look at the clock on the dashboard, but according to that it's already night time. Miles shrugs, helpful as ever.

Wait, I think. If it is Sunday – and not Saturday, as he told me – that could explain it. Maybe they only open for a couple of hours.

'I'll go and have a look,' I say, bursting out of the car and racing across the road. I hope to find the opening hours displayed. Instead there's a handwritten sign taped to the inside of the shop window: 'Closed due to family bereavement.'

I stand there on the pavement, staring at the purple felt tip words for a moment, unsure what to do next. I look up and down the street, hoping to see someone I can speak to, but there's no one. Then I remember the hardware store, which I've barely noticed, despite Miles parking right outside. I glance back across the street and see a large 'Open' sign.

Miles is watching from the car, but I avoid his gaze and

storm into the shop. There's an old fashioned bell on the door that competes for attention with the creaking of hinges as I enter the tiny space and stand at the varnished wooden counter. It's unattended and, as I wait for someone to appear, I eye the sparse selection of stock on display, resisting the temptation to look outside at Miles. It's a random collection of what must be popular items: screws, nails, nuts and bolts; an orange dustpan and brush; some tubes of silicone seal; hammers, screwdrivers and other household tools.

There's a door behind the counter, which is cracked open, but not so that I can see anything on the other side. I lean forward. 'Hello?'

'I'll be with you in a second,' a female voice replies from the other side followed by a loud banging noise, as if something has fallen over, and the muffled sound of swearing.

About thirty seconds later the door swings open and who should appear but the very person I came to find: the girl in red. Although she's not now – in red, that is. She's wearing a green fleece jacket and her hair's tied back.

'Oh,' I say. 'Hello. It's you. How did you get here so fast?'

'What do you mean? I was only out the back.'

'I, um—'

She flashes an insincere smile. 'Oh, I get it. You're making a joke.'

'Sorry?'

She stares at me, hands on her hips, and I find myself babbling. 'No. I, um. You know what I mean. I'm talking

270

about. You know. How you got back here. From the house on the cliff? Someone else gave you a lift, right?'

She shakes her head. 'Sorry, you've lost me.'

I can't believe what I'm hearing. Why is she pretending not to know what I'm talking about? And what is she doing working here rather than over the road?

Before I can think of what to say next, a car horn sounds. I turn around to see Miles make a 'what are you doing?' gesture through the window. 'One minute,' I mouth, holding up a single finger to emphasise my point.

Then, when I turn back to the counter, things get really messed up. The girl I was talking to is no longer there. Standing in her place, also wearing a green fleece, is a buxom middle-aged woman with short bottle-blonde hair and heavy make-up.

'What's going on?' I ask. 'Where did you come from? What happened to the girl I was talking to?'

'Are you serious?'

'No, really. What the hell? Did you guys swap over or something when I was looking the other way? Where is she? You're freaking me out.'

'I'm freaking you out? Look, I don't have time for this nonsense. What is it that you want?'

Several thoughts are churning through my mind now. Part of me is sure they swapped places when I looked the other way. And yet I only turned around for a moment. So what are the other possibilities? Well, what if the girl in red was never here in the first place? Perhaps I imagined her. Maybe I imagined the whole incident with her asking for a lift at the house. That would certainly explain why

271

we didn't see her on the way here. But that would make me crazy, right? Unhinged. The kind of person who might forget a whole week, as if it never happened; whose subconscious might block out his entire past for reasons unknown. The kind of person who might imagine having a daughter – a family even – when in reality he's a sad, single loser. What else? Could the person standing before me be some kind of shape-shifting monster, like you see in fantasy films?

That's not a path I want to go down. So I tell myself it must be the simple option: the one that doesn't brand me a crazy man or fantasist. They're playing a trick on me. Goodness only knows why, but I'm not going to stoop to their level. I'm not joining in.

Blondie is staring, waiting for me to answer her question. Hands on her substantial hips.

'I, er, was wondering if you knew what was happening with the shop over the road? It's closed.'

'There's a sign, isn't there?'

'Yes. It says something about a death in the family. Do you know any more?'

'You'd have to ask them.'

I resist the urge to point out the impossibility of that option and, instead, decide to ask her the question that's been on my mind all morning. 'This might sound odd,' I say, thinking that it can't sound much stranger than what's gone before, 'but could you please tell me what day it is today?'

'Seriously?'

'Long story, but if you could tell me that, I'll get out of your hair.'

'It's Saturday. Anything else? Maybe you'd like to buy something. We are a shop after all. Not an information service.'

I make my excuses and exit through the jingly, creaky door, wondering for the second time why they haven't applied any oil to it.

I didn't bother asking the date, as it wouldn't mean anything to me. I've no idea what it was the last time I remember being in the village. It's winter: probably towards the end, judging by the lack of dead leaves on the floor and relatively mild temperatures. But that's all I know, which is strange now I think about it. And yet, in the scheme of things, not the most important gap in my knowledge. Blondie also had a look about her towards the end of the conversation, like she might call the police or something. I didn't want to push my luck.

'What was that all about?' Miles asks as I open the car door.

'Sorry. I didn't mean to take so long. The general store's closed because of a family bereavement. There's a sign in the window.'

'Oh dear.'

'They didn't know any more about it in this place. It was all a bit weird in there, to be honest.'

'How so?'

It occurs to me that Miles would have had a decent view of what happened in the shop from his position in the driver's seat of the Land Rover. 'Did you see who I was talking to in there?'

'Yes, of course. Why?'

273

'Um, is she the usual person who serves you?'

'Yes. She and her husband run it, as far as I know. It's always one or the other of them. I don't think they employ anyone else. Was there a problem?'

'No, nothing. Not at all.'

I want to ask him if he saw the girl too, but I don't. I already know the answer.

'Let's get back to the house and have a look at those gutters,' I say, forcing a smile. 'Sorry about the wild goose chase. And for making you wait around.'

'Never mind, lad. You were only trying to help someone.'

I make small talk on the journey back to the house and keep smiling. It's the only way I can conceal the real conversation going on inside my head, which is as scary as hell. A rabid dog snarling at my ear.

What . . . the hell . . . is happening to me?

CHAPTER 24

Monday, 24 April 2017

Dear Sam,

See, I didn't make you wait long. Not even twenty-four hours. It's 1.35 p.m. Ruby and I have had our lunch and she's disappeared to her bedroom to read a book.

Yes, you heard me right. It's a novel she borrowed from Anna and, of course, that makes it far cooler than any book I could ever buy for her. She's had her head stuck in it most of the day, which is great, as far as I'm concerned. I'd much rather she was doing that than playing on her tablet or watching TV, which is all she usually wants to do, especially since breaking her arm. It's not like I can even suggest she goes out on her bike or anything at the moment.

Anyhow, it gives me a chance to carry on with what I was telling you last time. I left you on a cliffhanger regarding what happened with Rick on

Saturday. It does still feel strange telling you – my daughter – such matters. But we've already established the need for me to be honest with you, so I won't dwell on it. That said, things did get steamy and, while I'm happy to confide in you, I'm not going to go all *Fifty Shades of Grey*. That would be a step too far.

So what happened? Well, I told you last time how Rick and Anna came around and, after agreeing that she could stay for a sleepover, I invited him for dinner. The girls shared a pizza from the freezer, but I didn't have much in to make a meal for the two of us. Certainly nothing up to the standard Rick had set with his delicious roast. So we ordered an Indian takeaway. Rick tried to pay, but I insisted, especially in light of the huge bunch of red and pink roses he'd given me when he returned with Anna's sleepover things. Honestly, it was so big I had to spread the flowers across two vases: one on the dining table and the other next to the phone.

We ordered the food for 9.30 p.m., allowing plenty of time to get the girls away to bed. I did my best to make an occasion of it by laying the table and rooting out a nice bottle of wine.

'Well, this is nice,' Rick said, surveying the colourful spread of curry, rice, side dishes, poppadoms and chutneys, once I'd served up. 'Who else is coming?'

'Sorry? I, er—'

'Joke. I just can't believe how much you ordered.'

I felt my cheeks flush. 'Oh, right. Didn't want you

going hungry, did I? Especially after you did such a good job in the garden.'

He squinted at me across the table. 'So that's what this is. I see. Buttering me up so I might do it again, are you?'

I grinned and let myself relax into the conversation. 'Damn. You've found me out. And I thought I was being subtle. Wine?'

He looked at the bottle I was holding aloft with mock distrust. 'Hmm. Not sure I should risk it. You might take advantage if I don't stay in control of my faculties.'

'All the more for me, then,' I said, whipping the bottle away to fill my own glass.

'Hold on. Let's not be hasty. I'll risk it.'

'Are you sure?' I replied, buoyed by the two large gin and tonics I'd had while Rick popped home for Anna's night things. 'I can't promise I won't take advantage.'

By the time we finished the food – well, as much as we could eat of it – the wine was almost empty too and we were flirting outrageously.

'Shall I open another bottle?' I asked, sharing the remnants of the first between our two glasses.

'I was planning to drive back,' Rick said. 'Mind you, there's always a taxi.'

Or nothing at all, I thought, only just stopping myself from saying as much. You don't want to sound like a floozy, a shrinking part of my mind warned. Don't hand it to him on a plate: men like a challenge. But the voice speaking these words was fast fading.

'More wine it is,' I said, heading to the kitchen to grab it.

I'd just returned to the table and poured each of us another glass when the home phone started to ring.

'Hang on. I'd better just check who that is,' I said, dashing over to have a look at the caller display.

'Mum Mobile,' it read. That got my attention, as my parents had left on a month-long trip to New Zealand just before Easter and I hadn't heard a peep from them so far. I hadn't expected to. They're still very much in the 'no news is good news' camp and wouldn't usually bother unless there was a problem. You know what they're like, Sam. How many times a year did you used to see them: once, maybe twice? And usually it was us who drove the six-hour journey down south to their house, rather than the other way around.

Nothing has changed. They still think it's permanently cold and rainy in the north of England. They haven't given up hope that I'll move south again one day, even though I've lived here since coming to university at eighteen, well over half my life. If anything, we actually hear from them less than we used to do. They always seem to be away on holiday – a cruise here, a tour there. And when they are at home, they're busy socialising or going on day trips.

If I'm honest, I don't think they've ever really

known what to say to us since your death. Don't get me wrong, they were devastated. You were their first grandchild and they loved you more than you know. But their way of dealing with bad things has always been to brush them under the carpet. Stiff upper lip and all that; finding the positive in the negative; trusting in God's plan. In the depths of my grief, I was in no place to deal with that. None of it made any sense to me and I don't think my behaviour made any sense to them. So some extra distance grew between us.

I digress. The point is that when I saw it was Mum phoning – unexpectedly and all the way from New Zealand – I had to answer. Or rather I tried to answer but, feeling the effects of the wine and the G&Ts, I somehow ended up knocking over the glass vase of roses I'd placed there.

'Shit,' I shouted, frozen in shock for a moment by the loud smashing sound and the cascade of water, petals and stems over the phone. Then I noticed it was still ringing. So I picked the cordless handset up from the base unit with my thumb and forefinger, shaking off bits of glass before holding it up to my ear. At least it was still working in spite of the flower water. 'Hello?'

'Oh, you're there, darling. I thought I was going to get that awful machine.'

'Mum. Is everything all right?'

Rick had appeared by this time and was standing in front of me, surveying the damage.

'What happened?' he mouthed.

I shrugged and pulled my best 'I'm a clumsy idiot' face as Mum talked into my ear and Rick signalled for me to go through to the lounge while he cleared it up for me.

'Thank you,' I mouthed back at him as I continued listening to Mum, who was saying something about how they'd been in an accident.

'What kind of accident? What do you mean? Are you both all right?'

'We're fine, honestly. Nothing to worry about. It was a very minor coach crash.'

'A coach crash? Oh my God. Where are you now? Where's Dad? Is he okay?'

'Calm down, Maria. I'm at the hospital, but I already said that we're fine. I'm letting you know, that's all.'

'Mum, tell me what happened.'

'That's what I'm trying to do, Maria, but you keep interrupting.' You remember Grandma, Sam, she's can be quite direct when she wants to be.

She eventually explained that they'd booked themselves on a day trip around the capital city, Wellington, which had departed early that morning. About an hour into the trip, the coach had been in a collision with a lorry. It hadn't been that serious, but several of the party – mainly pensioners, by the sound of things – had suffered minor injuries. Dad, who'd been in the coach's toilet at the exact moment of the crash, had been thrown about in the small space and suffered a blow to the head and a few cuts and bruises. The doctors who'd checked him out thought he would be fine. But with it being a head injury, they wanted him to stay in hospital for twenty-four hours or so to keep an eye on him. It was all covered by their insurance, according to Mum, and she was hopeful they'd catch up with their travel itinerary in a couple of days. All the same, it was a shock.

Rick, who'd done a sterling job of tidying up my mess by the time I hung up, had managed to work out from my side of the conversation that there had been an accident. I brought him up to speed.

'So your dad's going to be all right?'

'I think so. Mum had me worried for a minute, though.'

'Was she injured at all?'

'She just banged her knee. If Dad had been in his seat at the time, he'd have probably been fine too. Listen, thanks ever so much for clearing up my mess. I can't believe I knocked over your lovely flowers. You must think I'm a right klutz. First the gravy and wine incident at your place; now this.'

'Not to worry. I rescued most of the roses, but I'm afraid the vase is in the bin. Is the phone still working okay?'

'It seemed to be when I was chatting to Mum. Why?'

Rick grimaced. 'Quite a bit of water got into the base unit. I did my best, but the LED display has gone off. I think the answerphone has had it.'

'Really? Oh, well. Mum will be pleased. She's always hated leaving messages on there. As long as the phone still works, I'm not too bothered.'

I used it to call Rick's mobile, to double check it was working, and it seemed fine, thank goodness.

'I didn't wake up the girls, did I? If they were asleep in the first place.'

'No,' Rick replied. 'I checked on them and they were both zonked out.'

'Are you sure they weren't pretending?'

He nodded. 'I double-checked. Where's your vacuum, by the way? I did my best getting the glass up with the dustpan and brush, but it could do with a proper going over.'

Something about the way Rick said this really turned me on. I guess I liked how he was taking care of me. Maybe it was something to do with the shock and relief of what I'd heard from Mum. Whatever the reason, I found myself grabbing hold of him and pulling him into what can only be described as a passionate embrace. It wasn't long before that second bottle of wine was empty and we were rolling around on the lounge carpet like teenagers and, well, I'll spare you the details, Sam.

All I'll say is that we had sex. Me and that gorgeous hunk. And it was great. Beforehand, I had been a little nervous about being naked and intimate with someone new – especially a man in such good shape. I'd like to say I felt guilty, especially after what Dan had said earlier, but in truth I didn't – at least not at that point. I got lost in the moment and enjoyed myself. The alcohol probably had something to do with it. I didn't even think about the bits of glass that might still be on the floor near the phone. Not much, anyway. I certainly didn't do anything about them.

You can remove your hands from in front of your eyes now, Sam.

The problem was we fell asleep in each other's arms afterwards, lying on the couch by this stage, and next thing I knew it was 4.30 a.m.

'Oops,' I said, disentangling myself from Rick and picking up the pieces of clothing darted about the lounge.

I woke him up and he was every bit as anxious as I was for the girls not to find out.

'I'll get in the car and drive back,' he said. 'I should be safe now. It's a good while since we finished the wine.'

'No, don't. You might wake them. Let's sneak upstairs to bed.'

'What?'

'No, not together. The bed's made up in the spare room. You go there first and I'll follow a few minutes later to my room.'

'How will we explain it?'

'We'll say you drank some wine and there were no taxis available. Keep it simple. They're only young, Rick.'

He looked doubtful.

'Come on. They'll probably be awake soon.'

'Right,' he conceded. He threw his clothes on and crept up the stairs.

Before doing the same, I quickly went over the area by the phone with the dustpan and brush and then a floor wipe. I would have liked to have used the vacuum cleaner, but I was afraid of waking up the girls. Rick had already done a good job, to be fair, and after a few minutes on my hands and knees, I called it a night.

The old me would have been there for ages, Sam, but I didn't allow myself to get OCD about it. That's not to say I didn't get up early the next morning to vacuum before the girls came downstairs. Of course I did, but that's just common sense. I couldn't risk them cutting themselves on a stray piece of glass.

Anyway, as I went to bed, still feeling flushed from my time with Rick, it struck me that he'd not so much as given me a peck on the cheek when he'd gone upstairs. I brushed it off. Put it down to the rude awakening. But still. It did seem a bit cold after what had happened between us.

Hold on. There's someone at the door.

I'm back now. Several hours have passed; it's almost 11 p.m.

It was Dan at the door. He wanted to mow the lawn for me, if you can believe it, and was surprised to find it had already been done. I could hardly not invite him in, could I? But it wasn't long until I wished

I hadn't. First of all Ruby told him that Rick had been the one who'd cut the grass. And then she said: 'He's my new friend Anna's dad. They both slept over last night.'

I was mortified. 'Anna came for a sleepover,' I explained to Dan. 'Rick stayed for some food and wasn't able to get a taxi, so he took the spare room.'

'Oh he did now, did he?'

'It's not what you think,' I lied to him when Ruby disappeared to the toilet a short while later. But he was having none of it, especially once he spotted the roses Rick had given me and put two and two together.

'So let me get this straight,' he said, his face twisted into a knot of fury. 'You knew that Romeo Rick was coming over yesterday when we spoke. You let me apologise and open up my heart to you. You gave me hope that we might get back together. Then you went and had your cosy little sleepover with lover boy. That's low, Maria.'

'That's not fair, Dan. It wasn't like that at all. Rick and Anna turned up unannounced.'

'Did you sleep with him?'

'What? That's ridiculous,' I said. 'Why would you ask me that?'

Not very honest of me, I know, but he put me on the spot and I feared how he'd react if I told him the truth.

'It's a simple question, Maria. Yes or no?'

Ruby walked back into the lounge at that moment,

thank goodness, saving me from having to give an answer. I knew it would be a short stay of execution, though, as there was no chance of Dan letting this drop. So I used the time I'd gained to come up with a story.

'You've got it all wrong,' I told him after sending Ruby upstairs on the pretext of showing him the book she'd borrowed from Anna. 'I got some bad news yesterday – from Mum and Dad. Rick was here when I took the call. He could see I was upset and stayed to make sure I was all right. That's it.'

'What bad news?' Dan asked. I told him, exaggerating ever so slightly to emphasise the point. Not good, I know. Really bad, in fact, but I needed something to distract him away from quizzing me about Rick. Something close enough to the truth to be convincing. It was the best I could come up with.

'I was telling your father what happened to Grandma and Grandpa,' I explained to Ruby when she returned.

'Grandpa's in hospital,' she said to Dan. 'But we don't have to worry. He's not going to die. This is the book Mummy was talking about. It's really good.'

The fire in his eyes had died down but not disappeared by the time he left. I didn't risk being alone with him any more, for fear of being asked that question again. I held Ruby close as we said goodbye at the front door.

'I'll call tomorrow,' he said. 'Check how your dad's doing.'

'I'm not sure I'll have heard—'

'Nonetheless,' he replied with a steely gaze. 'I'll call tomorrow.'

So now I've got to decide what to say to him, Sam. Do I keep on lying or do I tell the truth?

I can't believe I asked that after all those years I spent drumming into you that lying was bad. It still is. There's no excuse. But I'm trying to weigh up what will do the most damage: telling him now or not telling him and running the risk of him finding out in the future. The latter would be the worst possible outcome. But how likely would it be to happen? If I don't tell him, the only other person who could is Rick. Unless he tells someone else and . . . oh, this is ridiculous. Dan and I aren't even together any more. But the thing is, Sam – bizarrely – now that something has happened with Rick, I'm wondering whether it's actually Dan I want to be with.

It's crazy. I don't know what's going on in my mind. But hey, at least it's not OCD. With everything else going on, I've had no time for that. I've not even felt my usual urge to screw up this letter and start again.

I'm going to sign off now, Sam. I'll write again very soon. How else am I going to work out what to do?

Love as always,

M

Xx

CHAPTER 25

BEFORE

Sunday, 27 March 2016

Easter Sunday. The first without Sam. The next step in the painful trawl through the calendar leading up to the one-year anniversary of her death. Everything was the first without Sam. Last month's horrendous hurdle had been her birthday, on Valentine's Day. Before that it had been Christmas and New Year. Now this. Would it get easier as time passed?

And what about that awful feeling he woke up to every morning: the sinking realisation that his daughter really was dead; that it hadn't been a horrible dream? Would that ever stop or was he stuck with it for life?

Dan fell asleep every night hoping that he might dream of Sam being alive again. But he rarely did – not that he could remember, anyway. The only recent exception was a dream set in an airport. The two of them had been travelling together, only to be split up by security guards after their hand luggage was scanned. He'd been detained on suspicion of drug smuggling and a terrified-looking Sam had been ushered through to the departure lounge alone. Dan had woken up in a cold sweat at that point.

Usually she was dead in his dreams. In the kinder ones that meant, like in real life, she wasn't around. But in the nightmares, he'd encounter a chilling vision of her corpse, skin as white as the eyes were black, devoid of humanity. Sometimes he'd find himself buried alive alongside it, unable to escape the horror. On other occasions it would reanimate, like something from a zombie movie. And even as it hunted him down, he'd search for some trace of his daughter. He'd beg for a sign she was still in there, only for some animalistic groan to leave the monster's drooling blue lips.

It didn't help, of course, that he'd been the one who'd found her. He saw something that day which no parent should ever have to see. The image of that awful scene was burned into Dan's mind. He wished he could forget, but he couldn't. Throughout everything he did, it was always lurking in the background.

'Please not now,' Dan said to the empty bedroom as he felt his mind returning to that awful memory. He threw back the double quilt, wondering how long ago Maria had slipped out of her side of the bed, and put on his dressing gown, still fighting to shift his thoughts elsewhere.

His head throbbed. A mild hangover from the beer and whisky he'd drunk the night before. Nothing he wasn't used to. It was more unusual to wake with a clear head

289

these days. He often thought about having a booze-free day, especially when he woke up feeling like this, but it was usually a different story by the time evening came around. A couple of drinks took the edge off. And it was usually only a couple, apart from at weekends when it tended to be a few more. Dan was pretty sure he didn't have a problem. He had considered it privately – not that he'd admit this to anyone – and he'd decided that as long as he wasn't drinking during the day or doing it in secret, he was fine.

He almost bumped into Ruby in the hallway. She was also in her dressing gown and, judging from the barely open state of her eyes, had recently woken up.

'What's this mole doing walking around my house in Ruby's dressing gown?' he said, ruffling her hair. 'Where's my daughter? What have you done to her?'

'Daddy,' Ruby replied with a sleepy smile. 'Don't be silly.'

The two of them wished each other a happy Easter before heading downstairs together. Dan feared what they might find, but he was happy to discover Maria preparing breakfast. The dining table was already laid, including a chocolate egg for each of them, and the welcoming smell of fresh coffee and warm bread was wafting out of the kitchen.

'Good morning,' he said, finding Maria attending to a pan of boiling eggs at the hob. 'Happy Easter.'

She turned and smiled, giving him a rare peck on the lips before kissing Ruby on the forehead. 'Happy Easter, both of you. You're right on time. I was about to give you a shout. Breakfast will be served in, ooh, five minutes. Grab yourselves a seat and relax.'

'Are you sure?' Dan asked. 'Is there nothing I can do to help?'

'Nope. It's all under control.'

'Wow. I'm impressed. Hasn't Mummy done a great job?'

Ruby gave an enthusiastic nod as she headed back to the table and the lure of her chocolate egg.

'Which one do you think is yours?' he asked. 'I think the Hello Kitty one is probably mine.'

'Daddy! You're being silly again. Yours is the Yorkie, of course.'

'Really? You think so? How do you know that's not Mummy's?'

'Because it's your favourite. Hers is the Caramel, because that's what she likes.'

'You might be right.'

'Can I open my egg after breakfast? Oh look, it's got chocolate buttons inside. And there's a picture you can colour in on the back. Look!'

'Wow. Yes, of course you can open it after breakfast. It is Easter.'

'Yay.'

'Hold on. Be quiet for a moment. Can you hear that?'

'What? I don't hear anything.'

'It's like a scratching, sniffing kind of noise. I think it's coming from over there.'

Dan walked to the sideboard and put his ear against one of the doors, holding a finger up to his lips. He nodded, whispering: 'In here.'

'Daddy, you're tricking me. There's nothing inside.'

'No, really. I can definitely hear something. Come and listen if you don't believe me. Put your ear here, like I did.'

Ruby did as he asked and, without her noticing, Dan scratched the bottom of the unit, making her jump.

'What is that?' she asked, backing away, eyes wide open. 'Do you think it might be a mouse or – yuck – a rat?'

Dan could tell Ruby was anxious now, which wasn't what he was aiming for. 'No, no. Don't worry. It's not a mouse or a rat. I think it's something nice. Do you want to have a look?'

She shook her head. 'You do it.'

Dan opened the door and pulled out the foil-wrapped chocolate rabbit he'd placed in there the night before. 'Look. It's a golden bunny,' he said. 'Nothing to be afraid of, darling.'

'I knew you were tricking me. Was it you who made the noise?'

'What do you mean? It was obviously this rabbit.'

Dan made the rabbit snuffle around Ruby's neck, causing her to giggle. 'Oh dear. He says it smells of peanut butter there. I think you'd better have a shower after breakfast.'

'Daddy! I had one last night. And I do not smell of peanut butter.'

'I know. Only joking.' He handed her the chocolate. 'Here you go. Happy Easter.'

'Come on, you two. Food,' Maria said, carrying the eggs in one hand and a plate of hot cross buns and croissants in the other.

'Yummy,' Dan said. 'Come on, love. Let's sit down.'

They'd decided to spend Easter without any other family this year. There had been an invite to stay with Maria's parents for the weekend, but Dan hadn't fancied it and, luckily, neither had Maria. They'd blamed it on him having to work, although in reality he was only required in the office on Easter Monday.

He did feel a little bad for Ruby. Helen and Geoff were always great with her and it wasn't like she had much in the way of other family. Dan and Maria were both only children; on his side there was just his mum left. Thanks to the Alzheimer's, she rarely knew who he was these days. She'd actually confused him with the doctor when he'd called in to see her on Good Friday. His dad had died from a massive heart attack three months before Ruby was born. She had a few second cousins, but none lived nearby and she'd only met them a handful of times.

Because of their own backgrounds, Dan and Maria had both felt strongly about having more than one child. And they'd achieved that, only to have it torn away from them again. So Ruby would grow up as an only child after all.

That thought popped into his head as they had break-fast and, although he kept smiling for the others, it made him feel like beating his chest and screaming at the sky. Made his heart ache for Sam to be back there with them – her old seat at the table never looking emptier than it did at that moment.

'I really missed her today,' Dan said to Maria after putting Ruby to bed that evening.

She nodded but didn't reply. Kept on staring at the TV, which was tuned into one of the twenty-four-hour news channels.

'Why don't we talk about her to each other any more?' he asked. He'd held in his emotions all day, for Ruby's sake. Now he needed an outlet.

Maria sighed, turning her head towards him in slow motion. 'Do we have to do this now?'

'Yes. I think we do.'

'I tried really hard today, Dan. I wanted to make it a nice day for Ruby and I'm worn out.'

He perched himself on the arm of the couch, next to where she was sitting. 'I understand that, love. More than anybody. I thought maybe I could put the pain aside today, but she barely left my thoughts. I kept thinking back to all the previous Easters we spent together. I couldn't get past the fact she should have been with us.'

He turned to make eye contact with his wife, only to see that she was crying. 'I'm sorry,' he said, instantly feeling guilty. 'I didn't mean to upset you. You were great today, honestly. I—'

'What you described is how I feel every day, Dan. You go off to work – get away from it – but I'm here all the time, constantly reminded that she's not.'

'You could go back to work if you wanted to. It was your choice to stop.'

She shook her head. 'I wasn't here enough for Sam and look what happened. There's no way I'm risking that with Ruby.'

294

'What about if you found something part-time, so you only worked during school hours? That's not so uncommon.'

'As a solicitor? Are you serious?'

Dan sighed, running a hand through his hair. 'How about voluntary work, then? That would get you out of the house; you might even meet some new friends.'

'What's that supposed to mean?'

'Nothing. I'm just trying to help.'

'Well, you're not, Dan. You might be able to carry on doing things as you always have, but I can't. There's too much at stake. I'm not losing another daughter.'

'There's no need to be so dramatic, Maria. I was—'

'Dramatic? I don't believe you. Why do you always have to make everything worse?'

Dan stood up.

'Going for a fag, I suppose. The answer to everything.'

He didn't reply, knowing better than to rise to the bait, although Maria was right. He hadn't smoked all day. Now he was gagging for one.

He went outside to the car and pulled his half-empty pack and lighter out of the glovebox. He sparked one up from the shelter of the passenger seat, standing to smoke it on the drive, enjoying the head rush from the nicotine his body craved.

'Evening,' a neighbour he vaguely knew called out, walking past with his chocolate Labrador. 'Happy Easter.'

'Thanks. You too.'

It was quiet after that, as Dan liked it, giving him the chance to reflect. They'd had a nice day until now, despite how he'd been feeling. Following breakfast, there had been a leisurely period of lounging around, reading the papers and listening to music while Ruby ate chocolate and coloured in the picture on her egg box. Later they'd had an egg hunt around the house. Dan had done the hiding, with Ruby and Maria hunting; then they'd swapped and he'd been the one searching for the chocolate treats. In the afternoon they went for a walk along the river that ran through town, before enjoying a tasty meal at The Golden Dragon on High Street.

There had been plenty of light conversation between him and Maria, but he guessed that was more for Ruby's benefit than anything else. Without ever specifically discussing it, they'd both done everything they could to make it a normal family day for her. Maria had even avoided any of her weird obsessive behaviour. But now their daughter was in bed, it was business as usual: cold and lifeless, teetering towards dysfunctional.

As he so often did nowadays, Dan found himself regretting how the conversation had gone between them. Surely there was some way he could have handled it better. Why hadn't he put his arm around her, like he would have done without thinking in the past? She might not have brushed him off this time. It might have been enough to break through that barrier she'd erected around herself. It could have been a step forward.

But no, he'd gone for a cigarette instead. Now she wouldn't want to be anywhere near him. If he went within a couple of metres of her, she'd turn her nose up and complain that he smelled disgusting.

He took a final drag, stubbed the cigarette butt out on

the floor and disposed of it in one of the many wheelie bins tarnishing the garden. Maybe he could stop. That might help smooth things out with Maria at least. It was easy to think that way now he'd had his fix; if only it would last.

As he walked back inside the house, he decided to go for a shower before trying to make up with Maria.

He hated conflict between them. He didn't have any illusions of being able to talk her into sex, which had been off the cards for a long time. But a kiss and a cuddle would be nice. That was rare as hell too and he missed it.

When he found all the downstairs lights switched off and no sign of his wife, he knew she'd gone up to bed in a huff. Or locked herself in the bathroom while she soaked in the tub.

He weighed up whether or not to go upstairs and try talking to her. He almost did it. But the evidence of past experience was too compelling. It said enough that she'd turned off the lights when she knew he was still up, deliberately trying to annoy him. He could have still used the downstairs bathroom, where there was a second shower, but what was the point now?

Dan went to the liquor cupboard, in the same sideboard where he'd hidden Ruby's chocolate rabbit, and poured himself a large glass of whisky, finishing the bottle. It didn't take him long to drain, plonked on the couch, channel surfing, unable to find any programme that held his attention.

The drink had made him feel a bit better and he fancied

some more. Something else strong. So he walked back to the cupboard to see what was there.

Baileys, peach schnapps, port, amaretto and vodka. Not a very impressive collection. He and Maria had always been mainly beer and wine drinkers. And yet Dan had enjoyed a few whiskies of late. The bottle he'd finished had been a Christmas present from a contact at work.

He'd had a bad experience with vodka as a teenager, which had left him wary. But it was the only bottle that looked remotely appealing, so he pulled it out, found a new glass and mixed it with some ice and orange juice. Not bad at all, he thought, sipping it on the couch. Much easier to drink than whisky. Maybe it was time to re-evaluate those feelings about vodka.

He knew that pouring another one was a bad idea, especially with work in the morning, but Dan still couldn't face going upstairs. Maria had gone for a bath. He could tell from the various plumbing noises he'd heard. You got to know such things after living in a house for a while – particularly when you'd fitted much of the main bathroom yourself. There was a time when Maria had appreciated his DIY skills. Not everyone was lucky enough to have a husband as handy as him. There was a lot she took for granted.

He wondered if his wife still loved him. He was sure she must blame him, at least in part, for what had happened to Sam. How could Maria not speculate about his actions that day? He'd done so himself often enough: scouring the memory; analysing his every move.

So where did the two of them go from here? He couldn't

change things on his own. She had to want it as well. It occurred to him, not for the first time, that perhaps they ought to go for some kind of couple counselling. There was the guy he'd seen a few times about his depression, which he'd found helpful. But Maria didn't know anything about that. He'd hidden it from her. Why? Probably the same reason he'd declined the happy pills his GP had offered. Too much stigma attached and he didn't want to appear weak. Someone had to hold things together.

He'd have to find a different counsellor, but the idea felt like a good one in principle. A positive step forward. He'd have a look on the Internet at work tomorrow.

Not long after coming to that decision, Dan dozed off, with his latest drink balancing precariously on his knee. Somehow it remained there until 3.55 a.m. when, attempting to dodge a punch in a dream, Dan jerked forward in the chair. He awoke with the horrified belief that he'd wet himself. The reality – a lapful of vodka and orange – was still damn annoying. Not least because he was due at work in four hours.

'Bloody idiot,' he muttered, stumbling to find the kitchen roll. 'Stupid bloody idiot.'

CHAPTER 26

'Everything all right?'

'Sorry?'

'You seem a bit lost.'

'I, er—' I look around and can't understand what's going on. There are people everywhere. Travellers wheeling cases, studying information screens, queuing, using their phones.

The woman who spoke to me is wearing a hi-vis vest over a navy jacket and a sky-blue blouse; a photo ID pass around her neck says her name is Diane and she's a customer service assistant.

'Sir, have you already checked in? Do you have a boarding card I could look at? That way I can point you in the right direction.'

'Hang on,' I reply, patting my pockets.

'What about your—'

'Bag?' I say, finishing the sentence for her as I look down at the small shoulder bag at my feet.

She nods, the hint of a frown flickering across her forehead and then vanishing. It's replaced by a customer service smile: measured, robotic, friendly but professional.

I pull a folded piece of paper and a passport out of my jacket's inside pocket. 'Here it is.' Handing her the boarding card, I add: 'I'm flying to Eindhoven.'

'Very nice. I love Holland. We're not supposed to call it that any more, though, are we?'

'Do we know each other?'

'No, I don't think so.'

'You were going to tell me that your daughter-in-law is Dutch, weren't you? But she's lived here for a long time. She doesn't like people calling it Holland, as that's only a small part of the country. The proper name is the Netherlands.'

Diane scratches her temple. 'I'm sorry. Have we—'

'Is it right what I said?'

She nods.

'I knew it. Don't ask me why or how. It's like I've either got the world's worst case of déjà vu or something strange is going on.'

A huge man in a leather trench coat rushes by, running over my foot with the wheels of his case. I notice that – bizarrely – he's holding one of those retractable dog leads in his left hand. It stands out because of its fluorescent yellow colour. 'Hey!' I shout after him. 'Watch where you're going.'

He's familiar too, although for some reason I didn't expect him at that particular moment. I turn back to explain this to Diane, but she's gone. Nowhere to be seen. Charming. So much for customer service.

I walk towards the nearest information screen to see what's happening with my flight. I look at all the faces around me – business travellers, families, friends, love-struck couples – but there's no one I recognise. Then I feel a tap on my shoulder and turn to face someone who does look familiar.

'Hello?' I say to the girl facing me.

'Do you recognise me?'

'Um, yes, I think so.'

'Who am I, then?'

'I can't put my finger on . . . Listen, to be honest, I'm feeling a bit confused. I—'

A red arm whips up without warning and slaps me hard across my left cheek. 'You shouldn't be here. You need to go back. Right back.'

'What the hell?' I reply, dazed. 'You can't do that. I don't even—'

Slap.

She's done it again.

Harder this time.

Forcing me backwards.

'I said get out of here. Go on. You don't belong.'

'What?'

Slap.

'Will you stop doing that?'

Slap. Slap.

She's at it with both hands now. My head's hurting. I'm holding my arms out in front of me to stop her, trying to grab her hands, but she's too nimble. She skips out of the way and darts back in to do it again.

I can't believe no one's reacting. How can all of these people be oblivious to what's going on before them?

'It's because they're not real,' she says, slapping me for the umpteenth time.

Wait. How did she know what I was thinking? I didn't say it out loud.

'You didn't need to say it out loud,' she says. Or rather, she doesn't actually say it. Her lips don't move, but somehow I can hear her in my mind. 'Why would you? None of this is real. So whether you think or say something here, it's all the same.'

Her voice is calmly saying all of this to me while the slapping assault continues. It's as if the two things are unrelated.

'Stop slapping me,' I say, using my mind rather than my voice.

'Fine,' she replies at last. She lowers her arms and stops.

'What's going on? Who are you? Where am I?'

'You need to work that out for yourself.'

The two of us are standing face to face under the information screen, communicating telepathically. It must look as odd to everyone else as it feels to me. And yet they were happy to ignore me being assaulted, so I'm not expecting an intervention.

'What was all the slapping about?'

'I needed to get your attention. You're cruising towards the exit door when you should be finding your way back to where you belong. Where you're needed.'

'I don't understand. I don't know what you're talking about.'

'Get the hell out of here!' she screams into my mind.

It's louder than anything I've ever experienced before. As if a bomb has exploded inside my skull. Everything is noise and bright white light.

I'm thrown backwards and forwards. Every which way.

It's dark and there's a horrible stench of burning chemicals. I recognise it, I think.

'Hello. Can you hear me?'

It's a man's voice from somewhere behind. I want to turn to look but I can't move. Where am I?

Spider's web.

Glowing clocks.

'Can you hear me?' the voice, which sounds familiar, asks again. 'Hold on. Help is on the way.'

He's saying something else now, but I can't make it out.

I want to call out to him, but all that leaves my mouth is a low groan.

I feel dizzy.

Eyelids so heavy.

Can't . . . stay . . . awake.

'Morning, Jack. You're up bright and early.'

Miles is unloading a large bag of beans into the built-in coffee machine above the oven. I smile at him, say good morning and accept his offer of breakfast. But behind the facade I'm cracking up. How did I get here? I've no memory of waking, getting dressed and coming down-stairs. And what happened yesterday? Or the day before?

My memory's all messed up: confused by shadows of half-remembered dreams.

The last thing I remember for sure is being in the car with Miles in the village and that weird incident in the hardware shop. Was it real or a dream?

I should tell Miles what's going on. He is a doctor after all. But I'm not sure I trust him. I'm not convinced he's ever taken me to the hospital. He says I've been there, but I've no memory of it.

There's something off about all of this. What if he's drugging me? Mind-altering substances could explain a lot. Maybe even what I saw – or thought I saw – in the shop. How has this not occurred to me before?

I wait until he's finished with the coffee machine and then, as he looks at me, hold my hand to my stomach and wince.

'Problem?' he asks.

'Stomach cramps. Think I'd better get to the toilet.'

'Oh dear. Hope it's not the crab we had last night.'

Crab? I've no memory of that. Shutting the kitchen door behind me, I head to the foot of the stairs. I wait there for a moment, to make sure he's not coming after me. Then I slip out of the front door.

It's cold outside this morning, another biting wind blowing in off the sea. Again, I don't have my jacket with me, but there's no time to find it now. I have to get out of here. As far away as possible. And it has to be now.

So again I find myself heading towards Gigi, aka Miles's mud-caked green Land Rover. My heart is pumping away in my chest. I'm still not sure whether I have a driving

305

licence, but last time I was driven by Miles, I had a good look at what he was doing and it felt familiar. I reckon I do know how to do it. I'm hoping muscle memory and so on will take over.

I get to the car and it's open as usual. I even find the key in the glovebox without having to dig around too much. I slip it into the ignition and an overwhelming sense of panic kicks in. It grabs me by the throat so I can barely breathe, and presses me hard into the seat.

It triggers something else.

Throws me back into my mind.

'Hello. Anyone home?' I call as I enter the house after a busy day at work. 'Sam? Are you back yet?'

There's no sign of life downstairs, but when I walk into the lounge, I spot her handbag and her red summer coat thrown on the sofa instead of being put properly away. 'Bloody hell, Sam,' I say to the empty room. 'How many times?'

I'm tempted to go up and shout at her, but she's been a bit subdued recently and I don't have the heart. She's in her room, no doubt, away in a world of her own. Probably listening to music too loud on the headphones of mine that she commandeered after breaking her own.

The clock in the kitchen reads 4.15 p.m. Ruby's not due back from her holiday club bowling trip until 5 p.m. and Maria's expecting to be late, as usual. I put the kettle on to make a brew. Watching it boil, I think that I'll make Sam one and take it up for her. What has she been doing all day? It's only since she turned fourteen earlier this year that we've been allowing her to stay home alone over the school holidays. It seems to be working out. Well, I think it is, although it's hard to tell with a teenager. You just have to do your best to communicate what's right and wrong and hope they're not taking drugs and having underage sex behind your back. Sam isn't very communicative, though, and seems to prefer visiting her friends' houses to having them over here.

I make two cups of tea and put them on a tray with a couple of chocolate digestives. I'm going to try to have a chat with her; see if I can cheer her up a bit; clear away a few of those moody teenage cobwebs.

Ring ring. Ring ring.

I'm still sitting in the Land Rover and I can hear the sound of a phone.

It keeps ringing, on and on, until I find the source: a battered old Nokia mobile phone under my seat.

The name displayed on the screen is Sam.

Hold on. Wasn't that the name of the girl in the flashback I just experienced? The girl I thought of as . . . my daughter? My heart somersaults.

I press the green button to take the call.

CHAPTER 27

Wednesday, 26 April 2017

Dear Sam,

Let me start by saying that your grandpa's okay. I've spoken to Mum again a couple of times since my last letter and he's out of hospital now. The doctors say there's nothing to worry about. He'll be stiff and sore for a while, but that's it. The two of them have even had the go-ahead to continue with their trip. So that's all good.

Unfortunately, the same can't be said for matters closer to home. Somehow I've managed to go from having two men chasing after me to stuffing things up with the pair of them.

Before I get on to that, I have to warn you that the OCD isn't good today. I just read back what I've written so far and it's taking all of my willpower not to screw it up and start over. It's partly because of that blotch in the ink a few lines back, but I don't like what I've written either. I'm seeing Rosie for a session later on – the first in a while – and I feel like I need it.

If I did screw up this letter, I'd do the same again with the next one and the next one and the next one . . . until the bin was full. Then I'd be on to something else, like the scuff mark on the wall by the front door that I noticed earlier.

I'm trying to write my way out of caving in. I know if I push on, the urge will eventually pass and I'll be a step closer to freedom. But it's so bloody hard.

'Think of it like swimming out of a choppy sea,' Rosie told me in an early session. 'As you get closer to the shore, the waves will get smaller and smaller until eventually, all being well, you'll be striding out on to the beach.'

'And if I give in?'

'The current will carry you backwards and you'll have to start the journey to shore all over again.'

So let's push on. Back to my trainwreck love life.

I fobbed Dan off, if you remember, batting away his questions about Rick by moving the conversation to Mum and Dad's accident. By the time he phoned the next day, as promised, I'd already heard that Dad had been discharged from hospital. I told him so, no longer wishing to tempt fate by exaggerating their plight. As expected, we were soon back to the question of whether Rick and I had slept together.

I'd thought plenty since our last conversation, deciding that honesty was the only option. I'm sure that must sound hypocritical in light of my previous actions; I won't insult your intelligence by offering any defence.

I took a deep breath before answering. 'You're right. I'm afraid Rick and I did sleep together. But—'

I never got the chance to reel off the explanation I'd prepared, as he hung up on me. Who can blame him?

We haven't spoken since then. Ruby, who's not back at school until tomorrow, is with him today. Hence I can sit here at the kitchen table writing this at lunchtime. He didn't come to the door this morning. He pulled his car on to the drive and honked his horn to announce his arrival, not acknowledging me at all. I suspect he'll do much the same when he brings her home.

As for Rick, I don't have a clue what's going on there. I don't think I ever told you what happened with him on Sunday: the morning after the night before. He was weird, like a different person. He was already fully dressed when he came downstairs, shoes and all. I was sitting at the kitchen table watching the girls have breakfast.

I smiled. 'Morning. Did you sleep well?'

'Fine, thank you.'

'I've explained to the girls that you drank a glass too much wine to drive safely last night, because drink-driving is very dangerous.'

He ran his right hand across the dark stubble on his cheeks. 'Right.'

'Sit down, Daddy,' Anna said in between mouthfuls of cereal. 'Have some breakfast with us.'

'Yes, please do,' I said. 'Let me get you a cup of coffee. Toast? Cereal?'

He looked as awkward as hell standing there, finding things to do with his hands, eyes everywhere apart from in my direction. 'I'm okay, thanks. We need to get going, Anna. Daddy has things to do.'

'What things?' she asked. 'Can't I stay and play a bit longer?'

'No, love. Finish your breakfast and I'll get your stuff together. Is everything in Ruby's room?'

Anna nodded.

'Maria, is it all right if I go and—'

'Of course.'

He disappeared back upstairs, leaving me puzzled. Where was the man I'd spent a lovely evening with yesterday? I'd never seen him like this before, even when Ruby had fallen down the stairs. He'd been useless then, but not cold.

I followed him to Ruby's room.

'What's up?' I asked, finding him kneeling on the floor, rolling Anna's sleeping bag.

'Nothing,' he replied without turning to look at me. 'I have some work stuff to do.'

I stared at the closely cropped hair on the back of his head, remembering the way it had made me shiver when it had brushed across my naked body hours earlier. 'On a Sunday?'

'Yes.'

311

'Is this about what happened between us last night?'

'No. I . . . never mind.'

'What?'

He sighed. 'I wish you hadn't said what you did to Anna about me drinking too much.'

'What was I supposed to say? The truth? It's not like I told her you were drunk.'

'She's my daughter. I would have preferred to handle it myself.'

He continued stuffing Anna's things into her bag.

So where did this leave us? I was tempted to ask if he'd lost interest after getting what he wanted; if the sex had been that bad for him, although it definitely hadn't seemed that way. Instead, I slipped back down to the kitchen and pretended nothing was wrong.

The only hugs and kisses as we said goodbye were between the girls. I suppose that would have been the case regardless, considering the fact they were watching, so I didn't dwell on it.

I told myself Rick was tired and embarrassed. I thought he'd contact me later on and it would all be fine. However, it's three days now and I've not had so much as a text message from him. I thought he'd at least ask after my parents following the accident, but not a peep. I've not contacted him either. He was the one being offhand.

Anyhow, I'm dealing with it much better than expected. I should be feeling used; worrying about my sexual performance and other things I might have done wrong.

I'm not.

The old me would have been going crazy now. Especially with Ruby out of the house. But that's not the case. I know I told you the OCD isn't good today, but the important thing is that I haven't given in to it. I'm still in control, and that's what I'll be reporting to Rosie later on. I'll be focusing on the positive, like she encourages me to do.

The intrusive thoughts that come with OCD aren't unusual. Most people have them, according to Rosie, but aren't troubled by them. For me, there's that overwhelming desire to act; to address a perceived level of threat. Every time I resist and do nothing, that's a win.

When I see Rosie now, which is less and less often, it's mainly to report on my progress. I'm essentially fighting a duel with myself, but she's always there to arm me with new tools. Last time she mentioned learning some relaxation techniques; fingers crossed that will be on the agenda today.

As for Dan and Rick, hopefully I'll have more to tell you when I next write. I can't believe it's all so up in the air. I've got myself into a mess, haven't I? As I've been penning this letter, one thing has become clear: my relationship with Dan is by far the most important to me. That's what I need to fix.

I think having sex with Rick was something I needed to get out of my system. It was great, don't

313

get me wrong. But for all the animalistic passion, there was none of the honesty and intimacy of what I used to have with Dan. That develops over years of being together. I didn't know it was something I missed until now. My mind's been clouded for so long: first with my grief over losing you and then with my OCD. Finally I'm starting to see things clearly.

Rick still doesn't know about you, Sam. Not unless he's heard it from someone else. I haven't found the right moment to tell him. Even if I do, he'll never understand. Not like your father does.

So what are my chances of getting Dan to understand all of this? I'll have to give him time to cool off first. Then we'll see. Days ago he was trying to convince me to give it another go, but that was before I slept with Rick. Still, I don't regret telling him the truth; I couldn't have lived with myself otherwise.

That's all for now, Sam. I need to get myself ready to see Rosie. I'll write again soon.

Love as always,

M

Xx

CHAPTER 28

BEFORE

Thursday, 31 December 2015

'How's it going?'

'Not too bad. You?'

'Nearly there. A couple more pages to tie up. Then I'm out of here.'

Dan nodded. 'Me too.'

He wondered how much small talk it would take before Maurice got to the point, the real reason he was standing next to his desk, which they both knew was to crash a fag.

That was the lot, as it turned out.

'You don't by any chance, um, fancy popping out for a smoke, do you?'

'Have you got baccy?' Dan replied, barely keeping a straight face. It was fun to make his friend squirm.

Maurice shrugged, looking down at his feet. 'I haven't.

I'm a nightmare, aren't I? I bet your heart sinks every time you see me walking over. If I could just bum one more off you today, I'll buy you a pack next week, I promise. I'll even buy you a pint after work, if you like.'

'Go on then,' Dan said, standing up and pulling his jacket from the seatback. 'Seeing as it's you.'

There weren't many people who'd be able to get away with it like Maurice did. But he'd been a good friend to Dan in tough times, and he was always great company, so he'd earned special treatment. Besides, based on past experience, he would eventually buy Dan a pack. It might not be next week, but it would happen.

'Are you going to take me up on that drink, then?' Maurice asked once they got outside. 'It is New Year's Eve after all.'

'Yeah, I could probably fit a quick one in. What are your plans for tonight? Partying with one of your lady friends, are you?'

'Oh, we'll see. I'm weighing up a couple of options. I'm not a big fan of New Year's Eve.'

'Why?'

'Always a let-down. Everyone builds it up and then there's that awkward countdown to midnight. Once all the kissing and bad renditions of "Auld Lang Syne" are out of the way, what's left?'

'Nice weather for it,' Dan said with a shiver, huddling into his jacket in a bid to fend off the cold.

'What are you up to?'

'Not much. Maria and I are staying in. We don't feel like celebrating. We had to make an effort at Christmas, for Ruby's sake, but tonight is mainly for adults, right?'

Dan took a long drag on his cigarette before adding: 'Annual events, even the smaller ones like Bonfire Night, reopen the wound. Remind us of what happened; who's missing. Not that we ever forget. These times just accentuate the pain. Sorry, mate. I don't mean to be morbid.'

Maurice placed a hand on Dan's shoulder and gave it a firm squeeze. 'Don't be ridiculous. You know I'm here any time for you. What you guys have been through: there are no words. How are Maria and Ruby?'

'Ruby's probably managing the best out of all of us. At least on the surface. I thought she might get into trouble at school, that kind of thing, but there's been no sign of it so far. She hardly mentions Sam, which doesn't seem healthy to me, and yet I don't feel like I should be forcing our conversations that way either.'

Maurice nodded. 'How old is she now? Seven, isn't it?'

'That's right.'

'Poor thing. No one should have to go through that so young.'

'I know. I do worry that it'll come out when she's older. That she'll always be messed up by it on some level. I've done my best to make sure she doesn't blame herself. You know, in some kind of warped way.'

'And Maria? How's she coping?'

'Not well. It's hard to explain, because I don't really know what's going on with her. She's closed herself off, insisting on handling it alone. She's not interested in counselling or anything like that.'

'Tricky.'

'You're telling me.' Dan bent down and stubbed out his smoke under his shoe.

An hour or so later, Dan turned off his computer and, together with Maurice, headed back outside to his car. They were among the last to leave. Dan had half expected to receive a phone call reporting a breaking news story that couldn't be ignored, but thankfully it didn't happen and he was free to go.

'Red Lion?' he said with a straight face as Maurice peeled off towards his own car: an ancient green Volvo that he dubbed the Tank.'

'Yeah, right. You know you wouldn't catch me dead in that miserable excuse for a pub. White Horse?'

'Sure. I'll see you there.'

They met at the bar of the pub – a traditional but popular spot, small enough to always look busy – after both parking nearby.

Maurice was ordering their drinks when a burly bald chap walked up and thumped him on the shoulder. 'All right, Shanksy,' he boomed. 'Long time no see.'

'Who was that?' Dan asked him a few minutes later when they headed outside to the beer garden to huddle under one of the heaters.

'A guy I was at school with. I never liked him, to be honest, which was why I cut it short and suggested we came out here.'

'Really? You did a good job of hiding that. I thought he must have been an old friend.'

'No point being rude, is there? I haven't seen him for years.'

318

'What's with the name? Shanksy he called you, wasn't it?'

Maurice chuckled. 'That was my nickname once upon a time. Not one I miss.'

'Go on. You have to tell me why now.'

'Only if you promise never to use it or to tell anyone else.'

'Scout's honour.'

'Fine,' he replied, grinning. 'Bit of a funny story. There was a time at secondary school when I, um, got caught short. I'd had a bout of diarrhoea and didn't quite make it to the loo in time. I ran there in a panic and, for some ridiculous reason, decided the best thing to do was to stick my soiled underpants in the cistern and go commando. I don't recall how the story got out. I must have told someone who then blabbed. Anyway, I never lived it down. Shanksy came from Armitage Shanks, the toilet manufacturer; unfortunately it stuck.'

Dan laughed. 'No way. That's hilarious. But why would you—'

'No idea. Totally weird, I know. I wanted rid of them and that was the nearest option.'

A little later, puffing on another borrowed cigarette, Maurice asked how Dan was coping with the situation at home.

'I'm all right. As well as can be expected.'

Maurice lowered his voice. 'Are you still seeing, um—'

'The shrink? No, not for the moment. He did help, though.'

Maurice was the only person Dan had told about seeing a therapist. He wasn't as comfortable about the fact as he made out. He'd had six sessions, mainly to help deal with the depression he'd been feeling, and they really had helped. But it wasn't something he liked thinking about. It had occurred to him that maybe part of the reason he'd felt better was because he didn't want to be in therapy any longer. Who could say?

'Well, if you ever need anyone to talk to informally, don't hesitate. I'm happy to listen any time.'

'Thanks. I'll pay you in fags, shall I?'

Maurice laughed.

'Seriously, though,' Dan added. 'It's New Year's Eve. Let's talk about something else, like the couple of options you're weighing up for tonight? Come on, Shanksy.'

'Do not use that name, mate. Seriously. You promised.'

'Fine. But throw a bone to a sex-starved married guy. I need to get my thrills somehow.'

'A gentleman never tells.'

Dan grinned. 'I never had you down as one.'

'I'll tell you who isn't a gentleman: my daughter Sasha's new boyfriend, Oli. He's a cocky little shit. I actually walked in on them having sex the other day.'

'You did not.'

'Seriously. Can you imagine?'

Dan winced. 'How much did you see?'

'They were under the covers, thank goodness. I got back in from work early and heard music coming from her room. She wasn't even supposed to be at my place that day. She should have been at her mum's. I probably ought to have knocked, but I had no idea. She's only just turned eighteen.'

'What did you do?'

'Screamed in sync with Sasha and ran out of there. She came to see me after a few minutes, as mortified as I was and full of apologies, but when he eventually emerged, he was grinning like an idiot. Didn't even mention it, like he couldn't care less. Then he had the cheek to put his feet up on the couch, shoes and all. I don't know what she sees in him. He's obviously a player, only after one thing, but she fawns over him. I can't wait for him to move on, although of course I'd never tell that to Sasha. Honestly, I wouldn't wish a teenage daughter on anyone.'

Maurice saw Dan's face fall and instantly knew what he'd said. 'Oh, mate. I didn't think. I'm so sorry.'

'It's fine,' Dan replied after a pause. 'You shouldn't have to tiptoe around me.'

'No, but seriously. I take that back. I apologise.'

'Apology accepted. I know you didn't mean it.'

It did leave a sour taste in Dan's mouth, all the same. A reminder of what – who – was missing from his and his family's lives was all it took to cast his mind into a dark place. He felt a powerful urge to stay out and drink whatever it took to numb the pain; to forget his troubles for a few hours. At home, no matter how much you drank, there were reminders of Sam around every corner. He dragged himself back there nonetheless.

At least one person was glad to see him when he walked through the front door.

'Daddy,' Ruby shouted, jumping up into his arms. 'You're home.'

'Hello, gorgeous,' Dan beamed, troubles forgotten for a moment in his little girl's toasty embrace. 'What have I done to deserve this lovely welcome?'

Ruby shrugged as he plonked her down on the ground. 'Why are you so cold?'

'Because it's freezing outside,' he said, placing a hand on her hot forehead and making her squeal.

'Daddy! That's mean.'

At least she hadn't told him that he smelled disgusting. That was why he kept mints and a spray deodorant in the car, to cover up the cigarette smell. No need to impose his dirty habit on her.

Dan's parents, Bill and Margaret, had both smoked when he was growing up. He remembered hating the way they smelled afterwards and how he would refuse their hugs and kisses until it had gone away. They'd done it in front of him in the house, of course. That was the way in those days.

How quickly he'd moved from being an arch opponent of cigarettes to a young smoker. His first one had been swiped from his parents. He'd been thirteen and egged on by a school friend, and soon afterwards he was smoking daily, loving the buzz it gave him and the small sense of rebellion he felt every time he lit up.

Dan really hoped that Ruby wouldn't follow in his footsteps. To his knowledge, Sam never had, but he'd quit when she was only seven, soon after Ruby's birth, so at least he'd not been setting a bad example after that. He thought he'd kicked the habit once and for all, until his world collapsed and he ran back to his old crutch. Now he couldn't see himself packing it in again. He said all the right things to Ruby, about it being a dirty habit and how he wished he'd never started. But he knew that if she wanted to smoke when she was older, she'd do it regardless. He was still smoking despite his father dying from a heart attack.

Dan's mum had quit some time ago. Once the Alzheimer's had started, he used to joke that she'd forgotten that she smoked. He wasn't making fun of her; it was just his way of dealing with it. But such comments made others uncomfortable, like they didn't know if it was acceptable to laugh or not.

He'd been to visit her after work on Christmas Eve. The home she was in was only a few miles away from the office, in a peaceful spot overlooking a golf course on the edge of the city. It seemed nice enough, despite all the horror stories he'd heard about such places. He did feel bad about the fact she was in there, but what else was he supposed to do? She needed specialist care around the clock and didn't even know who he was half the time.

Making the decision to move her there had been a hard one, especially since he had no other siblings to talk it through with; no one else to share the burden. Maria had been very supportive, but she wasn't a blood relation. She hadn't been brought up by her. The Alzheimer's had been in its infancy when Dan's dad was still alive, but there had been a rapid decline after he'd gone.

It made Dan sad to think that Ruby had never known his father and that her only memories of his mother would be like this: a husk of her old self, ravaged by dementia.

He wished she could have experienced what he had with his grandmother – Gangy, as he'd called her. She'd often looked after him as a child and they'd had great times together: making marmalade, jams and cakes; taking long walks along the river; listening to each other's stories.

At least Sam had known his parents properly. She'd been heartbroken when her grandad had died, and Dan liked to think that, in spite of her illness, his mum had always recognised Sam. Margaret loved children but had thought she couldn't have any, until Dan came along in her mid-thirties. His father was nine years older.

'Our little miracle,' they used to call him. He'd hated it as a child, but now it made him misty-eyed.

'Bill, there you are,' she'd said as he'd walked into her room on his latest visit.

She often mistook him for her late husband.

'It's Dan, Mum,' he replied. 'Your son.'

She nodded. 'Have you mowed the lawn?'

'No, Mum. It's winter. The grass doesn't grow at this time of year.'

'Really?'

'Yes, it's Christmas Eve. You've seen all the decorations, haven't you?'

'Of course, dear.'

Dan hated these conversations. It was awful seeing her so confused; so helpless. Where had his mother gone? She was still in there somewhere, wasn't she?

'Is Danny coming to visit?' she asked. 'I never see him any more.'

'It is me. It's Dan. I'm here now, Mum. Listen, they

324

told me you've not been eating much. It's important that you do to keep your strength up. You'll get turkey and all the trimmings tomorrow. You like that, don't you?'

She smiled at him, but her eyes were vacant.

'Where's Samantha?' she asked him later in the visit.

'Sam couldn't make it today,' Dan replied, 'but she sends her love.'

'She'll do all right, that one.'

Dan winced at the tragic irony of her words but did his best not to let it show. He had tried telling her about Sam's death on a couple of occasions, longing for the kind of comfort a mother can offer her son, but it never sank in. Eventually he decided it was kinder that she didn't know the truth.

He'd stayed for an hour or so at the home, which as usual was roasting hot and smelled of bleach. Then he'd wished his mum a happy Christmas, receiving a confused stare in return, and left feeling miserable and guilty.

He'd not visited again over the festive period, which only added to the sense of guilt. Mind you, it wasn't like she'd notice.

'How has your New Year's Eve been so far?' he asked Ruby as he removed his jacket and loosened his tie.

'Good.'

'You went to Amelia's for lunch, didn't you?'

She nodded.

'Was it fun?'

'Yep.'

'What did you get up to?'

'Playing and stuff.'

'Where's Mummy?'

'She's cross with me.'

'Why?'

'I don't know.'

'Come on. You must have some idea. Have you had an argument? Did she ask you to do something that you didn't do?'

Ruby shook her head.

'So what happened?'

She looked at the floor.

'Come on, love. What was it? It can't be that bad.'

She answered without looking up. 'Mummy's hidden all the photos of Sam.'

'What?' Dan looked around and his heart sank as he saw that it was true. They'd all gone. As far as he could see, there wasn't a single photo of Sam left on display. 'Why has she done that? Where are they?'

Ruby shrugged. 'I dunno. I told her it was mean. I said it meant she didn't love Sam. That's when she got mad.'

Dan's mind was racing, trying to work out what on earth had happened. Surely she hadn't destroyed them. Just the idea of this made his blood boil, but he fought to suppress his anger; to keep his cool. There was no way she'd do that. No way. 'Where is she now?'

'In Sam's bedroom. I tried to go and see her there, to say sorry, but she told me I had to stay out.'

'Right. I'll go and have a word with her.'

'Can you tell her I'm sorry? I didn't mean it.'

'Of course. Don't worry, love. It'll be fine. Would you like a drink?'

326

'Yes, please.'

After pouring Ruby some cordial, Dan took a deep breath and climbed the stairs. The door of Sam's bedroom was shut. He gave a gentle knock and pushed it open.

'Maria. What's going on?'

He spoke in a near whisper, not wanting to startle his wife nor make things worse. He may as well not have spoken at all, for she showed no sign of having heard him. She was sitting on the carpet, facing away from him; staring at the large wardrobe full of Sam's clothes. At her side, to Dan's considerable relief, was a cardboard box full of the missing framed photographs.

'Maria?' he said, kneeling at her side.

Still she gave no indication that she'd heard him. Her body was rigid. Her face, visible to him now for the first time, was devoid of expression, like she was in a trance.

'Are you okay, love?'

Nothing.

He held his right hand out in front of her face, ready to click his fingers, to snap her out of it. 'Ruby said you were cross with her. She told me about the photos. I don't know what—'

'Why can no one ever leave me the hell alone?' she said in a violent crescendo from growl to scream, meeting Dan's gaze with wild eyes. 'Of course I'm not bloody all right. My daughter's dead.'

Dan's heart was racing, but he held his ground, fighting to keep his voice calm and steady. 'She was my daughter too. And Ruby's sister. We're all hurting, Maria.'

'Get stuffed! You're never here. What do you know?'

327

'I can see you're upset, Maria, but this won't help. Whatever's happened, we can work through it.'

'Sometimes I want to burn this room to the ground,' she said. 'Did you know that? I imagine myself pouring petrol all over the place; dropping a match and watching it go up in flames.'

Dan was shocked by his wife's words, but he'd seen her angry like this several times since Sam's death. He knew she could lose her temper, spout fury and vitriol, only to be calm again an hour later. As for the best way to deal with her now, he had no clue. He wished he'd never come into the bedroom in the first place. And yet here he was, staring into the eye of the storm. He wondered about backing away and leaving her to it, but she didn't give him a chance.

'I have to get out of here,' she said, snapping to her feet and racing to the door. 'I hate this bloody place.'

'What are you talking about, Maria?' Dan called after her. 'Where are you going? It's New Year's Eve.'

'Don't you dare touch that box of photos!' she shouted back. 'Just leave it alone.'

He followed her downstairs, nearly slipping in his haste. Maria already had a coat on and was scrabbling around the kitchen, looking for something. Silently signalling to Ruby that everything was all right, he asked Maria again what she was doing.

'Where the hell are they?' she yelled in reply.

'I don't know what you're talking about, Maria. Will you please calm down?'

'My keys. Where have you put them?'

'What? I haven't even seen them.'

She charged into the hall, muttering something unpleasant under her breath, and the next thing Dan knew, she'd gone out of the front door. Just as he was thinking to himself that it was good she hadn't found her keys, he heard the sound of a car starting. Out of the window he saw her reversing his Focus off the drive. She was away down the road by the time he got outside to try to stop her.

'Oh, come on!' he shouted. 'Really?' Kicking out with one socked foot, he stubbed his toe on a terracotta plant plot and yelped in pain.

'What's wrong, Daddy?' Ruby's anxious face asked from inside the open front door.

'I banged my toe.'

'Where's Mummy gone?'

'She had to pop to the supermarket. She won't be long.'

Hoping for his words to come true, Dan hobbled to his daughter, placed an arm around her and led her back inside. 'Come on, love. Let's sort you out some tea. What do you fancy?'

'Pizza?'

'That sounds like a good idea. I think we might have some in the freezer, but if not, we could always order a takeaway.'

'What about Mummy?'

'Sorry?'

'Can't she get some from the supermarket?'

'Oh right. I see what you mean. No, let's get takeaway. It tastes better, doesn't it? I'll order enough for all three of us and then Mummy can have some too when she gets back.'

'She's still cross with me, isn't she? Does this mean I'm never allowed in Sam's room again?'

'Oh, Ruby. Of course not. You can go in your sister's room any time you like. It's as much your space as it is any of ours; if it helps you feel closer to her, then all the better. None of this is your fault. Mummy's just feeling extra sad today about Sam, that's all. I'm sure she had a good reason for moving the photos and she'll explain it to us later. In the meantime, they're all safe and sound. She's put them in a box. We'll just leave them there for now, okay?'

'Okay.'

Dan could see tears forming in the corners of his daughter's eyes and he pulled her into a hug to comfort her.

'I didn't mean what I said to Mummy. I know she loved Sam.'

'Please don't worry about it, darling. She didn't mean what she said to you either. I promise.'

Dan sighed to himself. He couldn't bear it when Maria got like she was today, especially when it impacted on Ruby. He could understand his wife having bad days. He had plenty of those too, albeit in a more subtle way. He also understood that grief affected everyone differently. But she was like another person altogether on these occasions: manic, ferocious, irrational. It was horrifying to behold – and so different from how she once was. Maria used to criticise people who spoke out in anger, unable to control their temper. To do so now would be hypocritical.

Part of him was glad she'd gone. He'd rather she didn't return until she'd had a chance to calm down, but he knew she shouldn't be driving anywhere in that state. She was literally a road accident waiting to happen.

He wouldn't rest until she got back.

CHAPTER 29

'Hello?'

No answer. Sitting in the Land Rover, I pull the mobile phone away from my ear and confirm that the call has connected.

'Is anybody there? Sam?'

I hear what sounds like a gasp on the other end of the line.

'Hello? If you can hear me, please say something.'

Still nothing. I'm not sure what to do.

It occurs to me that it could be Miles. Maybe he's watching me from inside the house. Or even closer. The thought panics me and I find myself scouring the rear-view mirror. I look all around, searching for some sign of him. But what about the name displayed on the screen: Sam. Did I imagine it? Was it some kind of mental projection from the flashback? I look again at the screen and it's still there. I'm on an active call with Sam.

Mind you, that doesn't mean much. Miles could be

playing with my mind. If that is my daughter's name, I could have told him so before my accident. It would be easy enough for him to program any number he liked into this mobile and save it under her name. He told me that he didn't have a mobile, but if it's not his, whose is it? I don't know what to believe any more.

'Listen,' I say. 'I want to speak to you. I really do. But if you're not going to say anything, I'm going to have to hang up.'

'Wait,' the reply comes at last. A tiny voice. Female. Sounds a long way off.

'Okay, I hear you. I'm listening.'

'Who is this?' she asks.

'Sorry? I'm, er . . . Who were you calling?'

'My father. I was calling my father. I've been trying to get hold of him for a while.'

Her words set my heart racing. Could she really be talking about me? I want to believe so, but I daren't get ahead of myself. I remember Miles mentioning his daughter once or twice. Could this be her? What did he say her name was? I'm sure it wasn't Sam. Or was it? Why can't I remember anything? Why am I so bloody useless?

I'm looking forward through the windscreen and, all of a sudden, an image flashes in front of me – a spider's web. Just for a second. Startles me. Then it's gone.

'Hello? Are you still there?'

I shake my head. Rub my eyes with one hand. 'Yes, I'm still here. I was thinking, that's all.'

'What were you thinking?'

'Wait. I haven't even told you my name yet.'

333

'What if I already know your name, but it's not what you think it is? That leaves me in a fix. If I tell you, you'll think I don't know, because it's not the name you expect.'

'Why don't we start with your name, then?' I suggest. 'Is it Sam? I think it is, because I heard you gasp when I said it for the first time. Like you didn't expect me to know that.'

'Where did you get the name from?'

'It's displayed on the phone.'

She laughs. It's unexpected but warm and genuine. 'Oh, right. How funny. I love it when things are that simple.'

I scratch the back of my head nervously. 'So, Sam. Why are you calling me?'

I want to ask her if she's my daughter, but I don't dare. Not yet.

'Damn. I'm going to have to go,' she replies.

'What?' Panic grips me. This could be the key. I could finally be speaking to someone who knows me – knows who I was before my accident. I can't let her slip away.

'Keep hold of the phone, but don't let him see it. I'll contact you again soon.'

'Miles, you mean? Don't let him see it? Why not?'

But the phone's gone dead. Totally dead. There's no display at all on the screen any more, as if it's run out of battery.

'Shit,' I say, pressing the power switch and every other button I can find, but it makes no difference. Then I glance in the rear-view mirror and my heart sinks as I see Miles walking towards the car. I shove the phone into the pocket of my jeans and wonder what the hell to do next.

Part of me remains tempted to drive off. Miles is still a little distance away and I could probably make it. Probably. But I'm not confident enough in my ability behind the wheel. What if the muscle memory I'm relying on doesn't kick in? I need to find a reason to explain the fact that I'm in the driving seat with the key in the ignition. Well, that last bit is easily solved: I remove the key and throw it back in the glovebox. Now I have to think of something to tell him about why I'm sitting in his car.

I rack my brains for something – anything – and then it comes to me. I reach for the pocket of the passenger seatback, hoping and praying. My hand finds what it's looking for not a moment too soon, pulling it out as Miles's shadow announces his arrival at the side of the Land Rover.

I turn to face him and meet his puzzled look with a grin.

'Hi there,' I say, opening the door and climbing out of the ever mud-caked car. 'Damn. You caught me. I was about to drive off.'

'Sorry?'

'Only joking. I was looking for this,' I say, holding the portable radio aloft. 'I've been searching for it everywhere. Then it occurred to me that I might have left it here last time we went to the village.'

'Oh?'

'Yeah. I had it in my pocket. It must have fallen out.'

'Right. I see. How's the stomach? I thought you were—'

'Well, it all came out in one big gush. I feel better now, but ask me again in half an hour.'

Miles winces. Nobody likes to hear the details of someone else's diarrhoea. Not even a doctor.

'So what's the plan for today?' I ask.

'Um, I left you a note in the house. I thought you were upstairs. I need to head out for some supplies.'

'To the village?'

'No, the supermarket. Food stocks are getting low. You can come if you like.'

'Sure. I can do, if you need my help, although I would rather stay in the vicinity of a toilet for the time being. I wouldn't want to be caught short.'

'Fair enough. You stay here then, lad.'

'Stuff it. I'm being a wimp. I'll come. Let me grab my jacket.'

'No, no. That's not necessary. Better to err on the side of caution, especially if it was that crab we had.'

'Whatever you think is best. You're the doctor. I can get on with some stuff here in the meantime. Floorboards maybe?'

'Only if you're up to it.'

'Of course I am. I need to earn my keep.'

I enter the house a few minutes later, having waved Miles off. So what now? Things might not have turned out as planned, with him going off in the car and me being the one left behind. But it's not all bad. I have time to myself to find some answers; to better understand what's going on.

I pull the mobile phone out of my trouser pocket and have another look at it. It still doesn't appear to have any power. Is the battery dead? How many bars was it showing

336

when I was talking on it? I wish I'd paid attention. It certainly seems dead. I've pressed and held every button on the damn thing and nothing has made the slightest difference. It must be the battery. But how the hell do I charge it without a power cable?

'Great,' I say to my reflection in the small grey screen. 'How's Sam going to call me back now?'

'Sam,' I say, liking the way the name sounds. 'Sam, Sam, Sam. Who are you, Sam? Are you my daughter?'

And yet, if I did have a daughter, why would I have come here alone and not spoken of her? Am I the kind of person who abandons his family? I had a daughter called Sam in the flashback, right? Yes, I'm sure I did. But wait. She wasn't the only one. When I think about it, there were two daughters and a wife: I had a family. I'm certain of it. But what were the names of the other two? And which daughter was I with during that other memory I had, when we were trick-or-treating together? I don't have the answers. I trawl my mind, but nothing appears. As every moment passes, my recollection of this latest precious memory fades. It makes me angry. I mean, seriously, how can I not know these things? How could I not have mentioned them to Miles?

The more I think about it, the more all of this comes back to him. He has to have been lying to me. About how much, though? I consider what Sam said before hanging up. She told me not to let him see the phone. She had to have been talking about Miles. It was right at the moment he turned up. Maybe because she saw him coming, meaning . . .

I rush back outside, the biting wind seizing another opportunity to ridicule my lack of a coat.

'Hello?' I shout as loud as I can, my voice carrying over the cliff and echoing down into the sea below. 'Sam? Can you hear me?'

I say the same handful of words over and over, long pauses in between, but there's no reply. Eventually, I carry on regardless. 'Listen, Sam. I know you're here somewhere. If you want to speak to me, you're going to have to come out and show yourself. The phone's dead. I don't have a charger. Sam? I need to speak to you. I don't know what's going on; what he's doing to me. I want to remember, but I need your help. Sam, please. I know you're here. You have to be. How else did you know he was coming? You planted the phone too, right? You wanted me to find it. Sam? Sam?'

I'm out of breath. The cold's not helping and I'm nervous too. I feel like I'm on the verge of a breakthrough, but now she's not answering. Or maybe she's not here at all and I got it wrong.

I wait a little longer, walking up and down in front of the house, partly to keep warm and partly to see if I can see something. But it's just me and the elements, with the sea playing percussion in the background.

I decide to head back inside the house, but first I walk to the edge of the cliff. I peer over at the waves beating against the rocks far below; spitting their froth. My eyes are drawn to the bottom.

Down.

Down.

Down.

I imagine myself climbing over the pathetic fence, or kicking it away, and stepping out into oblivion.

Then I blink and wonder what the hell I'm doing. I take myself back to the house, trying to ignore the fact that my legs are shaking.

As soon as I'm inside, I head up the bare staircase and along the hollow shell of the landing. I know exactly where not to step these days, barely noticing what a dilapidated mess it looks; even the mildew smell has grown familiar.

I open the door to civilisation, entering the small corridor that houses my bedroom. But that's not where I'm heading. I stop in front of the door that leads to Miles's bedroom, but this time – bold in his absence – I don't hesitate. I grab the door handle, turn it and . . . it's locked.

Dammit. I look down and notice for the first time the keyhole under the handle. How have I not spotted that before?

I try the handle again to be sure it's locked and not just stiff, but there's no doubt. So what now? I've no idea how to pick a lock and not a clue where Miles might keep the key. If I had to guess, I'd say he has it with him, meaning I'm stuffed. I could kick it down, of course, but how would I explain that when he gets back? Especially if I don't find anything.

I'm desperate to get inside. The fact that it's locked adds to my conviction that there's something he doesn't want me to see. So how do I get a look without him knowing about it?

The answer comes to me all of a sudden and I race

outside. Heart skipping, I dart around the house. The aluminium ladder is in the usual place. We used it the other day to check the guttering. My job was to steady the bottom. Miles didn't think I was ready to climb a ladder again yet. Well, stuff that. How do I even know if the story of my accident is true? Maybe it was him who knocked me unconscious.

The ladder's lightweight for its size, so I carry it to the front of the house without too much effort. Extending it alone proves trickier, especially as the odd gust of wind blows in, threatening to knock me off balance. But eventually I manage to get it high enough and in the right position to lean it against the wall by Miles's bedroom window. I put my weight on the bottom rung and jiggle up and down a few times to sink the feet into the grass. That should keep it nice and steady, I think. Then I go ahead and start climbing, not leaving myself any opportunity for second thoughts.

I'm halfway up when I feel something vibrating against my leg. I stop, not sure what it is, until I hear the ringing noise too and remember the mobile phone.

Keeping my left hand gripped on a rung, I squeeze my right into the pocket of my jeans. Or at least I try to, but it's numb from the cold and pulling out the phone takes forever. When I eventually manage, I see the screen is working again and Sam's name is displayed on the caller ID. I try to press the green button to answer, but my stiff thumb slips and the mobile tumbles on to the grass below.

'Bollocks,' I cry out, climbing back down to retrieve it, only to find the battery has been knocked out in the fall.

As I'm fumbling to put the pieces back together, I hear what sounds like a car approaching in the distance. I freeze.

Surely it can't be Miles back already, can it?

Who else would drive all this way up the dirt track?

How do I explain this?

Wait. Maybe there's time to move the ladder before he arrives.

I stick the phone back in my pocket, place one hand on either side of the ladder and swing the top out towards me. That goes well. It's standing vertical, but the feet are still wedged in the soft earth under the grass and I have to try to shake them free.

At that moment another gust of wind comes in from the sea and catches me unawares. The ladder slips out of my hands and back towards the house, the top crashing into the window of Miles's bedroom and – to my horror – smashing the glass.

Then the mobile starts ringing again.

CHAPTER 30

Thursday, 27 April 2017

Dear Sam,

So that's the Easter holidays done. It was Ruby's first day back at school today. I thought I'd be glad to have some more time to myself, but as soon as I returned from dropping her off this morning, the place felt so empty. I wished she was still here with me.

It's funny, Sam. I often wonder how I ever used to fit in working full-time. To an outsider it probably looks like I have nothing to do all day, but you'd be surprised how quickly the time passes. I drop Ruby off at school at about 8.45 a.m. and I have to be back to pick her up for 3 p.m. When you factor in the driving, that's barely six hours I have to myself. Cleaning, shopping and household admin takes up a good chunk of that, believe me.

I am finding I have more spare moments than I used to now that I'm getting the OCD under control. It's stolen so much time from me over the past couple of years. I remember staring at the freezer door for hours one day. I was convinced it wasn't shutting properly and all the food inside was at risk of perishing. So I kept pressing it shut as hard as I could and then staring at the seal for a while before eventually pulling on it, with varying amounts of strength, to see how easily it would open again. God knows how many times I repeated that process. It was all down to the fact that I'd found a small patch of water on the floor, which was probably from a dropped ice cube. I only managed to tear myself away in the end because I had to pick Ruby up from school.

Anyway, there was a shock development on the Rick front today. I still hadn't heard from him since he slept over. Not so much as a text. Okay, I hadn't made any attempt to contact him either, but he was the one who'd been out of order. I'd been expecting him to offer some kind of apology for his behaviour that morning, but as the days passed, it became increasingly apparent that that wasn't going to happen.

I knew it was likely I'd see him again this morning and I was still weighing up how to react as I drove Ruby to school. One part of me wanted to give him a piece of my mind in the form of a blazing row (once the girls were out of the way and, preferably, not in front of the Queen Bs or their minions). Another part of me preferred the idea of maintaining my dignity by playing it cool and making no reference at all to his behaviour or what had happened between us.

His white Mercedes – back from the repair shop at last and looking pristine – was parked in the usual place. But when Ruby and I reached the school gates, it wasn't him kissing Anna goodbye. It was a woman: a glamorous brunette, early thirties with big brown eyes.

Anna saw us and waved. 'Hi, Ruby,' she said with a grin. 'This is my mummy.'

'So you're Ruby,' her mother replied with a smile almost as perfect as Rick's. 'Anna's been talking about you non-stop. I hear you two are great friends already. And how's your arm? Still in plaster, I see.'

'Yes,' Ruby mumbled before whispering something to Anna that made them both giggle.

Anna's mother turned her smile on me, holding out a hand in greeting. 'And you must be Ruby's mum. Mary, isn't it?'

'Maria,' I replied, shaking her hand and noting the immaculate gel nails: fuchsia to match her lipstick. I also noticed that we were being watched by Horsey and WAG. You remember me telling you about them, right? The two Queen Bs who snubbed me in the early days. They were standing together further along the pavement, talking in hushed tones. No doubt they'd worked out what was going on here – or whatever version of the truth best suited their malicious tongues – and they were watching with glee. Something to gossip about later with the others.

'I'm Lisa. Lovely to meet you.'

'You too.'

As we waved goodbye to the girls, I couldn't avoid an envious look at Lisa's petite figure in a knee-length floral summer dress. In my head she'd been less attractive.

'Anna looks to be settling in well. I'm so glad. It's always a worry when you move house. It seems like a nice school. Has Ruby been here since reception?'

'Yes,' I said, wondering what Lisa was doing here and feeling the scrutiny of the Queen Bs' eyes still upon us. 'Is this your first visit?'

'To the school? No, we all dropped in a couple of months ago, before we enrolled Anna. They gave us the guided tour.'

I'd actually been referring to the area, rather than the school specifically, but I didn't say so. Her being here struck me as odd. Rick had never mentioned anything about a visit. And where was she staying? Surely not with them.

'Where are you parked?' she asked.

'Next to you. You're in Rick's car, right? I see it's back from being repaired.'

A flicker of a frown crossed her forehead, but then she was all smiles again. 'Yes, of course. He was with you and Ruby when he had the bump, wasn't he? Shall we walk together?'

'Sure,' I replied, only too glad to put some distance between us and the Queen Bs.

I wondered how much of the truth Rick had told Lisa about our relationship. She'd phoned him that time when Ruby and I were round at the house for a meal. But did she also know, for instance, that Rick and I had gone out for lunch, just the two of us? And the rest.

I decided he'd probably said as little as possible, especially since she was being so friendly.

'I'm under orders to be extra careful on the roads,' Lisa added, rolling her eyes. 'You know what boys are like. I sometimes think Rick loves his car and his gadgets more than me. Is your other half the same?'

It struck me as an odd comment for an ex to make, but I brushed over it, saying something about all men being that way. 'Lovely morning,' I added, keen to avoid talking about my domestic situation.

'Yes, beautiful.'

'So how long are you here for?'

'I'm heading back to Brighton tonight. Work tomorrow, unfortunately, but at least it's only for a day. Then a nice long weekend, thanks to Bank Holiday Monday. It's a nightmare doing the long-distance thing, especially with Anna. But hopefully it shouldn't be for much longer. Rick's been great about it, but I can tell it's starting to wear him down. The sooner we're all back living under one roof, the better.'

Yes, you read that right, Sam, although no one would blame you for questioning it, least of all me. I couldn't believe what I was hearing. I was flabbergasted and it took every ounce of composure in my body not to let on.

Thinking back, I'm not sure Rick ever specifically told me that he was separated from his wife, but he definitely guided me towards that belief. There was never any suggestion of them living apart temporarily because of her work. He tricked me into thinking he was single. I would never have got involved with him otherwise. I hope you believe that, Sam.

It makes sense now why he was always so keen to avoid talking about past relationships; why staying the night made him so awkward. I keep thinking I should have seen the signs – that I was a fool for not realising the truth – but what's the point in dwelling on it? I've been had. There's no escaping that fact. But, well, I can't pretend I didn't enjoy myself in the process. And now at least I can focus on what matters: fixing things with Dan, your father. Getting our family back on its feet.

That's not how I felt at the time, of course. I was fuming. As I say, I did my best to internalise all of this, but it didn't totally escape Lisa's attention.

'Everything all right?' she said.

I think she'd asked me something before that, although I've no idea what. My mind was all over the place, trying to process what she'd revealed.

'Um, sorry, yeah. I've not been feeling well,' I fudged, placing a hand on my belly. 'Bit of a stomach bug. It seems to come in waves.'

'You do look pale. Can I help? Do you want to put an arm around me or—'

'No, I think it's passed now, but thank you.'

'Don't mention it. It's nice to meet a friendly face at the school gates. Mums can be so bitchy when they get together, especially about people they don't know. Honestly, they were awful at Anna's old school. I can't be doing with all that nonsense. How is it here?'

I wondered if she'd noticed our audience at the school gates. They were out of sight now, thankfully. 'Um, there are mums like that here too.'

'Shame. Oh well, at least I have you to point me in the right direction. Maybe we could go for a coffee once I move here permanently.'

I did my best to smile. 'Sure.'

I know, I know. Not a good idea. But what was I meant to say, Sam? Lisa seemed so nice. I hadn't wanted to like her, but I did nonetheless. In different circumstances I even think we might have been friends. I'm not stupid, though. I know it can't happen. It'll be hard enough trying to manage Ruby and Anna's friendship.

'It's a lovely spot here, isn't it?' Lisa went on. 'Close enough to the city for shopping, work and so on, but with a nice small town vibe. And so much countryside on the doorstep. My friends in Brighton are a bit snobbish about us moving north; they have no idea.'

I did lots of smiling and nodding, which was all I could manage in the circumstances. My mind was elsewhere.

I did consider telling Lisa everything as we finished our conversation at the cars. You could argue she has a right to know. But I decided not to get involved.

348

I don't want to be a home wrecker and I definitely don't want for any of this to become public knowledge. Can you imagine the field day the Queen Bs would have with it?

I do plan to say something to Rick, but I haven't decided what yet, as I need time to think about it. Doing nothing isn't an option. He'd take that as a green light to go ahead and do the same again with someone else. I've met his type before. It's a shame I didn't identify him as such beforehand. I probably could have if I'd been looking hard enough, but he caught me off-guard – and he is bloody good-looking.

So that's the end of me and Rick. If I'm honest with myself, I think it's for the best.

Moving on, Grandma and Grandpa still seem to be doing well. I've not spoken to them again since my last letter, but we have exchanged a couple of texts and the rest of the trip is going according to plan. They fly back in a fortnight; I doubt I'll hear from them again until they get home. Mum told me to stop fussing in her last message.

As for Dan, he still hasn't spoken a word to me since I admitted to sleeping with Rick. When he dropped Ruby home yesterday, he stayed in the car again, driving off as soon as I answered the door.

'What's up with you and Dad?' Ruby asked.

'What do you mean?'

'He's mad at you, isn't he?'

'Is that what he said?'

'No, but he didn't get out of the car to talk to you like he normally does. And he looked cross whenever I mentioned you.'

'I see.'

'I guess you had another argument. Was it about me?'

'No, of course it wasn't about you. Why would you think that?'

'So you did have an argument, then. I knew it. Dad's never going to move back home, is he?'

There were tears in Ruby's eyes, which made me well up too. I bent forward to give her a hug, but she pulled back, refusing to meet my eye. Reaching into her bag, she took out an envelope and handed it to me. 'Here.'

'What's this?' I asked as she ran upstairs. 'Wait, Ruby. Where are you going?'

'To my room.'

Several thuds and a door slam later, I sat down in the lounge and stared at the envelope. My name was on the front in Dan's handwriting. After staring at it for a moment, wondering what it might contain, I opened the damn thing. Inside was a note in black biro on a single folded sheet of A4.

Maria,
I'll pick Ruby up at 7 p.m. on Friday and will drop her home at 6.30 p.m. the next day. Text me if there's a problem.
Dan

Not exactly friendly, is it? I'd assumed we'd have to speak to each other to make these arrangements – hoping for a chance to say something more – but Dan had found a way to avoid such contact. Even his instruction to text him if there was a problem was calculated to avoid actual conversation. Mind you, what did I expect? Clearly Dan was going to need some time to get past my revelation about Rick.

Part of me was relieved by his note. Before opening it, I'd imagined all sorts. I'd even prepared myself for a formal start to divorce proceedings, although on reflection I'm sure he'd never hand me such a document via Ruby.

And yet, the more I thought about it, the cold functionality of what he had written bothered me. A heartfelt outpouring about his hurt feelings or even a furious rant about how much he hated me would at least have given me something to work with. I had no idea how to respond to this, so I left it a while. But once Ruby was in bed, I decided to phone him. I had a feeling he wouldn't take the call if he knew it was me, so I blocked my number.

'Hello?' he answered after three or four rings.

'Dan. It's Maria. Please don't hang up. It's important.'

'What? Is Ruby all right?'

'She's fine. It's—'

'Listen, Maria, unless this is about Ruby, I've nothing to say to you. I thought that would be clear from my note.'

'I didn't mean to hurt you, Dan. I really—'

He hung up before I had a chance to finish. And every time I tried calling back after that, I got voicemail.

'Come on, Dan,' I said, leaving a message on the fourth attempt. 'Please talk to me. I have things I need to say to you. I can't bear this.'

It's ironic, isn't it? Dan's stuck with me through all my troubles, putting up with my bizarre behaviour; my rants and rages. He's always been the one determined to repair our relationship, even after I threw him out of his own house. He's been desperate to talk about 'us' for ages. Now that I'm finally on board and beating my OCD, he won't speak to me.

I knew he'd need time and space – anyone would – but I didn't expect him to shut me off like he has. I never saw this coming.

I've no one to blame but myself and I don't expect you to feel sorry for me, Sam. But I am in a bit of a fix here and I've no idea how to get out of it. I genuinely want to sit down with Dan and try to work things out. It must all look very fickle. Like I'm a person who only wants what she can't have. But honestly, Sam, it's more than that. I feel like I've had an epiphany and finally seen what's been staring me in the face all along.

I pray it's not too late.

Rosie went through some relaxation techniques with me in our last session, as promised. I think now would be a good time to try out the mindfulness CD she gave me. It should help me unwind and take a step back from my problems, rather than slipping into OCD. If I'm lucky, it might even guide me towards some solutions.

Love as always,

M

Xx

CHAPTER 31

BEFORE

Tuesday, 8 September 2015

'I'm heading home.'

Maurice's words and the hand he placed on Dan's shoulder snapped his mind into focus. Sitting on the bottom stair, he'd zoned out, glad to escape the reality of what was going on around him.

'Sorry, I was miles away. Thanks so much for coming. It's appreciated.'

'Of course.'

Maurice was one of a small group from the office who'd attended the funeral, including Jane and other members of Dan's direct team. Talking to his fellow editor reminded Dan of the ill-advised decision he'd made to return to work a few days after Sam's death. He'd hoped it might give him some focus – take his mind off the gaping wound that was everywhere he looked at home – but he'd not even lasted two hours.

He remembered Maurice more or less picking him off the floor last week, when he'd broken down after going outside for a cigarette.

'You shouldn't be back at work. It's too soon. You're not ready.'

'I'll be all right in a minute,' Dan replied, embarrassed; fighting back the tears. 'I don't know what came over me.'

'Come back inside the office. Let me get you a coffee or something.'

Dan shook his head. 'No. I can't go back in there. Not like this.' He looked at the main entrance and saw someone else coming outside – a woman he didn't recognise. She had a pack of cigarettes in her hand and was heading their way. 'Shit,' he said, turning and heading for the car park.

'Where are you going?' Maurice asked, following him.

'To my car.'

'I'm coming with you, then.'

They stayed in there, smoking and talking, for nearly an hour. It was the first time Dan had really spoken to anyone about how he was coping. It really helped. Maurice was a great listener. Eventually, he reiterated that it was too soon for Dan to be back at work.

'Go home,' he said. 'Be with your family.'

'I can't. I'll have to tell someone.'

'I'll square it away for you. No one expected you back this quickly. Are you all right to drive yourself home?'

Dan nodded, taking a deep breath and looking away from Maurice as he felt himself welling up again. Maybe his colleague was right. If the mere thought of someone being nice to him was enough to set him off, editing a newspaper probably wasn't a good idea.

Back in the present, Dan reflected that today was the first time he'd seen Maurice since then. Although only a matter of days ago, it felt like ages. By the same token, it seemed almost inconceivable that only eleven days had passed since Sam's death. Had he really spoken to her less than two weeks ago?

'Have the others from work already gone?' Dan asked.

Maurice nodded. 'I was just talking to your mother-in-law.'

'Lucky you.'

He smiled. 'She and your father-in-law are staying here, I believe.'

'Only for a few days.'

'And your mother?'

Dan had explained to Maurice about the Alzheimer's when they'd spoken in the car. He'd been unsure at that point whether or not to have her at the funeral.

Shaking his head, he explained: 'I had a long chat with them at the care home and we decided it was better she didn't come. It feels wrong, but she wouldn't have known what was going on. They said it was likely she'd have got confused by the change of surroundings and could have ended up causing a scene. I've already told her twice about Sam's death now, but it's not sinking in.'

'How are you holding up?'

Dan shrugged. 'I've been dreading today. Now I'm ready for it to be over.'

'What a lovely service. I know that's what everyone says after funerals, but I mean it. When the choir from her school performed, it was beautiful. And the eulogy you and Maria gave was so touching. How brave of you both to stand up there like that.'

A numb weariness had set in after the raw emotion of the service and the short family-only cremation that followed. Dan had glided through the wake as if in a dream and now, as it was finally drawing to a close and the numbers in his home were thinning out, he wanted to sleep. To disappear from reality for as long as possible.

'I've never properly thanked you for how you helped me at the office the other day,' he said. 'I was a mess and you were fantastic.'

'It was nothing. I'm a father too. I can only imagine the hell you're going through.'

'I meant to speak to you earlier; it's been crazy. Will you thank all the others from work for coming too? I'll do it myself when I get back, but I want them to know that it means a lot. So many sent cards as well. It's over-whelming.'

Maurice nodded. 'Of course. All the best. I'll see you when you get back.'

'You don't have a spare cigarette, do you? I've smoked all mine.'

'I have some baccy. I can roll you one.'

'I don't want to put you out.'

'It'll only take a minute.'

He whipped out a pack of papers and got to work before Dan could argue otherwise.

'Here you go,' he said, handing over the roll-up in no time. 'Enjoy.'

'Cheers. Do you mind if I keep it until later? I ought to say a few more goodbyes.'

'Of course.'

After seeing Maurice to the door, Dan stashed the roll-up in the front pocket of his shirt. He circulated among the remaining guests, thanking them for coming; hoping they would leave soon.

Maria, he noticed, was deep in conversation with Mrs Forester, the head teacher of Sam's high school. Thankfully things looked a lot calmer than last time. He was considering joining in until Helen, his mother-in-law, beat him to it. Instead he headed upstairs to check on Ruby.

Her bedroom door was shut to keep the noise out, but when he opened it – taking care to be as quiet as possible – he saw the light was still on and she was sitting up in bed reading.

'Hi, love,' he said. 'Can't sleep?'

She shook her head, her eyes red and puffy.

'How are you doing?'

Ruby shrugged, not meeting his gaze.

'Fancy a hug?' he asked, sitting down next to her on the bed.

She nodded, throwing both arms around his middle and pressing her head sideways into his chest. Dan returned the embrace and, without further words, they stayed like

358

that, comforting each other, for some time. He felt like he ought to say something wise to help her make sense of what had happened, but he had nothing. There was no making sense of it. Sam's death was a horrendous waste of a young life. A life he should have been there to save. How the hell had he not seen warning signs?

'Daddy?' Ruby whispered. 'Do you believe in Heaven?'

'Um,' Dan grunted, clearing his throat and feigning a coughing fit in order to buy himself some time. What to say now? He wasn't religious at all. He was a card-carrying atheist. But he and Maria, a lapsed Anglican, had agreed to let Sam and Ruby make their own minds up. It wasn't something they talked about much at home. And the last thing he wanted at that moment was to deprive his daughter of any comfort she might find in the prospect of her sister being in a better place.

The best he could come up with was to turn the question back on Ruby, asking her what she believed.

'Well, Grandma says there is. But she and Grandpa go to church and we don't. Does that mean Sam won't be allowed in?'

'No, I don't think that matters. If there is a better place after this, then I'm sure your sister will be there.'

'Does that mean we'll see her again one day?'

'That would be nice, wouldn't it?' Dan replied, part of him wishing that he did believe in an afterlife, so that he could take comfort in the prospect of an eventual reunion.

'She was in my dream last night.'

'Really? That's nice. What was she doing?'

'I don't remember much. Just normal stuff, I think. But

it was like she hadn't died. Then I woke up and realised it wasn't true, which made me cry.'

It broke Dan's heart to hear these words leave his daughter's mouth. He could feel himself starting to cry, but he refused to give in to the tears, determined to stay strong for her. He didn't feel strong. He felt weak and helpless, like his very essence had been shattered into a million little pieces. But he was still a father – and that meant being a rock for Ruby whenever she needed him. That meant holding things together no matter what.

'You should have said something, darling. Did you tell Mummy?'

She shook her head.

'Please do tell one of us next time, Ruby. You don't need to go through these things alone. We're both here for you any time you need us, day or night. Okay?'

'Okay, Daddy.'

'It's good to think about Sam, though. She'll always be in our memories and there are lots of happy ones to help us get through the sad times. Do you know what I was thinking about earlier?'

'What?'

'Out of nowhere it came to me that when Sam was little, before you were born, she used to call handbags ham bags.'

Ruby gave Dan a blank look.

'Like they were made out of ham,' he explained.

'Oh, right. I get it now. It sounded the same when you said it.'

'Exactly. They do sound very similar, which is why we

didn't notice she was saying it. Then one day she and I were doing some Christmas shopping and I bought a new leather handbag for Mummy. Sam looked at me, dead serious, and asked why it was still called a ham bag if it was made out of leather and not ham. I didn't laugh in front of her, because I knew she'd be embarrassed, but it made your mother and I giggle for a long time afterwards.'

Ruby smiled. 'When did you think about that?'

'As we arrived at the funeral. I'm not sure what reminded me of it, but it helped with the sadness for a few minutes.'

'You cried a lot at the funeral, Daddy. I've never seen you do that before.'

Dan hadn't seen Ruby's comment coming and struggled to gulp down the huge lump in his throat. He took a long, deep breath and replied in as calm a voice as he could manage: 'I miss her terribly, Ruby. I wish she was still here with us.'

'Me too.'

Later, after everyone had left and they'd broken the back of the cleaning up, Dan, Maria, Helen and Geoff all turned in for the night.

After an hour of tossing and turning in the dark, Dan peered over towards the shape of his wife on the other side of the bed.

'Are you still awake, love?' he whispered.

She sighed. 'Yes. All your wriggling about and fidgeting isn't helping.'

'Sorry.'

She turned to the middle of the bed, groaning as if it

required great physical effort, and the whites of her eyes shone at him. 'I feel so empty. Like I've cried out everything that matters and nothing's left.'

Dan reached his hand out to hers, so their palms were touching and the tips of their fingers intertwined. He exhaled deeply. 'I know.'

The two of them had hardly spoken all day. Of course they'd been at each other's side, at least until the wake, but few words had passed between them. What was there to say? Nothing that would make any difference. Nothing that would change what had happened and bring their daughter back.

'What now?' Maria asked.

'We carry on. We have to for Ruby's sake.'

'What if I don't feel like carrying on?'

'Do it anyway.'

'I kept looking for them at the funeral, you know.'

'Looking for who?'

'The ones who did this to her. I was scanning all the faces in the congregation, wondering if any of them had the gall to turn up.'

'You shouldn't do that to yourself, Maria.'

'Why not? They killed her.'

'You can't say that.'

'You're defending them?' Maria asked, pulling away and raising her voice.

'Shh. Keep it down or you'll wake everyone up. No, of course I'm not defending them. I'm sorry if that's how it sounded. It's been a long, hard day. Let's not turn on each other. That's the last thing we need.' He leaned over and planted a kiss on his wife's forehead. It hurt to feel her recoil at his touch, but he let it pass. 'I saw you and your mum talking to Mrs Forester earlier.'

'Yes.'

'What did she have to say?'

Maria ran a hand through her hair. 'Nothing she hasn't told us already.'

'The investigation?'

'Still ongoing, apparently. She'll let us know as soon as it's done.'

Dan thought back to the last time the three of them had met, in Mrs Forester's office at the school, a few days ago. Maria had lost it, veering from crying fits to shouting and screaming, although ultimately things had calmed down. The head teacher had seemed genuinely devastated. She'd said she was determined to get to the bottom of whether there was anything the school could have done differently to stop it; whether there were any warning signs they should have spotted. And yet Sam hadn't even been at school when it had happened. It had still been the summer holidays then, although they were back now, one pupil short.

It appeared that Sam had given no indication to her friends or teachers of there being a problem. While frustrating, Dan found this tough to dispute, since neither he nor Maria had spotted any warning signs either.

He resisted congratulating Maria on keeping her cool with Mrs Forester this time, knowing she'd take it the wrong way. 'It was nice of her to come,' he said instead.

'Nothing's going to happen to them, is it?' Maria added after a lengthy pause.

363

'You don't know that.'

'Even you don't think they're responsible.'

Dan picked his words carefully. 'I think they're just kids, like Sam was. Kids are impulsive. They do things without thinking about the consequences and sometimes they go terribly wrong. But that's not the same as—'

'How can you be so bloody rational? Our daughter's dead. Don't you care?'

'Are you seriously asking me that, Maria?' Dan hissed, unable to stop the fireworks exploding in his head. 'I found her. I had her lifeless body in my arms. I can't unsee what I saw that day. It's there every time I close my eyes. And I don't know why she did it. I just can't understand how things got to that point without us realising. How did we not know that our daughter was suicidal? How the hell could we not see it?'

Only when he stopped his rant did Dan notice the speed and heaviness of his breathing. It sounded deafening as he stared through the dark at the outline of his wife, willing her to reply – to give him an answer. But there was nothing apart from a quiet sob.

'It makes no sense,' he offered after a long moment, calmer now. 'I know you want someone to blame. I understand that, believe me, but I honestly don't think the answer lies with these kids. It's not enough. It doesn't add up. There must have been something more. Come on, Maria, you have to know what I'm saying. Do you truly believe she took her own life because of a few nasty comments?'

'I don't know,' Maria whispered eventually. 'I just don't know why she did it.'

'I keep telling myself that she didn't mean to,' Dan said. 'That it was a cry for help and if only I'd—'

'Don't.' To Dan's surprise, Maria took back his hand and squeezed it. 'We can't think like that.'

'But if she'd meant to go through with it, she'd have left a note, right? Then at least we'd have understood what was going through her mind. The not knowing is tearing me apart. She must have felt like that for some time. She must have been depressed, but I didn't have a clue. I thought she was just being a normal teenager. Did she ever seem depressed to you?'

Maria shook her head. 'I can't do this now, Dan. I have to sleep. We buried our daughter today. I've nothing left.'

'Okay, love,' Dan whispered in her ear, kissing her wet cheek. 'I understand.'

After retreating to his own side of the bed, Dan lay there in the dark, trying to keep still, for what seemed like ages. Maria settled into the slow, measured breathing of sleep, but as much as he would have liked to do the same, it evaded him. His mind wouldn't stop. He knew his wife's question about whether he cared had just been the grief talking, but it had still hurt. He was grieving too. And he'd bent over backwards to keep her happy, doing things the way she wanted.

He hadn't wanted a church service. He hadn't wanted a big do at all. The crematorium chapel would have been enough for him, but he'd gone along with her wishes. It had also been Maria's idea to hold the wake at the house, while his preference would have been to hire a room: somewhere easy to escape from. But again he'd given in and let her have her way. He knew how important it was to their relationship not to start falling out so early in the grieving process; he'd sacrificed his own beliefs and desires for what he'd believed to be the greater good. He was desperately trying to hold things together – to be the strong one for everyone else – but it was so damn hard.

Eventually, careful not to disturb Maria, he crept out of bed and put on his dressing gown.

The cigarette Maurice had rolled for him was where he'd left it, tucked away on the shelf above the coat rack. He let himself out of the back door, still in his dressing gown, and lit up. It was harsher than he was used to, but he relished every bitter gasp and the resulting head rush.

He was about halfway through when someone switched the downstairs lights on. He assumed it to be Maria. Then he saw his mother-in-law staring out of the window, brandishing a wooden spoon.

'What on earth?' she said after taking forever to open the window.

'Is there a problem, Helen?' he replied.

'I thought there was a burglar.'

'And you were going to use the wooden spoon to stop them, I suppose.'

'I grabbed the first thing I could lay my hands on. What are you doing out there in the middle of the night?'

'I'm having a cigarette.'

'Goodness me. You look ridiculous.'

'Thanks.'

'I thought you gave that dirty habit up years ago. Why on earth have you started again?'

'Because my daughter's dead.'

'Don't you think you ought to be with your wife right now, instead of out there?'

Dan almost told her to go to hell, but in the name of family relations, he employed the last piece of restraint he had left. 'Let's not do this now, Helen. Go back to bed. There's no burglar; nothing to worry about.'

She opened her mouth, as if about to retaliate, only to shake her head, close the window and disappear back into the house, turning the lights off behind her.

Dan finished what little was left of the cigarette. He stared wistfully at the moonlit sky as the toilet flushed upstairs. He waited a little longer, to make sure the coast was clear, before going back inside.

He shut himself in the study downstairs and turned on the computer. Then, for the umpteenth time, he found himself trawling through the various social media sites where Sam had accounts. Multiple images of his beautiful daughter slid across the screen, blurring into one another. They were joined already by fresh images and comments from the funeral. So many of them. But he couldn't bear to look at these yet and scrolled past, back to the older stuff he now knew only too well.

Dan and Maria had searched these websites together at the start, as a way to try to work out what had happened. Maria had found her answer in the few nasty messages they'd uncovered from so-called friends – girls Sam had known since primary school. But as he'd just explained, Dan didn't buy into them being the cause. Certainly not the sole cause. The messages they'd found were mean, sure, but nothing out of the ordinary for teenagers. Sam was a sensible girl, wasn't she? Surely she could see past a couple of girls making fun of the way she dressed. The comments about her smelling of body odour and the nickname they'd given her, Sweaty Sam, had been more offensive. These had made him feel angry. He could understand her being upset, but surely not enough to want to end it all. Dan had been called worse during his own school days.

It didn't make sense. If she was upset, why hadn't she talked to them about it? Why was she so damn closed? She'd told them all sorts as a young child; by the time she was a teenager, she always seemed to keep things to herself. There was no convincing her that a problem shared was a problem halved.

As for the nasty messages, it wasn't like there'd been a catalogue of them. They'd only found a handful. If they hadn't been so recent, no one would have thought anything of them. But they were enough to convince Maria that Sam had been the victim of bullying. Her theory, expounded to Mrs Forester and anyone else who'd listen, was that it must have started before the holidays and continued online over the summer. She believed Sam had been dreading the start of term and became desperate for a way out. There was no evidence of this other than the nasty messages, though. And unless the school's internal investigation turned up something unexpected, Dan couldn't imagine it going any further.

He'd spoken to her two closest friends, Olivia and Amy, neither of whom had been involved in the messages. They'd been inconsolable at the funeral, but both seemed shocked by the suggestion of Sam being bullied. On the other hand, they did say she'd been quieter and more withdrawn of late. They hadn't seen as much of her as usual over the holidays.

So why did she do it? The question continued to haunt him. It was why he kept checking these web pages of hers, scouring them for some kind of answer. The police had ruled out foul play in her death. They'd not found any evidence of drugs or alcohol in her system. And she wasn't pregnant, thank God.

They'd not found any references whatsoever to committing suicide in her accounts. Initially, Dan had wondered how she knew what to do, but getting information was so easy these days. There was no trace of any such searches on the home computer or on her mobile phone, but that didn't mean much. You could access the Internet from almost anywhere. Free public Wi-Fi was readily available – and deleting your browsing history was as simple as a couple of clicks. Sam was tech-savvy enough to have covered her tracks.

One thing he had discovered was that the lead singer of a band Sam liked had killed herself. It had happened a month or so earlier, although Sam had never mentioned it to him or Maria. Since the group was fairly obscure outside teenage circles, they hadn't heard about it. Sam had mentioned the news in a couple of social media comments, but only to say that the singer, Kat Landon, would be missed and it was a tragic loss. Nothing to ring alarm bells. Dan hadn't even picked up on what she was referring to until reading an article in a music magazine from her bedroom. He'd put two and two together after recognising the band name, Thirteen, from a poster on her wall. That and the fact the circumstances of the musician's death were remarkably similar to her own, which he struggled to find a coincidence.

But it didn't explain why on earth Sam would want to copy her. How had she reached such a low point without him or anyone else noticing?

What had he missed?

Was it something he and Maria had done wrong in raising her?

Had she actually meant to do it? Or was it a cry for help; an experiment gone wrong?

If only he'd got there sooner. He might have saved her.

CHAPTER 32

'You need to get out of there.' The voice on the phone sounds tinny.

'Sam?'

'You know it is.'

'Where are you?'

'Are you listening to me? You need to get out of there. Now. He's on his way back.'

'Miles? I know. I heard the car, but where can I go? I'm in the middle of nowhere.'

There's no answer. I panic that the phone's gone dead again or she's hung up, but when I look at the screen the call is still connected.

'Hello?'

Still no reply.

'Sam, I get the feeling you're somewhere nearby. If you want me to get out, you need to help me. You need to tell me where to go.'

'Hide.'

'That's it? Some help you are.'

The car noise is really close now. It rises up and then stops, which I take to mean Miles has parked. I still can't see the car from where I'm standing, beneath his smashed bedroom window, but I know it'll be a matter of seconds until he comes around the side of the building; until he finds the ladder and sees the mess I've made.

I make a dash for the house. I don't know why exactly, as that's bound to be the first place he'll look. But the ground out here is so open and flat, there aren't many other options.

'Hang on,' I whisper into the mobile. I've no intention of trying to run with it against my ear, but I keep it clamped in my right hand as I tear through the front door.

I stare at the bare staircase curving up towards the first floor and make a snap decision to stay on the ground level. It should be easier to escape from here. I don't fancy trying to climb out of one of the upstairs windows. So I run past the stairs, heading for the kitchen. That leads to the back door, although I've never seen it used in all the time I've been here. I know it's locked and I've no clue where the key might be.

The kitchen is also likely to be the first place Miles will look for me.

Hold on, what am I doing? I think. Why am I running away from Miles? I might have smashed his bedroom window with the ladder, but what's the worst he's going to do about it? Why am I scared of him all of a sudden? Surely I can come up with an explanation that doesn't involve me trying to look inside his bedroom.

My gut tells me to keep on going, so I move along the downstairs hallway. It's as dilapidated and dirty as upstairs: the same musty mix of forlorn floorboards, part-stripped walls and inhospitable emptiness. I make my way into a large room at the back with an open fireplace and bay window. Miles once told me he intended this to be the main living room. For now it's an empty space. The only furniture, if you can call it that, is a shabby wooden stool standing underneath a bare light bulb in the centre of the room.

I shut the door behind me and put the mobile phone back to my ear. 'Are you still there?'

'Yes.'

'Why am I running away from Miles?'

'Where are you?'

'Inside the house.'

'Has he seen you?'

'No, I think he's still outside.'

'Good. You need to try to get to the car. Is there a way out of the back of the house?'

'The car? Listen, what's going on? Why am I hiding from him?'

'You need to get out of there. You need to get away from him.'

'Yes, I get that. I understand what you're saying. But you're not explaining why.'

'Do you trust him? Do you believe everything he's told you? What led you to the car before, when you found this phone?'

'I'm not sure. How do I know I can trust you? You're

a voice. You seem to be nearby, but you won't tell me where. I don't even know who you are, Sam.'

'Yes you do.'

I pause for a moment before replying. 'I think I do. But how can that be? Listen, where are you? Can we meet face to face?'

'I'm close, but there's no time to meet right now. You're asking the wrong questions. It's where you are that matters.'

'I've told you, I'm in the house.'

'Really? Are you sure?'

'What? I—'

I'm interrupted by the sound of the front door slamming shut. A moment later Miles's voice echoes through the hollow shell of the house. 'Jack, where are you? What the hell's going on?'

'Shit,' I whisper. 'He's here.'

I shove the handset into the back pocket of my jeans without waiting for Sam's response. There's no time.

I can hear the thudding of Miles's feet as he looks for me. A change in the sound signals that he's moved from the bare floorboards of the hall to the tiled floor of the kitchen. 'Jack, where are you? I'm getting worried.'

Is that genuine concern I can hear in his voice? The sound is muffled through the walls. I don't know what to believe any more. Part of me wants to face him; tell him the truth, or at least something he might believe that doesn't sound so weird. I could say I was going to wash the windows for him. They're always dirty because of the sea spray. I could say I was starting with his bedroom window to give him a nice surprise when he got home. There's no bucket of water or cleaning materials to back up my story, but I could claim I was placing the ladder first when the wind caught it. It's not that unbelievable. I reckon I could make it sound convincing.

But that gut feeling still holds me back. I slip off my shoes and, carrying them in one hand, tiptoe to the window.

More footsteps. He's back on the floorboards now. Is he coming this way? I freeze by the window as he calls my name. The footsteps stop. So does my heart. There's a long, excruciating moment of silence. Finally they start up again: thud, thud, thud. Moving away this time, thank goodness. Back towards the front door and up the stairs.

He must be going to my bedroom, which gives me a chance to get out of here. I could use the front door, but I don't want to risk that. I can see the Land Rover – Gigi, Miles's so-called Green Goddess – out of the window and I'm drawn to it. But if I'm going to try and get away in it, I need as much time as possible. The last thing I want is for him to see me crossing the front of the house out of one of the windows and to come after me.

So I go with my initial plan to climb out of this window, which will hopefully buy me more time. I examine it, glad to see no sign of any locks. There are two sections that should open, both old sashes like the one in my bedroom I couldn't shift.

Stay calm, I tell myself.

I slide open the fastener on the one in front of me and give it a shove. Nothing. Dammit. In the glass I see the reflection of my face, twisted in frustration, and then for a moment I'm somewhere else.

Darkness.

Burning chemicals.

Spider's web.

Glowing clocks.

'Can you hear me? Try to stay with us. You've been in—'

It's over as quickly as it began. I'm startled by the sudden brightness all around me and my reflection in the window. What the hell was that?

'Can you hear me?'

I can, but I don't know where it's coming from. So quiet.

I remember the phone in my back pocket. How could I have forgotten? I pull it out and hold it back up to my ear. 'Hi.'

'Finally! I was getting worried. What's going on? Where are you?'

'Still in the house.'

'Where exactly?'

'Downstairs. A room at the back. I was hoping to climb out of one of the windows, but—'

'Where is he?'

'Upstairs. Looking for me.'

'You need to get to the car.'

'That's what I'm trying to do. Hang on.'

I shove the phone back in my pocket so I can try the

other window. I can hear footsteps above me. It's only a matter of time until Miles checks down here. I need to get out now.

The fastener on this one is stuck, but after some frantic wiggling, I free it. 'Please,' I say under my breath before trying the sash. It slides up a couple of inches, enough to let the cold air rush in, and stops.

'No, no, no.' I grab the base of the part-open window with both hands and shove again with all my might. Paint and rotten bits of wood come off in my palms, but the pane shifts upwards several inches. Finally there's a gap just about big enough for me to squeeze through.

'Where the hell are you, Jack?' Miles's voice, sounding far too close for comfort, makes me jump. I take it as my cue to climb on to the window ledge and push my feet out of the gap into the fresh air. It's a tight fit, but with some twisting around, bending and breathing in, I make it outside. As soon as my feet hit the ground, I run straight for the Land Rover. It's only a short distance and I don't look back. If he's there at one of the windows or, worse still, already coming after me, I'd rather not know.

Swinging open the driver's door, I reach into my back pocket for the phone; it's not there. I pat myself down in panic, praying it's in one of the other pockets but finding nothing. Damn. It must have slipped out when I was climbing through the window. Looking round for the first time, I see no sign of Miles and decide to risk going back. But as I'm about to shut the door, I hear a voice. 'Don't bother. You don't need it.'

'What?' I scan the inside of the car, which remains empty, and spin around to check the vicinity. 'Who's there?'

'I thought we'd been through that.'

'Sam? Where are you?'

'Get in the car. He's not seen you yet, but it won't be long until he does.'

I lean inside.

'Sit down, for goodness' sake,' she says, as the penny drops that her voice is coming through the speakers of the car stereo.

'How are you doing that?' I ask, closing the door. My hands are shaking and sweat is forming on my palms.

'Later. Do you have the key?'

'Hang on.' I reach over to the glovebox and rummage through the junk.

'And?'

'It's not where he usually keeps it.'

Then I spot it. Still in the ignition. I can't believe I didn't look there first.

'Found it.'

'Great. Let's go.'

I wonder for an instant how Sam can hear me, but there's no time for that.

'Head down the track to the main road,' she snaps.

I bite the bullet and turn the key. Time to see if I can actually drive. You can do it, I tell myself. I'm not entirely convinced, but I push that doubt to the back of my mind and go for it.

I drop my left hand to the gear stick without looking

at it. My right foot finds the brake; my left the clutch. Mirrors, shoulder, handbrake. Yes, this is happening.

Wait. Seatbelt. Mustn't forget that.

And then I'm lifting the clutch, rolling backwards, turning the wheel. I ease to a stop. Find first gear. Deep breath. And . . .

Thump, thump, thump.

I nearly jump out of my skin.

'What the hell, Jack?'

It's Miles. Our eyes meet through the window. He's livid, foaming at the mouth. He wasn't there a second ago. Where did he come from? Now he's opening the passenger door. I panic. Floor the accelerator. Pull away before he has a chance to get inside.

I'm racing down the bumpy track and, glancing in the rear-view mirror, I see Miles picking himself up off the ground, red-faced and shaking a fist at me. I'm glad he's all right, but I need to get away from him, so I continue forward, as fast as I dare, glad to turn a corner and lose sight of him.

The passenger door flaps open, hitting a tree, as I take another corner. 'Crap,' I say, stretching over to pull it shut but not quite reaching.

'What's happening?' Sam's voice asks through the speakers.

'Nothing.'

'Doesn't sound like nothing.'

'It's fine,' I say, eyeing the mirror as I slow the car to a halt and reach over again, managing to shut the door this time.

I half expect Miles to appear behind me as I look back before pulling away again. But all I see is a rabbit, light brown with a bushy white tail, hopping across the track.

I push on, keen to get as far away from Miles and the house as possible.

After a few intense moments of concentration, glad I know how to drive but far from confident, I speak to Sam again. 'Where to at the main road?'

'Have you reached it already?'

'Not far. Am I heading for the village?'

'I'll let you know in a second. Bear with me.'

I see the road when I turn the next corner and, after a moment of elation, my heart sinks as a red tractor turns off it and on to the track ahead of me.

'Come on. You've got to be joking.'

'What's wrong?'

'A stupid tractor's appeared. It's blocking the way.'

I slow the car, scouring the track ahead for a passing place, but find nothing. I start checking my rear-view mirror again, even though I know Miles couldn't have caught up with me yet on foot. There's nothing to do but keep on going and hope for the fool in the tractor to get the message and back up. But it keeps on coming and, as we get closer to each other, I see the driver is waving at me.

'Bloody idiot,' I mutter. 'You can wave all you like, but you're the one who needs to get out of the way.'

Sam's gone silent. I'm about to ask her for directions again when the tractor driver comes into focus and I slam my foot on the brake in shock. What on earth? It's impossible. I shake my head, but he's even closer now and there's no mistaking him: Miles, still waving and wearing a manic grin. But how's this possible when I only just left him behind me, scrabbling around in the dirt? How can he be here now, coming at me from the other direction?

'Sam, there's something seriously weird going on. It's Miles. I mean, it can't be. I left him behind at the house, but . . . he's the one driving the tractor. And he's heading straight for me. What the hell do I do now?'

'Get away from him.'

'Where to?'

'Can't you reverse?'

It's banked up on either side of me and walled with thick hedgerows. Driving backwards along this bumpy, winding track is the last thing I want to do, but I'm out of options. The tractor's almost upon me and showing no sign of slowing. I slam the gearstick into reverse and, twisting my neck to see behind me, pull away. I only make it a few metres before one of my back wheels hits a pothole and the rear of the car spins out, jerking to a halt sideways in the track. I look out of my window, helpless, as the tractor keeps coming.

Miles is staring down at me from the cab, eyes wide and laughing. And then he changes right before my eyes into someone else: a huge man hunched over the wheel in a leather coat. His long grey hair flaps around the leathery, pockmarked skin of his red face. Only the manic grin remains the same.

He looks familiar, I think, as the tractor ploughs into me at full speed.

CHAPTER 33

Thursday, 4 May 2017

Dear Sam,

I can't believe it's a whole week since I last wrote to you. There's good news and bad news. I'll start with the bad, shall I? It's your father. He still won't speak to me and now he and Ruby have fallen out too. On Tuesday morning he sent me a text message (the only form of direct communication he'll have with me) saying he wanted to pick her up and take her out for a pizza that evening. I agreed, although goodness knows why he couldn't have done it over the Bank Holiday weekend instead. I was hoping it might afford me a chance to break the deadlock, but once again he refused to get out of the car when he picked her up and dropped her off.

Ruby was upset when she got home. I could see she'd been crying when I answered the door; she ran straight up to her bedroom.

'What's the matter, love?' I asked after following her upstairs.

'Nothing,' she replied, lying stomach down on the bed, face to the wall.

'It doesn't look like nothing.'

'Leave me. I'm fine.'

I wasn't taking no for an answer. 'If you don't tell me, I'll have to ring your father and ask him.'

'He won't even speak to you.'

'Is that what this is about?'

She claimed it wasn't, but I know her well enough to recognise when she's lying. 'Come on, Ruby,' I said, perched on the side of her bed, gently stroking her curls. 'You can tell me. Bottling it up will only make you feel worse. I want to help.'

'Fine. I had an argument with Dad.' She said it like it was no big deal, but a moment later she was bawling.

'Oh, darling,' I said, taking her into my arms. 'That's right, let all your emotion out. You'll feel better for it.'

After calming down a little, she explained that Dan had been really grumpy in the pizza place. A waitress had knocked over his drink and he'd shouted at her, totally overreacting in the situation.

'It was so embarrassing, Mummy. And then he told me off for the way I was eating,' she said, bursting into tears again. 'I don't even know what I was doing wrong. You know it's hard with my arm in plaster.'

I was fuming, wondering what the hell Dan was playing at, but I bit my tongue, saving it for later. The family dynamic was bad enough without me siding against him in front of her.

I listened to what she had to say, nodding support-ively, as she explained that the real row had come in the car on the way home. Dan had asked her to relay to me the arrangements for this weekend – when he'd pick her up and so on – and she'd said no.

'I told him I was sick of passing messages between you two and he should do it himself.'

'And what did your dad say?'

'He shouted at me.'

'Really?'

'Yeah. So I told him I didn't want to stay at his flat at all. I said I hated being with him.'

They were already in the driveway at this point, Ruby explained. She stormed out of the car and he drove off.

'I don't really hate being with him,' she said. 'I was angry.' Her lower lip was wobbling and I stroked her hair, feeling the softness of it under my fingers.

'I know, darling. Don't worry. Your father will understand.'

I couldn't quite get my head around what I was hearing. It really didn't sound like Dan. I'm not saying I didn't believe Ruby; of course I did. But I felt like I should at least hear his side of the story. I couldn't help feeling it was somehow my fault. What if my revelation about sleeping with Rick had driven him over the edge?

As soon as I'd got Ruby off to bed, I called his mobile. He didn't answer, of course, so I left a voice-mail and sent a text asking him to call me back urgently. Two days later, he's still not done so, despite several more attempts on my part to contact him. I even tried getting hold of him at work, but no luck there either. It's not on. Ruby's still really upset about what happened and it needs resolving. You can't treat a child that way. If he hasn't got back to me by tonight, I'm going to have to go over to his flat in person.

Hold on . . .

Sorry. I had to dash to get the landline. The answer-phone is still broken from that night I spent with Rick, when I spilled water all over it. Fool that I am, I thought it might be Dan. Speak of the devil and all that. Of course it wasn't. It was a bloody call centre.

So that's the bad news. On to the good, which concerns Rick. As I told you last time, I felt like I had to do something, even if I wasn't going to tell Lisa the truth. So last Friday lunchtime, after missing Rick on the morning school run and still not having heard from him, I sent him a text message.

Met your lovely wife Lisa yesterday. We swapped numbers. Think we'll be great friends.

The bit about swapping numbers was a lie, but it

had the desired effect. He was on the phone five minutes later.

'What are you playing at?' he snapped.

'Hello to you too.'

'Seriously. What's that text all about?'

'I was giving you a heads up, Rick. Shame you didn't show me the same courtesy before I met Lisa. Never mind. What an eye-opener. It's amazing how well the two of you get along since you separated.'

'What? We're not—'

'Yes, I know that now, Rick. I was being sarcastic.'

'I never—'

'Don't even go down that path. You may not have specifically said so, but you definitely led me to believe that the two of you were no longer together. Did it never occur to you that she and I would eventually meet and she'd learn the truth?'

'What truth?'

'That you're a lying, cheating—'

'I'll deny it. I'll tell her you're a lonely housewife who got obsessed with me. That you tried it on and this is your revenge because I said no. She won't believe you over me.'

'How many times have you done this before, Rick? You pretend to be such a great guy – this wonderful single dad – and it's bullshit. The minute you got what you wanted from me, you lost interest. I bet you've already moved on to your next target, haven't you? Who is it? Another mum from the playground? Someone at work?'

'Maybe it's because you were crap in bed,' he said. 'Did you ever think of that?'

'Wow. What a charmer. I should have realised the truth after seeing how useless you were when Ruby broke her arm. I ought to have trusted my instincts.'

'Leave me and my family alone. And don't you dare criticise my parenting. I'm a damn good father.'

'Not such a good husband.'

'You can't prove anything. It's your word against mine.'

'Does Lisa know you spent the night at my house? I could always tell her and then make some reference to the mole on your—'

'Don't you dare.'

'Or the way your voice rises like a girl when you get really excited. That might ring a bell.'

'Listen, Maria.'

'No, you listen,' I replied in what you used to call my 'stern solicitor' voice, Sam. 'You might be interested to know that I've recorded this conversation. If you don't want a copy of it ending up in your wife's hands, you'd better keep Little Rick in your pants from now on. It's purely for Anna's sake that I'm giving you this one chance. But if I get wind that you've been up to no good again, the gloves are coming off. Are we clear?'

My question was met with silence.

'I said are we clear?'

'Yes,' he replied in a pathetic little voice.

I hung up, pleased with myself. The bit about

recording the conversation was another lie, but he didn't know that. I doubt it will change him for good, but hopefully he'll think twice next time before cheating again.

That's it for me and Rick, as far as I'm concerned. I'm done with him. He's of no further interest. He's avoided me ever since then, even finding somewhere else to park near school. He'll probably warn Lisa off me.

Now I can see Rick for what he is, I know his type. I've worked with plenty of guys like that and they're masters of self-preservation. Lies trip off their tongues like their date of birth. If he hasn't already, I expect he'll discourage Anna from playing with Ruby too, which is a shame, but your sister will cope.

It's as we get older that these things tend to get more painful, isn't it, Sam? Like the girls who said those nasty things about you online. Girls you'd known since primary school.

I know I said I wasn't going to use these letters to talk about the difficult stuff, darling, but in our last session Rosie suggested that maybe now I should. I don't show these to her, by the way. I speak about them, but only very generally. The letters themselves are just for me and you.

There are some things I need to tell you, Sam, things that I've been bottling up for a long time. Ever since you died and the floor fell out of my world. Ever since I let you down so badly that you felt you had to take your own life.

I've said it before and I'll say it again now, because it's the truth: I don't blame you for what you did. There have been private moments when I've unfairly blamed your father – never vocalised, thank goodness. And of course I've blamed the bullies and their nasty comments. Most of all, though, the person I blame is myself. I probably always will. But for my own sanity and the rest of the family's sake, I have to learn to live with it and move on.

I can't change the past, but I can make a difference now. Particularly by not letting Ruby down like I did with you. And that means more than being home all the time. It means actually being there for her – mentally as well as physically – and trying to undo the damage I've done to our family unit.

So it's time for me to apologise to you, Sam. I need you to know how incredibly sorry I am for letting you down. Countless times I've thought back to that night, four days before you killed yourself, when you came to me, asked for my help, and I failed you.

'Mum?' you called from inside your bedroom as I walked along the landing. Ruby was already in bed and Dan had a late meeting at work.

'That's me,' I replied, sticking my head through the doorway, which I was surprised to find open for once.

'Could I talk to you about something?' you said, a glum look on your face. You were lying on your bed, knees raised. I queried why on earth you were wearing jeans when it was so warm and got a 'dunno' in reply.

'What's the matter?' I asked from the doorway. 'Can it wait? I've got a pile of washing to get through and then some work stuff to do after that.'

You shrugged.

'Couldn't you have talked to me during dinner? You hardly said a word.'

Then you came out with the sentence that's been stewing in my head ever since I lost you: 'I'm feeling a bit depressed, that's all.'

Why on earth that didn't ring alarm bells in my head, I'll never know. To this day, I can still hear the waver in your voice as you said it. I've played it over and over in my mind and each time it rips me apart to think I did nothing. I didn't even sit down to hear what you had to say. No, I was far too busy with my own thoughts, which were mainly work-related at that time.

'Depressed?' I replied. 'You've obviously got too much time on your hands. Try spending a day in my shoes. Seriously, I'd give anything to be a teenager again in the summer holidays. You kids are so dramatic these days. You don't know how good you've got it. Go and have a bath. That'll brighten you up.'

And with that I left, didn't I, Sam? You must hate me for that, but it can't be more than I hate myself. I didn't even give it a second thought, you know. Not until four days later. Then you did get my

390

attention – and how I wish you hadn't. I could have stopped it ever getting that far, couldn't I? If only I'd listened to you, my darling. If only I'd heard what you were trying to tell me.

I've never told anyone about that night, Sam. Not your father, not Ruby, not even Rosie in one of our sessions. I'm too ashamed.

I'm sure you never said anything similar to Dan, because I know he would have done something about it. He was always much better with you than I was. On the night of your funeral, he even asked me if I thought you'd ever seemed depressed. I wanted to tell him then, but I just couldn't. I've heard him question so many times why you didn't come to us for help, keeping it to myself that you did.

I don't know why you chose me instead of him. I never will. But letting you down is the greatest regret of my life.

One of my first thoughts after it happened was that I mustn't let Ruby down too. I see now that I have done, by letting the OCD take me away in my head so much; by driving Dan away. Pushing her father further from us hasn't been good for her, has it? I forced him to move out of the house and refused his attempts to heal our relationship. Now I've slept with another man and made things even worse, pushing him over the edge when I should have been pulling him back.

I often wonder if you meant to kill yourself or

391

whether it was a cry for help that went unanswered. At your inquest, the coroner ruled it was an accident, citing the lack of a note or any significant evidence from school or home to suggest you were suicidal. He didn't know about our chat. I couldn't bring myself to tell anyone, Sam.

In the immediate aftermath of your death, I needed someone to blame other than myself. I'd seen a programme on TV about cyber bullying and, after I found those nasty comments online, I decided that was it. Now, with hindsight, I don't think it was just one thing, was it? It's nice to have an easy explanation, but life rarely works like that. They were nasty, hurtful comments. But no evidence has ever emerged of them being anything more than that: an isolated incident rather than a bullying campaign. Maybe they were the straw that broke the camel's back. Or maybe that was me, brushing you off four days earlier.

I neglected you emotionally, Sam. And I'm not just talking about that one occasion. It was a long-term thing. I was far too busy with my work and my own concerns. I didn't pay enough attention to you and your needs, especially in those last few years. I was happy to let you be the sulky teenager who shut herself away in her bedroom. Other than nagging you to do your chores and your homework – willing you to achieve academically what your father and I had – how much did I get involved in your world? I was too busy being the high-flying career woman.

Look where that got me.

Anyway, this isn't about me wallowing in self-pity. It's about accepting the truth and moving on. There's one more thing I want to say to you, Sam, but it's gone 2.30 p.m. and I need to pick up Ruby from school. I'll finish later.

I'm back. It's just after 10 p.m. Ruby's in bed. Your father phoned earlier – at last – but we were at the supermarket. Typical. There was a missed call from him on the phone at quarter to five and another at ten to, but no message, as the answer machine is still broken. I don't know why he didn't try my mobile. I tried to call him back, but it went straight to his voicemail.

I told you there was one more thing I wanted to mention. It's about your friend Olivia. I bumped into her in the street a little while ago and we had a quick chat. A few days later she turned up on the doorstep and asked to speak to me. It was the middle of the day and I was home alone. I was surprised she wasn't at school, but she said she was on her lunch break and had a free period after that. She had something to tell me – something about you.

'It's been weighing on my mind,' she said after I sat her down in the lounge and fixed us both a cup of tea. 'I wanted to say something at the time, but I was too embarrassed. I did my best to forget about it, convincing myself it wasn't important, but since I saw you the other day, I've hardly been able to think of anything else.'

She looked so much older than I remembered. Well, she's sixteen now. It's amazing the difference a year or so makes when you're a teenager. How I wish I'd been able to see you grow in the same way, my love.

'There was something that happened between the two of us,' Olivia went on. 'It was about a week before Sam, er, died. She was round at my place. We were listening to music.' Olivia took a deep breath; ran a hand through her hair. Her face was flushed. 'Sorry. It's still embarrassing. I haven't told anyone until now. Even Amy doesn't know. I mean, it's probably nothing, but I feel I ought to—'

'Go on. Whatever it is. You can tell me, Olivia.'

'Right, I'll say it. We were lying on the bed and, I don't know where it came from. I couldn't say for sure who started it. Somehow we ended up kissing.'

'Oh.' I hadn't seen that coming.

'The thing is, it was as much me as it was her, but I panicked and pulled away. I made out like she'd forced herself on me and said it was disgusting. I asked her to leave. I can still see her face now. She looked so hurt. It was the last time I ever saw her. I was planning to make up with her, but . . . I really don't know why I did it. I should have told someone before, shouldn't I? Do you think that's why she killed herself? Do you think it's my fault?'

It took me a moment to register that she'd stopped talking and was now looking at me, waiting for a response.

'I'm not a lesbian or anything,' Olivia added, filling

the silence. 'And I don't think Sam was either. Not that I would have minded. That would have been fine. We were just, you know, experimenting. I really wish that hadn't been the last time I saw her.'

I signalled for her to stop.

'Sorry. I'm talking too much, aren't I? I always do that when I'm nervous. Are you mad at me for not saying something sooner? I should have told the police, shouldn't I?'

'Stop, please. It's fine. I'm glad you told me, but I'm sure that didn't have anything to do with it. Let it go, Olivia, and remember the good times. Dwelling on it won't bring her back.'

She burst into tears, so I gave her a hug. Of course, I don't know if what she told me had anything to do with your suicide, Sam, but I knew it was pointless her punishing herself over it. In many ways I'm glad she told me when she did, as my reaction closer to the time would have been much less calm.

I took the opportunity to ask Olivia if you'd ever mentioned having suicidal thoughts. It was something I'd asked her and Amy at the time of your death – and they'd said not – but I needed to be sure.

She looked horrified. 'No, honestly. Never. I wouldn't have kept that from you. You have to believe me.'

'What about when that singer from the band Thirteen killed herself? Did Sam say anything about that? I know she liked her. Did she give you any idea that she might want to copy her?'

This was something your father discovered after

you died, Sam. He insisted on mentioning it at the inquest, although the coroner argued there was no hard evidence of a link between the two tragic events. I've wondered about it before, stared at magazine pictures of the singer, Kat Landon, wondering what she'd been thinking, and whether it would bring me any closer to you.

Olivia shook her head as she wiped away fresh tears. 'No way. She was definitely upset about it, but she never said anything about wanting to do the same. If I thought for a second she was going to, I would have told you. I swear.'

I'd been OCDing over some grout in the bathroom when Olivia rang the doorbell. After she left, I realised how unimportant it was in the scheme of things. I was even able to leave it alone for a while. And do you know what? It was soon after her visit that I decided to seek the help of a counsellor. I'm not saying it was as a direct result of that, but it certainly helped me turn a corner.

I'm delighted to say I turned another corner today too, Sam. After I put Ruby to bed this evening, I went to your bedroom and took out that lovely school photo of you from about six months before you died. You know, the one when you had your hair up and a big grin. You said the photographer had pulled a ridiculous face to make you laugh. Anyway, it's back in pride of place on the wall in the lounge and I fully intend to return the others too. I know Ruby and your father will be pleased.

What I haven't done is tell Dan about Olivia's revelation. I meant to, but things have been so awkward between us lately. I've never found the right moment. I need to tell him. I know that – and I will. I'm going to tell him about the chat you and I had too. I've no idea how he'll take it, but he deserves to have the whole picture. Without honesty, we haven't got a chance of ever working things out. One of the hardest things for both of us has always been the uncertainty: the lack of closure, due to not knowing why you took your own life. Maybe telling Dan these things will help him to find some peace. I hope so. I wish I could give him the definitive answer, but I simply don't have it. The only one who does is you, Sam.

Finally, before I find myself in the Guinness World Records for writing the longest letter ever, I want to say one more thing to you, my love. It wouldn't have mattered to me or your father in the slightest if you were a lesbian. Perhaps you were; perhaps you were experimenting or confused. We would have loved you whatever. I only wish I'd shown you that when you were still here. Then maybe you would never have left us.

The phone's ringing. Perhaps it's your dad.

Love as always,

M

Xx

CHAPTER 34

BEFORE

Friday, 28 August 2015

'Hello. Anyone home?' Dan called as he entered the house. 'Sam? Are you back yet?'

There was no sign of life downstairs, but when he walked into the lounge, Dan spotted his elder daughter's handbag and her red summer coat thrown on the sofa instead of being put properly away. 'Bloody hell, Sam,' he said to the empty room. 'How many times?'

He was tempted to go up and shout at her, but she'd been a bit subdued recently and he didn't have the heart. She was in her room, no doubt, away in a world of her own. Probably listening to music too loud on the headphones of his that she'd commandeered after hers broke.

The clock in the kitchen read 4.15 p.m. Ruby wasn't due back from her holiday club bowling trip until 5 p.m.

and Maria was expecting to be late, as usual. Dan put the kettle on to make a brew. Watching it boil, he thought he'd make Sam one and take it up for her. What had she been doing all day? It was only since she turned fourteen earlier this year that they'd been allowing her to stay home alone over the school holidays. It seemed to be working out. Well, he thought it was, although it was hard to tell with a teenager. You just had to do your best to communicate what was right and wrong and hope they weren't taking drugs and having underage sex behind your back. Sam wasn't very communicative, though, and seemed to prefer visiting her friends' houses to having them over here.

Dan made two cups of tea and put them on a tray with a couple of chocolate digestives. He was going to try to have a chat with her; see if he could cheer her up a bit; clear away a few of those moody teenage cobwebs.

Ring ring. Ring ring.

He pulled his mobile out of his jacket pocket and frowned at the number flashing up: the office. Bloody hell. What did they want? He'd only just left. It was Friday afternoon, for goodness' sake. Couldn't they leave him alone for five minutes?

'Yes,' he answered.

'Dan?'

'Who's that?'

'Sorry to bother you. It's Jane.'

He already knew that. He recognised her voice. But he wasn't going to make it easy for her, even though she was arguably his best reporter: one of a precious few remaining from the pre-centralisation days.

Dan took a seat at the kitchen table and a sip of tea. 'What's up?'

'The council have been on. They're spitting feathers.'

His heart sank. 'What? Why?'

'It's about a reader's comment on the website.'

'Bloody hell. That's not our problem. Speak to the web team. They're supposed to monitor comments.'

'I know. I have. I've already told them to pull it.'

'Good. You did the right thing. So what's the problem?'

'It was Julia Walker who called.'

'The chief exec?'

'Yep. She was fuming. Demanded to speak to you.'

'What was in this comment?'

'It was bad. A proper rant about her deputy, Alan Smith. Libellous as hell.'

Dan sighed. 'What did it say?'

'Well, among other things, it accused him of embezzling funds and feeling up his female staff.'

He put his head in his hands. 'How the hell did that get through? Was the writer named?'

'No. Well, he – or she – called themselves Deep Throat. Very original. The web guys say they might be able to dig up some more info. At least an email address.'

'Tell me it's already been taken down.'

'Hold on.' There was a pause and the sound of keyboard typing in the background. 'Yes, it's been removed.'

'Good. Have you got a direct number for Julia Walker?'

'Sure.'

She gave it to him and asked if he'd like an email copy of the comment.

'Yes, please.'

'I'll send it now. Sorry to bother you.'

'No, you did the right thing, Jane. Good work getting it taken down so quickly. Have a nice weekend.'

Dan hung up. Julia Walker was hard work at the best of times. He wasn't looking forward to calling her. He decided to do it without actually reading the comment, so he could make it clear he was out of the office but taking the matter seriously. He'd call her from the car, on the way to pick up Ruby, which would add to the effect and hopefully buy him a bit of time. Delaying a proper discussion until Monday, once the dust had settled, seemed like the best option.

But first he wanted to say hello to Sam. He'd give her that cup of tea before it went cold; tell her where he was going. He removed his cup from the tray, had a sip and then headed upstairs with the remaining cup and biscuits.

'Sam,' he called as he reached the top of the staircase, walking carefully so as not to spill the tea. 'It's Dad. I've got a brew for you.'

There was no reply. Her bedroom door was shut, as usual, and there was no sound from within. His eyes were drawn to the charming sign she'd created: 'Sam's space. Stay out!'

Holding the tray in his left hand, he knocked with his right. He always knocked before going inside these days. She was a teenager after all. He didn't want to burst in unannounced at some embarrassing moment. There was still no answer, though.

'Hello,' he said in a raised voice, knocking again.

'Sam, it's Dad. I've got a cup of tea for you. I'm coming in.'

Still no reply. He dreaded to think how loud she had those headphones. She'd give herself tinnitus if she wasn't careful.

Dan grabbed the door handle and let himself in. 'Hello, Sam. I've—'

The tray fell from his hand, tea and biscuits tumbling through the air and crashing down on to the carpet. Pure instinct catapulted him across the room before his brain had the chance to catch up with what his eyes were seeing. What his mouth was yelling. Time stopped as he threw his arms around her inert form. Raised her up in the open wardrobe and tried to support her weight with his body. Banged her slumped head on the rail as he scrabbled with his hands to untie the leather belt. He struggled forever but finally yanked it free, exposing her neck, stretched and twisted to one side, a pale groove engraved in her skin.

She was on the carpet now – his beautiful girl – and Dan was kneeling over her, splashing tears on to her impossibly white face. Her drooling blue lips. Her blood-stained nostrils.

He was screaming for help. Searching for life. Shouting for her to come back to him. Lost in panic.

He had to do something.

He had to do something.

He had to do something.

Slapping himself around the face, he jolted his brain into gear. Back into the driving seat. He felt to see if she was breathing. If she had a pulse.

Nothing.

Dan pulled his mobile out of his pocket and dialled 999. Told them what they needed to know and begged them to hurry. Then he dropped the phone without ending the call and started CPR, hoping he remembered it right. Wishing he'd remained a first-aider in the new office, so his training would have been more recent. Knowing in his heart that it was already too late but continuing nonetheless, because the alternative was unbearable.

He didn't allow himself to think beyond the moment, for fear of losing his mind to panic again. He had to hold it together. So he stayed focused on what he was doing: thirty chest compressions then two rescue breaths; thirty chest compressions then two rescue breaths. Over and over, without any sign of recovery, until he heard the siren outside. He tore himself away from her – his precious Sam – just long enough to race downstairs, fling open the front door and run back again to carry on with the CPR.

'Up here,' Dan shouted as he continued with the chest compressions. 'Hurry.'

And then a green and yellow blur as the paramedics came in and took over. He stood back and crumpled into a heap against one wall; did his best to keep it together enough to answer their questions as they tried to save her. To do what he couldn't.

He prayed his heart was wrong. That they'd be able to pull her back with their knowledge and fancy gadgets. But he saw the truth in the pained expression on both of their faces. They were going through the motions.

This realisation shattered the defences he'd thrown up to keep himself going. In came the floodwaters of despair.

His precious Sam was gone.

How?

Why?

No, this couldn't be real. He had to be in a dream – a nightmare. His daughter would never willingly do that to herself. To her parents. To her little sister. She was a good girl. A sensible girl. She was happy. She loved her family. Wasn't she? Didn't she?

'You have to save her,' he blurted to the paramedics, scrambling to his feet. 'She didn't mean to. It's a terrible accident.'

One of them looked towards him. 'We're doing everything we can for her, sir. Please stay back and leave us to—'

He stepped forward. Caught a fresh look at Sam's contorted, lifeless body. Felt light-headed and . . .

Black.

When he came to, Dan was in bed. Thank God, he thought. It was a dream. Then his hearing kicked in and there was noise all around. Lots of voices. He was still in Sam's bedroom, lying on her bed. There were several more medical staff now, as well as police. Sam was being lifted on to a stretcher.

'What?' Dan slurred, trying to get up despite the fact that his head was pounding and he felt woozy. 'Is she—'

A woman's face. 'Calm down, sir. Please stay where you

are for a moment and don't try to get up. You passed out and banged your head. We need to give you a check over.'

'My daughter, Sam. Where are they taking her? What's happened?'

'I, er. I'm not—'

'I did what I could, but I couldn't help her. I should have got home sooner. I might have reached her in time. Does Maria know? What about Ruby? Someone needs to—'

He tried to sit up again, only to find himself pushed firmly back down. He hadn't been able to see the stretcher any more. What had they done with his daughter?

'Where is she?' he asked, struggling until the throbbing in his head forced him to stop. 'Where's Sam?'

'Please, sir. Do as I ask and stay where you are for now.'

'Is he awake?' a deep male voice asked. 'We need to speak to him. Find out what happened.'

'Yes, but he might have a concussion. He hit his head against the wall. Pretty hard, apparently. He was out for a while.'

'He's the guy who rang up, right? The one who found her hanging?'

'She's called Sam,' Dan cried out. 'My fourteen-year-old daughter. I need to know what's happened. Someone tell me. Did they resuscitate her?'

His words brought the room to a hush. There was some rustling around and mumbling and then another face – a middle-aged man – appeared.

'Hello.' He looked down at some notes. 'Mr Evans?'

'Yes. How is she? How's my daughter?'

'My name is Dr Shah. I'm terribly sorry but there was nothing anyone could do. I'm afraid your daughter didn't make it. She passed away.'

CHAPTER 35

I'm eight years old in a cool larder with my grandmother. She's tiny – only a little taller than I am – standing on tiptoes on a footstool, stretching up to a high shelf.

'Careful, Gangy,' I say, worried she might fall.

She turns and hands me the jar. Orange Marmalade, her neat handwriting reads on a small white label. There's no metal lid, like you get in the shops, but a special waxy disc and some see-through stuff held on with an elastic band.

'Isn't all marmalade made of oranges?' I ask her in my high-pitched little boy's voice.

'Sometimes I put ginger in it too,' she says, beaming that huge smile of hers at me like I'm the most important person in the world. 'I've even made it with lemon and lime,' she adds. 'But I'm not sure you'd like that.'

'I don't like any marmalade apart from yours,' I tell her.

She winks at me. 'That's my boy.'

'Please can I have some, Gangy, on a piece of toast?'

'Not now, love,' she replies, stepping down from the stool, wrapping her arms around me and ruffling my hair. 'There's something else we need to do. In the garden.'

'Are we going to pick some of your veggies? I love doing that.'

She shakes her head. 'Not this time. I want you to meet someone.'

'Someone in the garden? Who, Gangy? It's not a scarecrow, is it?'

'No, silly sausage. It's a real person. Someone nice.'

'Have I met them before?'

'You'll see.'

She takes me by the hand and leads me through the kitchen and out into the garden. But when I get there, it's not the place I'm expecting. We're on a clifftop. It's a bright sunny day and there's a light breeze.

'Is that the sea I can smell?'

Gangy nods, still holding my hand and leading me forward. 'That's right.'

'But hang on, you don't live by the—'

I turn back and her house has gone. There's a sprawling meadow behind us.

'Don't worry,' she says. 'Trust me. Everything will make sense soon.'

'Where are we going? There's nothing here. I thought we were meeting someone.'

'We are. Look over there.'

She points towards the edge of the cliff and there's a large tree that wasn't there a moment ago. From one of the lower branches hangs a swing made of an old car tyre and a chunky piece of rope. Someone's using it – swaying backwards and forwards – a girl in a red coat with long black hair, which flows behind her as she swings.

I look to Gangy for an explanation, but she's facing ahead, leading us towards this mystery person. We're almost upon her when we stop. Gangy turns to face me and squeezes my hand before letting go. 'You need to do the last bit alone.'

'What? Why can't you come? Where are you going?'

She leans forward and whispers: 'I want you to close your eyes and count to ten.'

'I'm scared, Gangy.'

'Don't be. I need you to be brave. Once your eyes are closed, I'm going to place something in your hands. You mustn't peek until you reach ten. Then you can look. It's my gift to you.'

I take a deep breath. I don't feel brave, but I trust her and don't want to let her down. 'Okay.'

She ruffles my hair and plants a tender kiss on my forehead. 'Close your eyes now and start counting out loud.'

I do as she asks. On the count of two, I feel a gentle tug on my right arm. She pulls it towards her, opens my hand and places something cool on my palm. Then she closes it again. I keep on counting out loud, wondering what she's given me. The top feels different to the bottom and sides. Some parts seem to move. Wait. I think I know what it might be.

I count nine and ten, open my eyes in sync with my

hand and see that I was right. It's a toy car – a silver one – which she's placed upside down in my palm. I flip it over and see that the windscreen is cracked in a shape that reminds me of something, but I can't put my finger on what. I want to ask her why she's given me this battered old thing, but she's gone.

'Don't you know why?' a female voice says from behind me, making me jump. I turn and see the girl from the swing. She smiles. 'Hello, Dad. Aren't you going to give me a hug?'

As the words leave her mouth, it's like a power jet flushes my mind. A huge blockage is shifted. For a moment it overwhelms me: the surge of information – of suppressed memories – sweeping back into place. I'm blinded by them. Stupefied.

'Are you all right?' Sam asks.

'I, um. I'm fine,' I manage eventually. 'I've—'

'Remembered?'

'Yes. Did you do that?'

She shrugs. 'Some of it was me.'

I look down and see that I have the hands, arms and body of a man. 'Oh my God,' I say, my voice deep once more. I rush forward to give Sam that hug. 'It's you. You're here. I never thought we'd see each other again. How?'

I stop talking and enjoy the moment in silence: the amazing feeling of having my daughter in my arms. And then my mind starts up again, crying out for answers. Hold on, I think. How can I be here with Sam? She's dead. She killed herself. How could I have forgotten that? How could I have forgotten who I was?

'What's going on?' I ask, pulling away. 'What is this place? You are Sam, right? I am Dan, your father?'

'Of course.'

'Sorry, but I had to ask. Everything's a bit, well, confusing. Was it you I was speaking to before – in the Land Rover? Wait a minute. How did I get here? There was a crash and then I don't know. What is this place?'

She shrugs and looks away towards the sea. 'It is what it is.'

'Listen, Sam. It's so amazing to see you again. There are no words to convey how much it means to me. It's a dream come true. But I don't know what you mean. And as happy as I am right now to be with you, how do I know you really are Sam? How can I be sure you're not a figment of my imagination? Where am I now? Am I dead? Can this really be the afterlife that I've never believed in? No, my mind must have created you. It's the only explanation that makes any sense to me. I must be unconscious or something. I bet I'm still in the car, aren't I?'

'Which car?'

'What do you mean? The Land Rover. The one I stole from Miles.'

'Really?'

'Of course.'

'You remember everything?'

'Yes. I think so.'

'So how did you come to stay with Miles?'

'We met one night in the pub. He was looking for a hand with the renovation and I needed somewhere discreet to stay, where I wouldn't get asked too many questions.'

411

'Why did you need somewhere discreet?'

'Um.'

'You don't really remember that, do you? It's what he told you happened. Like he told you your name was Jack.'

She has a point. When I think about it, I don't remember anything before waking up in Miles's house and him saying I'd banged my head. Well, nothing about Miles or that place. My previous memories are of my old life as Dan: grieving father; separated husband; newspaper editor. So how did I get from one to the other?

Sam is staring at my right hand. It's clenched around the gift Gangy gave me – the beaten-up toy car – and, following her cue, I look at it again.

'What's the last thing you—'

I gasp before she finishes the sentence. I remember walking out of work, picking up the duct tape and the length of garden hose from that awful flat and driving to the coast. Heading for the clifftop from that family photo. Trying to phone Ruby and Maria to say goodbye but getting no answer. And then . . .

I take in the scenery around me. There's nothing for as far as I can see apart from the two of us, the green grass and a glorious deep blue of merging sea and sky. The smell of warm summer sunshine combined with fresh sea air. The sound of gentle waves lapping against the rocks far below.

'Hold on a minute. Where's the tree gone?' I ask. 'And what about the rope swing?'

Sam shrugs. 'You tell me. I think it was a not-so-subtle reminder of how I died.'

The lightness of the way she speaks of her suicide shocks me. Images of those horrendous moments after I found her lifeless body flash into my mind, tearing my heart out all over again. I want to ask her why – to finally get some answers after all this time – but the thought is overtaken by shameful memories of my own journey to North Wales. I remember how I was planning to follow in her footsteps and end it all. To run away from my problems and leave Maria and Ruby to pick up the pieces. How could I do that to them when I know first-hand the pain it will cause; the scars it will leave? But something's missing. I can picture myself in the car, almost there, and then the image gets cloudy.

'What are you thinking?' Sam asks.

'I'm wondering where I am; how I arrived. It's not real, is it? I don't understand how Gangy's here one minute and then she's not. How I'm in her house and then in the middle of nowhere by the sea. And you. I saw you several times before this: walking along the clifftop; working in the village. Why did you pretend not to know me? Why didn't you say who you were?'

She doesn't answer me. Her eyes fall again on the toy car I'm still holding.

I sigh. 'Fine. All the answers are in the palm of my hand. I get it. So I guess I killed myself. Sucked in a load of exhaust fumes, like I was planning to, and now I'm dead. This is the afterlife, right? The one I don't believe in. This whole time – Miles, the ramshackle house on the cliff – it's been me kidding myself that I'm still alive. Because how could an atheist believe in life after death?

And the airport. Yes, I remember that too: departing to Eindhoven, a city with a name that means "End Lands". That makes sense now. I guess it was me trying to find a way to accept the truth; an analogy to help me grasp that I'm dead. But wait.'

I pause to weigh things up. 'You were there at the airport too, now I think about it. What was all that you said about going back; about how I shouldn't have been there? And why were you trying to get me away from Miles later on? If I am dead, how come I don't actually remember killing myself? What's going on, Sam?'

She reaches out and squeezes my hand. The one not holding the toy car. 'Open your eyes,' she says. 'It's not too late.'

She kisses my cheek and takes a step back. 'Look at the windscreen.'

I lift up the car, a miniature version of my own Ford Focus, and turn it so I'm looking directly at the broken windscreen. As I do, it dawns on me what the pattern of the breakage resembles. I look up to tell Sam and everything around me changes.

It's dark.

I gasp for air and there's a horrible stench: burning chemicals, powdery almost.

I . . .

Spider's web.

Glowing clocks.

Where am I?

Can't focus properly.

Can't move.

Trapped.

'Hello, are you back with me?'

A man's voice from somewhere behind. It sounds familiar. I want to turn to look, but I can't move.

Where am I?

'If you can hear me, I need you to try to stay awake.'

Spider's web.

Glowing clocks.

'Can you hear me?' the voice asks again. 'The firefighters have arrived now. We're going to get you out as soon as we can.'

Spider's web.

Glowing clocks.

The man lowers his voice, but I can still hear him. 'What took you guys so long? We need to get him out of here now. I don't know how badly he's hurt, but the car looks pretty crushed on that side. I can't get close enough without risking it tipping any further. He's mostly been unconscious.'

No, not a spider's web. It's the cracked windscreen of my car. Right in front of me, above the illuminated clocks of my dashboard and the deflated airbags that hide my injured body from view.

Why can't I move?

The accident. I remember.

I was on my way to kill myself, having waited for the cover of night. I swerved to avoid that man in the road. The tall guy in the long coat; the fluorescent dog lead in his hand. His eyes appeared out of nowhere in my headlights. What the hell was he doing there? Did I kill him?

Then the red truck sped around the corner, heading straight for me. I lost control, spinning and flipping the car off the road. At that point I must have lost consciousness.

Someone else says something I can't make out and then I hear the man again. 'I arrived just after it happened. I was driving by and stopped to help. The tall bloke being checked over by the paramedics was apparently walking his dog off the lead on the coastal path when it chased something into the road. He went after it – God knows what he was thinking – just as this poor guy came along in one direction and the truck came in the other. I've been here with him the whole time. I didn't dare risk getting into the car, for fear of dislodging it, but I managed to open the boot so I could talk to him; hoping he could hear me. He needs urgent medical treatment.'

I'm hanging over the side of the cliff, crushed into the front seat of my car. If I listen carefully, I can hear the sea crashing around on the other side of the windscreen. It's so hot. I'm covered in sweat.

Burning chemicals.

Shit. The car's on fire.

I don't want to die.

Ruby.

Maria.

Sam . . . Gangy?

Please don't let me die. I shouldn't have come. It was a terrible mistake.

'Help,' I manage to say in a gravelly whisper, my tongue like a sandpaper block.

416

'Help,' I try again, louder, although still no one hears me. 'Help!'

'Christ, that's him,' the man's voice says from behind me, moving closer again. 'Come on. Let's get him out of here. Hello? Can you hear me?'

'Yes.' The sound comes out weakly; my voice feels strange. 'Fire! Smell burning.'

'No, don't panic. There's no fire. You've been in a car crash. It's the airbag you smell. There's a chemical reaction when it deploys. Please stay calm. The fire lads are here, but just to get you to safety.'

His face – his short white hair – appears in the rearview mirror and I can't believe my eyes. 'Miles?'

'Yes, that's right. So I did get through to you! My name is Miles Jackson. I'm a doctor. Well, a retired one. I've been with you the whole time and I'll stay with you.'

Miles Jackson? I think. What the hell?

'I need you to try and stay awake,' he continues. 'What's your name?'

'Um, Dan. Daniel Evans.'

'Good. That's great. I can't tell you how glad I am to hear you speak. I want you to keep talking to me, okay? We'll have you out of there in no time. They're putting a winch on your car. Once you're back on the road, we'll have a proper look at you. Get you to a hospital. Dan? Are you still with me, lad?'

'Yes.'

'Good. Now sit tight. Don't try to move about.'

Talking is an effort. 'I don't think I can. Can't feel my legs. I'm scared.'

'Can you feel your arms?'

'Yes. I think so. But I can't move them.'

'Don't panic. Everything will be all right. Keep talking to me, yes?'

'Okay.'

'Are you in pain?'

'Head hurts. Think I banged it.'

'Anything else?'

'Thirsty. Really hot.'

'Sure,' he replies. 'It's been roasting all day. Don't worry. We'll get you some water as soon as you're back to safety. Do you have a family, Dan?'

'Wife and daughter.'

'What are their names?'

'Maria and Ruby.'

'Do you have a phone number we can get them on?'

I tell him the landline, the only number I can remember, although I suspect the main reason he asked for it was to keep me talking.

'Good. We'll call Maria once you're safe.'

'If I don't make it, tell them I love them.'

'Dan, you can do that yourself. You're going to make it.'

'Hope so.'

'What was that, Dan? I couldn't hear what you said. You're staying with me, aren't you?'

'Yes,' I reply. Or at least I think I do, but maybe the words never leave my mouth. I suddenly feel so tired. I can hardly keep my eyes open. Miles is shouting something at me that I can't quite hear.

And then I'm jolted back awake by a deafening metallic creaking noise.

The car's moving.

It's sliding downwards.

I'm finished.

But no. I got it wrong. I can hear the sound of machinery and shouting from behind me. The car's moving backwards. They're pulling me to safety. I'm bumping all over the place for a few moments and then it stops.

I'm back on the road. It's swarming with members of the emergency services. My eyes, dazzled at first by all the flashing lights, are drawn to the open back of an ambulance a little further along. It's illuminated inside and I'm relieved to see the tall trench coat guy in there with his red face and grey ponytail. He's having his leg examined by a paramedic, but he looks to be in one piece, thank goodness. A few yards away I spot a policeman holding a panting springer spaniel on a fluorescent yellow retractable lead. It must be the dog that ran into the road and sparked all of this, although it looks oblivious to the fact.

A face – Dr Miles Jackson's – appears at the side window. He gives me a thumbs-up. 'You're safe now, lad. Everything's going to be all right.'

I wonder how he can say that when he's not even checked me over yet.

And his eyes tell a different story. They look more concerned than relieved as they take in the damage to the car. What does that mean for me?

I still can't move. What if?

Don't.

Stop it.

I shut down another voice in my head reminding me that I've been drinking. That I went AWOL from work. That I still don't know if the driver of the red truck has come out of the accident in one piece, although I pray they have.

I'm alive.

That's what I have to focus on.

It's all that matters right now.

I'll deal with whatever else – the consequences of my actions – in due course.

I'm alive.

I've been given another chance.

That's infinitely more than Sam ever had.

It's way beyond what I deserve.

So let's make it count.

ACKNOWLEDGEMENTS

Thank you to everyone who has played a role, big or small, in the creation of this book.

First I must mention my amazing family: especially Claudia, Kirsten, Mum, Dad and Lindsay. You've been behind me from the very start of my literary journey, back when most people thought it was pie in the sky. You've always believed in me and championed my work, without shying away from telling me the truth when things haven't been quite right. Your love and support mean everything.

My literary agent, Pat Lomax, also deserves a big mention. You've been a fantastic guide and companion on the road from would-be author to published novelist. I massively appreciate everything you've done to help turn my dream into reality.

Thank you to my excellent editor Phoebe Morgan. It's been a pleasure to work with someone so enthusiastic, insightful and conscientious. Further thanks to the rest of the fabulous team at Neon/HarperCollins, including

Helena Sheffield, Natasha Harding, Kate Ellis, Ellie Wood and Helen Huthwaite, as well as Jo Marino and Alice Bland from Way To Blue.

I'm also very grateful to John Khatri for reading an early version of this story.

It's important that I recognise all the support I received from friends and wider family members when my previous novel, *Time to Say Goodbye*, came out. It's tough promoting a first book and your enthusiasm and help spreading the word, both in person and on social media, made a huge difference.

Finally, I'd like to pay tribute to everyone who read my debut novel – and especially those who wrote such kind reviews or contacted me directly to say they'd enjoyed it. It's amazing to be able to connect with readers and to hear that my words have meant something to them. I hope you like this book just as much.

How do you leave the person
you love the most?

Is there ever a right time to let go?

time
to say
goodbye

S. D. ROBERTSON

A heart-rending story about a
father's love for his daughter.